On impact, the jet spun end over end, sailed several feet back up as if preparing to take wing again into the starry spring night, and burst into a spectacular fireball.

Wreckage was found to a radius of eleven miles, and two of the corpses were so badly burned and dismembered that they had to be identified by dental charts.

The crash became an instant media sensation in Japan for three reasons. Seiji Muramoto was descended from one of the oldest and most powerful samurai noble families, and his wealth was reputed to be in the billions.

He left no will.

He had no heir.

Also by David Klass:

NIGHT OF THE TYGER

SAMURAI, INC.

David Klass

FAWCETT GOLD MEDAL ● NEW YORK

A Fawcett Gold Medal Book
Published by Ballantine Books
Copyright © 1992 by David Klass

ISBN 0-449-14708-8

Manufactured in the United States of America

First Edition: June 1992

For Valerio, Pia, and Alessandro

Prologue

The Lear jet lurched for the first time over Kakogawa. The five men in the cabin fell silent and glanced at one another nervously. Then, as the plane steadied, they assumed that they had left a bad pocket of air turbulence behind, and went back to business.

Matsuda knew that he was being tested. He was the youngest of the four regional chiefs by almost a decade, and he could feel the older men watching him carefully. Even though he was forty-two years old, his rise through the organization had been meteoric by Japanese standards. Now, in the presence of Muramoto himself, he had to demonstrate his competence, while at the same time conducting himself with the necessary modesty and deference toward his older colleagues.

Seiji Muramoto sat in the center of the customized cabin, scanning profit reports from the Seto Inland Sea Fisheries. At seventy-two, he was lean and wiry, with quick, bright eyes and long fingers which he flattened out on the desktop as he read. His blue silk *kimono* was simple yet elegant; on the right shoulder the Muramoto family crest of a dragon facing a crane was embroidered in silver thread. Every so often he picked up a small cup of green tea and wet his lips with the bitter liquid. "I want a week-by-week catch breakdown from Takamatsu and Imabari from December to April," he said curtly.

Without any hesitation, Matsuda answered. He used the highest possible honorific forms when he addressed the old man. "I thought such a further breakdown might be necessary, so I already had one drawn up. Please see if it meets your expectations." He passed several sheets of paper to Muramoto, and then handed out copies to the other regional chiefs, who scanned them at rapid speed.

Muramoto nodded. "Good, very good."

The old man's semicircular desk dominated the cabin. The top of the desk was polished cedar, and gleamed in the uneven illumination of the ceiling lights. Ten feet in front of the desk, by the doorway to the cockpit, a computer screen flashed changes in the New York stock market. The Japanese and Hong Kong markets were closed for the night.

The lights from the cities below glowed and then disappeared as the plane passed in and out of cloud banks, on its way from Fukuoka to Kyoto. It was cruising smoothly at forty-one thousand feet.

Matsuda and the three older regional chiefs all wore almost identical dark suits, white shirts, and solid-color ties. Even when Muramoto interrupted a report to ask a few difficult questions, the tone of the business meeting remained friendly. Each of the three older regional chiefs had worked for the Muramoto family for nearly half a century, and despite the presence of young Matsuda, there was a deep sense of kinship in the small cabin.

The second time the plane lurched, the dip was severe enough to splash green tea over old Muramoto's silk sleeve. Matsuda was out of his chair in an instant, a white handkerchief ready in his hands to dab up the spill.

"*Dame da na?*" the old man grunted at the sudden rough ride.

Then the engine began to vibrate. The explosion came a few seconds later. It was a single loud bang, and the entire jet quivered and pitched to one side. The three old regional chiefs were thrown to the floor, while Matsuda barely managed to cling to his seat. The overhead lights blinked out. In the darkness, Matsuda had a sudden fleeting vision of his young wife, Etsuko, as he had last seen her in Takamatsu a few hours ago. Her stomach was just starting to swell with their first child.

Old Muramoto himself was buckled securely into his chair. He grasped the edges of his desk with both hands and held on till his knuckles turned white.

A shrill whistling came from outside the aircraft.

Thousands of papers from business reports flew about the dark cabin like a flock of startled birds.

For several seconds the jet whirled wildly down through the night sky. The five men inside the cabin were jerked and shaken as the plane spun. They clung to seats in the darkness, listening to the whistling grow louder. A wire pulled loose, and orange and white sparks shot in all directions like tiny starbursts.

Then, bit by bit, the pilot regained a measure of control. The plummeting plane began to fly in erratic downward loops. As the loops became more regular spirals, the five men were able to catch their breath.

A buzzer sounded and emergency backup lights blinked on and provided a small amount of illumination. The copilot stepped out of the cockpit. "Compressor failure in one engine," he shouted. "A piece from the explosion must've sheared a control cable. No elevators or ailerons working. We're steering with the other engine, but we can only go in one direction. We'll try to crashland. . . ." Then he turned back to help the pilot.

The five men in the cabin looked at one another. No one spoke. The whistling from outside the cabin built steadily. It came from all directions at once, like the whine of a mosquito amplified a thousand times.

"Sabotage!" the regional chief from Kyushu suddenly hissed, anger and panic winding his voice tight. "Who would dare . . . ?"

"Until we land safely, the question of who is responsible for this is irrelevant," Seiji Muramoto told him in a voice that was remarkable for its gentle authority.

The man from Kyushu did not speak again.

They heard the faint whir as the pilot extended the flaps and landing gear to try to slow their descent. Almost immediately the flaps sheared off with several quick grinding thuds. A dozen or so metallic concussions ruptured the air as the skin of the aircraft popped in and out from the air pressure of the rapid descent.

At ten thousand feet there was another loud explosion. Muramoto, who had been a highly decorated pilot in World War II and knew quite a bit about aircraft, nodded very slightly as if accepting something. Too much strain had been put on the second engine. It had also undergone compressor failure, and the plane was now virtually impossible to steer. He unbuckled his seat belt and stood, gripping his desk for support. His austere face betrayed no fear, but rather every nuance of pose, voice, and posture reflected generations of stern family discipline.

"The fact that you gentlemen are with me on this flight is a final proof of your loyalty. You all have distinguished records of service.''

He managed a bow. The four men, clinging to their chairs, bowed back, much lower. They understood the grim reality behind such a speech, but they showed no fear. Matsuda again thought quickly of Etsuko. They had been married for less than a year. Ironically, his advancement to this inner circle and his presence on this plane were in large part due to the fortuitous marriage. His young wife was the grandniece of old Muramoto. Beneath her gentle exterior, she had a bit of the old man's iron will. Matsuda remembered the way her eyes had glistened with tears when they had exchanged wedding vows. The gaze she had directed at him beneath those tears had been strong and unwavering. They had had nine absolutely blissful months together. Matsuda told himself he had been very fortunate, and steeled himself for what lay ahead.

Still old Muramoto managed to stand, his shoulders back and his body ramrod-straight in the pitching cabin. When he spoke, his voice rose over the shrill whistling to fill the room. "There is a haiku of Basho's:

> 'Old friends say good-bye
> Forever—wild geese
> Wandering in cloud.' ''

For a long moment the haiku hung in the semidarkness, as time froze for the five men. The cabin was filling with smoke, so the poem's concluding line seemed hauntingly appropriate. Already the smoke, thickest near the ceiling, was clouding and blurring faces and figures.

Then the plane lurched so precipitously that all five of the men were hurled to the floor. The computer terminal in the corner broke loose and rolled around the cabin, its screen shattering into millions of tiny shards. The cabin underwent explosive decompression, and oxygen masks were automatically lowered. And the smoke poured in.

In the cockpit, the copilot's head snapped forward against a control panel, and he slumped down, unconscious. The pilot battled on with the control wheel, alone, and at the last moment managed to somehow pull the plane partially out of its nosedive.

A large, shadowy square of rice field lay near the slopes of Mount Rokko. He fought to bring the plane in as level as possible, and miraculously the jet swooped down on the wet paddy in a fairly flat descent. A split second before touchdown the plane rolled suddenly to the right, and the pilot threw his hands up in front of his face and let out a piercing death scream as the earth rose up to claim him.

On impact, the jet spun end over end, sailed several feet back up as if preparing to take wing again into the starry spring night, and burst into a spectacular fireball.

Wreckage was found to a radius of eleven miles, and two of the corpses were so badly burned and dismembered that they had to be identified by dental charts.

The crash became an instant media sensation in Japan for three reasons. Seiji Muramoto was descended from one of the oldest and most powerful samurai noble families, and his wealth was reputed to be in the billions.

He left no will.

He had no heir.

SECTION ONE

If you are in the line of fire . . .

1

A spring storm off the Chesapeake had thundered up the Potomac and was lashing Georgetown with a cold, pounding rain.

They had made love for nearly an hour on the rug in front of Jack's fireplace, and now they lay gently tangled, listening to the cascade of rain on the skylight twenty feet overhead. The once-blazing fire had dwindled to embers that occasionally managed to lick out quick tongues of red-orange flame. Faintly, in the background, the air conditioner purred on low. In these humid days of mid-May it was standard practice among the fashionable set in Georgetown to run one's air conditioner while a fire was burning.

Kate's head was nestled atop Jack's chest and her eyes were closed—he thought perhaps she had drifted off. He lay still so as not to disturb her, and thought again about the letter.

It had been waiting for him when he came home from work, mixed in with the usual collection of junk mail. Like most agents, he received his bureau-related mail, bills, and personal correspondence at work. In his branch of white-collar law it sometimes seemed an unnecessary precaution—the Wall Street insider traders he investigated hardly seemed the sort to track him down and try to take revenge. But the strong advice at Quantico—which almost all agents heeded after their training days—had been to keep anything that might identify them as to career or loved ones far away from their domiciles. Those friends and business acquaintants who had Jack's home address knew enough not to write to him there.

So what was this?

He had turned the small envelope face up and immediately recognized several irregular key imprints from the well-worn pica twelve-point of his father's antiquated Olivetti portable. He stood for nearly a minute in a sort of daze as anger, curiosity, and most of all, numbing shock mingled together.

9

It had been nearly three years. What could the old bastard want?

Kate shifted and her soft breath fell warmly against Jack's cheek. He glanced at her and saw that she was studying him through half-open lids. He kissed her on the forehead, and she rewarded him with a little smile. "What were you worrying about?"

"Nothing."

"You were grinding your teeth together. You had the strangest look of anger on your face."

He knew there was no point in lying. She was uncannily— sometimes uncomfortably—intuitive. "Got a strange letter to-day."

"Old lover trying to rekindle the flame?" Her green eyes sparkled playfully.

"Just the opposite, really."

"Old enemy out for fresh blood?"

He didn't deny it. "It was from my father."

Her head jerked up in surprise. "Really? That's great. I mean, isn't it?" She was very big on family ties. Her quick eyes studied his face intently, hoping for some sign of agreement.

He said nothing. The cascade on the skylight slackened off into a sputtering drizzle.

She rolled off him and sat up so that she was looking down at him. "I mean, isn't it nice that he wants to get back in touch? He's making an effort, Jack."

"Lie back down, sweetheart."

But she wouldn't let it go. "What did he want?"

"Damned if I know," Jack told her. He grabbed a handful of long auburn hair and tugged her gently back down. Her head came to rest on his chest again, and her arms looped loosely around his torso. His knuckles snowplowed over the slope of her neck to caress her soft cheek. From there, his fingers took the slow slalom route down to her hips, following the gentle curves of her lovely body.

"Well, what did the letter say?"

"I didn't read it."

"What do you mean, you didn't read it?"

"I threw it out."

Then there was a long silence. Her muscles tensed and her

breathing grew faster and deeper. It wasn't until he felt her tears that he realized she was crying.

Jack sat up and held her shoulders, looking into her soft eyes. "Baby? Believe me, he's not worth it."

She swallowed several times and moved her body back so that his hands fell away. "I'm not crying for him. I'm crying for me."

"I don't understand. This isn't a big deal. Don't make it one. . . ." Even as he tried to calm her, he watched as the sadness in her face changed to unmistakable fury.

She stood, walked to the couch where the amorous encounter had begun an hour before, turned her back to him, and began pulling on her clothes.

Jack took a few steps after her, feeling awkward, not knowing whether to comfort her or demand an explanation. "Listen to me for a minute, Kate. It was just a stupid letter from a son of a bitch. . . ."

She stopped dressing and looked at him. "Tell me you love me."

"What has that got to do with my father?"

Her green eyes glittered; she had never looked more beautiful. "We've been seeing each other for five months. You've never said it. If you love me, tell me."

He opened his mouth, but no words came.

"Right now."

"I . . . I just don't see why . . ."

"Fine. You don't have to say anything else."

She had almost all her clothes on now. He touched her arm very gently. She pulled back and spoke in an angry rush. "You have nothing to feel guilty about. You've been careful not to commit to a damned thing. We haven't even talked about marriage or kids or . . . anything. I absolve you of all guilt. Now I'm getting the hell out of here."

Anger came to his rescue as he ran to block the door. She tried to dodge around him, and he grabbed her and held her. *"Listen to me,"* he shouted. Then lower, "Listen. You don't know what it was like . . . and I'm not trying to use this as an excuse . . . but you don't. I'm glad you had it happy." She tried to twist away, and he tightened his grip. His voice swelled and trembled almost at the breaking point. "I don't want you to go. I'm doing the best I can. . . ."

She looked him up and down, from his toes to the crown of his skull where the black hair was just starting to thin a bit, and she exhaled. When she finally spoke, it was a chilling whisper. "Damn you for making me feel so good. Damn you for being everything I want in a man, and really not being anything at all." She broke free and moved past him to the door, and then turned. "I'm thirty-one. I don't have time to waste. Don't worry, there'll be someone else ready to take my place. I'm sure they'll be lining up for you. . . . 'Bye, Jack."

And she was gone. Jack watched her walk through the drizzle, get into her red Miata, and peel out from the curb. He closed his front door and stood alone in his apartment, naked, listening to the low hum of the air conditioner. He walked over and switched it off. Now the only sound was the steady pounding of heavy rain on glass. He pulled on his clothes, listening to the rhythm of the May storm. As he buttoned his shirt, he spotted the red ribbon Kate had worn in her hair that evening. It was half out of sight between two couch cushions. He picked it up—it was soft in his hand and smelled faintly of jasmine.

The familiar sweet smell caught him like a stiff right cross. He lurched to his bar and poured himself a double shot. He brought the whiskey to his lips and then pivoted in a half circle and, without drinking, hurled the glass against the paneled wall. Without stopping to throw on a coat or even take his service revolver, he headed straight for the door and the cold, stormy Georgetown evening.

The dark and the wet striking together had left Q Street strangely deserted. Elms on either side twisted up through the murk, raising their branches as if voting across the center of the narrow street. Jack headed east with long, loping strides, unmindful of the rain that pelted his face and quickly soaked through his clothes.

The usually busy intersection of Q and Twenty-ninth was empty save for a single taxi, which braked carefully to a stop in front of a fashionable row house to disgorge its well-dressed fare. A door opened, and for a moment there were the sounds from a private party: live piano music, drinks clinking, and a woman laughing much too loud. Jack turned down Twenty-ninth and speeded up into a fast jog. The exertion and the sting of cold rain against his face provided some relief. Soon the lights of M Street glittered ahead of him, and then he was running against the stream of traffic toward Foggy Bottom.

What had she seen? What connection had she made?

He pumped his arms and brought his knees up to the level of his waist in a half sprint. A mile flew by. He didn't remember turning onto Twenty-third, but he must have, because suddenly the Lincoln Memorial loomed in front of him. Thunder ripped overhead, and he took shelter inside the Parthenon-like temple that houses the statue. He was completely alone with the majestic likeness of the sixteenth president. Flashes of lightning animated the white marble to the point where it seemed at any second the great bearded head would turn and the heavy arms would rise up from the ponderous curule chair to instruct and admonish.

Jack shivered as he gazed up at the kind and strikingly paternal visage.

Damn her. On what basis did she judge him?

He wiped the wetness off his face, and his fingers traced the hook of his broken nose. *Did she know about that?* Did she know what it felt like to have your own father pound you into unconsciousness at the age of eleven? Did she know the fear of trying to fight back, windmilling childish punches till the taste of blood opened into blackness? Did she know what it was like to lie in bed at age eight with a pillow over your head listening to your mother sobbing in the next room?

He had visited Kate's family in Boston and met her parents and all five siblings—a merry, fun-loving Irish clan. They had feasted together and laughed together, and he hadn't been a bit envious— just glad for her. *But what could she possibly understand about him? And how dare she judge him?*

Another thought came to him, too painful to consider, and he was off again into the downpour, running alongside the reflecting pools that were overflowing so that his feet stamped in and out of puddles.

DAMN HER, SHE WASN'T WORTH IT! Except that he knew she was. And it had happened before, in one fashion or another. So it wasn't her, but him. And the real connection, the real thing she'd glimpsed . . . The real anger in her green eyes . . .

He ran from the thought, flying through the darkness, toward the floodlit white obelisk of the Washington Monument, a fitting phallic monument to the "father of our country." At the foot of the marble shaft he paused, and the thought came to him again: *. . . That the greatest curse a man could have wasn't impotence or childlessness, wasn't failure or poverty, but that there was something far worse and infinitely more damning. . .*

Once again he was off, a bit slower now, feeling the long, wet sprint in the aching muscles of his legs and in the breaths that heaved painfully in and out. But it was only as he neared Tenth Street and saw the cold concrete colossus of his own FBI building towering up into the night that he stopped and allowed the thought a firm beachhead.

To pass through the years without being able to reach out and touch in that way that he had heard so much about and knew must exist for others.

He walked closer to the concrete headquarters. It was surreal to be there without anyone else on the street. To be there without a gun. He shivered and wrapped his arms around his stomach for warmth.

For his long-suffering mother he had managed only sympathy, and a burst of pity during her final lingering illness. He had no siblings—an older brother had been carried off by a childhood disease at an early age. For his one surviving grandparent he felt respect and even a certain amount of affection, but their friendship was an uneasy one—he could only stand to see his grandfather a few times a year at most. And for his father, who had steered him toward this concrete building and this successful career just as surely as he had made a boy's life miserable beyond the telling, Jack felt a deep-rooted rage.

How dare Walter reach out to him through the years and the miles? Upon what father-son bond did he stake this claim? And why now, after so long? Why not let the enmity lie between them unspoken and unresolved, till time sent the old man off to join his wife in their small graveyard plot in Rose Hills?

Jack flagged down a cab and got in. His voice shook as he tried to give the cabbie directions. The ride home took less than fifteen minutes. He was shocked to find he had left his apartment door wide open. He got his revolver and then, shivering and holding the 9-mm Sig Saur at hip height, he searched quickly, room to room, before running a hot bath. He slipped out of the wet clothes and toweled himself off, and as the bath filled up, he walked into the kitchen and began rummaging through the garbage container.

There, covered with coffee grinds and stained with orange juice, was the envelope. He opened it with shaking fingers—incredible the influence his father still had on him—and extracted a single piece of paper and an airline ticket. He read:

> Jack,
>   Turn sixty next month. No party planned but would like to see you. Weather quite good here.
>
> Walter

Jack ripped the letter and tickets lengthwise and then in half again, and threw the pieces back into the garbage. Leaving his revolver on the kitchen counter, he walked to the bathroom and eased into the warm water. He slid down in the tub till the water lapped at his chin, and tried to think about nothing at all.

Most especially, he tried not to allow his mind to ponder the quite good May weather in Los Angeles.

2

The assassin took the *Shinkansen* bullet train from Tokyo to Atami, and then changed to a local train for the ride out to the tip of the Izu Peninsula. He wore the neat but casual clothes of a Tokyo vacationer, spoke to no one, bought nothing, and blended in so well with the other passengers that even his size drew little attention.

He was very big for a Japanese man. He might have been mistaken for a sumo wrestler, except that he didn't have a potbelly or a hair knot. Rather, he was perfectly proportioned—so much so that the symmetry of his build made his height far less apparent. His thinning black hair was cut short in a military-style haircut.

The ride to Shimoda took a bit more than two hours. The assassin watched the graceful resort spas roll by—Ito, Inatori, Inami, Kawazu. The small houses in the towns had white walls and red roofs, and were built so closely together that they seemed to lean on one another for support. Down by the water, tourist hotels with large neon signs fractured the view. Then, after Ito, graceful seaside villas began to appear, each with its acre or two of land.

A decade ago it would have been difficult to believe that any Japanese could be rich enough to own such houses with such tracts of land. Now the assassin saw many imported sports cars outside the villas.

At two he pulled out a rice ball and ate it in small bites. He would have liked to buy tea to wash it down, but of course, he couldn't buy anything, couldn't take the chance that some rural *soba* salesman might remember his face. He was taking something of a chance by even riding this train, but he wanted to get a feel for the Izu and its inhabitants before attempting such a dangerous assignment.

16

And the people who paid him respected the way he worked. Because he always finished off his assignments on time, quietly, cleanly, almost artistically. . . .

For the last thirty miles or so the *Izu Kyuko* train route led right along the coast, and at every turn a different beach or rocky promontory bordered the blue waters of Sagami Bay. The assassin opened the train window nearest him, swallowed deep breaths of salt air, and closed his eyes to concentrate. Death was near, and though he had killed hundreds of times before, he still found the proximity of bloodletting to be majestic and worth savoring.

His sword and a change of clothes were in a black leather bag between his feet. He worried that the Italian leather was too extravagant and might attract attention. This was his first trip to the tip of the Izu, and he had not expected the famed tourist area to be quite so provincial. He moved his legs forward, hiding the bag behind his feet and ankles.

These days most of his work was done in cities or overseas. It had been a long time since he had been this far out in *inaka*—the boondocks. He had been raised on a farm in a rural district of Tokushima, and the sights and smells of the Izu brought back many memories. An old woman stood near him hunched over nearly in half, her spine horribly bent from decades spent planting and harvesting rice. Down at the end of the car, a farmer sat wearing an enormous straw hat. When the train rolled past verdant mekon orchards, the assassin breathed deeply and remembered the rich soil of his father's Tokushima fields.

Shimoda was the last stop. The assassin left the station with the other passengers, and then struck off on his own down the narrow streets. He had never been to Shimoda before, but he had spent hours that morning memorizing maps, and he had a perfect short-term memory for places.

And for names.

And for faces.

The bicycle was waiting for him in the right spot, leaning up against a wooden fence. He climbed on and rode for almost an hour, to a copse of trees a half mile from Ida's villa. He pulled the bicycle deep into the thicket, and changed into loose-fitting dark black pants and a black shirt. Then he sat down and waited for darkness.

At eight o'clock he began to walk down the road toward the

villa. He kept to the tree line, and when a car appeared, he stepped back with a speed and grace that was remarkable for such a big man, and faded completely from sight.

He was shocked to find that the fence was not even electrified. Ida was indeed as big a fool as they said. The assassin had been prepared for electricity, but now all he had to do was climb in silence. In the moonlight he could see five feet of barbed wire at the top of the fence. He kicked off his slippers and flexed his toes and fingers.

He could pull screws out of boards with his toes. Or wind watches with them. Once he had used his toes to rip the intestines out of a man's stomach.

The assassin was over the fence in less than five seconds, without so much as a rattle of wire. He dropped the final ten feet and landed silently on the balls of his feet, alert to every sound and smell. Ida's passion for outdoor gardens was well-known, so the assassin knew there would be no dogs to contend with, only human bodyguards. He moved silently through the bushes toward the Italian-style villa that was lit by the moonlight and by the occasional flicker of a firefly.

He carried a single weapon—it was an old one with quite a bloody history. The seventeenth-century *ninja* assassin Satsuke Surutobi had commissioned the making of this sword, and had used it during his remarkable career. It was much shorter than a normal Japanese sword, with a wider guard and a thicker blade. One might have expected a weapon with such a history to have a haft encrusted with precious metals and gems. This short sword, or *shinokatana* as the *ninjas* used to call it, was simple, razor-sharp, and immensely practical.

Not that he considered himself a *ninja*. The great *ninja* schools of Ida and Koga were all but gone, and many of the finer points of the art of death had been forever lost. These days *ninjas* were almost cartoon characters, used by Hollywood and by movie studios throughout the Far East as the most exotic killers in their silly martial arts films.

He had studied *ninjitsu* as part of his martial arts training, but it had been the less dramatic elements of the old art that he had found the most useful. How to blend in with natural scenery so as to be almost invisible. How to understand high and low sight lines, and angles of view. How to apply makeup with unheard-of speed, and switch costumes in the blink of an eye. And, of course, the sister arts of medicine and poison.

No, he was not a *ninja*. If he had had a business card, it would have read simply "assassin." He killed people for hire, and he used some of the old methods because they were still the most effective.

The moon above the Izu was full, and the ring of luminescence that surrounded it suggested that tomorrow it might rain heavily. Later, clouds obscured the moon and a sea breeze whispered through the low bushes.

The assassin reached Ida's garden and became invisible.

At 5:32 the sun came up, and at 5:40 Ida's chief gardener walked out of his tiny cottage on the villa's estate, clippers in hand. He inspected the garden from the primary viewing point, making sure that the night wind had done no serious damage. He had a very well-trained and careful eye, but he did not spot anything amiss.

The gardener walked along the pond with a distinctive, measured tread, his shoulders hunched slightly as if he were cold. He stopped at the orange tree above the pond and began trimming the branches. He wore loose-fitting tan trousers, a white T-shirt, and a sombrero that he had brought back from a recent trip to Mexico. He worked standing up, his head bent in concentration, clipping so that the tree branch would not look in any way trimmed, yet would at the same time be shaped to fit the lines of the garden, and would lead the eye gently out to the Oribe-style stone lantern in the center of the pond.

The gardener's concentration was such that he did not hear the body approach him with great speed from behind, did not sense the short sword blade naked and poised, and did not lose his grip on his clippers as he fell heavily to the grass by the side of the temple pond. His hand jerked across a patch of moss, and then was still.

Two hours later Masao Ida—president and sole owner of Ida Computer Industries—left his villa for a morning walk. He brought only one bodyguard with him, for the tramping of too many feet interfered with his aesthetic appreciation of the garden.

He was a small man, just over five feet in height, and his energy and constant movement combined with his smooth skin to make him look much younger than his fifty-seven years. His sharply pointed nose and quick eyes gave his face a birdlike quality, and as he walked away from the villa in springy strides, he almost seemed a sparrow hopping over the lush lawn.

The lone bodyguard trailed him at a distance of about fifteen feet. The man was muscle-bound and heavy footed, and carried a semiautomatic in his hands.

They passed the chief gardener, who was kneeling down twenty feet from the path, facing away from them, pruning a small tree with great concentration. He was wearing his usual white T-shirt, with his sombrero over his face to hide his eyes from the sun. He grunted at Ida and the bodyguard and kept working.

When Ida got to the stone bench that sat in the primary viewing spot, his nervous demeanor changed. He stood very still, closed his eyes, and relaxed every limb in his body. He breathed regularly and deeply, and listened to the secrets the morning breeze whispered to him through the nearby bamboo grove. Then he opened his eyes, sat down on the bench, and looked out over his garden.

It was his life's work—he considered his computer company merely a bothersome necessity. There were, of course, much finer gardens in Kyoto, but in Shizuoka Prefecture this was undoubtedly one of the best.

In the soft morning light, the bushes that climbed wildly in ascending and uneven rows at the edges of the garden were like ocean swells, trimmed so that they billowed up steeply toward the clear blue Izu sky. Down lower, the lines of the foliage became more rounded and more tranquil as flowering hibiscus and low-hanging willows dipped into the almost glasslike surface of the pond. In the very center of the silver-green water the stone lantern anchored the surrounding bushes, trees, and pond with the eerie stillness of its ancient rounded shape.

There were three other main viewing points, set off by a clever use of the foliage so that the same tree became at once an integral part of one way of viewing the garden, and also a dividing barrier. When viewed from a different vantage point, the same pond and foliage seemed to express a completely different aesthetic concept.

Ida closed his eyes again, breathed deeply, and smiled. He tried to imagine his garden in a hundred years or so, when it would be grown in and have achieved some maturity.

The bodyguard did not fully turn as the old gardener sauntered by up the hill. He recognized the old straw sombrero and the gardener's slow and measured steps, and only turned to look when he caught the gleam of the sword blade out of the corner of his eye.

And by then, of course, it was far too late.

The bodyguard whirled around with great speed. As his arms began to raise the gun, the short sword had already stabbed through the center of his throat, neatly slicing his jugular. Guided by a firm and knowing hand, the sword cut cleanly through his spinal cord and was withdrawn.

Ida, meditating on the stone bench, did not turn.

The assassin approached through the short grass, swiftly and silently. "Masao Ida," he whispered when he was five feet away.

The industrialist turned, gaped, and fought for control. His eyes widened, and his mouth opened and then shut again as he saw the fresh blood dripping from the assassin's sword onto the mossy bank. "Who sent you?" he managed to whisper.

The assassin shook his head and stepped closer, cutting the gap between them in half. The way powerful men faced death was something he found quite fascinating, and he watched closely as Ida struggled to keep his wits about him.

"What are you being paid for this?"

The assassin shook his head.

"I will give you more . . . more than you can imagine," Ida whispered desperately. "You will never have to work again. I will give you all I have. . . ."

The assassin swung his sword in one powerful stroke from right to left, and Ida's decapitated head bounced off the stone bench and rolled onto the grass, his eyes still open, his lips still working, a faint hissing coming from his mouth.

For two long seconds the face on the ground stared up at the assassin as if still pleading to be spared. Then the expression suddenly became blank as death unhinged the quick black eyes and they rolled upward. The assassin bent and carved a Chinese character into the dead man's chest with the point of his sword. Then he turned and melted quickly into the bamboo trees that fluttered pleasantly in the morning breeze.

3

Jack turned the radio off and stepped on the accelerator as the highway emptied out past Alexandria. When he fought through city traffic he often played country-and-western and sang along with the hokey choruses in a slightly out-of-tune baritone. But when he had the chance to drive fast he preferred silence, so that he could hear the tires wrestling with the curves and massaging the straightaways.

Today he felt like driving very fast.

The blue Mustang surged forward, and the hardwood forests and rolling hills whipped past. It had been a hard week of work, and when he thought of his desk, piled high with contradictory depositions, the speedometer's needle dipped past eighty and he forced himself to take it easy. His special agent's badge would afford him little protection against a speeding ticket.

He crossed the Rappahannock at Fredricksburg, near the spot where George Washington supposedly threw a silver dollar across the river. In the Civil War this had been blood-soaked territory, almost exactly halfway between the two warring capitals. Now it was shady and quiet, and he inhaled deep breaths of the spring air as a road sign directed him on toward Richmond. For the first time in a week Jack felt himself begin to relax a little bit and enjoy the May sunshine.

He was glad he had decided to drive out into the country, although why he had decided to make this particular journey remained a bit of a mystery to him. He liked his grandfather well enough in small doses, but the old man's tendency to interrogate him about the likelihood of great-grandchildren in the near future was a bit annoying. It would be especially unwelcome today, when he still missed Kate so badly.

Jack coughed—he was just shaking the cold brought on by his

run through the rain a week before. A dozen times in the past week he had been tempted to call her, and finally he had gone ahead and done so. Their conversation had been awkward and brief. She didn't want to give it another chance. Good luck. 'Bye.

So why come to see his grandfather now, when the old man would be sure to hit that raw nerve? Jack turned off Interstate 95 and crossed the Chickahominy River. At any rate, the visit was long overdue.

A dusty local road took him along the bank to his grandfather's large white colonial-style house, where a bunch of ten-year-olds stopped playing football on the front lawn long enough to give his Mustang a good long look.

His grandfather saw him drive up and walked out to greet him. The old man looked as lean and wiry as ever. His left leg had been blown off at the knee five decades ago at Iwo Jima, but as he crossed the wide lawn, he walked with only a trace of a limp. His handshake was firm as his leathery lips twisted up in a small but pleased smile. "Welcome."

"Thanks. You look good."

"Can't complain." The old man pointed skyward. "Clouds from the west. Soon as the surface darkens, they'll start biting."

Twenty minutes later they were in his grandfather's motorboat in the middle of the Chickahominy, casting flies upstream and sipping cans of Coors. They hadn't seen each other for quite a while, but the old man didn't speak—he had never been one to break a silence. Once a conversation got going, he could keep up his end, but otherwise he seemed quite content to drift off into almost interminable silences.

On his fifth cast, Jack felt a hard strike and his rod bent almost double. He set the hook and began reeling, and about three minutes later he coaxed in a lovely two-pound brown which his grandfather netted. The old man shook his head as if witnessing one of the great mysteries of life. "It's enough to make a man give up fishing."

"What is?" Jack asked, putting the brown on a stringer.

"Haven't seen one that big in weeks."

"It's all in the technique."

"Hogwash," his grandfather said. "You don't know the first thing about river casting. But every time you visit you pull in lunkers left and right. It's like they're sitting down there waiting for you to come back."

"Maybe they are," Jack said, lowering the stringer into the water and picking up his rod. "Next I go after his big brother." He tried a cast, and the fly barely went fifteen feet. "So," Jack asked, trying to cover the disastrous effort with banter, "besides my lunkers, what's the hot news around here?"

His grandfather cast his rig far out with a deft flick of the wrist. "Read about you the other day."

"Me?" Jack stopped reeling.

"In the paper. Something about the Hwang case. You were testifying."

"Oh, that."

"Getting to be a big shot."

"That one just snowballed."

"I figure that's why it's been so long since you came out," the old man said with just a hint of reproach in his voice. "I reckon you're real busy."

"It's just been a few months."

The skilled old hands flicked the rod upward after every three or four turns of the reel, to twitch the fly. "Four getting on five."

"Sorry."

"Don't be. Just like to see you more often is all."

They fished in silence for a while, catching and releasing seven- and eight-inchers and keeping a couple of bigger ones. Jack caught by far the majority of large fish, and each time his rod bent with a strike, the old man grimaced and shook his head. The wind picked up and stirred tiny waves that splashed against the boat's side. "I got a letter from Walter the other day," Jack said.

His grandfather's eyes followed his transparent bobber as it curled in across the current, dipping in and out of sight. "Is that right?"

"Wants me to come to L.A. for his sixtieth birthday."

"Doesn't sound much like Walter." It was one of the few times Jack had heard his grandfather refer to his son-in-law by name.

"No, it doesn't," Jack agreed, anger creeping into his voice despite his best efforts to sound nonchalant. "Sent me tickets and everything. I ripped 'em up and tossed 'em, but . . . the whole thing is strange. Walter and I haven't seen each other in years. . . ."

The wind grew still stronger, so that it whipped the willows on the near bank. When the old man finally replied, it was only to change the subject in a particularly unwelcome direction: "How're you gettin' on with that gal you brought out here last time? Kate, right?"

"That's right."

"She's a peach."

"Yes, sir, she is." Even at the time, Jack had known it was a mistake to bring her out here. But she had wanted to meet some member of his family, and finally he had broken down and brought her out for half a day on the river.

"Not to push, but I wouldn't object to a great-grandchild one of these decades."

Jack cast far upstream and reeled in slowly. "I'm afraid you're going to have to wait a little longer. Kate and I broke up a week ago."

A big brown rose behind Jack's fly and then shied away. "When they're interested and they're following along behind it like that, slow it down and twitch a little," his grandfather advised in a sure, low voice. "A longer look'll give 'em confidence, and with a twitch or two for excitement, they'll strike for sure." Jack wasn't sure whether the old man was talking about fish or women.

Later, in the living room, sitting in a rosewood rocker sipping gin and watching a new group of neighborhood boys play tackle football without pads, Jack decided to try again. Sometimes the old man took hours to get back onto a subject. Sometimes days. A boy fell on the grass, ripping a gash through the turf with his heel.

"They're tearing the hell out of your lawn."

"Not a care in the world at that age. Lookit him pick himself back up."

Jack took a deep breath. The sun was just beginning to go down over the Chickahominy. "Guess I'm curious what would make a man like Walter reach out after years and years."

The old man put down his drink, and his eyes narrowed. "He's feeling lonely. Or he needs money. Or . . ."

"Or what?"

"Sometimes a mean bastard when he gets about Walter's age looks in the mirror and starts to see himself for what he is. And he thinks that he can set everything right real easy."

This time Jack could not keep the resentment out of his voice. "I can't believe that. Not Walter."

The old man was silent for a time, and his face seemed to grow as hard as the shell of a walnut. "I guess you came here for advice, so here it is. I raised my little girl right and I think it was all Walter's fault their marriage went sour. I only saw it from the sidelines—you grew up with it all around you, but I can guess how bad it was."

No, you can't, Jack thought while the old man paused to sip his gin. *I know you've seen a lot, but I bet you can't even come close.*

His grandfather lowered his glass. "Lord knows I've tried to lead a Christian life and I'm not proud of hating any man, but when it comes to your father . . ." He couldn't finish the thought.

"I know," Jack whispered.

"If I'm coming between a father and a son's last chance to reconcile . . . well, I guess that's a pretty awful thing to do. But when it comes to Walter Graham, I say stay away and enjoy your own life, and let him rot."

"Yeah, but . . ." Jack tossed his head in fury. "Look, I don't even know why I brought it up."

His grandfather watched him carefully and then nodded. "You don't owe him a damn thing, Jack. He owes you. He owes all of us . . . Oh, lookit what the poor kid did!"

A ten-year-old had been tackled too hard, and was crying as blood spilled down from his nose over his lips and chin. With surprising speed the old man walked into the kitchen, grabbed a towel and an ice cube, and emerged onto his lawn. He had a way with kids—the boy ran to him, and the old man wiped the blood off.

They ate the fish they had caught for an early dinner. The freshly caught trout was delectable in the light beer batter. There were also long garden string beans with melted butter and sourdough rolls. The screen was open, and sweet air from the river, heavy with the smell of tidewater and red mud, filled the dining room. "You're gonna be driving home through the darkness," the old man said. "Why don't you stay?"

"I like driving at night."

"Don't mean to pry, but are you sure it's over with that Kate gal?"

Jack nodded.

"I'm not sure you should have let that one go."

"Other way around," Jack said. "Not my choice. Can we talk about something else?"

"God didn't make men to go through their thirties on their own."

"Or their seventies," Jack told him with some bite in his voice, intentionally putting an end to their dinner conversation. After that they ate in silence, watching the last light swirl through the eddies.

They walked out to the car side by side, and the old man surprised Jack by giving him a hug instead of a handshake. "Come back soon. And get me a couple of great-grandchildren. I wanna teach my great-grandson the curveball, and I'm not getting any younger."

"I'll see what I can do," Jack said, feeling the plea of the old arms across his shoulders. "You stop being such a recluse. Get out a little bit. Come visit me in D.C. and we'll go chase some hot young babes."

Jack drove home through the darkness quite a bit more slowly than he had come, listening to classical music most of the way. He realized that he had gotten exactly what he had come for. Who better than his mother's father to voice a strong opinion on Walter Graham? It had felt good to hear the decent old man assure him that he had no filial obligation to answer his father's summons. There was no debt to pay, no duty to honor. So to hell with Walter—it was time to forget about that and get on with his life.

Now that Hwang Securities was finally wrapping up, there were even bigger things brewing. The Harburg Fiasco would make someone's career, and Jack knew he was well positioned for it. Lost for a time in a Bach fugue and the Byzantine inner workings of the justice system, Jack crossed the Potomac and headed toward the lights of the city.

4

The assassin picked the lock of the restaurant's back door, and entered through the kitchen. It was completely dark. He smelled the cat just as the cat smelled him, and they spotted each other at the same instant. The assassin walked over and petted the sleek gray tomcat behind the ears, and the cat slid up against his palm and purred.

He liked cats, liked the way they moved. But if he let this one live, it might give him away the next morning, so in a single quick movement his fingers tightened and he snapped the cat's neck. He took the small corpse outside the restaurant and threw it into a trash bin behind a shoe store, and covered it with boxes. Then he reentered the restaurant.

He explored the small dining room, noting the positions of the seven tables, and the remarkable amount of space and privacy given to each one. This was indeed a comfortable, well laid out, and spotlessly clean restaurant—he could see why it was Miura's favorite.

At ten o'clock the next morning the owner of the restaurant and his two daughters entered through the back door. They brought in a variety of fresh vegetables and garnishings, and several boxes of the carefully selected three- to five-pound *torafugu* from Shimonoseki. This was a specialty restaurant, and fugu—sashimi cut from just outside the poison gland of the deadly blowfish—was the only entrée they served.

They cleaned their restaurant from top to bottom, and would not have believed it possible that there was a large man hiding there unobserved, watching them.

At five o'clock Kenji Miura—president of Dai-Sei Computer Technologies—walked through the door with six companions. He always ate very early, so as to be done before the dinner crowd

28

began to fill the restaurant. Two or three times a week he had fugu here—in his opinion, the old chef was the finest in Tokyo. Two of the men from his party—the two bodyguards—did not come to the table but rather waited in the entry hall. One of the restaurant owner's daughters brought them chairs, and flirted with them just a bit. They sat at an angle so that they kept their eyes on Miura.

An American engineer, his wife, and his twelve-year-old son sat down with Miura and his wife at their usual table. The American was a world-class computer engineer, and his wife was young and pretty, and Miura found the whole arrangement to be very satisfactory except for the adolescent boy. Why did Americans insist on bringing their children on business dinners? It was bad enough that they insisted on bringing their wives. The boy simply would not sit still. "Is it poison?" he asked, again and again. "Is it really poison?"

So Miura finally told them a bit about fugu, and took some pleasure in scaring the boy. His English was normally awkward and halting, but he had explained the nuances of eating fugu to so many English and American visitors that he had the impressive-sounding scientific words down pat. "The poison is called tetrodotoxin. It's found in the liver and the ovaries of the blowfish. Once eaten, there is no known antidote. Death occurs quickly—from a collapse of the nervous and respiratory systems."

The boy stopped shifting on his seat. He looked at his mother, who said, "Dan, I don't know if this is such a good idea. . . ."

"Please don't worry," Miura told her. "Since 1949 all fugu chefs in Japan have had to pass a rigorous test administered by *Koseisho*. . . ."

Miura glanced at his wife, who supplied the English translation, "The Ministry of Health."

"Yes, the Ministry of Health," Miura continued. "Since licensing started, no one has ever died in a fugu restaurant. So there is no need to worry." He did not add that every year fishermen who try to prepare fugu dishes at home kill themselves and their families. Or that in 1975 a famed Kabuki actor insisted on being served fugu liver, and died horribly. Or that the Japanese imperial family is not allowed to eat any dish made from fugu. Ever. For any reason.

In the inner kitchen, the fugu chef worked by himself, concentrating on the delicate operation. When he was carving fugu he would not let his daughters into the tiny room where they might distract him, but rather passed the plates of carved and arranged fugu out to them through a small square opening.

First he cut off the fins of the fish, toasted them, and put them into four glasses. He passed the fins out to his daughters, who poured warm sake over them, and brought this first course of *hirezake* to Miura's table.

"Please drink deep," Miura told his guests, enjoying their discomfort a bit, now that the moment of truth had arrived. "If the fugu is good, this will be the best meal of your lives. And if the fugu is bad, taking a little helping won't save you. There is a saying in Osaka, *'Ataru to, ipatsu de shinu.'* He looked at his wife, who supplied a rough translation.

"In English you would say, 'If you are in the line of fire, the first bullet will kill you.' "

"Kampai," Miura said, raising his glass.

"Kampai," his wife said back.

"Cheers," the American scientist said without much enthusiasm.

Miura took a large sip of his *hirezake*. They all watched him carefully. He smacked his lips and smiled at them. "Ah," he sighed with pleasure. "Simply delicious."

In the inner kitchen, the assassin slowly lowered himself from the high cabinet where he had been lying flat amid old kettles and rusting pans. He immediately noted the knife in the sushi chef's hand—it was not a weapon per se, but all knives deserved respect. And the sushi chef clearly knew how to use this knife.

The assassin approached him slowly from behind. The chef was so engaged in his delicate carving operation that he did not sense the man standing just behind him, watching. The chef removed the poisonous liver and ovaries from two large tiger blowfish. The slightest slip of his knife could result in the death of his customers, the closing down of his restaurant, and a long jail term.

Not to mention his disgrace as a fugu chef.

He worked quickly. Once the liver and ovaries were out, he began to slice the meat of the fish, cutting very thin strips and then arranging them artistically in floral patterns on the four plates. Miura had a special plate for his double portion, and the chef arranged Miura's sushi with the extra care due one of his best customers.

The assassin knocked the old chef unconscious with the weighted haft of his sword. The blow drew blood, but it did not crush the skull—the chef would probably live. The assassin took the chef's knife and turned his attention to the ovaries and liver, which had been carefully placed on a side table for disposal.

In the dining room, Miura was in fine spirits. "Eating fugu is just like your eating oysters," he told the Americans. "Only do it in cold months."

"In months with *r*s, as you say," his wife explained.

"That is when it is safest. So you should thank me for taking you here when the water is still cold. See, I appreciate all that you did for my company. My advisers tell me that some of your ideas were wonderfully helpful."

"It was a pleasure," the American said. "Rarely do I get a chance to consult for such a flawlessly run company. Your new computer designs are absolutely first-rate."

"Now you're sounding Japanese," Miura said, delighted at the way the American had returned the compliment. "But look, our main course has arrived. My friends, here is *fugusashi*!"

The two young waitresses brought over the plates that had been passed out of the inner kitchen to them. The strips of fish were cut so thin, they were almost transparent, and were arranged in the shape of chrysanthemums. The artful food sculptures were made to look even more like real flowers by a clever use of such garnishings as daikon radish and Japanese leek.

"You will now taste the most subtle food in the world," Miura promised them. "*Itadakimasu*—let's eat." He picked up a sliver of *fugusashi* with his chopsticks, dipped it in the thin soy-based sauce, and popped it in his mouth. They watched him chew and then swallow. "Quite good," he announced, very pleased. "The flesh is firm and savory. Please . . ."

Miura's wife took a piece of the raw fish from her plate and chewed it. She nodded at her husband, and swallowed. "Yes, it is quite good."

The American engineer ate a piece, and when he swallowed, his wife started in her seat. "It's delicious," he told her. "Not a strong taste but a striking one. Try a piece, sweetheart. I'm sure it's okay."

"I'm not so good with chopsticks," the engineer's wife confessed to Miura. "Is it okay if I use my fingers?" She looked down at the chrysanthemum of fish slices on her plate. "I don't want to destroy such a beautiful work of art for just one piece. You've already eaten—may I try a piece from your plate?" Miura nodded, and she picked up a piece of the slimy raw fish from Miura's plate and dipped it in the soy sauce. She brought it to her mouth and felt the cold raw blowfish against her upper lip. Then she returned the fish to Miura's plate and looked at her husband. "Sorry, but . . ."

Miura gave a little laugh. "Many people fear fugu. There is an old poem, 'Last night I ate fugu with a friend. Today I served as his pallbearer.' But there is nothing to fear." He looked at the boy. "Go ahead, Kaplan-*kun*, you try it."

"No way," the twelve-year-old said, pushing his plate away from him. "I'm not eating that poison guck." He knocked over his teacup, and a small puddle formed on the table. One of the waitresses ran over and mopped it up.

There was a momentary awkward silence. "Do you eat any dangerous foods in America?" Miura's wife asked to break the awkwardness and draw out the foreign guests.

"Everything my wife cooks falls into that category," the American engineer said.

"Dan, that's not true. . . ."

The boy nodded that it was true.

Miura and his wife laughed politely. And while he was laughing, Miura dropped his chopsticks. Dropping one's chopsticks in a fugu restaurant is a very serious matter, and the old chef's two daughters came running over. The poison found in fugu first attacks the motor neurons, so that it is well-known among fugu enthusiasts that when someone drops his chopsticks, he is manifesting the first symptom of fugu poisoning. Occasionally in a fugu restaurant, a diner will drop his chopsticks as a practical joke, to alarm the chef and the people he is eating with. When the joke is admitted, there are smiles and laughs all around.

Miura was not prone to practical jokes. His wife half rose from her seat, watching her husband's face as he tried to breathe. The chef's two daughters also watched him, also frozen in place, waiting for him to grin and confess that he was joking. Instead, Miura made a move to rise from his chair, sank back down, and keeled over backward onto the stone floor.

Miura's wife ran over to him and was joined in her efforts to revive him by the two bodyguards. The American woman let out a scream that was heard in an eel shop five doors down the block. One of the waitresses hurried to the telephone to summon help while her sister ran to the inner kitchen to tell their father. She found the old chef still unconscious on the floor. Blood trickled down over his face from a cut on his scalp. A small Chinese character had been artistically cut into the skin of the unconscious man's cheek with his own fugu knife. The character stood out in red outline against the old chef's pale face.

The assassin waited in the darkness by the back door, listening. The screams told him that he had succeeded, and he let himself out and walked down the back alley. He passed the garbage bin where he had disposed of the cat's corpse and slowed for a second. It had been unfortunate that he had had to kill the cat.

Then he sped up again. He had one more rather difficult job to do, and then he would treat himself to a very nice vacation on Phuket or Macao or perhaps Sumbawa.

He liked to travel. He was smiling slightly as he turned out of the alley and began walking up the block in the opposite direction from the two police cars that sped by him toward the fugu restaurant. He enjoyed working in the United States, and he was looking forward to the unique challenges of his next assignment in Los Angeles.

5

As Jack worked the speed bag, he was very conscious of being the only white man in the gym.

He normally worked out at a yuppie health club near Dupont Circle, but today he needed a lot more than sets on the Nautilus and women in spandex giving him the eye. They had a speed bag at the Bureau gym, so he could have worked out there, but even the relative seriousness of the afternoon weight-lifting regulars wouldn't have given him what he wanted today.

He wanted to hurt. He needed a place where they understood edge.

This boxing gym wasn't Kronk or Gleason's, but it was plenty serious. The sunlight that managed to filter through the dusty windows illuminated the old pine floorboards the color of tobacco-stained teeth. The two heavyweights sparring in the fourteen-foot ring were grunting and sweating, and when they landed body punches, the thuds ripped through the high-ceilinged room. A single rusty fan rotated in a corner, near the ghetto blaster that thumped out rap music. The place reeked of sweat and liniment.

Every minute a bell rang, and every three minutes a buzzer sounded out the round time. An old trainer with a face like a catcher's mitt stood near the ring, calling out advice to the fighters. "The body, man. Punish the body. Double on that jab, for chrissakes."

Jack found his rhythm, and his fists beat the speed bag in time to the rap music. He lost himself for a while in the cadence. Right, left, right, left. His hands became a blur.

He had spotted her car in a parking lot from a distance of nearly half a block. He was good at that—at noticing cars and remembering phone numbers and picking faces out of crowds. More than once the talent had proven a curse. Keeping on the far side of the street, he had walked closer, till he was able to read the license plate as the valet parkers jockeyed expensive cars back and forth. It was hers, all right.

Right, left, right. Jack's fists made the speed bag sing. He had walked past the restaurant's front window twice, spotting her at a corner table on the second pass. In a single quick glance he took in the bright splash of auburn hair on an emerald dress, the familiar smile, and her handsome lunch date.

He was a well-known figure on the Washington social scene; he worked in a conservative think tank, was a fixture at Republican fund-raisers, and occasionally threw lavish parties of his own. He had entertained them as a couple at one of those parties, keeping Jack's glass filled while he told Kate the amusing little anecdotes he was known for. Even then Jack had had the feeling the son of a bitch was measuring her, filing her away like a campaign promise to be investigated at some later time.

As Jack watched, the conservative sleazeball took Kate's hand in his across the table and kissed it. She smiled and then turned her head and glanced right at Jack. He had stood there for a moment, frozen, and then wheeled away like a junior high schooler caught peeping in his neighbor's window, and hurried off down the block.

Right, left, right, left.

Sweat ran down Jack's forehead and his punches became quicker and more fluid as he loosened up. It wasn't just that she had replaced him so quickly. That was simply the pace of this town. Rather, it was the sight of her with such a slimebucket Capitol Hill wheeler-dealer—a man who could probably say, "I love you" out of both sides of his mouth at once.

And the fact that she looked so happy. Left, left, right. Even more than happy, satisfied. Content. As if she had found something she really wanted, which he hadn't been able to give her.

Right, right, right. Tripling up. Seeing Walter's face on the speed bag. *Jack?* Pow, pow, pow. *Jack? You haven't answered my letter.* Right cross, right cross. Rot in hell! I'm not even angry with you. I've forgotten about you. These punches are for someone else. Bam, bam, bam. *Jack, do you blame me for what you say today?* Bam, bam. *Don't you have the courage to accuse me to my face?* Punching with wild fury. Get the fuck out of my head! Right, right, right.

The music shut off then, and Jack realized that a man had walked over and was standing behind and to one side of him, watching. Jack slowed up on the speed bag and half turned.

The young fighter was his own height, with smooth black skin except for just a bit of scar tissue around the eyes. Muscles rippled as he took a half step closer and smiled. "You were talking to the bag, man."

"Helps me get a good workout."

"Looks like you don't need too much help."

"Yeah, well, it's been a while," Jack said. The place had gone silent. Everyone in the gym was watching.

"I see your shirt. How high'd you go?"

"State final."

"Where?"

"California."

"Since then?"

"Fought in college," Jack said. "Not much lately."

The young black fighter took a half step closer. "I need work. Wanna help me out?"

"I'm not in shape."

"Three minutes."

Jack hesitated. It had been stupid to wear this shirt. He had grabbed it without thinking, but he knew they thought he was showing off. "Okay. But go easy."

Five minutes later they were in the ring, wearing headgear and padded belts. "Three minutes," the old trainer shouted. "At the buzzer."

The buzzer sounded, and Jack knew he was in trouble right away. The young fighter showed no respect, no caution, no intention of spending a minute or so feeling him out. He flicked two jabs that Jack backed away from, and then came in fast and low to the body. His first right to the ribs made a loud popping sound and Jack stumbled back. He dug three quick hooks into Jack's stomach, and when Jack sidestepped to the right, the young fighter anticipated him and shot up with a quick left that caught him flush on the right side of his headgear and almost dropped him.

Jack blanked for a long second, but he had been hit hard before and knew enough to keep his hands up and backpedal.

The other men in the gym had stopped working out and were

standing around the ring, watching and occasionally shouting advice. "C'mon, Larry. Get right on his ass. Move upstairs. Work it."

Jack's head cleared. Larry was cutting down the ring expertly, shooting hard right jabs as he waited for the moment to come inside again.

The bell rang. Two minutes. The old trainer shouted. "C'mon, get off. Don't just run away. Let your hands go."

Larry shot a right jab up high and tried to come in behind it, and Jack was waiting for him. His right-left-right banged home on the side of Larry's head, and as the black fighter stepped back outside, Jack saw him grinning slightly under his headgear.

The second minute was jabs and counters, and while Jack got the worst of it, he also landed some clean shots. His hand speed was still there. His footwork was awkward and his timing was off, but when they both threw, he was getting off first, and everyone in the gym knew it.

They were both sweating now. Jack felt each breath ripping through his lungs.

Again the bell. "One minute," the trainer shouted. "Throw some fucking leather."

And Larry came for him. Jack picked off two hooks and ducked a straight right, jabbing, feinting, trying to keep the young fighter away. But Larry threw caution to the winds and came in like a young Roberto Duran, ready to take two or three good shots to get within range.

Leather for leather, Jack. Quit backing up and throw. It was a ghostly voice from his own corner—a remembered voice he had heard in countless Golden Gloves tournaments, egging him on, sometimes to frightful beatings. *Turn animal on him.* I can't. He's a pro. He'll crush me.

As if to prove the point, the young fighter hooked to Jack's stomach with a short right that lifted him off the ground and made his guts burn right through to his sphincter.

See? So what? You wanted this. Bullshit I did. *Bullshit you didn't. That's why you're here. Now, get in there and show him what you're made of or so help me, I'll whup you myself.* With thirty seconds left, Jack stopped backing up and let his hands go.

They stood toe to toe. Larry was clearly surprised at Jack's late show of bravado. Except for the explosions of their punches and

their loud grunts, the gym had gone quiet. Right, left, right.
Savoring the fury of the moment. Taking a solid punch and connecting with three in return. Bam, bam, bam.

*That's it! Stay on him, Jack. Leather for leather. You can take
him down!* No. He's way too tough. *You're faster and tougher.
Go for it!*

Right. Right. Jack's hands exploded against Larry's headgear
as the young fighter began to backpedal away from the furious
last-second assault. Jack pursued him relentlessly, and just as the
three-minute buzzer sounded, he nailed Larry with an uppercut
that lifted the fighter off his feet and sat him down in the center of
the ring.

Jack lowered his arms and helped Larry stand back up. The men
standing around the ring nodded their approval and went back to
their training. Jack felt dizzy and sick to his stomach from the
body punches he had taken, but he managed a nonchalant grin as
he and Larry left the ring together.

"When'd you start fighting?" Larry asked.

"Ten. Police Athletic League. You?"

"Eighteen. The service. You got quick hands. Ever fight pro?"

"No," Jack said. "My father did. He wanted me to give it a
try."

"Pretty white boy like you could'a made money. Let's try it
again sometime, huh?"

"Whenever," Jack said, choking back nausea.

"Have to warn you. Next time I get even and kick your honky
ass."

"Maybe," Jack said. "Or maybe I'll knock your ribs out your
asshole one by one."

They shook hands, smiling, and Jack managed to hold it together till he reached the toilet stall. Then he knelt to stop the
dizziness, and threw up long and loudly. *Jack? You did good. I
always believed in you. That's the one thing you can't take away,
and you know it yourself, deep down. I was always in your corner.
I was always there when you needed me.*

That's true. You always were.

I taught you how to fight for yourself. I made you a winner.

I sure feel like a winner. The odor of a harsh industrial cleaner
rose from the floor and the edges of the toilet bowl, mingling with
the stench of his own puke.

I deserve an answer.

Knees on the hard tile floor, sick with the pain and dizzy from the stench, Jack saw clearly that he would have to go to Los Angeles. Anger accompanied the realization, and another wave of nausea immediately followed it.

In a small villa on Shodo Island, between the main town of Tonsho and Kankakei gorge, Matsuda's widow nursed her double grief amid the colorful burst of spring azaleas. She would often disappear before sunrise, hiking off by herself through the blazing color of the flowers to the cool pine forest beyond. In the late afternoons or early evenings she would return, eat a few slivers of fish and sip some green tea, and then retire to her bedroom, frequently without speaking to any of the servants or well-wishers who came regularly to pay their respects.

At first they had feared for her life. The loss of her husband had devastated her—the loss of their unborn child two weeks later seemed to be more than she could bear. The miscarriage, no doubt caused by the shock of grief and the stress of mourning, had inevitably led to whispers about the possibility of suicide.

The baby she carried had been her living link with her husband, a part of his flesh and blood that had survived the plane crash and that she planned to nurture and cherish in his memory. When she lost the child she wept uncontrollably for days, refused all food, and fell into a delirium that her servants feared could only end by her taking her own life.

But her friends, several of whom regularly crossed over from Takamatsu on the hydrofoil to try to encourage her, doubted that she would choose the shortest path of escape from grief. She came from a long and noble line of fighters, and suicide, however honorable, was not in her nature.

She lost weight till her limbs became sticklike and her quick eyes burned feverishly from hollowing sockets. Her face, which had once been famous the length of Shikoku for its youthful vivaciousness, now presented a harrowing but in some ways even more striking tableau of mature sadness. Where there had been ebullience, there was melancholy; warmth turned to wistfulness; she let her hair down like a widow's veil and spoke only in whispers.

But there came a time when the servants began to see a marked change in her grieving process. She wept less and walked more. She began gaining back weight. Eventually she started questioning old friends and colleagues of her husband about the circumstances surrounding the plane crash, and about the violence that had erupted in its aftermath.

Etsuko Matsuda had always kept respectfully in the background while her husband climbed the ladder of power in the Muramoto organization, but now she began to display a forcefulness and political sense that impressed her husband's loyal friends and worried those who were trying to leap into the regional power vacuum created by his death.

A month after the plane crash, returning from a long stroll through the pine forest, she asked the bodyguard who lived at the villa to teach her to load and shoot a gun.

The assassin landed at Los Angeles Airport at noon.

He had spent the twelve-hour plane ride studying maps and guidebooks to the City of Angels, all of which he read in English. He was quite proud of his language ability. He spoke passable Cantonese and quite a bit of Korean, and while his English was accented, it was grammatical, and he used it with confidence.

Usually, when he was working, he had to cut back on his vocabulary so as not to leave too much of an impression. Despite studying English for three years in junior high school and three more years in high school, many Japanese businessmen and tourists are afraid to try their hand at English conversation and prefer to rely on tour guides and interpreters. So the assassin was careful to throw out the English maps and guidebooks in the JAL terminal.

He had memorized what he needed to know.

He changed a bit of money and was mildly surprised to get back nearly a thousand dollars. The exchange rate never failed to amaze him. When he had begun traveling on business, America had been considered almost prohibitively expensive.

V.I.P. Car Rentals had the Mercedes Benz ready for him, under the name of Nakamoto. A pretty young Japanese woman came to the service desk to assist him, so he did not speak a word of English. No doubt the police would check the airports in a day or so for anything suspicious. In his charcoal gray suit with a *Yomiuri Shinbun* folded under his right arm, he gave the impression of being a successful Japanese businessman, in America for a short trip.

The Mercedes Benz would stand out, of course. But there was a reason for that, so it couldn't be helped.

It was a big, late-model black sedan—a gangster car. The assassin took the Century Avenue exit onto the San Diego Freeway and headed north. The freeway was still pretty empty, and as the big car purred along at sixty-five, he found a fifties station on the radio. The assassin couldn't imagine living in Los Angeles, but it was a nice place to kill in. There was almost no sense of neighborhood watchfulness or neighborly friendliness, and the freeways were wonderfully convenient once an assignment had been completed.

Which would be handy, because this was going to be quite a tricky job. . . .

He got off at Wilshire and stayed on the ramp to the second exit—Wilshire heading west. Soon he was in Brentwood enjoying the palm trees that curved gracefully to surprising heights. He was proud to see that in this affluent little corner of Los Angeles there was a definite Japanese presence—he noted half a dozen Toyotas and Acuras, and two sushi shops.

She lived on Kiowa, near Bundy. The name struck him as strange and exotic-sounding. Kiowa. Was it a man's name? It was almost Japanese.

He drove past her house once, and saw that in terms of privacy, he could not have hoped for more. It was a two-story Spanish-style house with white walls and a red tile roof, set back from the street on what was, for Brentwood, a fairly large plot of land. Two rows of eucalyptus trees hid the house and particularly its windows from the taller condominium buildings on either side.

So no one would be able to see in.

His mind automatically registered the critical information: two streetlights split evenly twenty kilometers down the block on either side, three large windows on the first story facing the street, four smaller bedroom windows on the second level, a back patio—just barely visible around the side of the house—with wire screening, and a detached two-car garage with no light.

He would enter through the back patio, after dark. Her husband was supposed to be away, so it would just be her. If a mistake had been made and her husband was home, he would kill the husband first, very quickly.

The assassin turned onto San Vincente and headed for the beach, driving slowly and carefully.

He had never liked torture. Torture was always unpredictable. Killing was quick and clean—a real art—but torture was almost by definition slow and messy. And sometimes, no matter how much skill was used, the subject held out. And held out. The assassin had run into such frustrating cases before.

Tonight, given the nature of the information he was assigned to extract from the woman, he expected to encounter resistance. And there was the added fact that the woman had met him once before. It had been a decade ago, in Atami, and of course, she would never remember his face, but he had an almost superstitious dislike of being assigned women he had met before.

If the woman had read about Muramoto and the plane crash, or about the deaths of Ida and Miura, she would very possibly be on her guard and have a weapon handy. All of which meant that he would have to be careful. But then, he was always careful.

The first sight of the great blue sweep of the Pacific Ocean delighted him. He had grown up with an almost religious reverence for the ocean—for its beauty and power. The broad white strip of sandy beach stretched away to the north toward Malibu and to the south toward the Marina. He turned south.

He parked on Rose Street and was surprised by how surly the parking lot attendant was to him. In Japan an employee who gave such service to customers would have been fired immediately.

The assassin spent the rest of the day on Venice Beach. It was one of the few places in the entire world where he could relax while on an assignment. No matter what cultural or behavioral mistakes he made or what he wore or how he acted, at Venice Beach no one would notice him or remember him. Most of the people on the walkway looked bizarre, and many of them acted as if they were half-insane.

At an outdoor stand he bought himself a sleeveless T-shirt that said "Santa Monica Yacht Club." Farther down the walkway he bought reflecting sunglasses and a vanilla ice cream cone. "Chocolate sprinkles?" the slightly obese lady asked him.

"I beg your pardon?"

She showed him. "Yes, please," he said, delighted with the word. "Many sprinkles."

For several hours he walked along, watching the people and the acts. He loved the blond California girls with their tight bodies in bright bikinis, shaking their hips and their breasts as they walked in ways that Japanese women never would. Japanese women were taught from grade school to walk modestly, but American women sent out invitations with every step.

There would be no time on this trip to play with an American woman. Except, of course, for the night's assignment. He thought back ten years, and remembered a striking redhead with an hourglass figure and a warm smile. As he pondered what he would do to her, he felt the first faint stirrings of sexual excitement. He stepped off the walkway toward the ocean and waited for his body to relax.

That was another reason why he didn't like torture. Even among the highest professionals, it tended to bring out personal weaknesses.

Farther down the walkway, a bearded man juggled chainsaws. The assassin put a dollar into his hat. A contortionist kept up a constant patter as he tied himself in knots. A shirtless young black man lay down on shards of broken glass and had members of the audience walk across his stomach.

At six the assassin got back into his car and headed north, past Brentwood. He got a hickory burger, french fries, and a Sprite at a hamburger stand and again was amazed at the slowness and rudeness of service industries in America. How did the country function as a superpower if its inhabitants took such little pride in their work, and the service was so shoddy? He drove with his dinner up to a remote stretch of Mulholland Drive.

The entire west side of the city spread out beneath him. He ate slowly, already feeling the excitement building in the pit of his stomach.

As darkness fell, and the lights blinked on in the homes below, the assassin changed from his traditional business suit to his loosely fitting black pants and shirt. He also pulled on surgical gloves and a black plastic cap over his hair.

At midnight the Mercedes Benz rolled to a stop on Kiowa Street, fifty feet from the Spanish-style house. One light was on in the house, on the ground floor. From his extensive knowledge of architectural layouts, the assassin guessed that the lighted room was the kitchen. Perhaps she was preparing a late night snack. In any case, it was very good because the kitchen would suit his purposes quite well. Only the upstairs bathroom would have been better, and he could bring her there if he needed to.

The assassin waited in the car for fifteen minutes, watching the empty street. Occasionally a car passed by, but there were no pedestrians. That was yet another reason why he liked to work in Los Angeles—nobody seemed to walk, so there were rarely pedestrians to contend with.

Kiowa Street was dark and empty.

At twelve-fifteen the door of the black sedan opened and then shut again, noiselessly. A black shadow glided quickly across the street and melted into the shrubbery in front of a condominium.

The assassin made it to the screened-off back porch in less than ten seconds. He quickly checked for alarms—he was quite expert in detecting security systems—but the back porch was not wired. He picked the lock of the porch door without trouble, and slipped inside.

He moved forward in a low crouch, less than two feet off the floor, avoiding the high sight line that was so dangerous. Into the house, down a dark hallway, toward the triangle of yellow light unfolding from the kitchen. . .

At the door he paused, and glanced quickly inside.

She was standing alone at the counter, with her back to him. Her red hair was much longer than he remembered it—it reached almost to her hips. She was wearing a blue terry cloth bathrobe, and from this angle he couldn't be sure of exactly what she was doing. He smelled alcohol, and guessed that she was making herself some kind of drink.

Perhaps, if she had read about what was going on in Japan, it was a tonic to help her sleep.

The assassin stepped into the large kitchen, his sword in his right hand. He moved absolutely soundlessly, but at his second step she sensed his presence, turned, and looked him right in the face. She was quite beautiful, with big green eyes and a full figure. When she saw him, something in her eyes told the assassin that she instantly recognized him and understood why he had come.

He moved quickly across the tile floor toward her. As she backed away she surprised him by demanding, *"Yakusoku wa dooshita no?"* What had become of his oath of loyalty?

He was twenty feet from her, then fifteen. *"Omae wa gaijin,"* he grunted. You are a foreigner. *"Nihon no shikumi ga wakaranai, daroo?"* What can you know of Japanese oaths of honor?

As if in answer, she picked up the kitchen knife. It was long and looked very sharp, and she held it tightly in her right hand. The assassin slowed and approached more carefully, enjoying the almost laughable notion that she was going to try to fight him off with the kitchen knife.

Looking right at him, she raised the knife above her waist, and by the time he understood and dove in to stop her, it was too late. In one fierce motion she thrust the knife deep into her throat, and he dodged to one side to avoid the spurting blood.

One look told him that the self-inflicted wound was indeed lethal, and that she would not be able to tell him anything now, even if she wanted to. The only thing he could do was to leave quickly.

Still watching him, she swayed and toppled to her knees, the blood beginning to geyser from her neck. Then she fell on her side on the floor, still holding the knife with both hands.

Despite himself, the assassin was deeply moved. He bowed formally to her, and then turned and hurried out of the kitchen. He let himself out through the porch door, and ran quickly for his car. On those rare occasions when assignments went awry, long experience had taught him to get out quickly. Bad luck usually brought more of the same.

He hurried down Kiowa and then stopped short and melted behind a palm tree. As if to prove his theory, a strange-looking vehicle with an orange light on top was parked next to his car, while a young black woman wrote out a parking ticket. He debated killing her. Either way, it was very bad. He decided it would be wiser to let her live.

She finished writing out the ticket, stuck it under his right windshield wiper, and drove away. When she was out of sight he hurried to the car and checked the ticket—it was for parking two inches too far from the curb. He glanced at his watch and saw that it was twelve thirty-five. What kind of a country was this where service in parking lots and restaurants was so slow, but young women gave parking tickets after midnight for ridiculous infractions?

He got into the car and drove away at just under the speed limit.

They would not be happy about the ticket. Of course, they would not be happy about the suicide, either, but the ticket would be very bad. As the assassin drove back toward Los Angeles Airport for the long flight home, he ran the episode over and over again in his mind. There had been little he could have done differently.

Truly it had been a magnificent death. And while on one level it was surprising, especially for an American, on another level it was exactly what one might have expected from a woman with such a history.

6

The maid found Shannon Miles's corpse at two minutes after nine o'clock, and by nine-thirty Kiowa Street was crawling with cops. They cordoned off the house and yard, began checking the sidewalks and gutters up and down the block, and did some preliminary questioning of the few neighbors who were at home.

At nine-forty Detective Walter Graham arrived to take charge of the investigation. He looked the part of a homicide detective, as if the police department had sent down to Central Casting for a square-jawed, grizzled bear of a man. His once handsome face was lined and pitted, and his blue eyes were dull and rarely showed any emotion except a general weariness. Still, even in his decline, there was something riveting about Walter Graham.

The young cops searching the yard and the street bent to their tasks more diligently after he showed up. The word around the department was that any careless mistakes or goofing off during one of Walter Graham's investigations enraged the detective almost to the point of violence. Twice he had been reprimanded for threatening fellow cops, and there were rumors of even more ugly incidents that had been hushed up. On the other hand, Graham was widely acknowledged to be one of the best and most tenacious detectives on the force.

Sergeant DeLorenzo, who had been senior till Graham arrived, ran down what they had already learned in quick and precise sentence fragments. "Name's Miles, Shannon Alison. Caucasian, thirty-five. She died from a single knife wound to the throat—kitchen's covered with blood. Knife's still in her hands. Maid found her at nine o'clock, and ran screaming down the street. The manager at the condo next door called 911 and—"

"Who was first on the scene?" Graham interrupted.

"Garner. He's out searching the yard now."

47

"I want to talk to him after I see the body. Got an occupation yet?"

"Manager across the street knew a bit about her. Says she was a teacher at U.C.L.A. Art history. Moved into this house with her husband four years ago."

"The husband?"

"Also a professor. Dr. Everett Miles, forty-three."

"Art history?"

"Computer engineering. U.S.C."

"The Trojan and the Bruin. Found him yet?"

"We're checking. His department at U.S.C. says he's in South Bend, Indiana, at a conference, but they're not sure exactly where in South Bend or who to call to find out. . . ."

"Any sign of a break-in? Anything funny?"

DeLorenzo shook his head. "Nothing. Looks like she did it herself. She's not a pretty sight. . . ."

Walter Graham took out his first unfiltered Marlboro of the day, lit it, and inhaled deeply. "No, I don't suppose she would be," he muttered. "Let's go."

They walked into the house together. Shannon Miles lay on her back on the kitchen floor, staring blankly up at the white stucco ceiling. The large puddle of her blood had congealed around her, so that her long red hair seemed to trail off into crimson syrup. She still held the kitchen knife in her right hand, her fingers tight on the wooden handle. Her bathrobe had opened during her fall, and her right breast was bare to the nipple.

Walter Graham walked around the perimeter of the pool of blood, studying Shannon's corpse from different vantage points. He examined her for a long time without speaking. "Cute gal. Pity," he finally muttered. "Fell on her side first—see how the robe is open on that side. Then on her back. How long you think she's been laying there?"

"Five," DeLorenzo guessed quickly. He had been expecting the question.

The detective shook his head. "We'll see what the coroner says, but just looking at her, I'll bet seven to ten. Middle of the night. She wanted to die when it was quietest." He bent to take a look at the neck wound, and when he spoke again he sounded almost puzzled. "You wouldn't think she could'a got the knife in that deep. Couldn't have aimed any better."

He walked slowly around the ground floor of the house, stopping here and there to glance at a few titles in the floor-to-ceiling living room bookshelves, the vitamins and aspirin in the bathroom medicine cabinet, and the sheet music on the piano. DeLorenzo followed him in silence, watching him work. It was almost as if the detective were sniffing randomly, waiting to come across a scent he recognized.

After poking into every room on the ground floor, Water Graham walked up the carpeted stairs and stuck his head into every room on the second story. He took in the master bedroom with its four-poster brass bed and antique wooden furniture, the simple but tastefully furnished guest bedroom, and the two small studies.

Graham spent longest in the upstairs bathroom, running his eyes carefully over several rows of neatly arranged fairly standard household pharmaceuticals. Then, without a word to DeLorenzo, he returned to the kitchen and studied Shannon's corpse again as if looking for something he hadn't seen during his first inspection.

Graham's eyes swept back and forth very slowly from crown to toes to crown again. He sniffed twice, quickly, like a terrier. "No perfume. No underwear. No makeup. Not even lipstick. No valued possession or keepsake. No suicide note. She didn't give a damn who found her or what they thought. Or else she did the whole thing on the spur of the moment, without planning." His raspy voice suddenly thickened and he broke into a series of deep coughs. The coughs, in turn, gave way to some rapid-fire questions that Detective Graham seemed to direct more toward himself than to DeLorenzo and the other policemen in the room.

"Why the kitchen? Wouldn't it be more comfortable to kill yourself in a bedroom? Why with a knife? Wouldn't a U.C.L.A. professor be able to think of a less painful way? Why no note? She was married—didn't she have anything to tell her husband?"

"Maybe she boozed up beforehand," DeLorenzo suggested, pointing to the full glass on the counter. "There's a gin and tonic over there."

Graham shook his head. "Not the way she stuck that knife in. We'll see what the coroner says, but I'll almost guarantee you she was dead sober to get herself off so cleanly." He thought for a few seconds and then spoke quickly. "Here's what I want you to do. I want to talk to the maid first, then . . . what did you say his name was . . . ? Garner. I want every single neighbor on both sides of

Kiowa questioned. Most of 'em won't be home till five, but we can get a start on it. Did they hear anything last night? Quarreling? Crying? Did they see anyone enter or leave? Did any cars pull into the driveway?''

"Then you don't buy the suicide?" DeLorenzo ventured.

"Of course I buy the suicide," Graham snapped. "What's not to buy? She was found with the damn knife in her hand, wasn't she?"

"Yes, sir."

"I want the house searched top to bottom. Look for any signs of struggle, any bloodstains in any other room, any drugs or firearms. . . ."

Walter Graham broke off for a second, and wiped his forehead with a wrinkled handkerchief. Then he went on, "This is a high-security area, and I want to know about any funny business in the neighborhood, no matter how slight. Any other houses nearby report break-ins? Any private security patrols spot anything? Any fire alarms, or calls to hospitals? Were there any moving violations or parking tickets given on Kiowa right up to Barrington? Anything at all. Got it?"

"Yes, sir," DeLorenzo said. Then, "What about the husband?"

"He'll come back from South Bend as soon as he gets the news. I want to see him right away."

"You think he knows why she did it?"

Graham looked at the young cop for a long beat. "You married?" he finally asked.

"Yes, sir. Two years this June."

"If your wife stuck a kitchen knife into her throat one night, don't you think you might have an inkling why she did it?"

He walked away before DeLorenzo could put together an answer.

Dr. Everett Miles was not what Walter Graham had expected at all. The computer engineer rode into his office in a motorized wheelchair that he maneuvered by hand controls. His broad shoulders helped hide a large potbelly, and his boyish face was topped incongruously with short, curly white hair. "I'm Everett Miles," he said. "They tell me you're in charge of this. . . ."

"Walter Graham. Thank you for coming." The professor's

handshake had no grip at all—it was merely a quick touching of palms and fingers. Graham closed the door to his office and then walked back and sat down on the top of his desk, facing Dr. Miles. For several seconds the police detective and the scientist studied each other in silence.

Dr. Everett Miles was clearly going through hell. His eyes were red from crying, and his fingernails had been chewed very far down. His seersucker suit was wrinkled, his breath was stale, and Walter could tell from one look that Dr. Miles hadn't slept at all the previous night. "Take the red-eye home?"

"It was the first flight back. When I heard about . . . about what happened . . . I went straight to the airport." The fleshy arm on the armrest trembled slightly.

"Like some coffee?"

"No."

"A sandwich? I can send out."

"I can't keep anything down."

Walter nodded and launched into something of a set speech. "Dr. Miles, I know you've been through hell. I'm not much good at pussyfooting around, so I'll be as quick and as direct as I can. A few of my questions will be painful for you to even think about right now. Bear with me. We both want the same thing."

"I'll do my best," Dr. Everett Miles said. "It's just that this doesn't seem quite real. I keep thinking it's a bad dream and I'll wake up. . . ."

Walter recognized the plea for sympathy. Tears would come next—the man was likely to break any second. Better to plunge in than to waste time on further niceties. "Shannon was born in Massachusetts?"

"Weymouth. South of Boston. She grew up there. Her maiden name was Cleary. Her mother still lives in the same apartment."

"And her father?"

"Died a few years ago, of lung cancer. He was a chain smoker. Three packs a day."

Walter's cheek twitched very slightly at this, and he glanced quickly down at the yellow-brown stains on his own fingertips. He pressed on. "She went to Yale. Majored in East Asian languages. Then she went to Japan for a couple of years to teach. That all right?"

"Yes."

"What did she teach over there, anyway?"

"She taught English conversation in a Japanese public high school. She went on a big program, run by the government. Ended up in a coastal city called Atami, and had a wonderful time."

"Then she came back and enrolled in U.C.L.A. as a graduate student? About nine years ago?"

"That's right."

"She earned her master's, and her Ph.D., and was just starting to teach as an assistant professor?"

"Correct."

"When did you meet her?"

"Seven years ago. At a party thrown by a mutual friend on the U.C.L.A. faculty."

"And you were married five years ago?"

For the first time Dr. Miles's voice cracked when he tried to answer, and he ended up just nodding.

Walter knew the next one would hurt, but he didn't pull the punch in any way: "Was your health condition the same then as it is now?"

The man in the wheelchair looked up quickly, and his cheeks grew red. "I don't see how it's any of your business—"

Walter cut in fast and hard. "Spare me the indignation. Just answer the question."

"I was in this same wheelchair the day that I met Shannon. She was bright enough not to judge people by their physical handicaps, which, unfortunately, I can't say for everyone in our society. She loved me for who I was. She didn't want a rugby player—"

"For Christ's sake, put a lid on it, will you?" Walter Graham knew the next one would be as bad or worse, but he didn't allow the engineer even a moment's respite. "Do you know if Shannon had had any serious love relationships before she met you?"

Dr. Miles looked momentarily outraged, as if he was preparing to tell Graham to go to hell. A second look at the hard lines of the detective's face seemed to make him think better of it. He took a deep breath and said, "Two. We never discussed them in any great depth. She lived with a boy while she was in college."

"For how long?"

"I don't know. A year or two."

"Do you know his name?"

"Of course not. And she had a romance in Japan, when she taught there. And no, I don't know that name either. Shannon didn't talk to me about the men in her past, and I didn't ask." Dr. Miles paused and blew his nose. "Could we do this another day? I really don't feel like answering any more of your questions right now." The fat fingers moved on the hand controls, and the wheelchair slowly rolled toward the door.

"You can go when I tell you you can go," Graham barked. "We both want the same thing—to find out what was behind your wife's suicide—and I'm damned if I'm going to let you leave before I ask a few follow-ups. . . ."

The wheelchair stopped and turned, and Dr. Miles was suddenly so angry that he was half shouting. "Shannon didn't commit suicide. Don't ever say that to me again."

"Then you think she was murdered?"

"She would never have committed suicide."

"Did she have any enemies with reasons to want to hurt her?"

"No." Dr. Miles's indignant anger melted quickly to soft-spoken grief. "Everyone liked Shannon. She loved, and was beloved." The engineer broke into tears, and wiped his eyes and nose with his shirt sleeve. Walter Graham looked away out the window and watched cars pass by till the crying sounds stopped.

"Did she have violent or unstable acquaintances?"

"No."

"Did she have debts or was she involved at all with organized crime?"

"Of course not."

"Was she taking or dealing drugs?"

The computer engineer hesitated just for a second. "We smoked marijuana recreationally."

"How often?"

"Maybe once or twice a week."

"Did she have any family members with serious emotional or psychological problems? Had she quarreled with any family members recently?"

"No. Never."

"Were there any men in her life who she was . . . romantically involved with . . . besides you? Do you think she might have had a lover? A platonic friend she was starting to get in trouble with? Even another woman?"

Dr. Everett Miles pursed his lips as if the question seemed to sting a bit. "I'm quite sure there was no one else."

"Did she have health problems, or financial problems? Were there any serious rifts in your marriage?"

"The answer to all your questions is no. No, no, and *no*! I want to get out of here. . . ."

"Well then," Walter Graham said in a soft, faintly derisive voice, "it doesn't sound like you can suggest anyone who might have had any reason at all for wanting to hurt Shannon?"

"That's right. There was no one."

"Then why do you say she was murdered?"

"Because," Dr. Everett Miles said with great conviction, "she was happy and she loved me. And happy people who are in love don't kill themselves."

"I agree. They usually don't. That's all I need to ask you right now. Here's my card. Call me any time of the day or night if you think of anything. And make sure we have a phone number where I can reach you if I need to."

Dr. Miles turned the wheelchair and rode toward the door without speaking. Walter Graham stepped to it to let him out, and then walked back to his desk and lit a cigarette. The engineer's final point echoed in his ears: "Happy people who are in love don't kill themselves."

Walter Graham exhaled two thin streams of white smoke through his nose, and broke into a long fit of coughing.

7

She walked out with him all the way to the front door, and they stood on the steps looking down at the rush-hour traffic crawling by in both directions on Sunset Boulevard. It was six-fifteen, and about half of the cars had turned their lights on already. "Do me a favor, Walter?" she said. "Have some fun this week?"

He nodded. She was a tall woman in her mid-forties, and against all of his expectations, he found that he liked and respected her quite a bit. "I will," he promised.

"Treat yourself to a little vacation or something."

"Jack's coming on Thursday. Maybe we'll go throw a baseball around like old times. Y'know, I never expected him to come."

"I told you he would."

"That's true. You did."

"You're very hard on yourself, Walter. I'm sure he has a lot of fond feelings toward you."

"I'm not so sure about that. To tell the truth, I almost don't know what to say to him when he gets here."

"Why don't you start by telling him that you love him?"

Walter laughed. "He'd get back on the plane and go back to Washington."

"I doubt that. I know it's a hard thing to say, but I think you need to say it and he needs to hear it."

"Well, anyway, I'll try to have a good time."

"You do that," she said. "And I'll see you again on the fifteenth. 'Bye."

" 'Bye." He walked down the steps away from her. His car was a big old Plymouth Fury, ugly and powerful, and he stayed in the left lane as he drove west toward the ocean, getting up a little speed as the traffic thinned out after Barrington. He sped through

55

the Pacific Palisades—damn antiseptic yuppie breeding ground—
and turned left onto Temescal Canyon.

He parked a half block from Will Rogers State Beach, crossed
Pacific Coast Highway at the light, took off his shoes and socks,
and walked across the sand toward the setting sun. At the water's
edge he turned south, and followed the surf toward Santa Monica,
his eyes on the ocean.

A few surfers in wet suits waited by their boards as a long
succession of small waves washed in. Above their heads, two
gulls hovered, seemingly motionless in the purplish last light.
Much farther out, a twenty-five-footer tacked shoreward on its
long trip back to Marina Del Rey.

She was a good therapist and a damn fine woman, and maybe
if he'd gone to talk to someone years ago, his life wouldn't be so
completely screwed up. But he had never put much stock in ther-
apists. He had always thought that most shrinks in Los Angeles
catered to rich and spoiled celebrity kids and bored Beverly Hills
housewives and lonely old turds who needed to rent a friendly ear.

Walter Graham had always preferred to spill his guts to his
favorite bartender.

But after the last disciplinary incident, the department had given
him no choice, so he'd gone to see her. And it had become a
regular thing. Now Walter found himself looking forward to their
biweekly sessions and listening closely whenever Dr. Cooperman
spoke back to him.

She was right—he needed some fun. Something good, and
cheerful. Because he had never felt so low. Even when he'd lost
his firstborn son. Even during the divorce. Even when he'd heard
that his ex-wife was dying and that she didn't want to see him.
Never, ever.

Partly it was the diagnosis. He wasn't afraid of death and he
could endure pain as well as anyone, but he had seen a few people
with serious emphysema and knew what an excruciating way it
was to die. And he knew he would never be able to quit smoking.
Even now, as he walked along the beach, he craved a cigarette.

He dug his toes into the cold, wet sand and forced himself to
think about the case. Also depressing. Nearly a week had passed
since Shannon's death and there were no leads, no breaks—the
whole thing made no sense at all. And, unaccountably, Captain

Charles was leaning on him to leave it at suicide, wrap it up, and move on.

Those had been the captain's exact words: "Leave it alone as a suicide, Walter. Wrap it up quick and we'll give you some other ones to worry about."

Walter Graham did up his top button and began to jog. A young couple, wrapped in blankets, stared at him as he went by—a man in a jacket and tie jogging on the beach, carrying his shoes in his right hand. He slowed down after a hundred yards and began to cough. Stopping, he thumped his chest with his fist, and spit into the hissing surf.

Everything made sense about Shannon Miles except her death. She was healthy, had a good job, a nice home, lots of friends, and enough money. Her friends all said that she seemed happily married, and that Dr. Miles treated her like a queen. A small quantity of cocaine had been found in her upstairs night table, but not enough to even raise an eyebrow about. There was probably that much cocaine in half the apartments in Brentwood.

Her very best friends said that she had seemed a little depressed lately. A bit nervous. She had called two companies about having security systems installed. And her licensed handgun was found in the top drawer of her dresser, loaded but with the safety catch on.

All of which amounted to nothing substantial. Dr. Miles appeared to be wrong—his wife had indeed been happy and beloved and in love, but for some reason she had still taken a kitchen knife and in one swipe ended her own life.

And they might never figure out why.

He turned back toward the car. Christ, it would be good to see Jack. He had sounded gloomy over the phone, but perhaps that had just been a reflection of a serious mood. Maybe the little fart had found himself a girl. And maybe he was ready to leave Washington behind and move back out West. God knows there was a career all set up and waiting for him with the Los Angeles police. Damn, but they had a lot to talk about.

Walter lit a cigarette, took several puffs, and tossed it down on the sand as a deep, hacking cough made him crouch over and spit bloody phlegm. Suddenly he wanted very much to have a grandchild.

The traffic had let up a bit, and he made it back to Eighteenth

Street in Santa Monica in less than twenty minutes. His rent-controlled apartment was in an old building, next to a Honda dealership.

From long habit he stood outside his apartment for more than a minute, listening and checking a number of small details about the knob and the locks that would have told him if anyone had forced an entrance. Then he let himself in, ran a hot bath, and replayed his phone messages.

The first message was from Jack. He would arrive on Friday, but he wasn't sure which plane he would be on, so he would take a cab from the airport. Also, he didn't want to impose on Walter, so he'd made reservations at a Western Inn up the block.

The second message was from Sergeant DeLorenzo, and it made Walter stand very still. Dr. Everett Miles was dead. Apparently he had flown to Japan a few days after Walter had talked to him, and traveled to the city of Atami, where his wife had once taught. His body had just been found at the foot of a hundred-foot cliff, splattered on an ocean rock. His wheelchair had landed in the sand, and tests showed the braking mechanism still worked perfectly. So it didn't seem like an accident.

The Japanese police were investigating, but it looked to them like the suicide of a distraught widower.

"Do you know the Yiddish word *tsuris*?" MacCormack asked, scratching a red spot on the side of his neck.

Jack nodded.

"Funny, you don't look Jewish."

"Neither do you." MacCormack was Irish to the core, with a bluff, red-cheeked, jowly face partially hidden behind thick spectacles.

"As my Irish grandmother used to say, I don't need this *tsuris*," MacCormack said, pulling his hand away from his neck. He had bad skin and was always scratching one body part or another, and applying this cream or that ointment. His late fifties were not being kind to him. Jack saw MacCormack in the gym several times a week, but despite the special agent in charge's best efforts, he had already developed a rather large potbelly and the first faint ripple of a double chin. His general fleshiness, and his oversize eyes which glistened behind his thick spectacles, gave him a warm, almost grandmotherly quality.

"I'm not trying to give you *tsuris*," Jack told him, "but after the way Hwang wrapped up, I'm surprised you begrudge me half a week."

"It's exactly because of how Hwang turned out that I do."

"I don't understand."

MacCormack snorted. "Follow me to my office and I will be glad to make things crystal-clear."

Jack followed the big man down a long corridor to his impressive corner office. Signed pictures of presidents since Kennedy hung on the walls. Jack noted in a quick glance that Carter was the only one missing. Further signed testimonials ranged from J. Edgar Hoover to the Reverend Ralph Abernathy to Henry Kissinger. The lone diploma on the wall was from Harvard Law School, Class of '55. Jack had heard the big man had graduated number two in his class. He had quite a reputation around the Bureau as a superb lawyer, a fair administrator, and an all-around good egg.

MacCormack shut the door and gestured Jack to a seat. The big man sat opposite him—he was breathing a bit hard from the walk down the corridor. "It's precisely because you did such a good job with Hwang Securities that this is a problem."

"But I just need a few days. I haven't missed a day of work in months."

"It's not the time, it's the timing." The big man leaned forward and his chair groaned. "You've set yourself up for a plum, Jack. And that plum is ready to drop in your lap."

"The Harburg Fiasco?"

A small nod that said quite a bit.

"I thought that was still weeks away."

"We'll start moving any day now. Not a good time to leave town, Jack. You're one of our rising stars. This one could do it for you."

Jack swallowed. "I appreciate you looking out for me, but I've already made my decision. I need to take the trip."

MacCormack took the fleshy fold under his chin between his thumb and second finger and toyed with it for a few seconds, as if trying to pinch it away.

"I'll be back real soon." Silence. "It's not for pleasure. It's family business." Silence. "Look, I know I owe you an awful lot, and I'm sorry if I'm letting you down. But this concerns my father, and I sort of have to go.'' Jack knew that when one worked in the intelligence business, it was best to come clean.

The division chief seemed surprised. ''Your father? We've been working together for years and you've never mentioned a father.''

''Well, I've got one.''

''And one who apparently requires looking after.''

A question was buried in the statement. ''Yes, sir. I kind of think he may.''

''Well. I *kind of* understand then. But I guess I should tell you, this may force me to go another way with the Harburg investigation.''

''I hope not, but if so, I understand.''

''Right,'' MacCormack said. ''Right. Well, I've got another matter to attend to. Luck with Dad.''

''Thanks.'' Jack stood. ''And thanks for looking out for me.''

MacCormack waved him away. ''Between the two of us, I sort of appreciate your motives. I have a son about your age who lives in Dallas and never comes to see me. Guess your father just had the luck.''

I'd say your son had a lot more, Jack thought as he left the division chief's office and headed down the corridor. He tried not to even think about the possible damage he had done to his career in the past five minutes.

Jack landed at Los Angeles Airport at ten o'clock on a Friday morning. He was traveling light—he had just enough clothes for a long weekend crammed into a single large shoulder bag. He walked out the door under the Ground Transportation sign, flagged down a cab, and was soon on his way to Santa Monica.

Jack's fingers drummed a nervous rhythm on the back of the car seat. When the driver turned off the Santa Monica Freeway and began negotiating local roads that Jack remembered from years past, his heart started to race and he actually began to have trouble breathing.

He forced himself to sit back and take a dozen or so short, regular breaths. It didn't feel like a homecoming—it was more like returning to a war zone for the final battle. Dozens of memories from five, ten, and even twenty years ago suddenly clamored their separate agonies and angers at the fringes of his consciousness. The taxi turned onto Eighteenth Street and braked to a stop in front of a low, rather ugly concrete building fronted by scraggly pines.

Jack paid the cabbie and stood for a moment on the well-remembered dingy street, looking at the two- and three-level buildings that rent-control laws had kept absurdly cheap while at the same time plunging the block into a permanently shabby state of disrepair. He climbed the stairs to the heavy, steel-reinforced door, drew back his hand to knock, hesitated, and then smacked the door with his fist.

Five seconds passed. He found that he was holding his breath, and exhaled. Another ten seconds crawled by. He rapped with the brass knocker and listened for footsteps, but none came.

His father must have stepped out. Jack still had his own old key on his key ring—he tried it in the keyhole and was surprised to see that it fit. For all Walter's carefulness in matters of security, he hadn't changed the lock in the last decade. Jack let himself in and heard the singing. His father was in the shower, and very uncharacteristically the tough cop was singing an out-of-tune "Old Man River" in a raspy baritone that sounded like a cross between Paul Robeson and Bob Dylan.

Jack stood by the butcher block kitchen table, listening incredulously. No wonder Walter hadn't heard the knocking—just listen to the old bastard croon. It was a song and a singing voice Jack remembered from his early childhood. For a moment his feelings of anger melted away at the awful singing and were replaced by surprisingly strong stirrings of fond nostalgia. Impulsively he headed toward the bathroom. He opened the bathroom door, stepped a few feet into the small, tiled bathroom, and as his father finished a nightmare chorus of "But them that plants them are soon forgotten," Jack called out, "Just wanna tell you I'm home and happy birthday—"

With lightning reflexes Walter Graham swept the shower curtain aside and whirled toward Jack, a gun in his hands. Walter caught himself just as his trigger finger began to move, and for a second father and son stared at each other across the barrel of the 9-mm Beretta automatic. The old policeman slowly lowered his gun, and put it back on the shampoo rack. Without looking away, he reached to his right and turned off the water. "You almost did it that time, Jack," he said hoarsely. "So help me God, you almost did it."

Jack could only mutter, "I heard you singing, so I figured I'd let you know I was here. Sorry."

"Sorry?" Walter shook his head, and the drops of water flew off in all directions. "Why don'tcha get outta my bathroom and let me get dressed. Jesus H. Christ, I almost blew your fool head off."

Jack walked back into the kitchen and tried to calm down. His right hand shook, and he folded it into a fist and slammed it down on the table so hard, the salt and pepper shakers clattered. He hadn't been in the apartment more than five minutes and he was already mumbling apologies to Walter like a little boy.

The apartment was small and a bit shabby, but spotlessly neat. The floors were mopped, the dishes done and put away except for one breakfast bowl in the drainboard. A copy of the *Los Angeles Times* sat on the couch, open to the sports section. There were little red checks and circles next to some of the horses' names in the racing form.

The bathroom door opened and Walter Graham walked into the kitchen wearing jeans and a white T-shirt, a towel draped around his neck. "Hey. Good to see ya."

"Sorry about the shower . . ."

"Forget it happened. But don't ever, ever try to sneak up on me like that."

"I didn't think you'd bring a gun with you into the shower."

"Guy I knew in Narcotics—Phillips—got wasted on the can," Walter grunted. "Great cop, but he let his guard down with his pants." Walter paused and looked at Jack. "You know, you're lookin' pretty good for a Washington paper pusher."

They shook hands. Jack could never remember embracing his father the way he had embraced his grandfather. A tight hand-shake was almost too much.

They shared a lunch of beers and cold cuts. Jack had expected to find his father in some kind of serious trouble that would immediately explain why he had written what was virtually a summons. Instead, they talked about the football season gone by, and the baseball season just getting under way, and who was the best boxer around, pound for pound. The old man was a bit thinner and his hair a bit whiter than Jack remembered it, but otherwise he looked to be in reasonably good health.

It irked Jack to exchange small talk—he remembered Kate and felt like demanding to know why his father had broken the three-year silent truce. But instead of asking, he heard himself replying to his father's question about Japan. "No, I've never been. You thinking of taking a trip?"

"Maybe I'll have to. I'm working on a case, and things are getting damn funny. Never hit anything like it." Walter quickly told his son about the deaths of Shannon and Dr. Everett Miles.

"Why couldn't it just be a strange double suicide?" Jack asked. "You always told me the most obvious solution is usually the right one. She killed herself. He was so upset, he went to someplace with nostalgic memories and decided to join her. . . ."

Walter finished off the last corner of a roast beef sandwich and swallowed it down with a swig of beer. "Why did he go to Atami, Japan? She'd taught there, but it didn't have any nostalgic memories for him." His eyes half closed for a minute in perplexed thought. "Neither of them smell to me like suicides."

"Don't some suicides smell differently?"

"No, murders smell differently. Suicides all smell the same deep down. People send out warnings, there's a pattern of depression, they talk about it with family or friends, kinda talk themselves into it. And they always have motives and purposes. If the Miles gal wanted to punish her husband for some great offense, or if she'd been diagnosed for some incurable disease, it'd smell more like a suicide. But I know Shannon pretty well by now, and she sounds like she was doing just fine. I met her husband and he was upset, but he wasn't anywhere near suicidal."

"So then what? Somebody must've hated them pretty badly. . . ."

"I don't know," Walter admitted, and for the first time Jack heard his father's hacking cough. "Spring cold," the cop grunted.

"Been to a doctor?"

"Hey, whatta ya say we clean this mess up and go throw a ball around like old times? I got two mitts."

"If you want," Jack said, surprised by the suggestion. First "Old Man River" in the shower, then a father-son catch. The old cop was certainly mellowing with age.

On the drive to the ball field Walter returned to the Mileses' deaths and spoke of the frustration he was having in his investigation. "They keep telling me to wrap it up. Captain Charles must've told me six times already. Never felt this kind of pressure before. And the Japanese aren't helping one bit. I tried to talk to someone over there working on the Everett Miles case—no one will talk to me. I requested pictures of the cliff and the body. . . . Nothing. I put in for a trip to Japan myself—it was turned down. That's almost unheard-of for a senior homicide detective working on a case.''

"Did you ask why?"

"Captain Charles says they're suicides, and I should wrap up the case and move on. Says I'm obsessed with it." Walter Graham broke off for a minute to steer the old Ford into the field's parking lot. "So listen to this. Dr. Everett Miles was a computer consultant, right? Guess where he'd been doing a lot of his consulting the last ten years?"

"Japan?"

"Two companies in particular. Guy kept wonderful business records. Ida Computer Industries and Dai-Sei Computer Technologies. I requested information on those companies from the Japanese National Police Force—criminal dealings, Yakuza connections, whatever. I also asked them to find out the name of Shannon's lover from her days of teaching English at Atami High School. They didn't give me a thing. I complained to the Japanese consul here in L.A. about the lack of cooperation. They called my captain and told him I was poking into Japanese industrial and technological secret areas. And instead of telling them this was a possible double homicide, Captain Charles came down on my ass—told me I was obsessed by this case and I should just let it go as two suicides and move on.''

A five-year-old boy sped by the car, a Wiffle Ball bat swinging over his shoulder as he ran. They watched as the boy reached a green station wagon and his father scooped him up and held him aloft, both laughing in the early afternoon sunlight as the boy's mother looked on, smiling from the other side of the car.

"Sorry to bend your ear with this case," Walter said, his voice strangely choked. "Let's go have a catch." They left the car and began walking across the field toward an empty section of grass in deep center. "So you got a girl out in D.C.?" the old cop asked.

"Had one," Jack replied, a clear warning in his tone.

"Didn't work out?"

"Nope. Do me a favor and drop it."

"There'll be another one. Lots of fishes in the sea. You'd be good settled down. Hot meals and a squalling brat to come home to—"

"*I said drop it.*"

"Why're you so touchy? This gal break your heart or something?"

"Leave it alone or I'm leaving right now."

"Okay. Christ."

They walked on together in strained silence, their toes kicking up clouds of newly mown grass. They passed a touch football game, a long-haired high schooler throwing a Frisbee to his collie, who time after time snatched it cleanly out of the air, and a fat man hitting a plastic golf ball in thirty-foot increments up and back across the park.

Jack stopped first, and Walter tossed him a mitt and then walked on another twenty yards. Jack recognized the mitt from his junior high school days. It fit snugly—the leather was cracked in places, but the double stitching hadn't come out and the insides of the finger holes were worn smooth.

Walter put on his own mitt and slowly circled his right arm with the baseball gripped tightly in his long fingers. Even from twenty yards away, Jack could hear the joints of his father's arms and back crack as he limbered up. He stretched a bit himself, watching his father's stiff movements. Someday he would inherit that old body—someday he would have that deeply lined face and the grizzly white hair. . . .

Walter could still throw hard. Jack caught the first ball too close to the heel and it stung. He tossed back a high one, and Walter stretched up to get it. For about half an hour they threw in total silence, reenacting a ritual that had been a constant in their lives several times a week for years.

They threw each other high flies and grounders, and Jack was surprised at how well his father still reacted to bad hops, and how easily Walter turned for fly balls over his head. Whatever it was that was bothering Walter didn't seem to have anything to do with the old cop's health. As they walked back across the field to the car, Jack asked: "So what's up?"

"Whatta you mean?"

"Been a long time."

"Three years."

"You must've had some reason for writing to me."

"Let it sit till after dinner," Walter requested. "Better to talk over drinks."

They drove back home, and for most of the ride Walter continued talking about the Miles case. As Jack listened, he began to wonder if his father was indeed obsessed and a bit paranoid. He was on the subject of the parking ticket now—and his anger rang in his voice. "The night of the murder, just up the block from the house, a ticket was given to a rented Mercedes Benz sedan. Naturally I checked through the rental agency."

"Who was driving it?"

"The car was rented by a Mr. Nakamoto, or at least he signed for it at the airport. But the rental was apparently paid for beforehand, in cash, by a bar in Little Tokyo that's known as a front for the L.A. branch of the Inagawa Yakuza family. That's according to the rental agency's records—the bar denies any knowledge of renting the car."

"What about Nakamoto?"

"Fake passport. Someone used the name to fly from Tokyo to L.A. and then back again. That's it. Trail ends. Once again, the Japanese police have been no help at all. And on my side, everyone keeps telling me the whole rented car thing with the parking ticket was just a coincidence. Drop it, they tell me. Wrap it up as two suicides. I mean, for Christ's sake . . ."

Back in Walter's apartment they took showers, watched a Dodger spring training game on television, and decided on Italian food for dinner. They went to a small restaurant on Montana, in a neighborhood that Jack remembered as being shabby but that seemed to have become gentrified to a glossy yuppie chic.

Jack had linguine with scallops and shrimp. His father ate veal piccata, and washed it down with long drinks of strong red wine. During dinner they exchanged bits of information about mutual acquaintances from years past, and the old man inquired into different aspects of Jack's life in Washington. Jack knew his father disapproved of his career at the Bureau, and he would almost have preferred the old cop's usual style of blunt criticism to this endless series of probing questions. Whatever real problem Walter was having that this small talk was meant to conceal, Jack found the charade more and more irritating as time went on.

Several times toward the end of the meal his father put down his fork and knife and coughed for ten or fifteen seconds into his napkin. "So have you been to a doctor or not?" Jack asked him.

"It's just a spring cold."

"That's what the doctor said?"

"Told me to cut down on my smoking. I'm down to two packs a day. Said to get more exercise. I use this thing called the Stairmaster at the gym. Damndest machine. Know it?"

"Yeah, I know it." Jack took a deep breath. If it wasn't a health problem, there was only one other possibility. Better to cut right to it than to continue with this infuriating small talk. "So how much do you need?"

The old man lifted his head in surprise. "Excuse me?"

"Money. How much do you owe?"

"What makes you think I'm in debt?"

Jack didn't need to answer. The old man read it in his eyes.

"You thought that was why I wrote to you? 'Cause I needed money?"

"Do you?"

"What a hell of a thing to come out with."

"Well, then why . . . ?"

"Christ, this veal is good," the old man said in a rush, cutting off Jack's question. "Chef is Mexican, but he must have some Italian blood somewhere."

After dinner they walked up Montana to a little neighborhood pub called Father's Office that served a wide variety of outstanding domestic beers from microbreweries all through the Pacific Northwest. It was a dark place with little pretension and lots of character. The bartender was no college surfer boy like in the Westwood bars, but a middle-aged man sporting a marvelous bow tie who greeted Walter by name and shook hands with Jack. There were ales and wheat beers and porters on the menu, and after a sip of something called Old Foghorn, Jack had to admit, "I didn't know they made beers like this in the United States."

"Yeah, well, maybe they don't sell 'em in the places you hang out in Washington, D.C." Walter Graham took a long sip of his Liberty Timberline Ale and lowered the glass. "Jack, it doesn't sound like Washington suits you. Why don't ya come back out here? Trade in that damn desk job for a detective's shield."

Jack almost felt relief. "Is that what you called me out to Los Angeles to tell me? That you don't like what I do for a living?"

"What I'm trying to say is that I could help you. I know people.

With your education and my connections, you could go places I never could go.''

"I already have.''

"Not anywhere worth anything.'' The old man's voice went up. "Feds are just leeches sucking the blood of honest taxpayers. . . .''

"What would you know about honest taxpayers?''

"You could be a good cop instead of wasting your life. . . .''

"Wanna talk about wasting my life? I had a pretty good role model.''

Walter Graham swallowed, set his jaw against his upper teeth as if preparing to chew on something unpleasant, and said, "You really thought I asked you to come out here because I needed to borrow money?''

"Your letter wasn't exactly full of information.''

"Why did you come?''

"To find out why you wanted me to.''

"I need a better reason than just wanting to see my son after three years?''

Jack looked sideways at his father, down the bar. Walter was sitting with both elbows on the wood, his right hand wrapped tensely around the handle of his beer mug. The lines in the craggy old face seemed to have deepened into trenches. "Yeah, you do. Why'd you write that letter? What am I doing here?''

Nearly a minute passed. Walter almost looked afraid. "I . . . I got to thinking. . . .''

"About what?''

"I think about your mother a lot.''

"That's funny.''

"Why's it funny?''

"Because you didn't think about her much when she was alive.''

"Jesus, Jack, I'm trying. . . .''

"Trying to do what?''

Walter grabbed him by the arm and wrist, and his grip was surprisingly tight. The people sitting on either side of them at the bar glanced over nervously. Walter's raspy voice was dry as sandpaper as he said, *"You son of a bitch,* why do you have to make this so hard? You could help me a little.''

Jack pulled free then, and the effort upset a beer mug, which rolled off the bar and shattered on the stone floor. The act of breaking free terrified and at the same time exhilarated Jack—for three decades he had not had the strength to do it. For three decades this man had bullied him and hurt him, and it all came back to him in a flash as he broke the tight grip and half rose, ready to dodge a blow or even to return one. They were drawing open stares now, and the bartender was edging closer without wanting to get involved unless absolutely necessary.

"I don't know what the fuck you're talking about," Jack told him, "so I don't know how I can help you. All I know is that if you grab me again, so help me, I'll put you through the wall."

The bartender leaned across and said, "Walter, maybe you two need to talk outside."

"No, it's okay," Walter said. Then he looked at Jack. His lips moved, but for the longest time no words came out. Finally he managed to speak in a tinny whisper. "All I wanted to say is that . . . ."

"What? Here I am. Say it."

"You're all I've got left in the whole world."

Jack's surprise at hearing those words was overpowering. He looked into his father's blue eyes and felt such conflicting feelings of love and hate that he couldn't move a muscle or speak. His father looked like every tender word out of his mouth was a separate agony, but somehow the old man managed to press on.

"We've had our problems. . . . God knows I haven't been much of a father, but I want you to know . . . Jack . . . ." The tough old homicide detective's body quivered and he actually seemed to scowl as he forced out: "I want you to know . . . that I love you."

His father's admission shocked Jack and touched and infuriated him so deeply that for a time he lost control of his own actions. He felt himself lean forward slightly, and thought he might kiss the old man's forehead, but instead he heard a derisive laugh burst from his lips. His father winced and pulled away, but the laugh went on until Jack suddenly heard himself demanding: "How dare you?"

"Jack . . . ."

"So you're gonna set it right? Don't you think you're about three decades late? Do you have any conception at all of how you've screwed up my life? Hamstrung me emotionally? Do you want me to tell you what my mother—your wife—whispered just before she died?''

Walter sat looking at him, and slowly shook his head. He dropped a twenty on top of the bar, and they got up and left together without a word. They walked down Montana to the ugly black Ford, and the silence between them was so dark, it seemed remarkable that they could get into the same automobile.

"I can walk to my hotel from your place," Jack told him. "Just drive home."

Walter flicked on his lights and drove the mile in complete silence.

When they got out of the car, Jack felt an urge to say something reconciliatory, but he held himself back because this was still too soon. It had taken him thirty-three years to stand up to Walter Graham and tell him what he deserved to hear. There would be plenty of time to make up later. "I'll come by at nine if you want," he said in an empty, flat voice. "Get some breakfast."

"Do what you want," Walter Graham muttered, and without a good-night, walked away up the path toward his apartment. Jack watched his father's shoulders move back and forth and in and out of shadow as he walked the length of the shabby apartment building. Suddenly Walter looked to him like a tired old man, and when he turned away toward his hotel, he felt a nagging guilt.

He knew he had really wounded this aging man who lived alone on this shabby Santa Monica street eighteen blocks from the ocean. It was a dark and empty street, fronted by two- and three-story apartment buildings and lined by untrimmed bushes and low, twisted trees. All in all, a lonely and ugly street.

As Jack walked away, the strange events of the evening swirled around in his mind, reshaping and realigning themselves like the designs in a kaleidoscope. He already felt guilty over how he had reacted in the bar, and at the same time he was fairly sure that he had done the right thing. He ran his right hand across his forehead. From there it traced the bump of his broken nose, a living memory of Walter's savage side. There was also an ugly scar on his back from a beating with a belt buckle.

Jack remembered his grandfather's explanation that some mean bastards reach a point in their lives when they start to see themselves for what they are. And then like Scrooge on Christmas morning, they set out to put everything right in the blink of an eye.

The thought infuriated Jack to the point where he clenched his fists as he hurried up Santa Monica toward his hotel. Life wasn't a Christmas carol, and Walter Graham had spent years and years doing serious damage to some nice and utterly defenseless human beings. He didn't deserve to be able to put things right quite so easily.

Jack opened his fists and forced himself to walk a little slower, assuring himself over and over that he had satisfied his duty to the past. An abused, terrified child's voice had mandated his bitter laugh in the bar, a long-suffering woman in her deathbed whispers had helped frame his angry response to his father's protestation of love. Maybe tomorrow or the next day he would move toward some kind of reconciliation with Walter. But for tonight, let the old man stew. God knows he had caused enough pain in other people's lives. Jack reached his hotel, climbed three flights to his room, and within twenty minutes was fast asleep.

The knocking came first, and Jack rolled over onto his stomach and wrapped his pillow around his ears. Then the doorbell. Then the doorbell and the knocking together, and soon the pounding came so hard, it almost sounded as if someone were trying to break down the door. "Okay," Jack mumbled, and then much louder, *"Okay, will ya take it easy?"*

He glanced at the hotel's digital clock—it was 7:10 in the morning.

He stumbled out of bed, trying to clear his head, and walked to the door, dressed only in his briefs. He unlocked and unbolted it, and opened it on the chain. Peering out, he saw two Los Angeles cops in uniform and a distinguished-looking black man in a dark suit. The black man must have been at least sixty, and his white hair glistened with some sort of mousse. The triangle of a perfectly folded yellow handkerchief stuck out of his suit pocket. In a low, almost musical voice, he said, "Jack Graham?"

Jack's head cleared with surprising speed. "What is it? What's happened?"

"We need to talk to you. May we come in?"

There was something in the man's low voice that carried authority. Jack took the chain off, opened the door, and stepped back into his hotel room. The two cops and the man in the suit entered. Jack pulled on a bathrobe without thinking—all of his concentration was suddenly focused on the black man's face. He was quite good at reading expressions, and he saw that whatever was coming was going to be bad. Very bad.

"I'm Roland Charles, captain of Central Division Homicide, Parker Center," the black man said. "I'm afraid I have bad news for you."

Jack waited.

"Your father is dead."

Jack sat back down on his bed, the blood thundering in his ears. It took him ten seconds to ask "How?"

"Neighbors heard a single gunshot about five hours ago. The patrolmen had to break down his door to get in. They found him in the kitchen. He seems to have put his service revolver in his mouth and pulled the trigger. All the doors and windows were locked."

"No," Jack whispered, wrapping his arms around his body and holding himself, as if the hotel room had suddenly become very cold.

"I'm afraid it's true. I've just come from his apartment. Why don't you get dressed. I'll have one of my men go get some coffee, and we'll talk."

Jack showered and threw on some clothes, not really even knowing what he was doing. The shock was numbing—a single image kept replaying itself over and over again in his mind. He saw his father the previous night walking away from him down the path to his apartment, moving in and out of shadow, his shoulders swaying tiredly with each step.

. . . And he had wanted to say something friendly, something reconciliatory, but he had held back. . . .

One of the patrolmen returned with a pitcher of coffee and a bag of glazed doughnuts. Captain Charles sat in the room's armchair—Jack sat on the bed. "I worked with your father for many years," Captain Charles began in a tone that was polite, but also no-nonsense. "He didn't like me much, but I always admired him. Hell of a good cop. I'd like to find out what happened."

He paused and looked at Jack, as if expecting him to say something. Hearing only silence, Captain Charles plunged on.

"We know your father went to his regular bar last night. The bartender told us about you. He said that you and Walter had words. A neighbor says he saw you with Walter late last night outside the apartment. That means you were probably the last person to talk to Walter before his suicide. . . ."

"Walter wouldn't commit suicide," Jack said dully, his voice as empty as his eyes.

"Why do you say that?" Again, after waiting only a few seconds for an answer, Captain Charles broke the silence. "Were you and Walter close?"

"No, not really. I live in Washington, D.C. We hadn't seen each other for a long time before this visit."

"Well, there are some things you may not have known about your father. He was a private man, but we try to take care of our own, and we'd been worried about him for a while. His health wasn't good. Frankly, his smoking was slowly killing him. He'd just gotten a bad diagnosis earlier this week."

"Cancer?"

"Emphysema. Also, he was heavily in debt. . . ."

"He told me he had money," Jack objected. "He lived alone. He made a good salary. . . ."

"He had a longstanding gambling addiction," Captain Charles explained. "Mostly the track. We think he was at least ten and maybe as much as thirty grand in the hole. I guess you know about his drinking problem, but you probably don't know how much it had begun to affect his work. He was almost suspended a month ago—instead, we tried to steer him toward someone who could help."

"I didn't know any of this," Jack admitted in a near whisper. "I could see that his health wasn't good. . . ."

"So yesterday you came in from Washington, D.C.?" Captain Charles asked. "What happened?"

Jack told him, and as he described their argument in the bar and the way they had finally parted, it seemed to him that he was practically confessing responsibility for his father's suicide. His voice cracked several times before he finished.

Captain Charles's face showed absolutely no emotion as he listened to Jack and then asked, "What time was it when you left him outside his building?"

"Eleven, or a little after."

"And then you walked right back to this hotel and went to sleep?"

"Yes."

"That's all I need for now. Thanks—I know this must be a hard time for you. There's something I'd like to say. . . ."

Jack looked at him.

"Your father had a lot of problems and he'd been depressed for a long time. Don't put too much blame on yourself. Here's my card. Call me any time if you think of anything or if you just need to talk."

Jack took the card and put it on the bed. The detective stood up and headed for the door, and the two cops in uniform trailed him out of the room.

After the door closed, Jack sat on the bed with his head down and his palms over his ears. The image of his father's slow and tired walk away from him down the pathway once again came to mind, and this time the memory brought wetness to Jack's eyes.

It was the first time he had cried since his mother's funeral.

8

The *Los Angeles Times* called it a suicide. The paper ran a small obituary of Walter, noting his service in the Korean War, his decades on the force, his work in the Police Athletic League, and his decoration for bravery by the mayor.

Jack read the obituary on the beach, and then threw the paper in a trash can and went back to watching the waves. For hour after hour on successive days he paced back and forth along the sand from Santa Monica to Malibu, watching the Pacific wash up on the wide strip of beach.

The sounds of the waves were soothing, and he relaxed a bit near the open spaces of sea and sky.

During the years they had spent apart and not speaking, Jack had dwelled almost entirely on negative memories of Walter. Now, as he endlessly paced the beach, Jack could not stop himself from recalling other, less painful times they had spent together. The former pro athlete teaching him how to pop up and keep running after a bent-leg slide. The world-wise philanderer promising his son with a grin that if he asked the prettiest girl in eighth grade out on a date, she wouldn't laugh. The ofttimes broke poker player and horse track bettor paying a good chunk of his Dartmouth tuition. And the familiar voice coming from his corner in dozens of boxing rings, believing in him and urging him on, more often than not to hard-fought victories.

The sand got in Jack's shoes and socks, and his cheeks and hands became sunburned, but still he paced as if trying to walk away from something within himself. He remembered Walter grabbing him at the bar in a tight grip, and how he had associated that grip with the abuse he had endured during his childhood. Now it seemed clear that the old man had been reaching out to him with the desperate grasp of a long-unexpressed but deeply felt love.

75

And Jack had broken away and felt proud of it. He only stopped his lonely walks and spoke to people when he needed to make the funeral arrangements. Then, as soon as he could, he went back to the sky and sea.

They buried Walter on a sunny Wednesday morning. Jack was surprised at the turnout. Dozens of old and young cops from the department showed up in uniform. A number of them gave brief testimonials about the good work Walter had done in his community. Several victims of serious crimes told of how Walter had helped them and their families at the most difficult moments of their lives. Captain Charles himself delivered the brief eulogy, in which he called Walter a true-blue knight, with all the flaws and weaknesses of a warrior but with redeeming qualities of courage, dedication, and honor.

No mention was made by anyone of Walter's death—of a shameful suicide in a shabby apartment on a lonely Santa Monica street.

And then they shoveled the muddy earth down into the pit, and Jack stood there and watched till the coffin was gone from sight. Most of the mourners had departed when a tall, middle-aged woman came up to Jack and touched his shoulder. "I'm sorry to disturb you at such a moment," she said, "but I'd like to talk to you sometime. I'm Erica Cooperman—your father was one of my patients. Here's my card. Please call me."

Jack called her, and drove to her office on Sunset Boulevard. It was large and sunny, and the room Dr. Cooperman led him to was furnished with Italian black leather chairs and a sofa, and a rolltop writing desk. It was hard for Jack to imagine Walter sitting or even lying on that sofa, telling his secrets to this woman with the Berkeley diploma above her desk and the Pollack and de Kooning reproductions on the wall. It didn't seem like a room Walter would have been comfortable in.

"Would you like a soft drink?" Dr. Cooperman asked.

"No, thank you."

"You don't look well."

"I haven't slept in nearly a week," Jack told her. "I suppose you can guess why."

"Maybe, a little bit. Walter didn't talk about you much to me. We talked mostly about his problems. You were one of the bright spots in his life, and he kept you to himself."

Jack stood up and walked to the window. The office faced out on a tiny flower garden. A rosebush with pink buds reached almost to the sill.

"I liked Walter very much," Dr. Cooperman said. "I try to like all my patients, but sometimes it's hard. Your father I liked right from the start. He was smart and he was tough, and I found him to be very much an original. I was terribly sorry when I heard what happened. The last time I talked to him, he was looking forward to your visit. May I ask what happened when you came?"

Jack told her briefly, not sparing himself in the least. As she listened her face softened, and Jack found himself liking her more and more. He finished in a rush. "So I watched him walk away without saying anything, and the next morning the police came to the door of my hotel room and told me he'd shot himself. So tell me, Dr. Cooperman . . . you were his doctor. . . . Did I put the final nail in his coffin? I guess I must have."

Now it was her turn to get up and pace to the window. She spoke with her back to him. "I can't tell you everything I talked about with your father. It was private when he was alive, and it's private now. He had . . . many problems."

She turned from the window, and her long fingers were knitted together. "This is a very difficult line for me to draw—between ethical obligations to the dead and a desire to help the living." She was silent for nearly a minute. "I'll tell you this much. Walter was in a deep depression. It had been building for years. Perhaps your timing was bad, but Walter wasn't pushed over the edge by a single unpleasant night, but by years and years of problems, most of which were of his own making."

Jack thanked her with his eyes. "So you think my father was suicidal?"

"If I'd thought he was suicidal, or that he posed a threat to others, I would have been legally obligated to report it to the police," she said. "He was extremely depressed, but in my judgment at the time, he was not dangerous to himself. In that respect, I count this as a professional failure."

"So you believe he killed himself?"

"Of course, given the evidence. I believe it. What other choice is there?"

The visit to Dr. Cooperman helped Jack a little bit, but he continued to experience almost total insomnia. During the late hours when he couldn't sleep, he went to the run-down apartment on Eighteenth Street and sorted and threw out and boxed up Walter's papers and possessions.

Night after night as he cleared away layer after layer and closet after closet, Jack took a backward journey down every stage of his father's life. There were shoe boxes full of racing coupons, and mementos from Walter's marriage and Jack's childhood, and letters Walter had received from his parents while he was serving in the Korean War. A dozen or so news clippings recalled his brief career as a professional prizefighter. There was an old high school yearbook with a big picture of Walter Graham—the starting center of the state championship football team.

As Jack read, and as his mental picture of his father's life began to come more and more into focus, a growing doubt began to tug at him. At first he didn't listen to it, even squelched it on purpose so that he could continue flogging himself with guilt for his father's death. But there came a night when Jack sat alone in the semidark apartment and admitted to himself that he didn't believe it. Everything he knew about Walter Graham as a father, and everything he had learned about the man while going through his life's accumulation of possessions, told him that Walter would never have put his service revolver into his mouth and pulled the trigger.

He wouldn't have done it precisely because of his gambling debts and other problems—he would have seen suicide as a cowardly escape.

He wouldn't have done it to strike a last unanswerable blow of revenge at Jack—he would have seen suicide as a cowardly admission of defeat.

And he wouldn't have done it because of the sickness. One of Jack's earliest memories was of sitting in his mother's lap watching Walter box against a much bigger opponent. Even to this day Jack remembered how Walter had refused to take a backward step, but had always moved forward, and again forward, taking incredible punishment without flinching. Walter would have regarded suicide as akin to running out of the ring, and even when he was faced with grave illness, such behavior was completely contrary to his nature. Walter had always had the instincts of a fighter—he had always moved forward.

Over the next day or two as Jack finished emptying out his

father's apartment, his belief that Walter would not have committed suicide grew stronger. Walter's desk was filled with notes and documents concerning the Shannon Miles case. The Mileses' water bills and gas bills and telephone bills and tax forms going back several years were carefully sorted into manila folders and marked up with different-colored cryptic and nearly illegible notations. Walter had been working hard at checking every last lead, and even though Jack couldn't make heads or tails of his father's scrawled notes to himself, he could tell that the old detective had been working excitedly, even feverishly.

As Jack finished his sad task and removed the last boxes and clothes, he began to think about the implications of what he had come to believe.

If Walter hadn't committed suicide, then someone had entered his apartment during the night and killed him. Even sick and weakened, surely Walter would have been able to put up a fight against an intruder. Furniture would have been broken, and there would have been cuts and bruises all over Walter's body. It was almost impossible for Jack to believe that one man could have entered Walter's apartment without his knowing it, snuck up on him and overpowered him without a big struggle, and forced his service revolver into his own mouth. No one had that kind of strength or skill.

No one.

Perhaps it had been several attackers at once. But surely Walter would have heard a group of people breaking into his apartment. And there were no signs of anyone entering or leaving.

Frustrated, Jack pursued another line of thought. If someone wanted to kill Walter, it was probably because of something he had done or was trying to do as a police detective. The only case that Jack knew of was the Miles case. Judging by the paperwork all around the apartment, Walter's interest in it had been almost obsessive . . .

. . . And it had involved two suicides that looked to everyone else like suicides, but which Walter felt hadn't smelled right . . .

. . . And when Walter had tried to push the investigation, the same Captain Charles who had delivered the eulogy at his funeral had tried to shut him down . . .

. . . And Walter's request for a trip to Japan had been refused, pictures and information regarding Dr. Miles's death in Atami had not been sent, and the whole thing had felt strange to him. . . .

Jack collected all of the documents from the Mileses and all of his father's notes on the case in a large carton, and took them with him on the flight back to Washington, D.C.

"You look terrible," MacCormack said, closing the door to his office.

Jack shrugged. "I've been having trouble sleeping since my father's death. . . ." He rubbed his eyes and took the proferred seat. There was a short silence during which the portly special agent in charge studied him with concern. "Is there a problem with my request for three weeks off?" Jack finally asked.

"Not that I know of. Your supervisor says you have the vacation time saved up."

"Yes, I do."

"Then there shouldn't be a problem. You're not working on any case. Of course, I'll have to assign the Harburg matter to someone else. I held it for you, you know. Even the extra week."

"Thanks. I should've called you."

The big man knotted his pudgy fingers on top of his desk. "I think one can be excused for a lapse of professional decorum when one's father dies. And certainly one should take some time off to recover."

"Then, sir, if I may ask, was there any special reason why you called me in?"

"To give you a friendly warning. I understand that your father was a police detective working on a case involving Japan." The pudgy hands separated as the big man anticipated Jack's question and dismissed it with a wave. "Oh, don't bother asking how I come to know such a thing. Your supervisor is just doing his job checking up on you, and I'm just doing mine. The point is, your father died while working on that case, and now, according to the itinerary you handed in, you want to spend three weeks in the very same Japanese city your father expressed an interest in traveling to on his own investigation."

Jack kept quiet. When an agent takes a vacation, he is required to furnish an itinerary for his trip in case the Bureau needs to get in touch with him in a hurry about a case. Jack had intentionally been as vague as the rules allowed, and apparently his supervisor had found his sudden request for time off and the vagueness of his proposed trip to Japan suspicious enough to do some checking up.

"Very worrying. Forgive me for asking a personal question, but do you have any reason to think your father's death wasn't a suicide?"

"Nothing substantial."

"Anything insubstantial?"

"I just want to poke around as a private citizen and put to rest a few lingering doubts."

"I can understand that. And I'm sure you understand what concerns me as the head of your section."

"The Neutrality Act," Jack muttered.

"That's correct. I've been through some very nasty situations in the past, and I want to warn you. Should the Japanese government feel you're investigating in an official capacity and want to make trouble, they can lodge a protest with our State Department. The consequences for your career would almost certainly be disastrous."

"I'll be very careful."

The big man tugged the red spot on his neck. "You of course know that a violation of the Neutrality Act would also leave you open to criminal prosecution?"

"I understand the narrow line and I'll walk it."

"You can't bring a firearm into Japan. You can't identify yourself as an agent for any sort of investigative purpose. Given the fact that by your own admission, you don't think there was any foul play involved in your father's death, I'm bound to ask you if it's really worth going over."

Jack looked back at the kind gray eyes and nodded.

"I could still give you full control of the Harburg investigation." MacCormick's voice sank to a gentle plea. "I've seen these sorts of things blow up before. Stay, Jack. Don't risk it."

"No choice."

"Then I can only assume that you know something or feel something about the matter that you're not telling me." The big man shrugged. "I supposed that's all right. In your position, if it were my father, I might act exactly the same way. The FBI legal attaché at the Tokyo embassy is a man named Carson—I know him slightly. Would you like me to tell him you're coming?"

"Thanks, but please don't bother."

"He might be of some help."

"Not to me." Their eyes met. "I'll just be on vacation."

"And you just happen to be taking this particular vacation in a city called Atami, that your father wanted to poke around in?"

"It's a famous resort. I understand it's very popular for its hot baths."

The big man snorted and then stood up and held out a hand. "Consider me a friend. If you need more time or if you unearth something and want to go through proper channels at high speed, give me a call."

"Thank you, I will. Good luck with the Harburg Fiasco."

"Keep your nose clean," the big man warned as Jack left his office. "Because I'd hate to be the one to have to say, 'I told you so,' and drum you out of the Bureau."

After leaving MacCormack's office, Jack drove to the Hoover Building on the edge of the Capital Mall. He lugged the carton containing his father's notes on the Shannon Miles case through long corridors of offices and forensic laboratories till he reached a series of windowless rooms, each with a half dozen or so computer terminals.

This was the real grunt-work section of the Bureau—even the state-of-the-art computers couldn't stop mountains of papers from accumulating on the researchers' desks. It was lunch hour now, and the room Jack entered was completely empty except for Monroe, who sat hunched over his terminal, concentrating so hard that he didn't notice Jack approach. He only looked up when Jack set the carton down on his already cluttered desk.

Monroe took his fingers off the keyboard and slowly looked up at Jack. He was short and very thin, with nervous brown eyes that jumped to the carton and then back up to Jack. They had become friends as softball rivals and had worked together on three investigations.

Several years ago Monroe's young daughter had developed leukemia, and Monroe had done everything he could to get her treated by a renowned oncologist at a famous hospital. Jack had remembered that the father of one of his Dartmouth roommates was a chairman of the board of that particular hospital. He had made a phone call to his old friend, and two days later the famous doctor had taken Monroe's daughter off the bottom of his long waiting list and accepted her as one of his patients. The little girl had eventually gone into full remission, and Monroe felt that Jack had been at least partly responsible for saving his daughter's life.

"You look awful," Monroe said.

"Thanks. Do me a favor?"

Monroe glanced back at the carton. "I'm backed up for at least two weeks. I'll get Mindy to do it. . . ."

"It's got to be you."

Monroe pushed the carton with the heel of his hand and grimaced at the weight of the papers. "What is it?"

Jack looked around to make sure that the room was indeed empty and then told him the details from beginning to end. Monroe listened in silence, occasionally glancing down at the manila folders as if trying to peer inside them. When Jack was done, the researcher nodded. "What do you want me to look for?"

"Anything that you think Walter was looking for. There are papers there he never had time to check on. See if anything strikes you as curious."

"Can it wait a few days? I'm in the middle of two other investigations."

"I'll call you in a week or so," Jack said. "Thanks. Next time you hit one of those bloopers into center, I'll let it bounce."

"I hit frozen ropes," the researcher responded. "You really do look bad, Jack. Go home and get some sleep."

Jack drove home, packed some clothes, locked his gun in the desk in his study, and headed for the airport. He bought a tourist guidebook to Japan, and as he waited for his flight, he located the city of Atami, halfway between Tokyo and Shizuoka.

In his mind, he had only two choices. He could find out who killed Walter and why, or he could spend the rest of his life torturing himself with the notion that he had been in large part responsible for his own father's suicide.

SECTION TWO

The Third City of Pleasure in the World

9

The other boys made up names for him.

Some called him Little Dracula since he lived in seclusion in the oldest part of the castle, wore dark clothes with capes and hoods, and only appeared after the sun had gone down. Others called him the Star Gazer because a long telescope frequently poked out of his window, and on his nocturnal walks the other boys had seen him silhouetted on mountainsides in the moonlight, staring up at the stars. But most of them simply called him "The Mystery Boy," which was a remarkable title to have at the Creusot School, where there were as many family secrets as there were students.

The school building was a sixteenth-century castle, surrounded by Alps. The nearest major city was Interlaken, which could be reached by a hair-raising three-hour bus trip followed by a rack-and-pinion railway descent to the southern shore of the Thuner See. For ten months of the year the castle grounds and surrounding valley were white with snow. A number of the nearby Alpine peaks kept their glacier cover throughout the year.

The boys who came to the Creusot School hailed from all over the world and only had one thing in common—their parents were all willing to pay large sums of money for a superb European education and the tightest security of any private school in the world. So it was that the sons of African despots became friends with the grandsons of Nazi war criminals who had relocated to South America, and the sons of Islamic terrorist leaders learned their French and German grammar sitting next to the sons of deposed Latin American dictators.

Like the vaunted Swiss banks in nearby Geneva, the Creusot School accepted deposits from all corners of the world, asked very few questions, and guaranteed safety and security.

The security force of ten men was equipped with an extensive and absolutely modern arsenal. Two helicopter gunships sat on a landing pad next to the guardhouse and made several reconnaissance flights a day at irregular intervals all through the valley and the surrounding Alps. The guards carried Uzis and had been trained by a former colonel in the Mossad.

Enrollment at the school never dipped below seventy, and at times almost exceeded one hundred. Many of the boys received special language instruction or religious training at the request of their families, and at least five had their own personal bodyguards. But the boys all ate together and played together and studied together, and many unlikely friendships were forged at the remote castle. It was perhaps this sense of comradeship and school spirit that led them to view the boy who lived apart from them as such a sad and mysterious figure.

While they disagreed on what to call the boy, there was only one possible name for the old Japanese man who accompanied him on all of his evening walks, limping with every other step as he favored his right leg. The old man was simply "The Limper." An often-repeated school tale said that The Limper had once quarreled with one of the head security guards, and when they had come to blows, the old man had broken both the guard's arms in less than five seconds.

Once a week The Limper would walk away down the road into the tiny town of Creusot and return several hours later with a heavy brown bag. The boy never accompanied him on these walks to town.

Every so often a rumor swept through the school about The Mystery Boy's parentage, but the rumors were just rumors. The only thing definite that was known was drawn purely from inference—whoever the parents were who had condemned their son to such a childhood of isolation, they were vastly rich and inordinately cruel.

Jack didn't sleep at all on the plane flight from Los Angeles to Narita. He was sandwiched between a fat lady and a seven-year-old boy, and each time the lady shifted her bulk, the brat seemed to kick restlessly from the other direction.

Dinner was a suspiciously square-shaped steak covered with a brown glop that passed for gravy. Jack had two Budweisers with dinner and three whiskeys during the movie in an attempt to relax, but when the movie ended and the lights blinked off for the night, he found himself more wide-awake than ever.

He felt uncomfortable—in a strange way, almost naked—traveling without a gun. At the same time he knew that MacCormack was right; the prohibition against bringing firearms across international lines was one of the most strictly enforced sections of the Neutrality Act. When an FBI agent is assigned to Alaska and travels across Canada to reach his post, he is not allowed to carry his service revolver for even a brief trip across foreign territory. When the president travels abroad, his Secret Service contingent gives up its guns at the border and is rearmed by internal security forces of the host country.

On one side of Jack the fat lady was soon snoring in thick, throaty bursts, like a bulldozer clearing snow in a blizzard. On the other side of him, the seven-year-old slept silently with his body twisted around so that his face was buried in his seat. Jack switched on the overhead light and reached down to his bag for something to read.

He had a Japanese phrase book, and he tried to memorize the numbers to ten and a few useful sentences. According to the book, Japanese people would be very helpful if he made the slightest effort to speak their language. It surprised him to realize that despite Japan's emergence as a world power and the Japanese presence in America, up till now he had only known a handful of Japanese words: *Domo arigato* for "Thank you" and *sayonara* for "good-bye," and a couple of others.

Though Jack didn't speak any Romance language well, on trips to Europe he had found he could recognize hundreds of words in French and Spanish and Italian. But Japanese had no Latinate roots to work forward from—the etymology and the grammar and the sounds were completely alien. As he tried to twist his lips around *"Sumimasen. Kono hen ni, ii hoteru wa arimasu ka?"* for "Excuse me, but is there a good hotel around here?" he had a sense of how far the 727 jet was actually traveling.

He had never been to the Far East before. He knew very little about Japanese history and culture, except for the myths common in America. Japan was always pictured as a society of worker ants who never stepped out of line, and of obedient and servile housewives who were fifty years behind European and American women in fighting sexual discrimination. Japanese society was supposed to be remarkably closed and regimented.

Jack put down the phrase book, and listened as the fat lady's snores climbed a half octave. It might be difficult if not impossible for a foreigner to try to investigate a crime in such a tightly structured society, especially since he couldn't claim to be part of any kind of formal government-backed investigation.

He closed his eyes and put his head back, and tried to think of nothing at all. He remembered from some Dartmouth philosophy class that that was one of the tenets of Zen—to clear the mind of all thoughts and even of the activity of consciously trying not to think. But the more he tried to relax and clear his mind, the more doubts about what he was doing and memories of Walter and guilt over what had happened in Los Angeles danced about in his head. Finally he gave up, and began counting the fat woman's snores as he waited for morning.

Breakfast was continental style with orange juice, coffee, and a croissant, but lunch on the plane was Japanese. Jack had been to enough Chinese restaurants in America to feel comfortable using chopsticks, but he was baffled by the flat green sheets that came wrapped in plastic along with his ten pieces of sushi and his bowl of miso soup.

"*Nori*," the fat lady said knowingly. "Seaweed. Tastes like the bottom of a pond." Jack smiled at her and put the seaweed aside.

The plane landed at Narita right on schedule, and as Jack waited for his suitcase, he was conscious of drawing a number of curious stares. He was at least five inches taller than any Japanese man in the terminal, and his broad shoulders and classic Western features caught the attention of Japanese men and women alike.

He changed some money and then took a tram, a train, and a subway, following the few English signs and asking his way to Tokyo Station. The vast terminal building made Grand Central seem puny in comparison. Throngs of late afternoon commuters hurried through the endless corridors as announcers called out arrival and departure times in fast Japanese.

He finally stumbled on a tourist information office, and a young woman in a blue uniform hurried over to help him. In slow but grammatical English she explained that there were two ways of going to Atami. There was a local train that made the trip in just over two hours, and there was a bullet train that was twice as expensive but covered the hundred miles in less than fifty minutes.

Jack opted for the bullet train, and was soon standing on the platform watching the rocket-shaped lead car pull into the station.

The doors opened, but for one minute the waiting passengers stayed off as gangs of old women brandishing sponges and vacuums scoured every car. When Jack entered, he found the inside to be immaculate.

Within ten seconds of the time the women in the tourist information office had quoted him, the bullet train shot forward on its long journey west. Jack had difficulty believing the smoothness of the ride—the countryside flashed past, but the inside of the bullet train remained so steady that vendors were able to sell bowls of soup without spilling a drop.

A spring monsoon began as the bullet train left Shin-Yokohama. Rain cascaded down from a darkened sky, lashing the windows as an occasional peal of thunder rumbled overhead. The bullet train reached the coast, and through the curtain of rain, Jack saw the sea, tossing in whitecaps. A long tunnel cut the view and the sounds of storm, and then the train was in daylight again, pulling into Atami Station.

Carrying his one suitcase and shoulder bag, Jack followed the crowd down through the three-story station, passing food stalls with plastic models of different dishes displayed in their windows. In front of the station, a long line of taxis waited, their window wipers swishing back and forth in the downpour.

An old man in a black uniform with white gloves stood at the front of a long line of travelers, helping them into taxis and speeding the process along. When Jack's turn came, he found himself loaded quickly into the backseat of an old cab. As soon as the door was closed, the driver sped away from the station, half turned, and asked, *"Doko desu ka?"*

"Just take me to a hotel."

The driver pulled over to the curb. He hesitated. "English, no," he said. "Sorry."

Jack flipped through his phrase book. *"Hoteru.* Any *hoteru."*

The driver looked at him a second more, shrugged and began to drive. They pulled up outside a large hotel on a narrow street where a doorman waited under an umbrella to help guests into the lobby. At the registration desk, a young male hotel clerk threw him two glances and then approached nervously.

"I'm sorry," he said haltingly. "I can't speak English. Sorry."

"I just want a room," Jack said, surprised at the lack of English conversation ability in Atami in such tourist industries as the taxi and hotel trades. Nearly everyone he had asked for train directions in Tokyo had been able to speak some English. His simple request didn't seem to register at all with the young clerk.

Jack turned to the travel dictionary in the back of the phrase book. *"Heya. Ichi heya."*

The young man nodded. He swallowed, but when he finally spoke, his English was not at all bad. "Japanese style okay?"

Jack nodded. "Anything."

A septuagenarian maid led Jack down a long corridor to his room, a teapot in her hand. She opened the door, and he followed her inside. As she poured him a cup of tea, he looked around the small room. The floor was made of some kind of straw matting, stitched in even squares. There was a night table and a small desk, but no bed. The maid asked Jack something in Japanese, and he answered by putting his palms together and miming going to sleep. Then he gazed around the room, pretending to search for a bed.

She grinned at him, walked to the closet, and pulled out a futon mattress. In seconds she had covered the futon with sheets and a thick coverlet. "Thank you," Jack said, "that will be great. Thank you." He offered her a small bill as a tip, but she backed up, bowed, and withdrew without taking the money.

Jack closed the door, took off his shirt and pants, and stretched. It felt as if he had been awake forever. Sipping the tea, he walked through the bedroom, passed the toilet, which was in its own tiny, closetlike room, and found the bath. The tub was much taller in height and much shorter in length than an American bathtub, and was set up in such a way that it faced the room's only small window. The window was of smoked glass, and rain beat on the outside of it with torrential fury.

Jack fiddled with the controls for several minutes till he figured out how to fill up the tub with hot water. He slowly lowered himself into the tub till he was immersed up to his chin, his knees drawn up halfway to his chest. Lying naked in the strange room, he felt the absence of a gun nearby—he remembered Walter's story about his friend on the force who had gotten wasted on the can. Jack forced himself to lie back, close his eyes, and relax.

He lay in the tub for a long time, watching shadowy outlines of raindrops slant down across the translucent glass. Then he got out, dried himself off, and headed back into the little bedroom. He checked to make sure that the door was locked, turned off the light, and climbed beneath the thick futon coverlet. In the quiet of the dark room, he could just hear the steady whisper of the rain against the bathroom window. After more than a week of terrible insomnia, he did not expect to fall asleep, but almost as soon as he closed his eyes, he slipped off into the blissful darkness.

Jack woke at five the next morning, after fourteen hours of dreamless sleep. He used the hand shower attachment to rinse himself off, shaved, and set out to explore.

The city of Atami looked marvelous in the stillness of the spring morning. The resort city was built on the lower slopes of steep mountains that ringed an almost semicircular bay. About midway to the sea the sharp mountainsides became more rounded, and white homes appeared in clusters between the green foliage and tan rock outcroppings. The city proper was perhaps a two-mile stretch following the coastline all along the bay. Down by the water's edge, colorful ten- and fifteen-story hotels looked down on a sand beach.

Jack walked downhill on a random path that brought him near the train station. Junior high and high school students were streaming toward the station from all directions, and a number of them stopped to gape and point him out to their fellows. The boys wore black military-style uniforms while the girls wore blue skirts and white blouses. *"Eh, gaijin, gaijin,"* a number of them shouted, and then hurried on to catch their train.

Jack soon left the train station behind and reached the center of town. A banner stretched across the top of the main thoroughfare with writing in Japanese characters, and "Atami *Ginza*" in English at the very bottom. The streets in this central *Ginza* area felt almost European—they were narrow and winding, and coffee shops and restaurants and boutiques stood one next to the other in a colorful collage of small-city commerce.

Between the *Ginza* district and the waterfront was a three-block stretch of older wooden buildings, many of which seemed to be bars or massage parlors or nightclubs. A number of the clubs displayed signs picturing seminaked hostesses in inviting poses. One bar featured a large wall mural of a huge octopus with its tentacles across the breasts and between the legs of a terrified naked woman.

Jack reached the beach, which was completely deserted and littered with trash. A mile out in the bay, a small island floated just above the horizon. As Jack watched, a ferry pulled out from the long Atami pier and headed slowly for the island, sounding its horn as it approached three fishing boats.

From this vantage point on the beach, Jack saw that the city of Atami had a remarkable symmetry. The graceful villas stitched precariously between the rugged peaks, the winding streets that threaded their way down the seams of mountain ravines to the more gentle slopes, and the tall, brightly colored hotels beaded side by side along the deep blue sea all seemed wonderfully suited to the scale of the bay and surrounding mountains. It was as if the city had first been sketched by an artist to fit the scenery, and then had been built according to his aesthetic design.

To the north, the sand beach gave way to precipitous stone cliffs, and Jack wondered if Dr. Everett Miles had fallen from them toward the gentle bay. Beneath the jagged cliffs, the sea foamed around sharp rocks.

At nine-fifteen Jack set off in search of the Atami Police Station. He passed a tiny bakery, entered, and delighted the woman inside by pointing to several large, waferlike cookies. Nibbling the cookies as his breakfast, he walked slowly back uphill, pausing to ask occasional passersby *"Keisho-cho?"* which his phrase book gave as Japanese for police station.

The station building was near the *Ginza,* in the center of town. It was a square three-story concrete building with a revolving door leading into a large reception lobby. Jack straightened his tie, ran his comb through his hair, and entered.

Several secretaries typed away at computer terminals off to one side of the high-ceilinged reception area. One of them spotted Jack and whispered to her neighbors, and in seconds they all stopped typing and watched him. A young policeman in a navy blue uniform walked over and spoke quickly in Japanese.

"I need to speak to someone about the death of Dr. Everett Miles," Jack replied in English. "Sorry, but I don't speak a word of Japanese."

The young policeman hurried away and soon returned with a slightly more senior officer, and the exact same scene was repeated. The third officer who was summoned gestured for Jack to follow him into the station.

Jack was led down a hallway and up a flight of stairs to a second-floor office where an older man with a deeply lined face and silver hair rose from behind a desk to greet him. The older man's English was so slow that each word seemed a separate sentence. "I am Hashiro Sato." He handed Jack a business card.

"Jack Graham." Jack took out his Bureau ID and passed it to Sato. The silver-haired man glanced at it and grunted a few words to one of the younger officers, who immediately hurried out.

"Tea?" Sato asked.

"No, thank you."

"Coffee?"

"No."

"Please wait."

Jack sat down in a straight-backed wooden chair. He took advantage of the wait to look around carefully. Sato's office was a study in contradictions. An old sword hung on a wall above a fax machine. On the opposite wall a colorful demon in a scroll painting scowled down at a computer terminal.

The door to the office opened and the officer walked back in, followed by a young policewoman. She was tall for a Japanese woman, and as she came through the door, Jack was struck by the beauty of her face. Her lips were full, her nose flat yet delicate, and her bright black eyes darted over him in a lightning examination. The masculine cut of her navy blue uniform did little to hide the curves of her figure. She said *"Ohayo gozaimasu"* to Sato, who returned her greeting with a string of grunted monosyllables and handed her Jack's Bureau identification.

She studied the card for several seconds, and then looked up at Jack. "Hello," she said, in remarkably unaccented English. "I am Misako Watanabe. Captain Sato has asked me to translate."

Jack was struck by her poise and confidence in this room full of men, almost all of whom must have been her superiors. "I'm here about the deaths of Shannon Miles in Los Angeles and Dr. Everett Miles here in Atami," he told her, being careful not to mention any sort of official investigation.

She translated, and Sato nodded and spoke quickly.

"Captain Sato remembers you, Mr. Graham. The Japanese National Police Division in Tokyo forwarded your request for pictures and details about Dr. Miles's suicide. Captain Sato says he hopes the materials and pictures we sent were useful."

Jack managed with an effort to keep the surprise out of his face. If they had mistaken him for Walter, perhaps he should play along. He made a snap decision not to mention that the pictures had never arrived in Los Angeles. "The materials were excellent. Please thank Captain Sato for all his help. I'll be in Atami for just a few days. I wondered if anything new has surfaced in the Everett Miles investigation here."

Once again the translations went back and forth. "Captain Sato says that the Japanese National Police took over the investigation. It was an unusual—" for the first time, Misako struggled with a word "—jurisdictional decision. So Captain Sato cannot tell you much. But he says that if you need any help while in Atami, you should come to him."

"Thank you," Jack said to Sato, and bowed. *"Domo arigato."*

"Doo itashimashite," Sato said, bowing back. He spoke a few more lines to Misako, and her face visibly tightened. At the last thing he said to her, the other Japanese men in the room chuckled, and she looked as if she would explode at them, but she managed to contain it.

"Captain Sato invites you to go drinking with him tomorrow night. He also asks if you would like to have me help you as a translator."

"I would love to go drinking with him. And having you with me would be enormously helpful," Jack said. "If you're willing?"

She shrugged angrily.

Jack said good-bye and thank you to Sato, and after handshakes all around, he and Misako walked out of the office. As soon as they were alone in the hallway, she said, "The name on your identification is Jack Graham. The request we had for help from Los Angeles was from Walter Graham. Why did you pretend to be him?"

"He's my father. . . ." Jack's voice trailed off. She was watching him closely, and he saw suspicion in her quick black eyes. "It's complicated. I'll explain later."

He waited for her in the lobby while she got a jacket and her purse, and then they left the station together. "Where did you learn such excellent English?" Jack asked when they were out on the street.

"In college. I spent two years as an exchange student in Madison, Wisconsin. Don't feel that you need to compliment me on my English."

They walked a half block in silence. Jack finally stopped and looked at her. "Frankly," he said, "I get the idea that you don't like me or you don't like helping me or something. I don't want to force you to be my translator.''

She hesitated. "May I answer frankly also?"

"Please."

"I was first in my class in high school. I graduated with honors from Kyoto University, the second most famous college in Japan. I made the top five percent at the police academy." She broke off for a second. "When I came to the force here, the older men asked me to make tea for them. I didn't join the police force to make tea, but I had no choice. It's been a battle to get treated with respect, but I'm finally working on some important cases now. So when Captain Sato asked me to be your translator—well, I didn't join the police department to be a translator. But I have no choice."

"I see. I sympathize. But I do need your help." Jack looked at her, and she finally nodded. "Captain Sato said something else to you, that made the men laugh?"

"He made the kind of joke that Japanese men make. He said that you were very good-looking, so I should enjoy helping you, and maybe I would learn something about . . . large American guns. . . ."

They looked at each other for a long minute. "I'm sorry they treat you that way," Jack said. "Listen, when you saw that I wasn't Walter Graham, why didn't you catch me on it inside the office? Why wait till I was outside?"

"Because I was called in as a translator," Misako said. "A translator doesn't make comments or give advice. A translator merely puts one language into another. So it wasn't my job to point out anything."

Jack smiled at the edge of sarcasm in her voice, and for a brief second her face softened and he thought she might smile back at him. "I need to go to the cliffs where Dr. Miles fell," Jack told her. "And then I'd like to go to Atami High School and talk to anyone who might remember Shannon Miles from her teaching days. Will you do me a favor?"

"What?"

"Don't be just a translator for me. When I do something wrong, tell me."

"All right." This time she did give him a slight smile. "If you want to go to the cliffs where Dr. Miles died, we're walking in the wrong direction."

10

The walk to the cliffs took them out of the city, along a steep coastal road. As they climbed higher, the view of the Atami waterfront grew spectacular. An old ferry left its slip and with several blasts on its horn, began its slow journey toward the island a mile or so out in the wide bay. The throaty blasts from the ferry's horn mingled with faint strains of carnival music from a seaside amusement park just off the quay. As Jack looked down, five children, colorful dots against the black tarmac of the amusement park lot, ran toward a large Ferris wheel which turned slowly against the morning breeze.

It was not yet ten, and the sun was already uncomfortably hot. A lizard scampered across the road ahead of them and darted into cover on the other side.

Jack glanced at Misako. She walked swiftly uphill, her feet rising and falling with graceful precision while her long black hair billowed backward in the breeze. He marveled at her near perfect posture as she fought upward against the slope in the midmorning heat. Did they teach girls to walk that way in Japanese schools, he wondered, or had she picked it up somewhere else? Perhaps she had studied dance; there was an almost balletic elegance in the controlled movements of her fingers and arms and the way she held her shoulders and chin.

Misako felt his stare and turned, and he said, "I'm glad we didn't take your car. This view is incredible. I hope you don't mind the walk."

"No."

"When you went to Madison as an exchange student, did you study at the University of Wisconsin?"

"Yes."

"For two years, did you say?"

"Yes."

"How was it?"

"Cold."

He pressed on, determined to break the chain of curt monosyllables. "I always thought Wisconsin was lovely in the winter. I grew up in Los Angeles, and when I went east for college, I just loved the winter. I spent one white Christmas in Milwaukee."

She hesitated, and her voice softened and became a tiny bit more human. "Yes. I liked the snow, too."

"It never snows here?"

"Almost never."

"What did you study at Wisconsin?"

"Linguistics."

"And how did you find American college students?"

"Lazy," she said, and as if to accent her point, she sped up a bit. Jack hurried to keep up. They rounded a bend and reached a fork in the road. Several brightly colored signs and a large pink neon arrow pointed toward a wide paved driveway that led up to the crest of a nearby mountain. In a commanding position atop the mountain, an old-style castle rose in looming silhouette against the blue sky.

"What's that?" Jack asked, stopping to look up at the castle, and using the brief pause to catch his breath.

Misako showed no effects at all from the brisk hike. Her breathing was even and her voice steady as she stopped, glanced up the slope, and said "*Atami-jo*. Atami castle."

"Great spot for it. It must've done a good job defending the city in the old days."

"It's not old. It's a fake," she said. "For tourists." ·

"No kidding? What's inside?"

She hesitated. "I don't know how to say it in English. It's a museum of cultural . . . pornography."

"I've never been to one of those. Is it interesting?"

"I've never been, either," she said. "Honeymooners come to Atami and go there. And sailors. And Tokyo salarymen on business weekends for *enkai* . . . big company parties. They enjoy the museum, and geisha, and other things. . . ." She broke off and started up the road again in fast steps.

Jack hurried to keep pace with her. "So Atami has a real sleazy side?"

"It has more geisha than any city in Japan except Kyoto."

"I always thought geisha were trained musicians and dancers. Is it just a fancy word for prostitutes?"

When she answered, there was an unexpected tone of sharpness in her voice: "Maybe tomorrow night when you go drinking with Captain Sato and his friends, you will find out."

They walked in silence for a while. Traffic passed intermittently in both directions on the narrow, winding two-lane road. After about half a mile more of steady climbing, they rounded a small promontory, and suddenly the city of Atami disappeared behind them, and a picturesque bay opened up in front of them. Hundred-foot cliffs dropped down to the shallows all around the bay, giving the otherwise cheerful little cove an ominous quality. The gray rock walls bit down on the sparkling blue water and frothing surf like great toothless jaws.

"We're getting close to the cliff where Professor Miles fell." She pointed to a spot where the coastal road dipped down to the very edge of a rocky precipice. A magnificent hotel was built into the side of a cliff so that its rooms followed the sheer rock face all the way down to a gleaming green tea garden at the very bottom that was continually showered with sea spray. "That's the New Akao."

"Looks expensive."

"Very expensive. Occasionally members of the imperial family have stayed there." As they neared the hotel, Jack saw two door-men in fancy uniforms helping elegantly dressed guests out of their cars. Young parking attendants hurried back and forth between the main entrance and the parking lot.

Beyond the hotel, the coastal road twisted down till it ran for a long stretch just alongside the edge of the cliffs. Jack and Misako hurried forward and were soon alone on the narrow pedestrian pathway. Beneath them, waves crashed in against the pocked faces of huge, weather-worn bay rocks and sizzled out to sea again through caverns and fissures.

"I take it Dr. Miles was staying at the New Akao?" Jack asked, glancing back at the hotel.

"No. He was staying at a cheaper hotel in town."

"How did he get all the way out here? Was someone driving him around?"

"We don't think so. We think he came by himself."

Jack stopped walking. Sweat trickled down off his forehead into his eyes. He blinked, and shaded his eyes from the hot sun. "He came all the way up here from the city in his wheelchair? The same way we just came?"

"He could have. It's less than three miles from the hotel he was staying at in Atami to here. If he went slowly . . ." She stopped walking and pointed to a spot on the nearby cliffs. "That's where he fell off."

Jack left the pathway and walked across fifteen feet of sand and gravel to the very edge of the cliff. He glanced back toward the New Akao—a rock formation completely screened off this spot from the nearby hotel. The sand and gravel made the footing treacherous. In patches, scrub grass and scraggly brush clung to the top of the rocky precipice.

Jack looked down at the waves crashing on the jagged boulders far below. "What time of day did he fall?"

"Just after sunset."

In his mind's eye, Jack imagined the wheelchair slipping and sliding from the path across the sand and gravel, reaching the edge, and then the quick plummet into semidarkness. The fall to the rocks beneath would have taken seven or eight seconds. "Where did the chair land?"

Misako walked out next to him and pointed down. "In the sand. It was in perfect working condition, including the—how do you say it?—braking mechanism."

"So he didn't roll over the edge by accident?"

"No."

"Where is the wheelchair now?"

"The Japan National Police took it. He landed on those rocks. Do you say 'headfirst'? His back was broken and his skull was crushed. Some Boy Scouts spotted his body a short time later. Now, here—" and she led him back halfway to the path and pointed to a patch of scrub brush "—is where we found his watch."

"Here?" Jack asked, managing to control his surprise. "To me the watch is one of the most interesting things about this whole case. Tell me all the details you can remember."

She looked at him. "It was a Timex. A leather band. The band was broken. . . ."

"How?"

"Torn. Or do you say ripped?"

"Either is fine. Was the watch still running?"

"Yes."

"There wasn't anything wrong with it?"

"No."

"And the Japanese National Police have the watch also?"

"Yes, they took over the investigation. They have everything."

"No one at the hotel saw or heard anything?"

"No. We checked extensively. It was all in the report. . . ."

"And there were no footprints, no signs that anyone had been up here with Dr. Miles?"

"Nothing. Are you ready to go back? I have some work to do this morning."

"One sec." Jack walked to the edge of the cliff again and gazed down at the jagged rocks where Dr. Miles had landed. He closed his eyes and spent a long minute trying to put himself in the widower's place—depressed, heartsick, confined to a wheelchair, sitting and listening to the roar and hiss of the waves as the sun set. . . .

A gull shrieked so far in the distance, he could barely hear its cry above the surf. As he stood there, the acrid salt tang crept down his nostrils and he could taste the sea air on his tongue. What was it that his father had said? All suicides smell the same deep down. . . . It's murders that smell differently. He opened his eyes, looked down at the jagged rocks a final time, and then turned back to Misako. "Okay," he told her, "let's go back."

They walked back past the New Akao, and rounded the promontory. It was much easier going downhill. Jack felt his strides lengthen with the slope; he noticed that Misako's graceful steps remained short and precise—the same as they had been on the way up the hill. "Thanks for bringing me up there," Jack said as they began the long descent toward the city. "You know this case better than I do. I'd like to know what you think."

"About what?"

"Do you buy it?"

She looked perplexed. Her mastery of English apparently didn't extend to popular idioms. "Buy what?"

"Do you believe it? Do you believe that Dr. Miles came all the way to Japan to commit suicide?"

Misako's quick black eyes glittered. "I don't know enough about Professor Miles to even begin to judge. . . ."

"He could have been suicidal," Jack told her. "His wife,

whom he loved, had just died. Either she killed herself or she was murdered—either way, it must have been pretty rough for him. He did his mourning all alone. His health wasn't great. So he came all the way out here—to a place his wife had loved and talked about and that therefore had some nostalgic memories for him, and he threw himself off. . . . Do you believe that?''

She watched him carefully.

''And since he wanted to die alone, in peace, he chose the one place where the cliffs are screened off so that no one from the hotel could see him, or try to stop him. And before he threw himself off the rocks, he ripped off his watch and tossed it away.'' Jack broke off. ''Do you buy it?''

''The way you are saying it, I don't think I want to buy it.''

''Then there's only one other possibility.''

''Dr. Miles was murdered,'' she said in a low voice.

''Yes.'' Jack nodded. ''He was pushed. He came out to these cliffs with someone, or to meet someone, and there was a struggle—maybe not much of a struggle considering that he was in a wheelchair, but the poor guy did his best and went down swinging. His watch was ripped off in the fight . . . and then he was thrown off, headfirst toward the rocks, and his wheelchair landed in the sand, braking mechanism intact. . . .''

''That's not what the Japan National Police concluded.''

''What do you think?''

She did not answer, but her eyes showed a complete willingness to consider other possibilities. ''Who would want to kill Professor Miles?''

Jack hesitated. ''Someone he knew,'' he finally said. ''Maybe professionally, maybe personally. Someone he came to the cliffs to meet, when the sun was going down. Someone he trusted.''

''Who?''

Misako's question hung in the air as they made their way from the outskirts of the city toward the *Ginza* district. The narrow streets were much busier at the noon hour. Diners hurried in and out of *soba* shops. As they reached the downtown area and made their way toward the old police station, Jack tried a different tack. ''Let's say for a second he hadn't been an American. If you'd just found a Japanese body on those rocks—no clues, no motive, nothing to go on—who would you start with? Who would pop into your mind? Who goes around pushing people off cliffs in places like Atami?''

"Yakuza," she answered quickly.

"Here in Atami?"

"Atami is a famous city for Yakuza. They hold their conventions here."

"In public?"

"Of course. Sometimes thousands of them come. They stay in the best hotels."

"Forgive an ignorant question, but why don't you arrest them?"

"For what?"

"Aren't they criminals? Mobsters?"

They reached the big, square police station and stopped just outside the swinging doors. "When it comes to organized crime, things are very different between America and Japan," she told him. "For many, many years the most powerful Yakuza leader in Tokyo paid the Tokyo police chief a publicized visit every new year to wish him well. Now I should go back to my work. Will you need me tomorrow?"

Jack nodded. "I'd like to visit the high school where Shannon taught. If you're free . . . ?"

"Come to this station at ten. I'll be waiting. And don't forget, Captain Sato wants to go drinking with you tomorrow night."

She was half in the door when Jack asked, "Why don't you come drinking with us?"

The suggestion seemed to surprise her.

"I mean, to be honest, I'd rather go drinking with you than with Captain Sato. Why don't you come? We can talk about snow in Wisconsin and linguistics and organized crime. It'll be fun."

"I am not invited."

"I'll tell Sato it was my idea—that I asked you to come along to translate. . . ."

"I don't drink," Misako said. "But thank you for asking. You will see that Captain Sato has very definite ideas about what kind of female . . . companionship is appropriate when men go drinking. Good-bye, Mr. Jack Graham. See you tomorrow at ten."

The assassin was traveling in full disguise and his car had dark-tinted windows, but even so, when he reached Atami he was very careful. Atami was a dangerous city for him—one of the few places in the world where dozens of people could identify him from the old days. Some of them might even see through his fake beard, mustache, sunglasses, and makeup. So he kept to the smallest side streets as he cruised through town.

He was surprised at how happy it made him feel to return to the famous hot spring spa. It was too bad he had come to work and not to play.

There is a saying in Japan that there are only three cities of pleasure in the world: Hong Kong, Rio de Janeiro, and Atami. The assassin had been to all three, and he much preferred Atami. You could get anything here if you knew whom to ask. Even after all these years he was certain that with two or three phone calls, he could have a girl—or for that matter, a boy, or even one of each—delivered to him in less than an hour.

He loved the mixed flavors of the city, the way the MOA Art Museum, one of the very best museums in all Asia, sat on one mountaintop while the museum of cultural pornography stood halfway across the bay on another crest, as if the two structures were proclaiming suzerainty over domains whose borders were, at best, indistinct. Expensive restaurants and chic international boutiques stood less than three blocks from a seedy red-light district. He loved the mixed clientele of the waterfront hotels, the sumo wrestlers and artists and famous actors who strolled around at night in bright cotton *ukatas*, rubbing shoulders with rich businessmen and gangsters and high- and low-class prostitutes.

Most of all, he loved Atami's underworld history, which for him added an almost nostalgic charm to the city's ambiance. It was here that the great Kakuji Inagawa used his Yokohama gang to wrest control of vice and racketeering on the Izu Peninsula from the Korean and Chinese gangs. And it was here, in Atami, in 1963, at the Tsuruya Hotel, that Yoshio Kodama, the *kuromaku* of *kuromaku*, persuaded the seven great crime bosses of Japan to put aside their personal rivalries and join together in *Kanto-kai,* a federation of crime kingpins.

The nostalgia also had a personal side. The assassin had spent many memorable evenings in his early twenties in Atami, feasting on fresh seafood as the sun went down and then satisfying his unusual sexual appetites after dark. It was here that he had received his very first murder contract, at the age of twenty-one, and it was here in Atami that he had first met old Seiji Muramoto.

The assassin drove up into the hills to the south of the city, and turned off the road onto a winding private drive. The Italian-style villa he finally pulled up at was surrounded by tall cedar trees, and by rows of bushes that effectively screened the house and grounds off from the surrounding hilltop mansions.

He got out of the car, moving slowly, like the middle-aged professor he was dressed up to resemble. He adjusted his eyeglasses, ran a hand lightly over his beard and mustache, and then carried his bags slowly toward the villa, stopping several times as if to catch his breath.

It was only inside the villa that he straightened up, took off the beard and glasses, and wiped away the makeup. All was exactly as he had requested. A dinner of cold fish and lightly steamed vegetables had been set out for him on the table. The vegetables were still warm. Next to the food was a large manila envelope and some handwritten notes on yellow lined paper.

The assassin nibbled a spear of asparagus as he studied the notes. He knew the hotel—it was an unusual one for an American to choose. Perhaps a taxi driver had randomly brought him there from the station. He ran his eyes down a long list of times and locations, memorizing the hotel room number, the check-in time, the time he had left the hotel the next morning, the bakery where he had stopped to buy breakfast, and so on. The notes were good—the watchers had done a thorough job. But of course, in Atami that was the easy part.

The assassin slit open the manila envelope and examined several enlarged snapshots. He studied the muscle tone in the American's arms and shoulders, and read an impressive conditioning into the way his broad chest tapered to narrow hips. Given the requirements of this particular mission and the American's size and physique, the initial approach would have to come from behind. The element of surprise, always crucial, would in this case be absolutely indispensable.

For several long seconds the assassin studied the American's face. It was not a particularly happy face, but there was an alertness to the bright black eyes that held the assassin's attention. And then there was the nose. The nose could not be discounted. The assassin examined it with care, trying to guess if it had been broken more than once. If not, the doctors had been very sloppy.

But then, doctors were generally sloppy in America, overpaid and overworked, competent but rarely inspired. The dozen or so times when he had needed plastic surgery, he had gone to a small, highly exclusive clinic outside Brussels. There were also supposed to be several true artists in Brazil, if one trusted the South Americans, which the assassin did not. . . .

Along with the pictures, the manila envelope contained some brief biographical information. He mouthed the name, Jack Graham. Gray-ham. Probably English. Born in Los Angeles. Single. With looks like that, it must have been a struggle to stay single. Thirty-three. The assassin smiled grimly.

Thirty-three.

The age Christ died at. The assassin had completely rejected the Christianity that his mother had picked up from an Assemblies of God missionary and indoctrinated him in throughout his childhood, but he retained from those late night Bible readings a certain fascination with details relating to the Flagellation and the Crucifixion.

He studied the face in the picture once more. Except for a slight thinning of black hair around the crown of the skull and some barely perceptible wrinkles about the eyes, Jack Graham could have been in his midtwenties. It was a good age to die, thirty-three. Just when the momentum of early manhood slows and stops, and the first few tentative steps backward are taken on the long, sad retreat of middle age. The assassin had killed many strong men in their prime, saving them the decades of decline and decay—it was one of the few areas in his life where he saw virtue and even a kind of public service.

He put the pictures and the biographical sheet back in the manila envelope, and turned his attention to the cooked fish. Holding the entire small fish in his hand, he turned it to face him and looked into its dead eyes. With the tip of his tongue he pried out a tiny eyeball, balanced it between his upper and lower molars, and bit down on it. The tiny salty explosion melted deliciously onto his tongue.

Jack decided to eat a quick dinner at the first place he came to, and sample the city's exotic nightlife some other time. He felt drained and tired, and didn't know whether it was from the long plane trip and stress he had been under for weeks, or the constant struggle of operating in a total alien culture where he had trouble communicating even the most basic requests. In any case, he craved another good night's sleep.

As he left his hotel and began looking for a place to get a quick bite, he glanced up and down the street several times. Except for three old women gossiping outside a rice shop and a crowd of slightly drunk businessmen, the side street was quiet and empty. Still, for reasons he couldn't quite explain, Jack felt uneasy. All day long he had had a growing premonition of danger, and a much more definite feeling that he was being watched.

Of course, as the only foreigner in Atami, he most certainly was being watched—he drew constant stares. But on the fringes of this harmless attention he felt—or imagined he felt—the more calculated scrutiny of professional surveillance. There was certainly nothing he could put his finger on; perhaps he was just becoming a bit paranoid. Nonetheless, as he spotted a busy-looking corner tavern and sniffed enticing smells of roasting meat, Jack threw one last look up the block. Then he entered through a narrow sliding door, which he closed carefully behind him.

It was a small place, with sawdust on the floor and several calendars with pictures of Japanese girls in bikinis on the walls. At the front, near the sliding door, a metal grill stretched above glowing coals that sizzled as fat slowly dropped down on them. A long wooden counter with bar stools ran from the grill two thirds of the way down the restaurant. At the back, three low *kotatsu* tables sat on a slightly raised platform.

Half a dozen men in work clothes sat at the counter eating skewers of meat and exchanging comments on the night's sumo fights. When Jack entered the restaurant, the conversation at the counter subsided as the men all turned to eye him curiously. He chose a stool far down the counter, and tried to ignore the stares. Bit by bit, the normal activity and hubbub of the restaurant resumed.

The master of the place, a man of at least sixty with massive forearms and hands crisscrossed with tiny scars and burn marks, stood by the fire, chatting easily with his customers and occasionally throwing sidelong glances at Jack. He left the conversation at regular intervals to take wooden skewers of different meats out of a metal vat, dunk them in an earthenware bowl full of sauce, and arrange them on the grill over the coals. When the kabobs were cooked, his wife took them off the fire, put them on plates, and brought them to customers along with large mugs of beer.

After noticeably hesitating, and conferring with her husband in whispers, the old woman brought Jack a napkin, some chopsticks, and a small plate of pickled radish. "I'd like a beer," he said, and mimed drinking from a mug.

There was a minor uproar at the counter as the regular patrons, who had been watching the encounter, laughed and exchanged remarks in fast Japanese. Perhaps, Jack thought, they were speculating on what kind of beer Americans liked to drink. The old woman gave him a gap-toothed grin. At least half of her teeth were missing—apparently the "Japanese Miracle" didn't extend to dentistry. She hurried to the refrigerator and brought him a large bottle of Asahi beer and a glass mug. She filled up the mug for him, pouring carefully. Aware that everyone in the bar was still watching, he brought the glass to his lips and took a large drink. Suddenly all eyes in the bar left him and jumped to the color TV.

On the TV screen, two enormous wrestlers, naked except for flimsy-looking loincloths that barely covered their genitals, waited at opposite sides of a circular ring. A brightly costumed older man, whom Jack took to be the referee, gave a hand signal and shouted something. The two wrestlers rushed together, butting heads in the center of the ring with a sharp cracking sound. In a maneuver that seemed impossibly fast for such giants, one of the wrestlers combined a twisting dodge with a slapping push that sent his opponent sprawling in less than a second.

In the restaurant, a loud clamor greeted the result. As the match was played over and over again in slow motion and the men at the counter loudly picked it apart, the master took five skewers of meat out of the vat and ambled over to Jack. *"Konban wa,"* he said.

Jack smiled. "Hi. Nice place you got here."

"No English," the master announced.

"No Japanese," Jack told him.

The master shrugged and held out the five skewers of meat for Jack's inspection. Chunks of chicken and beef were easily identifiable. Tiny carcasses of what looked like pigeons were strung together on another skewer. The final two types of meat, Jack couldn't identify—they looked like innards, perhaps liver or kidney. Jack pointed to the chicken, and the master nodded and grinned. *"Yakitori,"* he said.

"Yakitori?" Jack repeated. "Good?"

"Good," the master told him, and headed off toward the grill. Jack watched him take ten skewers of chicken out of the metal vat, dunk them in sauce, and spread them out over the flame.

One of the Japanese workmen at the counter looked up as the chicken sizzled. He was a young-looking sixty with grizzled white hair and tired eyes, and he reminded Jack quite a bit of his father. He was chain-smoking, and drinking quickly and without apparent pleasure. While his neighbors on either side joked and commented on the sumo action, the older man kept silent, his eyes flicking from the TV screen to the end of his cigarette to the wooden bar top in front of him.

Watching him, Jack wished for the thousandth time that he had reached out to his father while he was alive. How many nights had Walter sat alone at his favorite bar in Santa Monica, keeping his own silent company? Twice a week? More? Jack wondered whether hard-bitten loners who seem perfectly content to go their own way ever really desire solitude, or if they've merely adapted to loneliness and learned to put a brave face on, hiding their pain behind stylized facades of masculine toughness, and cigarettes, and alcohol.

Or do some of them really prefer to be alone? Had Walter? What ghosts had kept him company in his apartment on Eighteenth Street? His parents, who had lost everything in the depression and both died young? His wife, whom he couldn't stand to live with but most certainly had loved, and whose death he had mourned? His firstborn son, to whom he had given his own name, and who had died after only six months of life?

Jack exhaled and pressed down on the wooden bar top with his elbows. And then a diagnosis of emphysema. And then he had come to visit, and then . . .

Could it possibly have been loneliness and deep depression, all ignited one night by a spark of rage? Alone, at the kitchen table, Walter's police revolver loaded in front of him, miserable about his health, furious at Jack, a sudden rush of adrenaline sweeping through him, his fingers darting down and then back up, the pistol stock smooth in his palm, the cold barrel suddenly in his mouth, his finger tightening on the trigger . . .

And as a final thought? Relief? Fury? Fear? Or gratitude that he had found a shortcut away from such pain?

Here in Japan, wasn't suicide considered an honorable way to leave the world? Even, in cases, a heroic way? Jack had read new stories about Japanese mothers who kill their own children before committing suicide, believing they are fulfilling their final duty as parents. And there were the kamikaze pilots, placing love for country and emperor above their own mortality, choosing to leave the world in the prime of their lives, in a final fireball of will-power. . . .

Jack sipped his beer and thought of Dr. Miles, at sundown, on the edge of a precipice. What had the engineer been thinking about during the long flight to Japan, and on the trip to Atami? He closed his eyes and recalled the sheer rock face of the cliffs and the jagged rocks below. The surf sang its siren song. No doubt the engineer had been recalling days in the sun that were now all behind him and perhaps imagining years of dark loneliness that lay ahead. . . .

And then suddenly a rush of terrible clarity—the boldness of despair—hands reaching down and moving the wheelchair forward, once around, twice, the momentum unstoppable now, and the final moment of tottering on the edge, the incredible knowledge that it was really truly happening, a stab of fear, an impulse to stop, to go back, and then the long tumble into the maw of eternity . . .

Jack was shaken out of his morbid thoughts by the old woman, who clinked two small plates of chicken skewers down in front of him. *"Dozo,"* she said. *"Yakitori."*

He sampled a piece of chicken and smiled at her, and then nodded at her husband, who stood by the grill, watching. The sauce gave the grilled meat a delicate, almost sweet taste. Jack chewed and swallowed, and the old woman looked satisfied and walked away. Jack bit off a second piece and chewed. . . .

Any way he figured it, it was impossible to make it all add up. As isolated incidents, he could account for any of them, and even begin to understand some of them. His father was easy—his own guilt helped. It wasn't too much of a stretch for Dr. Miles. As for Shannon Miles, he didn't really have enough information, but maybe there had been something in her life awful enough to make her plunge a kitchen knife into her neck. But three suicides? Or if something untoward had happened to Dr. Miles, two suicides and a related homicide?

Jack finished the chicken, drained his glass of beer, and stood up. The old woman hurried over. *"Domo. Ni-sen roppayku yen,"* she said.

Jack handed her a ten-thousand-yen note, and she scampered

away with it. She was soon back with change. He had read in his guidebook that there was no tipping in Japan, but it seemed very odd to pocket all the money and head for the door without leaving anything.

"*Mata, dozo,*" the old woman called after him.

"*Domo arigato gozaimashita,*" the master said with a wave.

As Jack left through the sliding door, he caught one last glance of the old Japanese workman sitting at the bar, sipping his beer, not talking to anyone or looking at anyone—all alone in a crowd of people.

Jack walked back quickly. The dark side street was quiet. Somewhere in the distance, a large dog made low, almost wolflike sounds, halfway between barks and growls.

Tomorrow he would see about the school. Misako had been a great stroke of luck. Her English ability and her familiarity with the town were invaluable. As Jack walked, he cautioned himself to be on his guard with her. She was almost too helpful, too pretty, too perfect. Come to think of it, his entire meeting with Captain Sato right down to his being mistaken for Walter had gone a bit too well for comfort. Was Sato just being helpful, or was there another game being played? It was easy to feel paranoid walking home through a dark city in a foreign land.

As Jack neared his hotel, an old blind man hobbled out of a dark doorway ahead of him, tapping with his cane on the pavement. He paused at the curb to listen for traffic, and then cocked an ear as if he had heard or sensed something very faint yet disturbing. For a second the old man hesitated at the edge of the street, his cane twitching in midair like an antenna.

Jack understood the blind man's hesitation—once again he had the strange sensation of being watched himself. He pivoted around to survey the street behind him, but it was dark and empty. He stood looking down the gloomy side street for several seconds and then, satisfied, turned back toward the hotel. The blind man had reached the other side of the street and was slowly vanishing into the darkness. Jack followed him into the murk, reached his hotel without further incident, and soon slipped off into a second night's deep sleep.

11

The secretaries on the first floor of the police station greeted Jack with nervous smiles and a cup of green tea. One of them spoke into an intercom, and less than a minute later, Misako came down the stairs. In her navy blue police uniform she looked exactly the same as she had the day before, except that she now wore small, elegant silver earrings. As she smiled at Jack, she gave his jacket and tie a quick examination.

The tie won a second look. It was a thin, gray silk Armani—one of the best he owned.

"I dressed up a bit for school. Can we walk?"

"No, we'll take my car," she said, leading him out the door. They headed for a parking lot behind the police station. "I called ahead and told them we were coming." The gravel of the parking lot crunched underfoot.

Two policemen passed them, heading into the station, and said, *"Ohayo gozaimasu,"* to Misako, who returned the greeting. They sized Jack up in a way that made him wonder if she had a boyfriend in the department.

"So, any tips for me?" he asked her. "How does one act in a Japanese high school?"

"They are very different from high schools in America," Misako told him, heading for a little red Toyota in a corner of the lot.

"You mean, kids in Japan study?"

She gave no indication that she understood he was trying for humor. "When I was in high school I studied six hours every night."

"What did you do for fun?"

"I was in the science club."

"Was that fun?"

"Not really," she admitted. After hesitating, she said in a much lower voice, "I played the flute. I enjoyed that."

113

Her car was immaculately clean inside and out. She popped a CD into her car's player and backed out onto the street. Jack couldn't identify the music she had chosen. It was lushly orchestrated yet subtle—his best guess was Debussy, but when it came to classical music, he knew his best guess was a long shot. Misako drove the same way she walked—gracefully and very quickly. They were soon out of the city, on the same coastal road they had followed the day before.

As the city of Atami disappeared behind them, he took the long shot. "This is lovely. Debussy?"

"Ravel. *Daphnis and Chloe*. Third movement. It's one of my favorites."

"Can you play the flute part?"

"No." She let out a long breath. "Maybe, a little. I stopped practicing when I joined the police."

"Why?"

Her tiny silver earrings quivered as the car hit some bumps. She met his gaze and then looked back at the road. "I wanted to give all my energy to my job."

They drove past the New Akao, and the spot where Dr. Miles went off the cliff. "I thought about some of the things you asked me yesterday," she said. "Some of them were good questions."

"Wish I had some good answers."

"Maybe today."

"Maybe." The little red car sped forward, following the curve of the pretty cove. "I thought about what you said, too," Jack told her. "I mean, about the Yakuza presence in Atami and how organized crime is different here from America. I have to admit I don't understand how a Yakuza leader can walk into the Tokyo police station and give New Year's greetings to the chief. Or how Yakuza can have crime conventions right out in the open. I mean, if they're criminals, how can they operate in full view of the public and the police?"

She reached over and turned off the music, as if unwilling to keep talking over it. "Do you know where Yakuza come from?" she asked him.

"You mean historically?"

"Yes."

"I have no idea. I didn't know they had their own history."

"Japan is so old, everything has a history. Even the Yakuza.

They say they started nearly four hundred years ago, at the time of Ieyasu Tokugawa." She paused and looked at him. "You know Tokugawa?"

"I told you—nobody learns anything in American schools."

"Tokugawa is one of the most famous men in Japanese history. Before him, there was a long period of civil war in Japan. Each local lord had a little army of paid samurai. They fought against one another all the time. Then, in 1604, Ieyasu Tokugawa unified Japan and became shogun. Finally most of the local fighting came to an end. There was peace and . . . how you say it? A central government?"

"Yes. The people must have been happy."

"There was one group who was not happy. Many thousands of trained samurai became unemployed."

"So they became the Yakuza?"

"No, most of them gave up fighting and took regular jobs. But some of them formed groups of *ronin*—samurai without masters—and roamed around Japan plundering towns and doing whatever they wanted. They were trained to fight, so they continued fighting. Young men of the larger towns got together in groups to fight back, and protect their homes. They practiced sword fighting till they were as good as the samurai. To the people of their towns, they were brave heroes."

"And the Yakuza claim to be descended from those guys who protected their towns?"

She nodded.

"But that was hundreds of years ago. Now aren't they just common gangsters?"

"The Yakuza work hard to make it look like they are still protecting and serving the Japanese people. After the war, during the occupation, the Japanese police couldn't protect the Japanese people from Korean and Taiwanese gangs. In Tokyo and Kobe and other cities, the Yakuza fought with swords to defend the common Japanese people. There are thousands of movies and comic strips and novels about Yakuza heroes—they are always very popular."

"Sounds like you have a soft spot for them."

"A soft spot?"

"It sounds like you like them."

"No," Misako said decisively, "I don't like the Yakuza at all.

But many police do. And many soldiers, too. Politically Japanese soldiers and police are right wing, and the Yakuza have always been for the emperor and preserving Japanese traditions.''

''And in reality? What do they really do to get their money?''

''Drugs,'' she said. ''What you call 'speed' in America, we call 'shabu' or 'white diamonds.' Most of it comes from Pusan in South Korea to Shimonoseki. Also prostitution. In Japan it is called 'selling spring.' And gambling, selling protection of bars and nightclubs, and lending money with high interest rates. All of it is controlled by the Yakuza.''

''And at the same time they're patriotic and defending the common people?''

''Yes.'' For the first time, she caught his sarcasm and tossed it back. ''They say that they walk on the sunny side of the street so that ordinary Japanese people can walk in the shade. We are lucky to have such public servants.''

She turned off the coastal road onto a steeply climbing narrower drive. They drove past a terraced mekon orange orchard and crossed an old wooden bridge above a bubbling stream. On either side of the road, clumps of bamboo swayed gracefully in the morning breeze. Near the top of the hill, they went around a steep curve of the winding road, and suddenly saw three white concrete buildings, connected by tunnels and passageways. ''Atami High School,'' she announced. ''Shannon taught here for two years.''

The school buildings were old but perfectly kept up. A dozen or so students were out in front of the school's circular drive, sweeping dust from the pathway and clipping bushes and picking up small bits of litter. One by one the students looked up, saw Jack and Misako, and gaped at Jack. *''Ehh, hontoo? Gaijin!''*

''Why are they staring at me like that?''

''Because you're tall . . . and foreign.''

''What are they saying? What's that word, *'gaijin'*?''

''It means foreigner—person from the outside,'' Misako told him, sounding slightly embarrassed. ''They are just surprised to see you at their school. Come.''

They walked through the sliding doors of the main entrance and saw hundreds of tiny cubbies, almost all of them containing pairs of shoes. Misako led Jack over to a special rack, and selected the largest blue slippers for him. They were at least three sizes too

small. He put his own shoes in the cubby, and crammed his toes
as far into the blue slippers as he could.

"Can you walk in them?"

"Sure," Jack said, experimenting. If he dragged his feet a
little, the slippers stayed on.

Misako exchanged her shoes for some pink slippers, and led
him into the main office. Three secretaries and two male office
workers, the latter wearing almost identical blue polyester suits,
looked up from their various tasks and gaped at Jack just the way
the students had outside. Misako said something to them in Japanese, and one of the men nodded, replied in a polite tone, and led
them toward a side door.

"The principal is not here right now," Misako explained to
Jack. "They will go and find him. In the meantime, we should
wait in his office." The side door led into a spacious and comfortable office that looked out through picture windows at a baseball field and a cinder track. A large, antique rosewood desk filled
up one corner of the room. The rest of the office was set up as a
reception area with a couch and two armchairs arranged to provide
guests with a view out the windows.

On the walls of the office, stern-looking photographs of Japanese men, dressed and posed formally, hung side by side. Jack
walked around the room, studying the sober photographs. The
first few were lithographs from the earliest days of photography—
the last few were in color. All of the men in the portraits were over
sixty, and most of them looked over seventy. They all wore dark
suits and sat posed at the same antique wooden desk that was in a
corner of the office. "Is this the hard-ass teachers' hall of fame?"

"The what?"

"Who are these guys?"

"They are the principals of Atami High School from the time
the school was founded," she told him. "That was the first principal," she said, pointing to a faded lithograph. Her finger followed the succession of photographs all the way to the color
portrait on the other side of the room. "And that is the current
principal, Mr. Kobayashi."

"Is this a particularly old school?"

"No. Many Japanese high schools have this kind of tradition,"
Misako told him. "Our colleges are not so good, but our high
schools are . . . very strong."

118   David Klass

She stood and joined him staring at a particularly sober-looking principal of school days long past. The old disciplinarian had fierce black eyes, a starched collar that almost seemed to be choking him, and lips so tight and thin, they looked as if they would shatter if he tried to force them into any other expression than condemnation. "I heard Japanese schools are tough," Jack said, his eyes on the stern face. "I guess I see why."

She nodded, also fascinated by the face in the photograph. "So many American writers describe the success in Japan since World War Two as a miracle," she said in a low voice. "When I was in Wisconsin I read some of those books—they kept looking for one hidden factor to explain our 'miracle': the Japanese way of doing business, the Japanese mind, Japanese logic. . . ."

"We grew up believing that America was the richest, strongest, all-around number one country in the world," Jack told her. "The last ten years or so, when we heard that in area after area, Japan was passing us, it seemed hard to believe. A lot of Americans wanted to identify a cause or a reason—something you have that we don't. I mean, Japan was in ruins after World War Two. And now it's the richest country in the world. How do you explain it?"

"I don't believe in miracles," Misako told him. "But if you want to know how we were able to recover so quickly and make such great economic progress in such a short time, just look at their faces." Jack followed her eyes from portrait to portrait. "Our economy and our industry were, as you say, in ruins, but our tradition of education was unbroken. Our schools have always been the best."

The door opened to admit a frail-looking old man in a dark suit. Jack recognized Principal Kobayashi's wizened features from the color portrait on the wall, and gave him a deep bow. The old principal bowed back. A middle-aged Japanese man hurried through the door behind the principal and approached Jack nervously. His eyeglasses rode uneasily on his small nose, and he seemed to adjust them every few seconds with his right index finger. When he spoke, his English was choppy but grammatically sound.

"I am Hiroshi Endo, an English teacher of this school. This is Principal Kobayashi. Please sit down."

Jack and Misako sat on the couch. Principal Kobayashi chose an armchair, while Mr. Endo remained standing. The principal spoke and then took a business card out of his pocket and handed it to Jack. "He says, welcome to our school," Endo translated. "That is his *meishi* . . . business card. He asks, how can he help you?"

Jack glanced at Misako. Even though her English was incomparably better than Mr. Endo's, she showed no inclination to speak. He wondered if her silence was due to modesty or a desire not to show an English teacher up at his own profession, or because she was a Japanese woman showing the expected deference to men. In any case, Jack decided to follow her lead and work through Mr. Endo. "Have you heard about the deaths of Professor Miles, and of his wife, Shannon, back in America?"

"Yes, of course," Endo said. "When the professor died, there were stories. Even in the *Asahi Shinbun*. About him and about his wife. She taught here, long ago. Very sad."

"Did you or Principal Kobayashi know Shannon when she taught here? Her last name in those days was Cleary."

Mr. Endo translated the question for the old man, who shook his head. "When Shannon taught here, we were teaching at other schools," Endo explained. "Japanese schoolteachers are transferred every few years. From one high school to another. Before I taught here, I taught at Ohito. Before that, I taught at Shuzenji. Mr. Kobayashi was the assistant principal at Kanami before he came here. So we didn't know her."

"Aren't there any teachers who've been here for nine or ten years, and might have known Shannon?"

As Principal Kobayashi and Mr. Endo went over a faculty list, a small, gentle-looking woman in her forties entered carrying a tray and four cups of tea. She gave a cup to each of them, and Jack was surprised when she asked shyly but in quite passable English if he wanted cream or sugar. He thought he detected a faint British accent in her pronunciation.

As soon as she was done serving tea, she headed for the door, but before walking through it, she paused. She stood there for a long second, watching Jack and Misako, as if gathering her courage to speak to them. Then Mr. Endo announced, "We think there are only two. A physics teacher and a business teacher." As Jack and Misako gave him their full attention, the little woman slipped meekly out the door and away down the corridor.

"Can I talk to them?" Jack asked Mr. Endo.

"They both are in the middle of teaching classes now. They can meet you soon, during lunch period. Also, maybe you want to meet Eric Gleason. He's our American teacher. He does the same job now that Shannon did nine years ago. He can tell you what it's like being an American in Atami."

"Yes, I'd like to meet him."

For a while they sipped tea in silence. Jack found the silence awkward, but he noticed that none of the Japanese people in the room seemed to feel the need to break it. Instead, they just sipped tea and studied one another. A full minute crawled by. Jack glanced at Misako, who looked back at him and took a tiny sip of tea. Another long, silent minute passed.

In the distance, Jack heard a faint mechanical drone. At first he thought he might be imagining it, but the sound got steadily louder until Mr. Endo put down his teacup and stood nervously. He muttered something in Japanese to the old principal, who also seemed upset. Suddenly three teenage boys on minibikes crested the lip of the athletic field and roared directly across the soccer field. Students on the field scattered, shrieking. Two gym teachers gave chase on foot.

Old Principal Kobayashi put down his teacup and said something, his lips tight and his tone grim. "Principal Kobayashi says he's sorry you had to see this, but we have a problem with juvenile delinquents," Mr. Endo translated. "Most of our students follow the rules. The principal suggests you might like a tour of our high school?"

Jack agreed, and soon he, Misako, and Mr. Endo were walking through the spotless corridors. The high level of the education, compared to American public high schools, struck Jack at once. In an art class, thirty students drew a live model, and all the sketches Jack saw displayed a thorough knowledge of anatomy and at least a partial grasp of spatial foreshortening. A math class drilled in what would be second-year college calculus in America. In the English language lab, forty-five spanking new computer terminals and screens gave the room a high-tech feel. Students practiced "th" and "r" sounds while watching native English speakers pronounce the same words on the computer screens.

As they walked down the spotless corridors, it soon became clear to Jack that while the education was still obviously first-rate, the history of stern discipline represented by the photographs on

Principal Kobayashi's wall was under siege, if not facing an all-out rebellion. While most of the students were dressed neatly in severe, almost military uniforms—blue for the girls, jet black for the boys—and went without jewelry, makeup, long hair, or anything else that could create an individual style, a large minority of the students were openly challenging the conformity of the system in one way or another. Some of the girls had streaks of colored dye in their hair and punk haircuts, and a number of the boys wore oversize, baggy pants and brightly colored tank tops.

Jack's treatment by the students varied from the gasps and rude stares he encountered in almost every classroom to groups of students who ran up to him and blurted out random phrases in English at him to get some kind of reaction. No matter how he responded, the students laughed and shouted to one another as if a rare animal were on display. Once, traversing a long hallway while the classes changed, Jack was completely surrounded by male students, one of whom actually yanked on his suit jacket in a display of daring that was acknowledged by his fellows with cheers and hoots. Jack shoved him away, and the students backed off a few steps, but they seemed to completely ignore Mr. Endo's angry admonitions.

"Very sorry," Mr. Endo said as they walked back toward the principal's office. He wiped his forehead with a handkerchief as if the insubordination had made him perspire. "As our principal explained, we have a problem with school violence."

"Believe me, in America when we talk about school violence, we talk about guns and knives," Jack told him. "Your school is very good. And your students behave well."

"Twenty years ago, yes," Endo said. "Even ten years ago. But now we have a terrible problem, all over Japan. Families can't control their children. The children want everything. They want to be free like the teenagers they see in American TV and movies. They don't follow the rules. Terrible. Terrible."

Back in the principal's office, one of the two teachers who had been at Atami High School when Shannon Miles taught there was waiting nervously. He was a short, pudgy, white-haired physics teacher in a lab coat who never looked directly at Jack but addressed his responses to Mr. Endo as if Jack's lack of Japanese set him apart in a completely different dimension.

He hadn't known Shannon well, he explained, and he couldn't

remember much about her after ten years. She had been pretty, friendly, and popular among the students and the teachers. Her Japanese had been excellent. And she had played on the teachers' volleyball team. He spread his palms flat on the sides of his white lab coat and smiled apologetically. That was really all he could remember.

Jack asked a whole series of specific questions about Shannon's professional and personal life, and received only shrugs in return. When he asked if she had ever gotten into trouble with the Yakuza or with the police, Principal Kobayashi, who had been slouching, revived noticeably, and Mr. Endo's eyebrows shot up in surprise. The physics teacher shook his head and then gave a long, stumbling answer in the midst of which Jack thought he caught the word "rendezvous." Mr. Endo translated the answer to mean that as far as the physics teacher remembered, Shannon had never been in any trouble or involved with the Yakuza or anything like that.

When Jack finally told him he could go, the physics teacher apologized for not being more help and then turned and hurried out.

Jack had high hopes for the second teacher, who had a lecherous side he didn't seem to feel the need to keep hidden. As soon as he walked into the office, his eyes took a quick sight-seeing trip over Misako's body. As he talked to Jack and Mr. Endo, he managed to throw her a number of quick glances, and every few seconds he wet the corners of his lips with the tip of his tongue. His name was Mr. Nishimura, he was a business teacher in his midthirties, and in response to Jack's first question, he admitted that he spoke some English but said he would rather answer questions through an interpreter.

"Ask him if he remembers Shannon Cleary," Jack instructed Mr. Endo.

Mr. Nishimura grinned and answered for himself in broken but quite passable English. "Oh, yes, Shannon. I remember. Long red hair. Long legs. Very beautiful. Very glamorous. Like a movie star."

"Did she have a boyfriend?"

Mr. Nishimura nodded and this time made use of the interpreter to answer. She had one back in America. Some boy who had been her boyfriend in college. She talked about him often. "Too bad, *nee*?'' Mr. Nishimura added on his own, with a quick look at the other Japanese men in the room.

"Did her American boyfriend ever visit her in Atami?"

Mr. Nishimura thought and then shook his head. Not that he remembered. Shannon had been a frequent subject of gossip among the other teachers, and if her boyfriend had visited, the news would have spread quickly.

"Was she particularly friendly with any Japanese men? From the school or from the town? Was there any gossip about her being involved with anyone in Atami?"

The gossip, according to Mr. Nishimura, was that she didn't like Japanese men. Several of the male teachers tried to flirt with her, and had been politely but firmly rebuffed. Mr. Nishimura recalled a year-end *enkai* drinking party when the entire faculty went to a resort hotel on the tip of the Izu Peninsula, near Shimoda. After rounds of beer and sake, two drunken teachers had made passes at Shannon. According to Mr. Nishimura, she had taken great offense and actually slapped one of them for putting his hand on her thigh. The glint of anger in his eyes as he finished telling the story made Jack suspect Nishimura himself had been the culprit.

"Was she involved with the Yakuza, or did she get in trouble with the law in any way?"

Of course not, Mr. Nishimura answered quickly. In a city as small as Atami, if she had done anything wrong or associated with the wrong people, everyone would have known about it. Just take what happened at the Rendezvous Club, he pointed out. Shannon, seeking dinner late one night when all the restaurants she usually frequented in Atami had closed, had walked into an establishment of dubious repute. It was sort of a private club, Mr. Nishimura explained with a grin. "Very special club." Principal Kobayashi twisted uneasily on his seat.

"What happened?" Jack asked.

Mr. Nishimura shrugged and finished the story quickly. The owner of the club had struck up a conversation with Shannon, and eventually offered her a part-time job as a special late night hostess, apparently suggesting that it would be a good chance for her to practice her Japanese. Shannon had mentioned the job offer to someone at school, and there had been an uproar. The owner of the club had been disciplined, and the principal had felt it his duty as her surrogate father to give Shannon a stern warning about even walking through the door of such places.

"So she didn't take the job?" Jack asked.

"No. It was just a mistake."

"Do you know if she ever went back to that club, or any club like it?" Jack asked Mr. Nishimura.

"I never saw her there," he said with a smile, and threw another hungry look at Misako, who stared back at him blankly. "Shannon was a good girl. She followed all the rules."

"Did she have any . . . hobbies? Any special activities inside the school or out?"

Mr. Nishimura mentioned the teachers' volleyball team. She had been quite a good player, he said. Besides that, her only interest had been learning Japanese. His desk had been on the same row as Shannon's, and he had frequently seen her drawing *kanji* characters or studying Japanese grammar from thick textbooks she had brought from America. She was a fanatic about perfecting her command of the language, and devoted rare free time at school to practicing calligraphy.

Jack thanked Mr. Nishimura, who came up with "My pleasure" in response. As he left the office, Mr. Nishimura cast a final look at Misako and ran his tongue quickly over his lower teeth.

Box lunches arrived simultaneously with Eric Gleason. He was nerdish and seemed much too young to be working overseas by himself. His handshake was oily, and his owlish little face was pocked by a bad acne problem.

"The L.A. Police sent someone all the way here?" he asked Jack. "That's intense. We don't get many Americans in Atami."

"Don't some American tourists come?"

"Once in a while I see one or two. Mostly Atami is for Japanese. That's why it was so weird when that professor died here. I mean, it was like an American tourist finally comes here, and right away he falls off a cliff."

"Tell me about the job. Do they treat you well? Do they pay you enough?"

"They pay great. I've been here almost a year, and I want to stay for at least one more. I save five hundred bucks a month, and still I've traveled to Hong Kong and Thailand, and I'm gonna go to Bali soon. And if I wanted to, I could make even more money teaching side jobs, but I don't need it and they ask us not to.''

"What kind of side jobs?''

"Everyone wants to learn English. People are always asking for lessons and offering to pay. But *Mombusho*—that's the Japanese Ministry of Education, that pays us—doesn't want us working on the side. So I don't. I make more than I need as it is.''

"Ever hear of a club called the Rendezvous?''

Eric Gleason thought and then shook his head. "It sounds like one of those strip clubs, down by the water. There are dozens of them, and some of them take French- or American-sounding names to try to be exotic.''

They opened their box lunches and ate together as they talked. Inside the rectangular gray plastic lunch box Jack found a breaded pork cutlet on a bed of lettuce. Smaller compartments held potato salad and pickled radishes.

"Where do you live?'' Jack asked as he tried to pick up a precut sliver of pork chop.

"*Kyoin jutaku*—public teachers' housing. It's a nice apartment, on the very top floor of the building. Two of the rooms have ocean views.''

"It's assigned to you by the city?''

"Yup. The city owns the building. The rent is real reasonable.''

"Do you happen to know if Shannon lived in that same apartment when she taught in Atami ten years ago?'' Jack asked, playing a wild hunch.

Eric Gleason thought about it and slowly nodded. "I think all the American teachers starting with Shannon lived in the same place.''

"Why do you think that?''

"'Cause when American teachers go back home after their year or two is up, they sell as much of their furniture and stuff as they can to the next person coming over. And then they leave a lot of junk that they can't sell.''

"Kind of like hand-me-downs?''

"Yeah, that's right. There's stuff in my apartment that I've inherited from just about all the other guys and girls who've taught here before.''

"And you found something from Shannon?''

As Eric nodded, Jack sensed a quickening of interest on the part of Misako. She leaned slightly forward in her chair, and her eyes watched Eric expectantly.

"She left a few books. Reason I know they were hers is that they had her name in them. Real boring stuff. A dictionary. A thesaurus. Grammar texts. I can see why she left them."

"I'd like to look at them."

"No can do. I tossed them."

"You threw them out? Why?"

"Place was a mess when I moved in. I had lots of books and stuff of my own, so I just threw out a lot of the old clutter."

"And you haven't found anything else that belonged to her? Any of her old letters or teaching manuals?"

"Nope. Nothing like that." Gleason used chopsticks like a native Japanese, picking up tiny pieces of slippery pickled radish and conveying them effortlessly to his mouth. "Sorry. I like to live in a neat apartment, and it was just a sty."

"Do you think any of the neighbors might have gotten to know Shannon well? Have any of them mentioned her to you?"

"Most of my neighbors are teachers who've just been working in Atami a few years. I've heard a little bit from them about the two guys who taught here before me, but nothing about Shannon."

"Has anyone from the town approached you about anything at all that made you feel funny?"

"Like what?"

"Like there was something illegal going on?"

"No. Never."

"Have you ever encountered the Yakuza?"

"I've seen their cars when they have conventions here. It's really intense. Big black Cadillacs and Continentals—you never see big American cars like that in Japan normally. And the guys inside the cars wear dark suits. And sunglasses, even at night. It's intense."

"But they never try to talk to you?"

"No, not at all. They just stay at the major hotels. They're tourists here, just like everybody else."

"What about the social life for an American teacher here?"

"You mean, like, do I scam on the Japanese women?"

"How much freedom do you have? What kind of social opportunities do you think someone like Shannon would have had?"

Gleason finished his lunch and closed his lunch box. He slid his wooden chopsticks back into the paper holder they had come in, and put them on top of the lid. "That's a tough one," he said. "Japan's changing pretty fast in terms of how much personal freedom they're willing to permit, but by American standards, it's still in the Dark Ages. Ten years ago it must've been even worse."

"Worse how?"

"Teachers are supposed to live model lives. I feel like I'm watched all the time, and I know they cut me some slack 'cause I'm a guy. I bet for a girl with this job ten years ago it must've been real bad. Shannon probably felt like she was in a goldfish bowl."

"So there was no way she could've kept a relationship secret?"

"In Atami? No way. Her neighbors would've seen, her students would have seen—pretty soon everyone would have known. Listen, I walk into the Yaohan—the department store—to buy a flashlight, but I don't know how to say it in Japanese, so I do a little mime. The salesgirl understands, I get the flashlight, no problem. The next day at least fifteen different people come up to me in school and tell me the Japanese word for flashlight. That's what it's like."

Jack thanked Eric Gleason, exchanged another oily handshake with him, and then the young American was gone and Mr. Endo was asking if there was anything else Jack needed to do at Atami High School. Jack turned to Misako, and smiled. "Did I miss anything?"

"The office lady," she whispered back.

"What?"

"The lady who poured the tea for us. She spoke English. She might've known Shannon."

"If she'd been here when Shannon was here, wouldn't they have told me?"

"You asked for teachers," Misako reminded him. "She's not a teacher."

The office lady was sent for and soon hurried in. She arrived with a tea pitcher in one hand, and a small manila envelope in the other. She began the interview by pouring new cups of tea for them, and asking if they needed anything more to eat or drink. She did not seem frightened or intimidated at being called in for questioning. Her natural grace and graciousness, though muted and deferential from long habit, were quite striking.

Mr. Endo introduced her as Mrs. Mitsuko Taniguchi, office lady, and then remained silent for the rest of the questioning as it soon became clear that her spoken English was at least as good as his own. She was, however, so soft-spoken that Jack often had to strain to catch all of her answers.

"I learned to speak English in England," she explained. "My family lived in Bristol for three years, when I was a little girl. My father was an engineer. At the shipyards."

"How long have you worked at Atami High School?"

"Seventeen years."

"So you knew Shannon Miles?"

She smiled at the memory the name conjured up, and nodded. "Her name then was Cleary. Shannon Cleary."

"That's right. Were you friends with her?"

Modestly, "Yes, a little."

"Tell me about her." The open-ended invitation brought only silence. Jack became more specific to help her. "Was she happy in Atami?"

"Very happy. Many of the teachers were her friends, and all her students liked her. She had a beautiful new apartment near the MOA Art Museum, and her Japanese got very good. Yes, I think she was happy. When she had to go back to America early she was very disappointed."

"Why did she have to go back early?"

"Her mother got very sick, so she had to go back three or four months early. She wanted to stay, but her mother had been ill for a long time and Shannon was afraid her mother might be near death. She explained it to us at a big teachers' meeting. Everyone at the school understood."

"Did she have a boyfriend in Japan?"

Mrs. Taniguchi hesitated. "I don't think so. No."

"Do you know if she had one in America?"

"I don't think so."

"I heard that she talked a lot about a boy she went to college with."

"Yes." Mrs. Taniguchi nodded. "It was her old college boyfriend. But I think everything between them was over before she came to Japan. That was my . . . impression."

"Why?"

"Because—" Mrs. Taniguchi groped for words "—she always spoke about him in the past tense."

"Why did she talk about him at all?"

"Because . . . because, I think, many of the male teachers at Atami were watching her and . . ." She stopped and glanced at the principal and Mr. Endo, as if uncomfortable at having to impugn Japanese males in their presence. Then she looked at Misako, who smiled at her, and she seemed to gather strength. "They wanted to chase her. And she wasn't interested. So, I think, she told some of them about her boyfriend back in America."

"So they'd leave her alone?" Jack asked, remembering Mr. Nishimura of the lecherous roving gaze.

Mrs. Taniguchi nodded. "Yes."

"One of the teachers we've talked to said he thought Shannon didn't like Japanese men. Was that your impression?"

"Maybe."

"Why did she feel that way?"

Mrs. Taniguchi lowered her eyes, obviously very conscious of her male superiors. Around the walls of the office, the stern principals of years past glared down as they, too, awaited her answer. Jack noticed for the first time that they were all pictures of men—in all its long history, Atami had never had a woman principal. "I think she was very much a feminist," Mrs. Taniguchi whispered. "She didn't like the way women were . . . are . . . treated in Japan." The tea pitcher in her hand trembled slightly.

"There must have been other American teachers nearby. Was she friendly with them?"

"There were a few in Numazu and Shizuoka City. I don't think Shannon was close friends with them."

"Did she have anything going on in the city of Atami? A second job, a relationship, volunteer work . . . ?"

"I don't think so. She worked very hard at her Japanese studies. And she loved Japanese art. She went to the MOA Art Museum often. On weekends she went to galleries and museums in Tokyo."

"Did she get involved with the Yakuza at all?"

Mrs. Taniguchi repeated "The Yakuza?" to make sure she understood, before shaking her head. She seemed amazed that Jack would even ask such a question about Shannon.

"Did Shannon ever have any problems with the police? Do you think she could have gotten involved with some bad people by mistake?"

"No. Nothing like that."

"I hear there was an incident involving a club called the Rendezvous."

"I remember that. It was just a mistake."

"So Shannon never went back there, after the mistake?"

"Of course not. No. She followed the rules."

"Is there anything else you remember?" Jack asked her. "Anything at all that happened while she taught here that seemed strange or secret or hard to explain? Think for a second. Anything?"

"No. I'm sorry I can't help you more." A quick expression of profound sadness passed over the gentle woman's face. "I liked Shannon very much. I read about how she died. You think she was murdered?"

"I don't know," Jack said, but she read his suspicion in his eyes, and shuddered.

"How terrible. Who would do such a thing to such a beautiful person?" Mrs. Taniguchi held up the manila envelope. "Would you do me a favor?"

"What?"

"These are pictures of Shannon from when she taught here. Since she was the first American teacher at Atami, our school library kept them all these years. Perhaps her family would like them now. If her parents are still alive, they must be feeling terrible grief. Would you bring them back to America and try to give them to the Cleary family for me? I've written the last address we have for them. I would send them myself except that I'm afraid they might no longer be at this address. . . ."

Jack glanced at the address—it was in Weymouth, Massachusetts. He took the envelope and promised he would do his best to track down Shannon's family when he got back to America.

In Misako's car, as they sped back toward Atami, Jack opened the envelope and took out a half dozen color photographs. In the top one Shannon was jumping to spike a volleyball, right fist in the air, red hair sprayed out behind her. In the next few shots she was competing in races in a track-and-field day—her mane of long red hair and her long legs and athletic body giving her the quality of a young filly loping around happily at full canter.

The final shot had the look of a farewell photograph. Shannon, in a green dress, posed with a half dozen girl students, and all of them were teary-eyed. "Looks like they were sorry to see her go," Jack said.

Misako stole a quick look at the photograph and nodded. "Shannon was very nice, I think."

"Except that she was kind of harsh on the subject of Japanese men."

"Perhaps after your drinking party tonight, you will be able to understand her feelings about certain kinds of Japanese men a little bit," Misako suggested.

Jack watched her till she glanced away from the road at him. "Misako, today, when I met you at the police station, the men there looked at me in a way that made me think maybe you have a boyfriend on the force."

"No, they were just wondering who you were." Her gaze was steady. "I have no time for a social life."

"You don't date at all?"

"Never," Misako said. "No time."

"And that extends to American law enforcement officers who would like to take you out to dinner?"

She looked at him, and if she hesitated, it was only for the briefest heartbeat. "Thank you, but I'm very busy now."

"Even if we talked about the case during the meal? A good dinner might inspire us."

She shook her head. "I do my best thinking when I'm hungry. And alone."

They rode in silence for a while. "I know it's none of my business," Jack said, "but it seems a shame that when you joined the police, you gave up your music and having a social life and everything."

"I get a great deal of . . . satisfaction from my job," she said, guiding the car up to the curb. "And in Japan, in my field, if a woman is to be taken seriously, she must be serious. Here is your hotel. Have a nice evening." She switched on the blinker and came up with a strange smile for him. "Thank you for asking me out to dinner. I'm sure it would be fun. But I would rather keep our friendship purely professional, Jack."

"I like it when you call me Jack."

"Tell me, Jack, did you really think if Shannon lived in that apartment, some of her possessions might still be lying around? For a Japanese, such a thing would be unthinkable, after ten years and many different teachers living there in between.''

''Some American kids just out of college are slobs. If they pass on hand-me-downs from year to year, I thought we might get lucky. Anyway, it was worth a shot.''

''Yes, it was worth a shot. Good-bye, Jack.''

Almost as soon as he was out the door, she roared away from the curb. Jack watched her little red car zip in and out of traffic till it disappeared from sight.

12

The eel restaurant was clean and crowded, with chrome chairs and Formica-topped tables. There was no menu, or at least they didn't bother to show one to Jack. At the back of the restaurant, in tanks along the wall, hundreds of eels swam back and forth twisting and slithering in bunches beneath the bright lights.

Captain Sato brought two colleagues along, Lieutenant Suzuki and Detective Noguchi. Both men were dressed in dark suits, and both spoke fairly good English. Their party of four was immediately seated at a front table—from the way everyone in the restaurant treated them, Jack saw that Sato commanded quite a bit of respect. Soft Japanese music played from two roof speakers, and as Jack watched, it seemed to him that the throngs of eels twisted together and unknotted in rhythm to the music.

The soup arrived first, a light but tasty broth with a foul-looking gray-black organ floating in the middle of it that Jack's companions identified for him as the liver of the eel he was about to eat. They all ate their eel livers with great relish, and with many misgivings, Jack picked his own out of the bowl and popped it into his mouth. It was as bad as it looked, slightly chewy in an unpleasant way with a taste halfway between chicken liver and tripe. With a concerted effort Jack managed to swallow it down, and washed out his mouth with several large swallows of beer.

Jack had never eaten eel before, and when his portion arrived on a bed of rice, he was pleasantly surprised by the wonderful taste. The meet was sweet and succulent, and so tender, it flaked into pieces when he touched it with his chopsticks. One huge bottle of Sapporo Beer after another arrived at their table. The music shut off, and a TV in the corner of the restaurant was switched on to the day's baseball highlights.

Both of Captain Sato's colleagues seemed to be rabid fans. As they ate, they threw constant glances at the TV set. The older of the two, Lieutenant Suzuki, had the look of a high school wrestling coach who can still lick any member of the squad. His biceps bulged beneath his rolled-up sleeves, and his neck was so short and wide that his chin seemed to sprout directly out of his broad shoulders. "Japanese baseball is weak. American baseball is number one," he proclaimed after a black American player whom Jack remembered vaguely from the major leagues several years ago hammered a fastball out of the stadium on the highlight show.

It had been that way from the moment they had sat down—instead of talking about the Miles case or Jack's presence in Atami, they had traded generalizations about Japan and America back and forth, almost as a substitute for light conversation. Jack decided to let them set the pace and tone of the evening—for the moment he was content to finish his eel.

Captain Sato's English had gotten progressively better as he drank more beer. In the police station he had been reluctant to attempt more than a few words, but after a half dozen beers, he had become almost garrulous. "Japanese baseball should be for Japanese. Now, too many Americans." He glanced at Jack, as if he were somehow responsible. "We need to go our own way. Then Japanese baseball could be as strong as American baseball. Strong but different. *Nee,* Noguchi?"

Detective Noguchi was tall and well built, with the look of a swift center fielder and hawklike eyes that the beers didn't seem to dull. He was just a few years older than Jack, and his spoken English was by far the best of the trio. He was properly deferential to his superiors in word and manner, but on the subject of baseball he seemed to have the right to politely disagree. He shook his head, his eyes on the TV screen. "There will never be a Japanese heavyweight boxing champion. And there will never be Japanese baseball players as good as American players. We have lightweight boxing champions and lightweight baseball players."

Captain Sato frowned and turned to Jack. "You played baseball?"

For a moment, Jack was curious how Sato knew. It must be merely a guess, he decided. A healthy American man must have played baseball at some point. "In college, yes."

"Please tell my friends that size is not so important."

"Size is not so important," Jack told them obediently, swallowing a chunk of eel. "Speed and skill matter more."

"I have seen pictures of famous American home run hitters," Detective Noguchi replied. "Babe Ruth. Willy McCovey. Reggie Jackson. They were not small. They did not look fast."

Jack looked at Sato and shrugged. "He's got a point."

Captain Sato drained his beer glass, and Noguchi hurried to pour another one for him. Their ritual of pouring for one another mystified Jack. He couldn't figure out who should pour for whom, and when it was correct to do it. All he knew for sure was that they were all refilling his own glass at every opportunity, as if in a concerted effort to get him drunk. "You went to Atami High School today?" Sato asked.

"Yes."

"Did the students seem small?"

"Not particularly. No."

"As big as American high school students?"

"Looked about the same."

Sato nodded, pleased. He spoke in Japanese, and Noguchi translated. "He says that Japanese students today eat more meat than he did when he was young. He says his generation didn't eat enough protein. Japanese children today eat much more meat and grow much taller."

"So we will have big Japanese baseball players," Sato concluded happily. "As big as Americans."

"Big Japanese girls, too," Lieutenant Suzuki added, cupping his hands to his chest. "How do you say?"

"Breasts."

"Yes," Lieutenant Suzuki said, his cheeks a bit flushed from a dozen or so glasses of beer. He lowered his large arms to the table, and when his elbow hit the edge, the dishes rattled. "I like big breasts. You?"

"I'm not against them," Jack told him.

"Today you went to Atami High School with Misako Watanabe. From our office. A very pretty Japanese woman. Yes?"

Jack felt the three of them watching him. "Yes," he acknowledged.

"She has large . . ." Suzuki once again thumped his chest.

"They looked pretty big," Jack agreed, picking his words carefully. "She's very pretty."

"She is *onna zakkari*," Suzuki said. "You know what that means?"

"No," Jack said.

Suzuki looked at Noguchi for help.

"Onna," Noguchi said, "means woman. *Zakkari* means . . . What do you call it when a flower has opened?"

"Full bloom?"

"Yes. *Onna zakkari* is a woman who is in full bloom."

"Very full bloom," Lieutenant Suzuki repeated with an enthusiastic sweep of his arm, nearly overturning his beer glass. "But this flower doesn't want to be . . . harvested."

The other two Japanese men chuckled over Suzuki's choice of a word. "Harvested, *nee*?"

"This flower just wants to sit in the garden and look pretty," Suzuki continued. "Japanese women like American men very much. Maybe this flower likes you?"

"Sorry, no luck," Jack told him. Was he under suspicion for messing with the local women? Or had they put her with him on purpose, as a kind of experiment to see if he could loosen up the office prude? Either way, he didn't like it. "If you want to know, I asked this flower out to dinner," he told them. "She turned me down. Said she's too busy with her job."

"So, *nee*?" Suzuki mumbled. His peers made similar grunts, as if to ask what else was new.

"She is very good at what she does," Jack said. "Thank you for assigning her to me. It was a good choice—she's helped me a lot the last few days."

Sato put down his beer glass and held his palm over the top for a second, apparently signifying that he was done with refills for the time being. As if taking a cue from his captain, Detective Noguchi asked Jack, "What did she help you find out about Professor Miles's suicide?"

The mood at the table became less jocular. They watched him carefully. Jack had the fleeting suspicion that all the boisterous beer drinking and camaraderie and generalizations about America and Japan had been building up to this question—that the whole thing was preplanned so that after a half dozen beers, he was suddenly alone on center stage. "If you want to know, I don't think Professor Miles committed suicide," he told them, looking from face to face. "For that matter, I don't think Shannon killed herself either."

A roar sounded from the TV set as a player made a spectacular play. Heads turned in the restaurant, but at Jack's table the three Japanese policemen seemed to have lost their interest in baseball and were watching him in silence.

"So they were killed?" Sato finally asked, speaking softly but with an undertone of controlled anger.

"Unless there's another possibility. Yes, I think they were both murdered."

Captain Sato spoke quickly in Japanese, and his voice had an edge. When he finished, Detective Noguchi translated. "He says that Atami is not New York. People don't come here to visit and suddenly get murdered. He says you should know that every year there are twice as many homicides in New York City as there are in all of Japan. Dr. Miles was a college professor. Who would want to kill a college professor in a wheelchair? No one in Japan. No one here in Atami. It doesn't make sense."

"You're right," Jack admitted, looking right back at Sato, "it doesn't make any sense. Professor Miles told American police that Shannon had a serious romance when she lived here in Atami. A Japanese boyfriend. No one at Atami High School knows anything about her having a lover."

"Then there wasn't one," Noguchi said. "If there was, everyone at school and in Atami would have known."

"But why did she tell her husband there was one, if there wasn't?"

"Maybe she made it up," Suzuki suggested. "Women make things up."

"Why would she? I've heard of women covering up past romances to protect their reputations, but I've never heard of a woman inventing one and telling her husband about it. He idolized her—she didn't need to make him jealous. Why did he come here after she died? And then there's the Yakuza—they have a presence here, they hold their conventions here, but everyone says Shannon wouldn't have gotten involved with them. Why not?"

Sato smiled at Jack's reference to the Yakuza, but it was a smile without warmth. "Maybe you know the Yakuza from the Hollywood movie? I remember. Starring Robert Mitchum and Tanaka

Ken. This is not Hollywood.'' He paused—his eyes glittered hard and bright. ''You say people are not telling you the truth here. But everyone is helping you. You came to me. I gave you one of my best officers. You went to Atami High School. They tried to help you. The JNP conducted a thorough investigation and decided it was a suicide. Maybe there are no answers. Sometimes, you know, that is the case.''

The table had gone very silent. Suzuki was frozen in his seat, eyes on the eel skeleton on his plate, while Detective Noguchi watched the confrontation sitting straight and unmoving, his palms pressed together as if in prayer.

''Okay,'' Jack finally said. ''You're right—everyone here has been helping me. And I do see and admire how safe it is in Japan, compared to America.'' He managed a smile. ''Anyway, it's too early in the evening to talk business. I liked it better when we were talking about baseball and breasts.''

There was a moment of silent tension. Then Sato smiled back, and the corners of his wrinkled face lifted as he finally laughed out loud. The other two policemen joined in. ''Yes, *ikimashyoo*, let's go,'' Sato said, standing up. Jack wasn't surprised that they left without paying the check. He had grown up among policemen— apparently free meals were part of the job benefits on both sides of the Pacific.

They headed toward the line of car headlights that snaked along the highway above the beach. Beyond the narrow strand, the bright lights from the oceanfront hotels swam back and forth on the night waves. They stopped at some lighted batting cages a few hundred yards from the ocean. ''Now,'' Captain Sato said, ''let's see American and Japanese baseball.''

Once again Jack had the curious feeling that the night had been choreographed and that they were playing out a preplanned scenario. The talk of baseball in the eel restaurant had neatly prefaced their finding these batting cages.

In a few seconds Jack found himself facing a pitching machine while Detective Noguchi thumped a bat on the plate in the neighboring cage. Suzuki and Sato watched from outside the netting. The beers had left Jack just a bit light-headed, and he missed the first two pitches the machine threw at him. From the cage next to him came a steady ping, ping, ping as Detective Noguchi's aluminum bat ripped one line drive after another. Jack cursed and tried to concentrate on the next pitch—he had apparently been set up against the local hotshot.

Fifty feet from the cages, in the night shadow of a roof overhang, the assassin leaned against an old stone wall and watched and listened to the ping, ping, ping as aluminum bats struck rubber-coated hardballs. A sewer rat scampered along the stones near him, on its way to the wharf. His eyes flicked down to watch the dark shape scuttle from shadow to shadow. He knew the rat wouldn't bother him and also had no fear of him—on this night they were both hunters.

Ping, ping, ping. Shouts of encouragement sounded from the two older men, who watched from behind the cages. It was a good night for such a job—in midweek and cold enough so that even on the main streets there were relatively few pedestrians.

The assassin had no use for baseball—it was far too slow and too peaceful for his tastes. He loved to watch world-class full-contact karate, had a passion for Thai kick-boxing, and on a recent assignment in England, had watched his first rugby match and enjoyed it immensely.

The only part of baseball he liked at all was batting. Anything having to do with hand-eye coordination fascinated him, and he liked the duel-like aspect of the pitcher-batter confrontation. Now, from the shadows, he watched Jack carefully, noting the bat speed he generated by turning his hips, and his complete concentration. He knew that Jack must have had many beers in the eel restaurant, yet his coordination was only the slightest bit off. Soon Jack began nailing every pitch. The assassin nodded to himself, and touched the sword that was hidden inside his black shirt.

The son was strong and fast; the father had been a strong man, too. They were really very alike—in their movements, in their faces, in their muscles and bones. For a second the assassin remembered the look in Walter Graham's eyes at the moment he had killed him. It had been a fascinating look—no fear at all but only the purest distilled rage.

It would be most interesting to look into the son's eyes.

After three dozen pitches, Sato and Suzuki applauded loudly, declared the contest a tie, and slapped Jack heartily on the back. They all set off once again down the block toward the ocean.

They turned into an alley that led to a narrow, gloomy, winding side street. The air was thick with the sharp tang of ocean salt, and every other doorway seemed to be the entrance to a bar or nightclub. Pictures of naked women were taped to the inside of blacked-out windows, and sailors and middle-aged men in robes and businessmen in dark suits came out of doorways and went into other ones.

They finally turned into a narrow doorway screened off from the street by a hanging curtain. The nightclub was dark and boxlike, with a half dozen tables on one side and a fully stocked bar on the other. On the walls of the nightclub were dozens of shelves containing hundreds of numbered bottles of different kinds of whiskey, some full and some partly empty. Two of the tables in the nightclub were occupied by groups of men who stared briefly at Jack as he entered and then went back to their drinking.

The owner of the bar, a gnomish figure in a black silk dinner jacket, waved to Sato and called something out in Japanese. Sato returned the greeting. Immediately two Japanese women, one young and plump and the other midthirtyish and heavily made-up, hurried to their table. Apparently the two women knew Sato, Suzuki, and Noguchi well—good-natured banter passed back and forth.

Sato said something to the plump younger woman that made her giggle and give him a light slap on the cheek. He caught her arm and tried to pull her down on his lap, and as she resisted, he ran his hands over her buttocks and around her thigh. She squealed, squirmed free, and returned to the bar with the other woman to fetch their drinks.

"Whiskey water, okay?" Sato asked Jack.

"Sure. Whatever."

Suzuki jerked his head toward the two Japanese hostesses and raised an eyebrow questioningly. "Nice?"

"Very pretty," Jack said politely.

Sato pointed to the younger of the two women and wagged his pinky back and forth as if he were letting Jack in on a secret.

"We don't have that gesture in America."

"It means his 'mistress,' " Noguchi explained.

The word was new to Sato. "Mistress?" He tried it out a few times and then frowned with distaste. He evidently preferred wagging his pinky. "I like women," Sato said. "But he—" and he pointed to Suzuki "—is always hungry."

Suzuki laughed. "Very hungry. I taste the food from many countries. Japanese, of course. Thai. Chinese. Philippine. Once I even had a chance for an American."

His comrades looked at the big man doubtfully.

"It's true. A blond dancer. In Tokyo *Ginza*."

"What happened?"

"Too expensive," he said. "One month's salary. You have experience with blond girl?" he asked Jack.

"Yes.".

"Redhead?"

Jack nodded again, thinking of Shannon Miles. No wonder she had spread the myth of an American boyfriend. As the first American teacher in Atami, and with her long red hair, the attention she drew must have been unrelenting.

"What are blondes like?" Suzuki asked. All three men leaned slightly forward for his answer.

"Very nice," Jack said. "Very soft. Very sexy." He looked at Suzuki. "Which country's women did you like best?"

"Thai and Japanese," Suzuki said definitively, as if he had given the matter much thought. "Thai are most wild. I make them scream. They make me scream. But Japanese are the best. We have a saying in Japan, 'Who is the happiest man in the world?' "

Jack shrugged. "Who?"

"I don't know his name," Suzuki finished, "but he eats Chinese food, drinks German beer, has a Japanese wife, and lives in America."

Sato grunted something. The Japanese men all nodded. "Captain Sato says, maybe he doesn't live in America anymore," Noguchi explained to Jack. "That saying is old. He says maybe now the happiest man has a Japanese wife and lives in Japan."

The two hostesses returned to their table with a three-quarters-full bottle of Johnny Walker Black and a tumbler full of warm water. Jack had never mixed his whiskey with warm water before and found the taste a bit nauseating. After a few sips he got used to it to the point where he was able to swallow it down fairly easily.

With the added stimulus of the whiskey, the evening got progressively wilder. A microphone was brought to their table, and the Japanese policemen each sang a popular song to the applause of the other tables. They pressed Jack to sing an American song, and when he finally agreed, they handed him a long song list and asked him to choose. The only American songs on the list were "Diana," "Yesterday," and "Heartbreak Hotel." He chose the last, and he was just drunk enough to do an enthusiastic Elvis right down to a hip grind or two at the end. When he finished, there was loud applause, and as the heavily made-up hostess took the microphone from him, her thigh rubbed against the side of his leg.

"So when do you finish here and go back to America?" Sato asked him. The little man had drunk as much as any of them, but only showed the effects of the alcohol in his slightly slurred speech. His movements remained crisp and precise, and Jack felt a sharp purpose in the occasional questions he asked.

"I don't really know."

"You have more questions about Professor Miles?"

"A few."

"Where will you go next?"

Jack shrugged. "Where would you go if you were me?"

"Back to America," Sato told him with a hard smile.

"Tell me, if the Japanese National Police hadn't taken the investigation away from you, wouldn't you have a few more questions, too?"

Sato's hard smile became brittle. "No," he said. "You are . . . can I say, chasing shadows?"

"You can say it, but shadows don't rip the watches off men before pushing them from cliffs. Professor Miles struggled for his life, and lost. Someone pushed him."

"And his wife?"

"She had no reason to kill herself. It doesn't add up. I'm gonna stay in Atami till it makes more sense."

"You may be here a long time, then," Sato told him. "Maybe you will never go back." It sounded almost like a threat.

"Maybe," Jack agreed. "Who knows?"

The two hostesses returned to their table to flirt and pour drinks. Sato seemed to be their particular favorite, but Noguchi and Suzuki got their turns, and at one point in the evening the heavily made-up hostess sat down on Jack's lap and smiled at him. "Hello." Her breath smelled of lipstick and liquor.

"Hello," Jack said.

She swayed backward so that he had to put his arm around her back to support her. When he did, she smiled at him and slid her right hand under the table. She ran her fingers quickly down his thigh till they brushed his crotch, and said something to the others at the table that elicited loud laughter.

"She says Americans have big fishing rods," Noguchi translated.

Jack looked at her. She was still smiling at him. Two of her teeth were missing—he wondered if they'd been knocked out. "Tell her that Japan has some tasty-looking fish."

Noguchi did, and she laughed. Her fingers, hidden from view by the tablecloth, ran up his thigh again in quick stutter steps and then stopped to take measurements. Jack drew in a breath, and his arm tightened around her back.

She smiled at him and spoke again.

"She wants to know how you like your fish cooked?" Noguchi told Jack.

"Tell her that in Japan, I like it raw. As long as it's fresh."

Everyone at the table laughed. Detective Suzuki nearly fell out of his chair. "Yes, yes, if it's not fresh, the smell alone can be very dangerous. In that case, you must use soy sauce."

"Or throw it out and find another meal," Sato advised.

They finished off the bottle of Johnny Walker and ordered another one. Sato pulled the younger hostess onto his lap and pinched and probed as she squealed and squirmed. Jack tried to guess her age—she could be anywhere from twenty-three to thirty.

"This is good, old-style Japanese girl," he told Jack, his hand momentarily slipping under the hem of her dress. She grabbed his wrist and pulled his hand out, and he let it sit on her upper thigh as he launched into a drunken speech about America, slurring his words a bit: "American women are too strong. I went to America two years ago. For vacation. I stayed in New York City one week." He shook his head at the memory. "So dirty. A man in Times Square wanted to sell me a gun. On Broadway a teenager said, 'Cocaine, twenty dollars.' Grand Central Station, so many men sleeping on the street. Not safe to walk. Very bad."

"And you don't have those problems in Japan?" Jack asked, sipping what felt like his twentieth glass of whiskey of the night. His own speech sounded strange in his ears, and he had to make an effort to finish words. "No street crime? No homeless? C'mon . . ."

Sato shook his head. "We Japanese follow the rules." His hand strayed again, and this time the hostess let it explore a few seconds longer before she fished it out. "Japanese are clean, safe . . . can I say disciplined? It is our nature."

By midnight they were all very drunk. Jack had trouble sitting up straight, and Lieutenant Suzuki's face was so flushed, it seemed to be glowing like a red lantern. Noguchi's head kept nodding forward toward his chest—every ten minutes or so he forced himself to revive with a visible effort. They exchanged a final round of drunken toasts, with Jack raising his glass to Japanese tuna, fresh or with soy sauce, and Suzuki in turn toasting "blond American women, big breasts, I pay one month's salary, no problem!"

Once again they left without paying anything—Sato evidently had an understanding with the owner of the club. The three of them staggered down the narrow street and paused near the end to urinate in unison through a wire fence. When they reached the main street, Lieutenant Suzuki left them, slapping Jack on the shoulder in a hearty farewell that nearly knocked him over.

Four blocks from the hotel, Sato hailed a taxi and said his good-byes. Jack had very mixed feelings about this tough little police captain who didn't seem to like America much but had his own numbered bottle of American whiskey on reserve. Now, both very drunk, they exchanged bows and hearty handshakes. "Your hotel is close," Sato said. He pointed. "You know?"

"Sure," Jack told him, ". . . few blocks. I'll be okay. Thanks . . ."

Sato got into the taxi, and it screeched away from the curb.

Noguchi and Jack walked on in silence. "I can get back to the hotel," Jack told him. "Don't worry. . . ."

"I walk this way. To the end of this block," Noguchi said, stumbling a bit. He put his arms out to steady himself. "We drank very much."

"Too much."

"Tomorrow morning will be hard."

"When do you have to   in?"

"*Shichi-ji*. Seven."

"Jesus."

"Yes, Jesus," Noguchi agreed drunkenly. "I don't want to wake up. Jesus." He was reluctant to let the word go. "Jesus, Jesus, Jesus."

"You looked good swinging that bat. You played pro?"

"What?" Noguchi's feet slid a bit and he almost went down.

"Professional baseball?"

"Just in college," Noguchi said. "Here is my street. Good-bye. See you soon." He shook hands with Jack. "You know your hotel from here?"

"Sure."

"Straight. Then left."

"I know. Thanks. Good night."

Noguchi turned off, and Jack was alone. The street was completely empty. The thought of the soft futon waiting for him in his room carried Jack forward, step by staggering step. He hadn't been this drunk in years. It felt almost like coming home from a college frat party—in some ways, Sato and Suzuki had had the mentality of college fraternity brothers.

As Jack neared the corner where he would turn left, a dark shape emerged from an alley and glided quickly and silently toward him from behind. Jack saw the figure approach out of the corner of his eye and registered that it was a man, dressed in black. Even drunk, Jack wondered how the man could move so quickly without making a sound. He began to turn toward the figure.

The man dressed in black reached him with a burst of speed and extended a hand, which seemed to merely brush the back of Jack's neck. Steel-like fingers found three pressure points at the top of the spine. Jack's whole body went rigid. He almost blanked at the pain. It was a pulsing current of agony that never let up, like a continuous electrical shock. The pain was so excruciating that Jack could not even summon a scream.

Keeping his fingers on the pressure points, the man in black wrapped his free arm around Jack's waist, picked him up without any apparent effort, and began carrying him toward the alley.

Jack tried to stop, to slow him down, to put up some sort of struggle, but his limbs would not respond. In the tiny corner of his mind that continued to function, he realized that he was being taken off the street to a place where he would be killed.

They reached the mouth of the alley, and the man carried Jack twenty feet into darkness. And then, suddenly, remarkably, the pain stopped as the man took his hand from the back of Jack's neck and spun him around. Instinctively Jack tried to raise his right hand to ward off the first blow, but he was far too late. The chop with the heel of the palm caught him in the Adam's apple and knocked his body several inches into the air. Almost at the second his feet returned to the ground, a knee driven forward with great power crashed into his groin, and five lightning-fast punches pounded one after another into his midsection.

Jack blanked. When he cleared, the man in black was pinning him to the wall with his left hand. His right hand held a short sword. The surprise attack and the beating had rendered Jack helpless. All he could do was stare back into the eyes of his attacker. He felt himself being studied, probed, by a gaze positively unearthly in its lack of humanity. Then the sword darted forward and Jack heard himself make a sound in his throat as the blade sliced his left cheek.

Again the black eyes studied him. Jack saw in the cold gaze that the next sword thrust would be the finisher. Rage swept through him—blind anger and fear drawn from a primordial source he had never tapped into before. Without consciously willing it, he exploded suddenly with a final struggle for life.

Jack's hands came up, and as his right fist knocked loose the arm that pinned him to the wall, his left hand pushed the attacker back half a step.

It was a futile effort. The man in black moved more quickly than anyone Jack had ever seen before. A spinning roundhouse kick caught Jack full in the face and broke his nose. As Jack's body smashed backward into the stone wall, the man in black regained his pinning hold and drew his sword back.

Jack knew fear then, the icy certainty of his own death. A death scream welled in his lungs, but no sound came, except the gunshot that rang out suddenly in the dark alley and knocked dust from the rock wall just behind him. At the sound of the gunshot, the man in black whipped his sword arm forward and then disappeared into the darkness with the same unearthly speed with which he had first materialized.

Jack's mind registered that he had been stabbed in the chest. As he slid down the wall of the alley and began to blank, he saw Detective Noguchi run toward him from the mouth of the alley, his revolver in his hand. The tall detective said something to Jack, but the words were mere sounds whispered down a long tube, and the detective's face was also a blur, distorted and out of focus. Jack struggled on the lip of the precipice for one last second and then tumbled down the long slope into darkness.

SECTION THREE

Beating the Bamboo Thicket

13

Etsuko Matsuda moved from the fortified villa on Shodo Island back to Shikoku proper, ignoring the advice of her advisers and security people. They said they could not guarantee her safety— the power struggle within the organization was virtually over, and her husband's old rivals, backed by the new leadership on Hokkaido, would stop at nothing. She silenced them by pointing out that she could not possibly remain absent and expect to tap old loyalties and carry on her struggle. Better to return, fight, and if necessary die honorably, the way her husband had, than to live in safety and isolation.

So she returned to Takamatsu at twilight, crossing the Inland Sea by speedboat. Once back on the main island, she seemed to remain perpetually in the world of twilight, hiding and conducting clandestine meetings with old supporters. They moved her frequently from house to house and city and city, often waking her in the middle of the night because something seemed amiss and it would be better to move on. She never complained, but threw herself into the struggle with remarkable energy.

The change in her character was evident to all. From remaining in the background and following the wishes of her husband, she learned to give orders with a quiet authority that admitted no disagreement. She always dressed in black and never went anywhere without her gun. She relished occasional bold public forays into cities and towns to demonstrate her independence and fearlessness. Sometimes she even arranged to hold meetings in well-known spots, which is how on one particular evening her inner circle of supporters and advisers found themselves in the famous floating teahouse on the south garden of Takamatsu's Ritsurin-Koen Garden discussing the American.

She simply could not fathom the American, and asked repeatedly what was known about him. How could he not be working for the American government?

By all indications, they told her, he was on some sort of personal crusade.

Was he crazy, then? Was this the American cowboy mentality taken to extremes? Should they discount him as a nut?

By all accounts, he was quite sane.

Then the Inagawa were helping him?

No.

Of course they were. How else had he survived the attack?

Admittedly it was a mystery.

She wanted to question the Inagawa directly about this.

They would see, but such a meeting was probably impossible to arrange. And the Inagawa's loyalties were a matter of conjecture.

Things had reached such a point?

Yes. Things were very bad and getting worse.

Was there any more news from Los Angeles? Were the police still looking into the matter?

Only on the wrong side.

Well then, from that wrong side, had anything been found?

The search of Shannon's possessions and papers was continuing but apparently had not yielded the expected information. One theory was that the American detective had taken certain key items from Shannon's house, but so far nothing of value had been found among his personal effects either.

Was it possible that the detective had passed whatever he had taken from Shannon's home on to his son before his death?

The possibility had been investigated and discounted. The son's apartment in America and his hotel room in Atami had both been searched, with no result.

She seemed almost angry. All lines of inquiry seemed to lead to this mysterious, blundering American. What was his name?

Graham. Jack Graham.

And was it possible, she asked, that this Jack Graham had any idea what was really going on? Could he just be *playing* the fool?

For once, her advisers all agreed. She saw their heads shake one by one.

"Don't talk," the man in the wool suit said. "Just listen." He was well over six feet tall with a long neck, a sharp beak of a nose, and clumps of reddish brown hair. Looking groggily up at him, Jack was reminded of an ostrich. "I'm Guy Brown, from the American embassy," he explained in a voice that was both friendly and officious. "I'm here because the ambassador has taken a personal interest in your . . . case. I'd like to do all I can to ensure your quick recovery and expedite your safe return home."

He took a few steps forward. He even moved a bit like an ostrich, his head bobbing up and down with each jerky step. Jack felt a slight headache gaining strength—the pounding was annoying but bearable. He tried to concentrate on what the bureaucrat was saying. Every time he moved at all in the hospital bed, ripples of pain spread out over his upper body. Three tubes ran from his chest to oxygen and fluid-collection containers near the floor.

"I know you probably don't feel lucky just now, but the doctors say you were," Guy Brown announced, pulling up a chair next to Jack's bed. He sat, crossed his legs, and flicked some dust off one of his shoes with the back of his palm. "Whoever stabbed you went for your heart and just missed. Punctured a lung—they say you'll be up and walking in a few days if you follow instructions and don't get in any more fights." He grinned, and Jack almost vomited.

Jack blinked at the bright ceiling lights. It came back to him quickly, for the first time—the man in black, the surprise attack, the alley, the sword blade, and then the gunshot. The memory flash brought with it a sudden realization about his attacker and the significance of the attempt on his life. Jack closed his eyes, burying the thought from Guy Brown's prying gaze.

"You okay?" the tall man asked nervously. Jack managed a little nod. "You were out for about six hours, maybe seven. The doctors did some cutting and sewing. I guess they'll tell you all the details later, but the bottom line seems to be that the lung's okay and there's no permanent damage. They said you'd be waking up 'round nine. You're a few hours ahead of schedule."

Jack glanced around the hospital room. It was small and bare, very clean and completely empty except for a TV on a stand, some medical equipment, the chair Guy Brown was sitting in, and Jack's own bed. From a crack between two curtains, morning light unfolded a white diagonal across the gray floor.

"Took us a while to find out who you really were," Guy Brown continued. "People in Atami thought you were LAPD. Apparently Carson, the legal attaché at the embassy, knew you were here, but he's in Okinawa this week. It was quite a mystery for a while. If you don't mind my saying so, you took a real risk, and I'm not just talking about your health."

There was a short silence during which Jack returned the bureaucrat's unfriendly gaze. Finally Guy Brown spoke again. "Truth is, I was prepared to come out here and read you the riot act. Even if the LAPD thing was a mistake made by the local authorities, you've played hell with the Neutrality Act. The Japanese are real sensitive about their internal affairs—'specially these days. It wouldn't have surprised me if we'd had to send you home under guard. But . . ."

He shrugged and smiled thinly. "You seem to have a friend in a high place. Your chief—" he searched for the name and then found it "—MacCormack, in Washington, has pulled more than a few strings . . . and as I said, you got lucky. Japanese decided to let it drop. Everything's squared away for you to go home, soon as you're ready to travel. The JNP will take it from here—they're waiting outside to ask you questions."

Jack's eyes flicked to the closed door. Then he looked back at the embassy man, who was adjusting the knot on his tie.

"The doctors say you can fly home in a week or so. I got you a reservation on JAL. The Bureau picked up the check. First class . . ." Guy Brown paused—first class obviously meant something to him. "Like I said, you got friends in high places. They could do the plastic surgery here in this hospital, but I figured you'd probably rather have it done stateside."

Jack half sat up and asked, "What plastic . . . ?" The effort at movement and speech sent a wave of white-hot agony flashing down from his chin to his groin. The pain knocked him back onto the bed and he lay there, gasping.

"I told you to just keep still. You were intubated and extubated, and God knows how many of your ribs are busted. Just don't speak or move around. Your face will need plastic surgery—here, see for yourself." Guy Brown held up a mirror. Jack's broken nose had not been bandaged or put in a cast—the swelling was tremendous. Blue and purplish abrasions ran from his nostrils up to his lower eyelids. A rhombus-shaped symbol had been carved into the skin of his right cheek. The cut looked deep and ugly.

"Don't ask me what that is," Guy Brown said, following Jack's gaze in the mirror. "Whoever attacked you did a little artwork. The investigation is completely out of my jurisdiction. Maybe Lieutenant Sasaki of the Japanese National Police can tell you when he talks to you." Guy Brown lowered his voice. Another glance at the closed door. "He's one of Japan's best. A real rising star. Now, if you need anything in the three or four days till you go home, that's what I'm here for. Here's my card." He took a business card out of a black leather holder and put it down on the bed table. "Your boss, MacCormack, told me to tell you to relax and rest. Sounds like good advice. I'll catch you later."

Guy Brown turned to go. Jack tried to sit up again in bed, but he couldn't raise himself more than a few inches. The pain hit him from everywhere at once: his ribs, his legs, even the back of his neck. He managed to get out, "I'm not going home," in a rasping whisper before he sank back.

"Sure you are. I told you, the JNP will handle the inquiry into what happened to you and why. Believe me, they'll do a thorough job—'specially in a case like this involving a foreign agent. Your boss at the Bureau wants you back home." Guy Brown smiled his patriotic smile. "And you need some medical care in the good old U.S. of A."

Jack shook his head.

"Well, we can talk about it later."

Jack shook his head.

"I'm not gonna argue with you in this condition," Guy Brown said. "The reservation'll be waiting for you. You got lucky this time. I don't think you should push it another inch. See ya later."

He left, and immediately a young Japanese man entered and closed the door. He was of middle height, strikingly handsome, and dressed immaculately in an imported brown summer suit with a narrow beige necktie. Jack had seen enough young hotshots at the Bureau to know immediately that this young man was used to getting his way. When he reached Jack's bed he bowed once, quickly, and then got right to business.

"No need to talk," he said in very natural-sounding English. "Please, just lie still. I am Sasaki, Hideo. Lieutenant, Japanese

National Police. We are so sorry for what happened to you. I talked to Captain Sato and the other men you were with. Now we need to talk to you a little bit, and then you can go back to sleep.''

Jack wondered about the "we"—Sasaki was the only other person in the room.

"This means yes." Sasaki nodded his head, up-down. "And no." He shook it side to side. "If you feel pain, stop and we'll find another way. If you're too tired, we'll try again, later. Okay?'' His smile was flashy and well practiced—it belonged on a politician or a movie star or atop a Christmas tree.

Jack moved his chin up-down. It was a small movement and there was no pain.

"Good. Were you attacked by one man? You're sure he was alone? And this one man was Japanese? Will you be able to recognize a picture of him?''

Jack hesitated. He thought back to the alley. The attack was a painful blur. And then he remembered his attacker's eyes—the hard, probing gaze, studying him even as the sword drew back for a final thrust. The thought came to him again—the one he had had upon first waking up—and once again he buried it. He nodded to Sasaki.

"Good," Sasaki said. "Was he taller than me?" He slowly raised his hand over his head till Jack nodded. "Really, that much taller? And older than thirty? Thirty-five? Did he say anything to you? Make any sound at all?''

Jack thought back to the alley and shook his head. The entire struggle had been in silence.

"He cut you with a knife?''

"A sword," Jack whispered. He found that if he spoke in a low voice, while lying completely still, there was little pain.

"Don't talk. Please. So he had a sword." Sasaki gave the tiniest of frowns—it seemed somehow unnatural, like a poker player reacting to a particularly bad hand and instantly catching himself. "When you got to Japan you changed some dollars into yen? May I ask how much you changed?''

"Five hundred," Jack told him. "A dollar doesn't get you very many yen.''

"Five hundred dollars," Sasaki repeated. "And you kept this money with you? At your hotel you used cash?''

"Yeah."

"The night before the attack, you had dinner in a *yakitori* restaurant. Again, you paid in cash?"

Something in Jack's gaze as he nodded made Sasaki break off and explain, "We can't totally forget the possibility that it was just an attempted robbery." He saw Jack's reaction and held up his hands. "I don't think so either. But you had a lot of cash. Many people saw you spend it. You played baseball, went to a hostess bar. You were coming back from a tough part of town, drunk, at night; the street was dark. You were by yourself. . . ."

Jack continued to stare at him, and Sasaki smiled. "Okay, let's forget about the robbery idea for now. Let's go back to the man who attacked you. Do you think he followed you from the bar?"

"I don't know. We'd been drinking. . . ."

"Captain Sato says you had very much to drink. Were you carrying a gun?"

"I couldn't bring one into Japan."

"And you didn't try to get one here? For protection?"

"For God's sake, I was going drinking with the police chief. Why should I have felt I needed a gun to protect myself?"

"And you have no idea who in Japan would want to hurt you?"

Jack slowly shook his head.

"Okay, that's enough for now. We'll have some photographs to show you soon. We're looking into the Yakuza. That mark on your cheek could be one of the Inagawa family's . . . trademarks. We'll find out. Apparently you were asking all over Atami about the Yakuza. Even in a country as safe as Japan, one must be careful." Sasaki paused and flashed his handsome smile. "Tell me, the day of the attack you went to Atami High School and talked to some teachers and to Eric Gleason, the American teacher, about Shannon Miles. Did you find out anything useful or interesting about her?"

"No."

"The young American, Eric Gleason, didn't know anything? I understand he lives in the same apartment she lived in."

"He didn't know anything."

"Too bad. I will be back soon to show you some pictures. Please get a good rest."

"Where am I?" Jack whispered, propping himself up slightly with his elbows and gritting his teeth against the stabbing pain.

"Atami Hospital. You're safe. There is a guard outside your door. Please try to sleep now."

Sasaki left, closing the door behind him. Jack lay in bed in silence, pondering the absurdity of some of Sasaki's questions. An American lawman comes to Japan to investigate two murders, is attacked by a sword-wielding professional killer dressed like a *ninja*, who carves up his face, and they were considering robbery as a motive? Now, when he was alone in the room, his headache seemed to grow stronger till he stopped analyzing and just lay there staring up at the ceiling.

It hurt when he closed his eyes; it even throbbed when he breathed too deeply. An old doctor and a young nurse came in and checked the drainage tubes and took his pulse and temperature. The doctor spoke to the nurse in fast Japanese, and Jack looked from one face to the other, trying to read something about the seriousness of his condition. "Forgive my bad English," the doctor finally said to him, producing a Japanese-English dictionary from a pocket in his white coat and clinging to it as if for support. "I studied in college, many years ago. You have—" he hesitated, and consulted the pronunciation in the dictionary "—pneumo-thorax. A tear in the lining around the lung. It is not serious. Now, please rest."

It was only after they had left and the headache lessened a bit that Jack remembered the realization that had first come to him in the presence of Guy Brown. It was a thought triggered by the hazy memory of the attack on the side street, of the pressure points in his neck that had rendered him completely helpless, and of being carried like a rag doll with his feet off the pavement while his whole body was rigid.

When Walter had been found dead in his locked apartment, Jack had had a great deal of trouble believing that his father had been murdered. There would have been signs of a struggle. Walter would have heard someone entering or approaching. No one possessed the kind of strength and speed and skill necessary to force Walter into that chair, to force his own police revolver into his mouth, without so much as a glass being broken or a chair overturned.

Now Jack knew that there was such a man, out there somewhere. Every time Jack moved and felt the pain, he thought of the man in black—of the way he glided when he moved, of his paralyzing grasp, and of his probing, almost hungry gaze.

The knowledge frightened Jack, and on a deeper level it thrilled him. The attack by this man could only mean that somehow, without quite knowing where he was going, Jack was blundering along on the right path. It took away the last lingering doubts he had that his father's death had been a suicide, and that he was partly to blame.

And it pointed the way toward the possibility of someday avenging his father's murder.

The city exterminators came in the afternoon, when Eric Gleason was away at school. They came in a city truck, with the landlord of teachers' public housing to let them into Eric's apartment. While the exterminators worked, the landlord stood outside, and explained to the busybody of a downstairs neighbor who just happened to pass by that Eric had complained at school of a *gokiburi* infestation, and this was a free service the city was providing its resident foreign teacher. He added that there was no reason to talk about it with the other tenants—if the infestation was found to be serious, they would come back and look at other apartments.

The downstairs neighbor bowed and nodded and went on her way. She knew the story was fabricated—the flying cockroaches were a chronic problem for everyone, and when the weather started to warm up, nothing could be done about them. The landlord knew that just as well as she did, and he knew that she would know it. So he was really telling her that something was going on that was none of her business.

She paused at the landing of her floor and listened, but the men on the floor above her were not conversing. Finally she headed for her own apartment and tried to put the whole thing out of her mind. Like most Japanese busybodies, she had a very keen sense of what lines were not to be crossed, and she knew that this particular warning not to gossip had to be heeded.

Inside Eric's apartment, the search was conducted quickly, neatly, and very professionally. The bookcases and the storage closets were the main focus, but every photograph and scrap of paper was quickly examined and then carefully put back in its place. The only discovery that aroused any interest was Eric's cache of *Playboy* and *Penthouse* magazines, which he kept in his bottom desk drawer, secreted under several thick books of English grammar.

By Japanese standards it was a very large apartment for a single man—three tatami rooms, two of which had full views of the bay. The searchers were appalled by the slovenliness and strange living habits of the American—he didn't put his futon away during the day but left it lying on the bedroom floor, and it didn't look like he had scrubbed out his *ofuro* in weeks. And here was the city of Atami, wasting this apartment on him when it could have housed a Japanese family of four.

In less than half an hour the JNP searchers knew that there was nothing in the apartment that had belonged to Shannon Miles. If she had left any secrets behind her, intervening occupants of the apartment had long since disposed of them. Still, the Atami policewoman had been correct to tell them about the possible lead. Apparently the American, Graham, was naive enough to trust her, and dumb enough not to follow up a possible breakthrough he himself had unearthed.

The men in pale blue exterminators' uniforms locked Eric's door on their way out, got back into the city truck, and drove away quickly.

The next time Lieutenant Sasaki returned to Jack's hospital room, he brought several hundred photographs and a new theory. He handed the pictures to Jack one by one, and Jack patiently studied them and handed them back. Some of them won a second look, but none of them warranted a third one.

When they had exhausted the pile of photographs, Sasaki put them aside and started in on his new suspicion. "When the man in black came up to you in the street, he attacked from behind?"

Jack nodded.

"So he didn't see your face, in the street? Could he have thought you were someone else?"

"Who?"

"It's just an idea. But you were out with three police officers. They are all senior—they have enemies, men they've sent to prison. Two of them are almost your height. Lieutenant Noguchi looks very much like you from behind. Same build. Maybe the man who attacked you meant to attack one of them.''

''We were face-to-face in the alley,'' Jack whispered through clenched teeth. ''He knew it was me.''

''I've been to that alley. It's dark at night. Maybe he couldn't see. Anyway, once he had you there with him, he couldn't let you go. It's a possibility, *nee*? He got the wrong man and didn't know what to do.''

Jack whispered, ''He was a pro. He knew what he was doing. Do you?''

''Yes,'' Sasaki said, the flashy smile flickering on his lips for just a second, and then shining forth in all its accustomed splendor. ''We hope to have made some progress by the time you leave Japan.''

''We?''

''The Japanese National Police. We have been in touch with the Los Angeles police, and they are still looking into the case of Shannon Miles. And we are taking a close second look at the case of Professor Miles, so after you leave, we will stay in touch. . . .''

''I'm not leaving.''

Sasaki paused for a second. ''You have great dedication,'' he said, ''but you are hurt badly. It will be easier for you in your own country. I give you my personal promise that I will push forward with all energy.''

Jack looked at him till Sasaki turned his head and glanced toward the closed door. ''Maybe it's true that someone in Japan wants to hurt you,'' Sasaki told him in a different voice. ''Maybe even kill you. For example, the Inagawa Yakuza. I don't know why, but if it's true, then we must consider . . . There is a police guard outside your door now, but once you get out of this hospital, we can't protect you all the time. You should go home.''

''I didn't ask you to protect me.''

''You are very tough. But you are in Japan, on a visa. Your well-being is our responsibility. We have a responsibility to you and to your government, too. But—'' he shrugged ''—I don't know about things like visas. That is for other people. For us, we must try to find who did this to you. I will be back soon with more pictures. Please, get rest.''

That night a nurse gave Jack some pills that knocked him out.

He slept deeply and dreamlessly, and woke up feeling much stronger.

After a breakfast of warm soup, the old doctor gave Jack a thorough examination. The doctor's favorite English phrase was "Does it hurt here?" and the examination became a litany of that same question and yeses. When the old doctor was done, he reeled off a list of the different injuries Jack had sustained, from broken ribs to a mild concussion to the contused lung. "If you rest," he assured Jack, "you will be okay. Yes?"

"Okay," Jack promised him, lying back and pointing to the tubes on his chest. "When will you take these out?"

"Maybe tomorrow," the doctor said. "Please rest."

Late that afternoon, Misako surprised Jack by paying him a visit. She showed up in a flower-print dress, holding a bouquet in one hand and a copy of the *Japan Times* in the other. It was the first time he had seen her wearing anything but a plain police uniform. The soft cotton fabric made her look very feminine. She had washed her hair before coming—it was braided in back and hung down almost to her hips, where it was tied with a red ribbon.

As she walked in, the sight of his bruised face and the tubes in his chest stopped her for a second. She drew in a breath.

Jack grinned, and the wound on his face throbbed. "Hi." He managed a slight wave. A bolt of pain made him stop and lower his hand.

She recovered quickly. "Hi. They say you shouldn't move around."

"Thanks for coming."

She found a jar for the flowers, and then sat down next to his bed. She was no longer shocked by his bruises—they seemed to interest her. She threw a particularly long glance at the cut on his cheek.

It was easy to be bold when he was flat on his back in a hospital room. He whispered, "Still handsome?"

She rewarded him with a little smile. "You look terrible."

Jack propped himself up three inches to explain. "He got me from behind. And he had a sword. Otherwise, he'd be here instead of me. . . ."

"If you don't lie back and keep quiet, I'll leave."

He clamped his mouth shut and watched her.

She arranged the flowers she had brought with care. "I brought you today's English newspaper," she told him. "Printed daily in Tokyo. I thought maybe you might need something to read."

Jack thanked her with his eyes.

"What else do you need?"

"Some music . . . if you have an old tape player or a radio."

"I have a tape player. What kind of music?"

"Anything," Jack said. "Classical. That stuff you were listening to in the car. Debussy . . ."

"Ravel," she corrected him for the second time. "I'll bring both. So that you can learn the difference."

He grinned at her, and she looked back at him impassively. She could stare directly back into his eyes without flinching or looking away or appearing uncomfortable.

"Was the story about my attack in the news?"

"Not much. A few papers carried stories about an attack on an American tourist. None mentioned your name or that you work for the FBI." She paused. "It's very strange—the Japanese press is worse than the American press in finding out about sensational stories. Usually they would pursue a story like this very vigorously."

"What about at the Atami Police Station? Any gossip?"

Misako seemed genuinely confused. "I can't understand it exactly, but many people there . . . dismiss it. Some say it was just a robbery. Others say the man who attacked you meant to attack Lieutenant Noguchi. He has been in several dangerous cases."

"He's the one who fired the gunshot? How did he find me?"

"He was worried that you might not be able to find your hotel. So he came back after you, heard the struggle in the alley, and fired one shot. I think he saved your life."

"Yes. Please thank him for me." Jack paused and lowered his whisper so that she had to lean slightly forward. "Why do you think they're not taking the attack seriously at the Atami Police Station? You can see how badly I was hurt."

"Yes. I don't know." She stood. "The JNP has taken over the case. I should go now." Her tone was businesslike, but he thought he saw a playful coyness in her pretty eyes. "You need to stop worrying and rest."

"Will you come visit me again? And bring some music?"

"If I have time."

"I promise to learn the difference between Ravel and Debussy."

"I'll try to come."

"It gets lonely lying here."

"Try not to think about women. You'll get your strength back faster."

"It's hard not to think about women. All the nurses keep coming in to see me. I think they just want to get a look at an American body."

"It's a nice body," Misako said, and touched him once, gently, on the shoulder. Her fingers were warm. "Now make sure it heals quickly." She turned and walked out the door, and closed it gently behind her.

The day the police seals finally came off the last doors and windows of the white stucco house on Kiowa Street, a FOR SALE sign went up on the front lawn. The police vans that had carted off so many of the Mileses' effects stopped pulling into the driveway, and police cars stopped cruising down the side street from Barrington to San Vincente every hour or so.

Four members of the Brentwood over-forty tennis set remarked on the sign as they trudged back from a late afternoon at Barrington Park. "It'll go for at least three quarters of a million," one of them said, her Prince racket thunking against her rather flabby thigh with every step.

"Be lucky to get five hundred with the market this bad," her doubles partner, whose husband was a high-powered agent, corrected her. "What I can't understand is why it took them this long to finish with the house. I mean, how long can it take to dust for fingerprints and check for bloodstains?"

"Maybe they weren't just searching," the youngest member of the foursome suggested hesitantly. "I mean, one of them actually moved in for a while. Like he was waiting for something."

"What?"

"I don't know. A phone call or a letter . . ."

"He probably just needed a place to live rent-free for a while," the wife of the agent told her cynically. "What I don't understand is why they had to take so many of their things away. They must have emptied the whole place out. Do you suppose they're having a police rummage sale and this is how they get their stock?"

"Anyway," the woman with the beefy thighs said, heading to the sidewalk to avoid a Wiffle Ball game in the street, "that nightmare seems to be over. Let's hope someone nice moves in. *And you kids be careful of traffic. Why don't you go play at the park?* John, have you done *all* of your homework?''

The Wiffle Ball players ignored her. They had also noticed that the seals had been removed from the Miles house, but its open, empty condition only added to its already formidable mystery. The word among the under-twelve-year-old Brentwood Wiffle Ball set was that the house was haunted by many demons. When an errant ball rolled between two bushes on its front lawn, the batsman responsible had to be triple-dared into retrieving it. After finding the ball, he ran back out of the shadows with his little arms pumping and his eyes fixed on the nearest streetlight.

Coincidentally, that very afternoon a FOR LEASE sign also went up in front of Walter Graham's old apartment on Eighteenth Street in Santa Monica. The once shabby apartment had been cleaned and freshly painted. Several police vans had been seen one morning carting away all of Walter's papers and possessions. And when the vans left, and the police seals were removed, Walter's lingering ghost seemed to depart with them—the shabby street seemed somehow brighter, as if a pall had been lifted.

14

Under the care of the old doctor and half a dozen curious young nurses, Jack recovered quickly. On his third morning in the hospital the old doctor clamped the tubes and removed them. With the tubes gone, Jack found he could sit up in bed without too much pain, if he moved slowly and didn't twist from side to side. He asked for a telephone, waited patiently as the operators made the transpacific connection, and finally identified himself to MacCormack's secretary. She seemed to be half expecting his call. "He's been very worried about you," she said. "I'll put you right through."

As soon as he heard Jack's greeting, the old Bureau chief's voice began to rise. "Are you okay?" He didn't even wait for an answer. "What the hell kind of a bloody *schemozzle* have you gotten yourself into?" MacCormack demanded in his curious Irish-Yiddish blend. "Interpol wants to know who the hell you are. Some *meshuggener* from Los Angeles who just happens to be a police captain says you're interfering with an ongoing LAPD investigation. The Japanese came so close to pressing a charge with the State Department, it's hard to believe we talked them all out of it. You said you were going to be low key. . . ." There came a silence as the old Irishman paused for breath.

"I was being low key," Jack told him. "This wasn't my fault. I was attacked from behind. . . ."

"That's not the way I heard it. I heard you got stinking drunk, threw money around, some guy showed you a knife and tried to lift your wallet, you played the tough guy and tried to fight him off, and he damn near offed you. Now, how the hell do you expect me to explain—"

"It was a sword," Jack interrupted.

"A what?"

"It wasn't a knife. The guy who attacked me had a sword."
MacCormack pondered that one in silence.

"He was a pro. It was a hit all the way."

"So you weren't drunk? That story I heard was crap?"

"I was drunk, but there's no way in a million years it was a mugging. Who've you been talking to?"

"Half a dozen sources are telling me the same thing," Mac-Cormack growled. "Anyway, we'll have plenty of time to straighten this out once you get your *toches* back home."

"I think my *toches* should stay in Japan."

MacCormack could not keep the worry out of his voice. "Why? You are getting better? They said there was no danger. . . ."

"Sure, I'm getting better."

"Well then, what the hell? Embassy said you wanted to come home. Said you needed some plastic surgery when you got back. We even booked you a flight."

"I never told anyone I was coming home."

"Well, whoever said it, it's not such a bad idea." The old man's voice softened almost imperceptibly. "Come home, Jack. Get better. Leave this whole mess alone while you still have your health and your career."

Jack took the plunge. "I just need a few more weeks here. To follow up some leads. Then I'll come home."

"You have leads?"

"There are some questions I should ask. . . ."

"And there are some that I should ask. Like, what leads and what questions and why do you think things aren't the way everybody else says they are?"

"I'll tell you soon as I know anything definite. . . ."

"You took a sword in the ribs and you don't know anything definite?"

Jack waited, feeling the curve of the phone receiver on his palm.

"I've already stuck my neck out for you," MacCormack growled.

"I know," Jack said. "If I had something right now, I'd give it to you. But I don't yet. Meanwhile, I've got the feeling that I could be deported any second. Can you buy me just two or three more weeks?"

There was a long hesitation. "Can you stay out of trouble?"

"I can and I will," Jack told him. "Thanks."

Jack hung up and looked out the window at the square of blue sky between the white curtains. Two weeks wasn't much time, particularly if he had to spend much more of it lying in bed. The conversation with MacCormack had crystallized a suspicion that had occurred to Jack several times before. Why exactly had Chief Sato and his two friends pumped so much alcohol into him that night? It had rendered him almost defenseless, just before an attack. And in a neighborhood with so many winding streets, how had the man with the sword known just where to wait, and when?

Jack used the thought that he might have been set up to buffer the pain as he swung his legs over the side of the bed and gingerly lowered them to the floor. The first twinges needled his ribs. He forced his mind to think of Guy Brown, and Lieutenant Sasaki's flashy smile. Why were they trying to dismiss the whole thing as a mugging when there was obviously far more involved?

The pain was bearable as he transferred more and more of his weight to his legs. What could Shannon Miles and her husband have known, and Walter been close to finding out? Jack was finally standing, bracing himself on the edge of the bed with both arms. He remembered Captain Sato at the hostess bar telling him that if he stayed in Japan till the whole thing made sense, he might never leave. Had it been a joke, a threat, or a prophecy? Or all three at once? Jack took his arms away from the bed and dared a tiny step.

The pain in his chest and sides made him sit back onto the bed as tears welled in his eyes. For a moment he thought he might pass out, but as he sat very still, the pain slowly subsided. A knock sounded on the door of his room. After twenty seconds, Jack managed a "Come in" between gasps.

Misako entered, and closed the door behind her. She was wearing a knee-length blue skirt and a white blouse, and she looked prim and businesslike. In her right hand she carried an old cassette player while her left hand held a plastic bag with a half dozen tapes. "Hi," she said, obviously surprised to see him sitting upright. "Shouldn't you still be in bed?"

"You're just in time to help," Jack told her. "I'm trying to learn how to walk all over again. Will you catch me when I fall?"

"No," Misako said. "Lie back in bed. I'll play some music. I brought you some tapes."

Jack slowly pushed himself up again, conscious that Misako

was watching his struggle. When he was upright he winked at her, clenched his teeth, and struck out toward the far side of the room. He managed two tottering steps before he began to sag. She caught him and half carried him to the bed. She was much stronger than she looked—the last couple of steps, she supported nearly all of his weight.

She lowered him to the bed, both of them gasping. "Are you okay? Should I call a doctor?"

Jack lay back. "No. I'm okay. Thanks. Sorry to fall on you." He took several short breaths. "The good news is that they took my tubes out." A few more breaths. "And I'll be staying around Atami for a few more weeks. So as soon as I get out of here, we can start . . ."

Something about the look in Misako's face made him stop talking and watch her. She shook her head. "We won't be working together anymore. Captain Sato wants me to stop."

"Why?"

She plugged in the tape player, and the same lush music that she had played on her car's CD filled the hospital room. "That's Ravel," she said.

" 'Scuse me, but screw Ravel. What's with Sato?"

She shrugged. "He talked to the JNP. And to someone in Los Angeles."

"Captain Charles?"

She shrugged again. "They can't make you leave Japan, but they're not going to help you anymore. And that's all I know. I shouldn't even be here. Captain Sato was quite definite."

Jack looked at her. "But you are here."

Misako slowly nodded.

"Because you wanted to bring me some music tapes?"

She reached down and shut off the Ravel. "I wanted to say good-bye. It has been interesting working with you." Her small fingers clasped and unclasped.

Jack remembered doubting whether he could trust her or not. Now, watching her, he believed her totally. "It's been interesting working with you, too," he told her.

"Thank you." Her fingers found the hem of her blouse and twisted it nervously.

"Now that we won't be working together, would you consider going to dinner with me?"

"Yes," she said. "But I can't. Captain Sato wishes us to . . . sever our acquaintanceship. That was my strong impression when I talked to him. So I have to say good-bye."

"He runs your personal life, too?"

"In Japan," Misako said, "it's common for an employer or senior manager to exercise influence over the life of a . . . subordinate."

"For Christ's sake . . ."

"I didn't make the system. This is where I live. I should go now."

"Well, will you at least tell me something before you walk away through the door?"

"What?"

"Not much." Jack tried to control his anger. "Just, what the hell's going on? Why did Captain Sato pull this about-face and stop cooperating? Why does everyone want me to go home? Why did the JNP take over the case of Everett Miles and just bury it? Like you said, this is your society and your system and you understand it, so please explain it to me. What's the deal?"

"I can't tell you that, because I don't know," Misako said in an even, low voice. "Captain Sato is an honorable man. I've known him for five years. You are also sincere." She slowly raised and lowered her shoulders, her eyes on the window, her voice becoming distant as if part of her had already left the room. "Really, that's all I can tell you."

"Well then, let me ask you something else. What can you tell me about the Inagawa Yakuza?"

That caught her attention. Suddenly she was on full alert, her bright eyes riveted back on his face. "The Inagawa? Why?"

Jack brought his finger up to his cheek. "I hear this might be their calling card. Do you know about them?"

"Of course."

"Who are they?"

"The Inagawa are one of the oldest and strongest Yakuza families in Japan. Their base is Yokohama, but they are spread out all over Japan."

"The night Shannon Miles was murdered in Los Angeles, a ticket was given on the street outside her house to a black Mercedes Benz sedan," he told her. "The Mercedes was rented by a

bar in Little Tokyo that has well-known connections to the Inagawa Yakuza.''

Her face tightened as she registered the information. "Who was
driving the car?''

"Someone traveling on a fake passport. The car was paid for in
cash beforehand. The bar later denied any knowledge about it. My
father was looking into the whole thing. . . .''

She saw something in his face that made her step closer to the
bed. "What happened to your father?" she asked.

"He was killed. Shot with his own gun. The police called it a
suicide. I don't think it was.''

"I'm very sorry,'' she whispered.

"Me, too,'' Jack told her, his voice thickening. It took him a
few seconds to speak again. "Anyway, next thing I know, I got
the Inagawa coat of arms carved into my cheek. So naturally I'm
a little curious about them. Do they have a presence here in
Atami?''

She nodded.

"What businesses?''

"Pachinko parlors. Hotels. Gambling. Massage parlors.''

"And Captain Sato knows about them and about the other
Yakuza in the area, but he doesn't do anything?''

"What could he do?''

"Kick them out. He seems to genuinely care about keeping
crime low in his city. The night we went out drinking, he quoted
me all sorts of figures about how many fewer homicides there are
in Japan than America and how much safer the streets are here.
Why doesn't he just boot them out?''

Misako glanced at her watch, and then at Jack, apparently
undecided. The longer she remained in the room, the more uncomfortable she seemed to feel. "Let me explain something to
you,'' she finally said, sitting down on the corner of his bed so that
her knee brushed his ankle. "And then I really have to go. I must
warn you that what I'm going to say will make no sense to you.''

"Go ahead anyway.''

"The reason the streets in Japan are so safe,'' Misako said, "is
because of the close relationship between the police and organized
crime. Everyone understands this, but no one likes to talk about it.
In fact, just for show, every once in a while there are crackdowns

on Yakuza offices. The gangs are tipped off beforehand, and everything of real value is taken away. A few guns are left behind, to be found. The real bosses go into hiding, but younger family members let themselves be caught. Some of them go to jail, and when they come out, there are big *Demukai* celebrations that the state's efforts at rehabilitation have failed.''

"So it's just a game?"

"Not a game. Just a very different way of handling the problem of crime. In America you say you want to stamp crime out. In Japan we acknowledge that crime is present, has always been present, and always will be present. Perhaps vice is part of the nature of man. So we might as well admit that. Since crime will always be present, we have found the best way to handle it and keep it in limits is to . . . institutionalize it, so that even the Yakuza leaders have to worry about their reputations and their role in society. I can't explain it any better. But the Yakuza themselves keep small crimes from happening on their . . ."

"Turf?" Jack suggested. "They police their own turf and that's why the streets are so safe?"

She nodded. "Sometimes they go too far and the system breaks down. And sometimes one Yakuza family fights another. But mostly the system works. Now I really must go."

She stood, and Jack sat up. "Thanks," he said. "It does seem strange to me, but now at least I understand it a little."

"Where will you go next?" she asked, straightening the sheet where she had sat.

"You mean when I get out of here? I'm gonna shake the tree."

"I don't understand."

"My father was a tough, mean man," he told her, "but he was a very good cop. Probably about as good as they come. And he used to have a bunch of sayings that I heard again and again when I was growing up. One of them was 'If you need to find the hornet's nest in a hurry, git your ass up and shake the whole damn tree.' ''

"I see," she said. "In Japan we say, 'To drive out a snake, beat the bamboo thicket with a stick.' But you don't know where you're going to shake this tree?"

Jack saw no reason to tell her. If he was going to be going it alone, he might as well keep his own counsel. "No."

For a moment her face softened with concern. "Well, please be careful not to get stung."

"Y'know," Jack told her, "we wouldn't have to have dinner in Atami. We could go to Tokyo or wherever. For that matter, we can cook ourselves. I'm pretty good with Italian. . . ."

"I don't think it's a good idea now," she said, finishing with the sheet and preparing to leave. "Maybe sometime. Please don't worry about returning the tape player and the tapes. They're old—I only listen to CDs now. Good-bye, Jack."

Jack reached for his wallet on the bed table and held out a business card. "My home number is on the back. Call me next time you're in Washington, D.C. We'll go to an Orioles game or something."

She took his card, hesitated, and then made up her mind and took one of her own business cards from her purse. She wrote her home phone number on the back, and handed it to him. "If you get into any very serious trouble and need a friend," she said.

"You're the only friend I've got in Japan."

"Then you're in trouble," she said with a smile. She held out her right hand and Jack shook it, and neither of them let go for several long seconds. "I'm very sorry about your father," she whispered. "He must've been a nice man to have such a son." Her palm was warm and soft, but her grip was firm, and she looked right back into his eyes.

When they finally let go, she turned and walked quickly out the door without looking back.

15

The Club Rendezvous was just a few blocks from the train station, on a street that bordered the seedy section of town yet still looked decent and safe. The solid-looking two-story brick building that housed the club was well kept and set off from the street by a row of tall bushes.

Jack stood next to one of the bushes, running his eyes down from the small pink neon sign that flashed the club's name in both katakana and French to the bas-relief fleur-de-lis that enlivened the upper facade to the hand-printed menu taped to the outside of the heavy wooden front door. He knew that nearly a decade before, Shannon had walked through that oak door. As he looked up at the building through the twilight, Jack tried to decide whether she could really have mistaken the club for an acceptable place to try to find a late dinner.

On one side of the club was an Italian restaurant—the Capri—with terra-cotta walls, a poorly rendered and slightly askew fresco of the Mona Lisa above the entrance, and a roof that dipped down in front to where it was supported by a miniature plaster colonnade. Two doors down from the Club Rendezvous on the other side, the Boutique Casablanca featured pink minarets and teardrop-shaped windows covered by intricate arabesque metal grillwork. On this street of wildly overenthusiastic borrowings from abroad, the Club Rendezvous had a certain restrained dignity. Jack decided that it was indeed possible that Shannon had simply made an error in judgment in entering.

He pulled open the heavy wooden door and started up the steep steps. It was quite dark, so that he had to keep his right hand on the banister for support. He climbed slowly, avoiding jerky or stressful movements that might aggravate his injured ribs. In his mind's eye he imagined Shannon, hungry after a long day of

172

teaching, making her tentative way up this same dark passageway.

At the top of the stairs, a hanging curtain granted entrance to a carpeted antechamber that in turn led to the large main room of the club. As Jack walked through the antechamber, the club was completely silent, but just as he stepped through into the dimly lit main room, loud jazz began to throb from ceiling speakers.

A dozen or so men and three women were in the main room, all of them seated around a long wooden bar that faced toward an empty stage area. Most of the men wore business suits and had apparently come here from work. From the way they leaned over the bar, Jack saw that several of them were in advanced stages of intoxication. The women wore short, brightly colored skirts and were apparently paid hostesses, serving much the same function as the two women had in Sato's whiskey bar, except that the young women in Club Rendezvous were prettier and better turned out.

One by one everyone in the large room turned to look at Jack as he entered. He ignored them, walked through a cloud of cigarette smoke to an empty spot at the bar, and sat down. The bartender ambled over to him. He was a frail little man in his late fifties with thinning white hair, incongruously bushy white eyebrows, and a perpetual slight scowl that made it look as if he had just tasted something unpleasant. He studied Jack for a second and muttered a couple of quick monosyllables in Japanese.

"Hi," Jack said loudly, turning his head to give the old bartender a clear view of his scarred cheek. "Do you speak English?"

"No," the bartender muttered. "Japanese."

"I'm looking for the Inagawa," Jack said, speaking slowly and loudly. "Need to talk about this little decoration." He tapped his cheek. "And I'd like to ask some questions about a girl named Shannon. American. Red hair. Cute." From his jacket pocket he took the photograph that Mrs. Taniguchi had given him of young Shannon in a green dress, saying good-bye to her students. He held it out for the bartender. "Remember her?"

The old bartender's eyes flicked down to the photograph and then back up at Jack. His scowl deepened till the corners of his mouth were pointing almost straight down. *"Nan da yo?"* he growled.

"A beer," Jack told him brightly, taking out a ten-thousand-yen note and placing it on top of the bar. *"Biru."*

The bartender looked down at the bill and then back up.

"Any kind," Jack told him. "Sapporo. Kirin. Suntory. What-ever's cold. And I wouldn't mind meeting the guy who owns this joint. Also, if you happen to know a big Japanese fellow—'bout this tall, carries a sword, eyes like the angel of death, professional *ninja*—I'm looking for him, too."

The bartender took the ten-thousand-yen note and walked away. He returned a few seconds later with a large Kirin beer, a small glass, and a heap of bills and small change. He stood with his fingers on the wood of the bar, staring at Jack. Jack smiled back at him, filled the glass, and raised it up to his lips. "Cheers."

A very drunk Japanese businessman standing ten feet down the bar from Jack gestured toward him and said something in guttural Japanese that made the men around him laugh while the women giggled and covered their mouths in embarrassment.

"And your mother likes it that way, too," Jack told him good-naturedly, raising his beer glass in a mock toast.

The drunk Japanese businessman raised his whiskey glass in return and let loose another burst of what Jack took to be profane racial epithets. He pointed to Jack's scarred face and broken nose. This time, all the people around him laughed.

"And I did the same thing to your sister," Jack said back with a smile, "except that she made me pay for it."

The businessman staggered down the counter till he and Jack were only two feet apart. His breath reeked of whiskey, and there were stains on his red tie where he had spilled while sipping. "Haroo," he grunted.

"Haroo," Jack grunted back.

They studied each other for a moment. Then the drunk businessman broke into a wide grin and made an obscene gesture, curling his right index finger onto the top of his thumb to form a loop and sticking his left index finger through the loop to simulate sexual intercourse. Then he pointed to one of the pretty hostesses and cocked an eyebrow at Jack.

Jack was unsure what was being implied or offered. He inspected the indicated hostess, grinned his approval to the businessman, and then gestured for the old bartender to pour the man another whiskey and take the money out of his heap. Suddenly the whole crowd at the other end of the bar seemed to adopt Jack in unison. Other men came over to stand near him and thump him on the back while the young hostesses hovered nearby, smiling at him and making sure that all the men's glasses were full.

The crowding made Jack a little nervous. He felt the thumps on his back reverberating through his rib cage. He was at the point of forcibly breaking free from the crowd when the lights dimmed and the jazz shut off. All eyes swung to the stage area as a spotlight flicked on and two young Japanese women, holding microphones, stepped out into the light. They were dressed to appear as girlish as possible, and their singing voices were high-pitched and co-quettishly playful. They seemed to share the same small repertoire of cute poses and facial expressions, which they each ran through several times during their song.

When they were done, they curtsied and left the stage. The circumference of the spotlight dwindled till it was big enough for only one person, and a new, steamy striptease music came over the speakers. A large girl, dressed completely in black, sashayed onto the stage. For a few seconds she stayed out of the spotlight, and the men at the bar craned their necks to see her clearly. The music quickened. Suddenly she flitted directly into the circle of light, seemingly drawn to it like a giant black moth emerging from night shadows.

Jack was rocked by the sudden realization that she was blond and Caucasian. The men around him all stopped drinking and watched as she lowered her gown's shoulder straps on first one side and then the other, till the dress was held up only by her very ample breasts. She was a large girl, big-boned and thick-hipped, with wide, rounded shoulders and long blond hair which she showed off by tossing her head as she swayed to the beat of the music. Her fleshy face with its ruddy complexion visible through layers of makeup still showed occasional flashes of a sort of Ruben-esque cherubic seductiveness, but she was losing even this dubi-ous charm quickly, and Jack saw she would soon be left with the sex appeal of a potato.

As she began to sway, she ran her eyes casually out over the men at the bar and spotted Jack, and for a moment she looked surprised. Then her gaze left him to fix on a point somewhere in the middle of the room, and a vapid smile rose to her face and settled into place between her florid cheeks.

Her performance was halfway between a dance and an unveil-ing. She reached behind her back and unzipped the gown, and was able to shake it completely off her body by a series of fast gyrations, finally stepping out of it. Underneath the gown she wore a white slip, cut low over the breasts and high above the knees and tied in front with a blue silk sash. She pulled on the bow several times, loosening it and teasing the audience, before she finally undid the sash with a yank and let the white slip join the black gown on the floor of the stage.

She was left in a dark bra and black bikini bottoms, and for a while didn't seem particularly inclined to take either off. She danced abominably—totally without grace or a feeling for the music—and each time she raised and lowered one of her large feet onto the stage, there was an audible clump. Finally, urged on by shouts from the men in business suits, she reached behind her and unhooked her bra. Her exertions had made her perspire, and for a few seconds the black brassiere clung to her gleaming skin, peeling away bit by bit as she shook her shoulders.

When the bra finally came off, she immediately cupped her palms over her breasts, and only lowered them when begged to do so by several men who had moved to the front of the bar, near the stage. The music raced toward a crescendo. She kicked out her legs to either side in an awkward cancan, and then as the spotlight dwindled further and the music hardened to a drumroll, she took off her bikini bottoms and tossed them to one of the businessmen. She was now naked except for only the smallest of black G-strings, and she began to bump and grind her hips faster and faster.

A drunk businessman staggered toward the stage and tried to catch hold of her, and without breaking step, she put her hand squarely on the center of his chest and pushed him back toward his comrades. He regained his footing and made another assault, this time followed onto the stage by a less drunk friend. Cheered on by the men at the front of the bar, they trapped her between them and seemed at the point of tugging off her G-string when a bouncer walked out of the shadows, took her by the arm, and half escorted, half tugged her off the stage. The strip music continued for a few more seconds, and then stopped abruptly.

Jack ordered a second beer and drank alone. The two Japanese girls came back onto the stage wearing a bit less than they had the first time around, and began another song. A few more Japanese men staggered into the club, already drunk, and joined the crowd before the stage, pointing and making loud, lewd comments. Jack was at the point of leaving when the blond stripper stepped out of a side door and headed right for him. She was wearing the black gown she had started her dance with, and took a long drag on a cigarette as she joined him at the bar.

She exhaled and smiled. "Gave me a turn, love. Don't see many round-eyes here. Enjoy the show?" She gave his scar a quick look as she put her elbows up on the bar next to him.

Jack nodded politely. Her teeth were yellowing, and several of them looked chipped. He was good with accents, and his first thought was cockney. After hearing her speak a few more words, he knew she was not English but Australian. "What are you drinking?"

"Gin," she said, "but don't bother. They give me what I want. Hope I'll get pissed as a parrot and one of 'em'll hop on for a free ride. Not much chance o' that."

He held out his hand. "I'm Jack Graham. From Washington, D.C."

She looked down at his hand and almost laughed. "Aren't we bloody formal. I'm Barbara Gordon from Grafton."

"Where's Grafton?"

"In the middle of nowhere," she said. "Nearest place you've heard of to it's Brisbane. Five hundred or so miles north of Sydney."

The bartender brought her a tall glass of gin and walked away. All of the Japanese men seemed to be giving them a wide berth, as if by virtue of their communication in English, the two of them had somehow temporarily placed themselves off limits. She took a long sip of the gin and put it down on the counter.

"So, what are you doing here?" Jack asked her.

She stared back at him for a second, and then lowered her voice as if letting him in on a secret. "When I was seven, me mum gave me ballet slippers. Ever since then, I wanted to be a dancer. . . ." Then she lost it and broke up into loud guffaws that almost sounded like groans. "What'm I doing here?" she repeated over and over again. "That's rich, that is. Let me get you another one. Nobuo."

She waved the sour-faced bartender over and spoke to him in Japanese. He brought Jack a beer, gave the two of them a malevolent look that seemed to be left over from World War II, and walked away.

"Don't be pissed off," she told Jack as he poured himself a glass. "I was just having a bit'v fun. If you want to know, I'm with a group of girls—another one from Grafton, one from Walaroo, and one from Geelong. We work with a booking agent in Sydney. He sets up . . . tours . . . of performers for Asian countries. We started in Luzon. Then Seoul, and Bangkok, and now here. Luzon was a hole, but since then, it hasn't been half-bad. You should'a seen some of the private parties in Bangkok. . . ."

"Where are the three other girls?" Jack asked her.

"Two of them are at other clubs here in town. One of them is up the coast. Place called Ito."

"And the people in this club like having a foreigner dance here?"

"It's not really much about dancing, love," she told him with another broad smile. She stubbed out her cigarette and immediately took out a replacement. Jack lit it for her. "Thanks. I think they just about always have foreign girls here. There was a Philippine girl before me. They didn't treat her well, I hear."

"So if they could get an American girl, maybe not a great dancer but pretty and young and a redhead, they'd go after her?"

His question made her move a half step away and study him carefully. "Shopping one around, are you then? I wouldn't have thought it."

"No, matter of fact, I'm a cop," he told her, watching her face. Barbara Gordon from Grafton would not give him much trouble about the Neutrality Act. "I'm looking into a murder that happened here in town."

Her features didn't change at all, but he saw a sudden wariness narrow the edges of her eyes. She had talked to police many times before. "Why're you here?"

"The woman who was murdered came in here a few times. It was a long time ago, but I think our friend behind the bar remembers. I bet the owners do, too. Do you know who owns this place?"

"No," she said, "but I'll give you some advice for free. This is my second time 'round this club circuit in Asia." She checked to see where the bartender was. "Get along in Japanese pretty well, huh?" she asked as she casually swept the room with her eyes.

"Very well," Jack told her.

"Bit of Korean, too. And Tagalog. I don't get anywhere with Thai. I pick up other things, too, 'cause I keep my eyes open and my mouth shut." She leaned a bit closer to him, her right hand on the gin glass, which rested on the bar. "I've seen some of the blokes that run these operations. You don't want to come in here asking questions."

"Yes I do," Jack told her. "Matter of fact, if you know these guys and can speak to them in their own language, maybe you can pass on a message for me. I want to ask about a girl named Shannon, and I want to talk to the people behind the people that run this place. Also, tell them I'm kind of curious about the Inagawa. Got it all?"

She studied Jack for a long second and then smiled. "Got it, love. Now I've got to get up onstage again and do my act. Before you leave, do you want to go downstairs?"

"What's downstairs?"

She looked at him to see if he was serious, and then shook her head. "Know what a soapland is? Place for a bath and a nice rubdown. Tomoko." One of the prettier Japanese hostesses hurried over. "Why don't you bring Mr. Graham downstairs and show him a little Japanese culture."

"I don't think so. . . ." Jack began, but Tomoko had already put her arm around his and was tugging him toward the side exit.

"You came to the club, you might as well have a rendezvous," Barbara Gordon told him, running her tongue over the outside of her chipped teeth. "Go ahead. She speaks some English." She saw Jack resisting and winked at him significantly. "Maybe you'll learn something." She went back to her gin, and Jack let himself be gently tugged to the side door. It opened for them just as they reached it, and then closed behind them as they started down a steep flight of stairs toward a faint pink light.

The ground floor of the Club Rendezvous was partitioned into a dozen or so small private rooms, each of which was lit by pink neon lights very similar to the pink neon sign on the outside of the front facade. The air was thick with the smell of steam and suds. Tomoko led Jack by the hand into one of the rooms, and slid the door shut behind him. It was a small space, perhaps fifteen feet square, with a recessed tub in the middle, a tiny refrigerator in the far corner, and a low couch between the bath and the door. A pulley mechanism was fastened to the ceiling above the couch, so that a chain hung down from one side of the pulley wheel and a strangely shaped piece of leather hung down from the other. Tomoko flipped a switch and the same canned jazz that had played when Jack walked into the club filled the little room. She smiled at him.

"I just want to ask you some questions," Jack said, producing the photograph of Shannon. He handed Tomoko the picture, and as she inspected it, he watched her carefully for any sign of recognition. "I'm willing to pay for information," he said, taking out his wallet. Her face remained blank as she handed the photograph back to him, and let her hand trail down his shoulder to the muscles of his right arm. "Who owns this place?" he asked, still holding the wallet and feeling awkward.

Tomoko brought her index finger gently to his mouth, sealing his lips to silence. Her other hand came up to his face also, and for a moment both of her small palms were warm on his cheeks.

Looking down at her, Jack felt a touch of dizziness. Sweet lilac-scented perfume rose up from her body. Her dress was cut so low that when she bent forward, he could see her small breasts to the nipple. She saw him glance down and then back up, and she offered herself to him with a single tiny smile.

"Do you speak English?" he whispered, his voice unsteady.

"Twenty-five thousand yen," she whispered back, reaching out and taking the wallet from him.

"You speak pretty well," Jack grunted as she selected the bills she wanted, holding them up for him to see. "How long have you been working here?"

She sealed his lips again with her finger, and then took off his jacket, placing it neatly on a chair before kneeling and starting to open his belt buckle. She deftly opened the clasp and unsnaked the belt from around his waist. As his belt came off, she ran the fingers of her free hand lightly back and forth over his groin, teasing his pronounced swelling into a full erection. *"Umai, neeei!"* she said, sounding pleased.

Jack had never paid a woman for sex in his life. Walter had done it often after his wife had died, and perhaps as a reaction against his father, the mere thought of paying a woman had always disgusted Jack. He could see no pleasure in such an encounter, and he had no desire to risk picking up a disease. Now, almost naked, he took Tomoko lightly by the arms and raised her to her feet. He was breathing hard, and there was a growing tension all down his stomach as his eyes ran up and down her slim body of their own volition. "I don't want this. . . ." he managed. "I just came to ask you . . ."

Her fingers slid inside his T-shirt and up behind both shoulder blades, enjoying his muscles one by one. Then her hands moved around to the front of his chest, and romped about in his forest of chest hair. "Monkey man," she whispered, delighted. "Sexy." She lifted his T-shirt up and off, standing on her toes to pull it over his head so that the tips of her breasts rubbed his chest. Then she dropped to her knees to take off his pants, her face close enough so that he could feel her hot breath through the fabric. In a few seconds she was sliding his briefs down over his erection, which drew repeated stares from her.

She stood, facing him, and shed her low-cut dress with a single graceful motion. Her naked breasts were pert and firm, and her sleek body widened slightly to provocative hips, a scarlet triangle of bright silk panties, and long, thin legs. Her eyes locked on his, she slowly peeled down the scarlet bikini bottoms to reveal a vagina shaved of all pubic hair. Still looking up at him, she took his penis in her hand and stroked it very gently several times, as if making friends. Then she led Jack over to a tiled washing area near the bath and gestured for him to sit on a low plastic stool.

While Jack sat on the stool, she used a large yellow ladle to scoop hot water out of the bath and pour it over his head and shoulders. She soaped him thoroughly with a sponge, paying special attention to his chest and groin. Every time he felt himself beginning to lose his erection, Tomoko seemed to sense it, take him in her hand again, and stroke till he was rock-hard. When he was thoroughly soaped, she rinsed him off with the ladle, giggling happily as the soapy water cascaded down over his forehead and nose.

After he was all rinsed off, she led him over to the bath and helped him in. She pushed gently on his shoulders, and Jack obediently sank down into the steaming water—it was about as hot as he could stand it, and his erection shriveled. Tomoko left him for a moment to turn down the music, which was a bit too loud, and then joined him in the bath. She took his hands in her own, seemingly marveling at the breadth of his palms and the length of his fingers. Then she placed his palms on her breasts, and when he began to caress her, she tilted back her head and moaned impressively, if not entirely convincingly.

After the hot bath, while he toweled himself off, she walked to the refrigerator and opened an icy Kirin for him. His body had a warm glow inside and out, and when he took a gulp of the beer, he felt the freezing liquid sliding down the length of his throat. She led him over to the couch and made him lie on his stomach. The couch was small for him—his arms dangled down from the front while his feet hung off the back.

From the wall near the refrigerator she took a little kit, not unlike a fisherman's tackle box. She put it down on the floor near him, and Jack glimpsed different oils and lubricants and individually wrapped condoms. She selected a container of oil and squeezed a fair amount into each of her palms, and then brought her cupped palms to her breasts. When her breasts glistened with oil, she knelt behind him and gently lowered herself toward his back till her nipples brushed his shoulder blades. Holding herself up from the bench with her arms so that no part of her body except her breasts touched him, she began moving back and forth above him, spreading the fragrant oil across his back with the softest possible contact imaginable.

Jack closed his eyes and enjoyed the tantalizing sensation of her now fully distended nipples making parallel tracks across his skin. He could feel her hot breath on the nape of his neck, and every once in a while her body dipped down for a second and her hips and pubis slid over him, her skin warm and smooth.

When he was well oiled, she crouched above him and rubbed him down, from the top of his scalp to the soles of his feet. Her gentle fingers proved remarkably strong, and when she folded them into little fists to pound out knots of tension, her punches became a cadence, thumping along with the jazz from the ceiling speakers.

Finishing with his back, she helped him turn over and worked on his thighs and neck, avoiding his bruised ribs and chest. Jack opened his eyes and looked up at her as she knelt between his legs, stroking his upper thighs and gently caressing his testicles higher and higher until she reached the shaft of his penis and took it in her right palm.

When he reached for her, she stepped away, but it was only to select a condom from her kit box. She expertly rolled the sheath onto him, at the same time lubricating herself with a bit of oil. Then, looking down into his eyes, she inserted one leg and then the other into the piece of leather that hung down from the pulley wheel. Jack saw that it was actually a sort of harness, cleverly shaped to spread her legs without becoming an obstacle. Once inside the harness, she moved her body into position above him, seized his erection, and held him where she wanted. In one heart-stopping moment she impaled herself completely upon him and they both gasped.

For several minutes they bucked together and apart, his hands on her hips guiding her up and down. She handed him the chain hanging down from the pulley wheel, and when he tugged on it, she was pulled up toward the ceiling and her legs were spread wide above him. He found that he could hoist and lower her with an almost effortless movement of his right arm. The pulley and harness mechanism allowed deep penetration while at the same time keeping the weight of her body off him. As she was lifted and lowered at greater and greater speed, she began to breathe faster. When she was rising and falling like a piston, she tilted her head all the way back and moaned more convincingly than before.

Jack was lost in a warm, sensual world, her thin body seemingly weightless above him so that it was all he could do not to hoist her through the ceiling or lower her through the floor. He shut his eyes against the weeks of worry since Walter's death and the days of pain and boredom in the hospital, and lost himself in the escalating rhythm and the moans and the gasps till everything came together for a long, shuddering second and then exploded. His hands slid down her hips to her thighs and finally dropped off her knees till his arms hung straight down, exhausted. He opened his eyes and looked up at her as she stood off him and climbed out of the harness, her body wet with oil and sweat.

They rinsed off together, using the yellow ladle, and he tried to talk to her again. "Do you understand my English?"

She nodded.

"Did you know Shannon? The American girl in the picture?" "No."

"Who owns this place? The Inagawa? Is there one man? I just need a name." He touched her cheek. "Please."

She shrugged.

"Listen, I'm a police officer and . . ." Jack broke off as a commotion started outside in the hallway. There was suddenly the loud stomping of heavy footsteps, and a series of thuds as, one by one, sliding doors were thrown open and then slammed shut again. Jack looked at Tomoko; she withdrew to the farthest corner of the room and stood watching him with her back pressed against the wall.

Besides the sliding door to the hallway, there was no way out of the little room. Jack stepped to the door, but whoever was outside was only a few feet away. There was not time to make a break for it—better to let them come to him.

He moved to one side of the door and pressed his back up against the wall. The sliding door was thrown open and a burly man stepped into the room. Jack threw a quick right that caught him on the side of his head and decked him. Tomoko screamed as three more men hurried through the door with guns drawn. Jack backed off and stood looking at them. The second man through the door had the look of a low-grade thug, with broad shoulders and a dull pug face. He held his revolver at hip height pointed at Jack's stomach as he reached down with his left hand and helped his fallen comrade back to his feet.

The third man was older and shorter, and looked as if he had had a very painful career. A long scar started beneath his thinning hair and ran down the left side of his face to his jaw. His nose had been broken so many times that it had the globular shapelessness of a lump of tofu, while his eyes were surrounded by scar tissue. The fourth man was tall and somber-looking in a black suit with a black shirt underneath, a white tie, and sunglasses.

Jack took the tall man to be the leader, and finally broke the silence by asking him: "What do you want?" There was absolutely no response. "Money?"

The tall leader glanced at the older man with the scar, who turned to Jack and said in colloquial English with a strong Brooklyn accent, "Put yer clothes on. We're goin' for a ride."

Jack stepped over to his clothes and began pulling them on, at the same time sizing up his chances of making a break for it. In his condition, against armed thugs, he saw that he had virtually no chance. "Where are we going?" he asked, pulling up his trousers.

The tall man in the suit walked to face him, smiled, and snapped a karate kick into his groin. Jack doubled over and sank to his knees. The two thugs advanced to either side of him and lifted him back up. They draped his shirt over his shoulders, and half carried, half dragged him toward the door.

Facing backward into the room as they pulled him out, Jack saw Tomoko wave her right hand at him in a slightly mocking farewell. Then Jack was dragged out into the empty corridor toward a doorway, beyond which he heard a car motor idling.

The Cadillac smelled of lemon air freshener. It had leather seats and tinted windows, and whoever was driving seemed to enjoy taking the corners just a bit too quickly. Almost immediately after loading Jack into the backseat, they had blindfolded him, so after the first few quick turns, he completely lost his sense of direction. He had seen all four men get into the car with him, but once they started moving, they drove in complete silence.

The wheels finally shrieked to an abrupt stop and he was bundled out and spirited up a flight of steps, through a hallway, into an elevator. The elevator could not have gone more than two floors when it jerked to a stop and he was hustled down a long corridor and finally shoved through a door. Rough fingers removed his blindfold, and he looked around.

He was in a small, carpeted office with white walls and a single small window. The curtains were completely drawn over the window, and the three standing lamps that provided illumination left patches of shadow on the walls. In the best-lit corner of the room, a large executive-type desk was surrounded by several flat-backed chairs. Behind the desk, a row of shelves held books and papers and several glass vials filled with colorless liquid. Flesh-colored objects floated on the bottoms of the vials—Jack looked more closely and realized they were severed finger joints.

The two burly thugs led Jack over to one of the straight-backed wooden chairs and pushed him down into a sitting position. The tall man who had kicked Jack and the short one with the scar stood near him, apparently waiting.

"What's the deal?" Jack asked. His voice rang strangely in the silence.

No one bothered to look at him.

Jack turned to the little man with the scar and addressed his next question to him directly. "Who's running this show?"

The little man's eyes were fixed on the door, and he gave no evidence of even having heard Jack speak.

"Where'd you learn such good English?" Jack asked him.

"New York," he grunted, finally looking over.

"What school?"

"Attica."

Suddenly all of the Japanese thugs visibly tensed as the door opened and a powerfully built man in his fifties strode through. He wore a double-breasted pinstriped suit that accented his bull-like shoulders, and his hair was cropped so close to his head, it gave him a military demeanor. The four men bowed low to him. He nodded back, walked to the leather swivel chair behind the desk, sat down very slowly, lit a cigarette with a silver lighter, and finally turned his eyes to Jack.

"Who are you?" Jack asked.

The man with the scar translated his question, but the bull-like man would not be rushed. He spotted a thumbprint on his cigarette lighter and meticulously wiped it away with a white silk handkerchief. Finally he spoke in Japanese, his voice low and the words coming fast and confidently. At one point Jack caught his own name, but the rest of the Japanese went by him.

"He says it's more important that he already knows who you are," the little man with the scar translated. "You are Mr. Jack Graham, from Washington, D.C. He wants you to know that you are among people who wish you only success. He says the . . . interests he has the honor of serving have nothing against Americans. He likes Americans. He says he has seen all of the *Godfather* movies many times, and he thinks they are the best movies Hollywood ever made."

"Tell him *Casablanca* is the best movie Hollywood ever made, and he didn't kidnap me at knife-point to discuss cinema. I wanna know what the hell's going on."

Once again the translation passed back and forth, and the kingpin nodded and spoke. "He says, you are right, now is not the time to talk about movies, so why not talk about Shannon Miles?"

Jack sat forward, his eyes on the big man who puffed on his cigarette and looked back at him through the smoke. "How does he know Shannon?"

The answer was so long that the kingpin paused after every few sentences so that the translator could give it to him a bit at a time. "He knows everything that happens in Atami. He says Shannon was a very unusual girl. More Japanese than American. The face was American, but the soul was Japanese. He says you should always remember that about her.'' The translator paused for another burst of Japanese. ''He says you have some good ideas, but you must be careful not to be fooled by people who want to trick you or scare you. The . . . interests you have been asking about have nothing to do with this. We are public servants. When the sun is hot, we walk on the sunny side of the street so that the public can walk in the shade. We would never get involved in this. He says Shannon went into the Club Rendezvous only once, by mistake.''

''He's talking about the Inagawa? That's who you are? That's who he is?'' Jack touched his cheek and looked at the bull-shouldered kingpin. ''You say you're not involved, but isn't this your calling card?''

The kingpin replied emphatically, and the translator relayed his words in a slightly louder voice. ''He says no. Someone is playing a very dangerous game. They are using us. This is not the first time. It has happened both in Japan and in America. Cars have been rented, names have been used—it has caused great concern. We had no involvement with Shannon. We had no involvement with her husband. We have no wish to hurt you.''

''Why should I believe that?''

When he heard the translation of Jack's question, the bull-shouldered man stubbed out his cigarette and grunted a quick reply. ''Because,'' the translator explained, ''if he wanted to hurt you, we could kill you right now. No one knows where you are. No one would know where to look. It would be easy. But when this conversation is over, he will let you go. And he will even give you good advice.''

''First, ask him something for me. The man who attacked me was a pro. This tall. Built like a tank. He had a short sword, but he almost didn't need to use it. He dug his fingers into my neck, and my whole body went limp. If your boss knows everything that happens in Atami, does he know that guy?''

When the small man translated Jack's description of his attacker into Japanese, it had a pronounced effect on all five of the Japanese men in the room. The thugs looked a bit scared, but the kingpin nodded, smiled slightly, and spoke.

''He knows a man like that,'' the translator told Jack. ''A very dangerous man. The technique of paralyzing by attacking nerve

centers is called *koshijutsu*. A small group of *ninja* called the
Gyokko-ryu developed it centuries ago. Today, even among experts, almost no one would know how to do it.''

"Well, the guy who attacked me knew how to do it just fine.''

The translator listened to some more Japanese from his boss and
told Jack, ''He says, he has heard that you were drunk when you
were attacked. If you are going up against such a man, he says
you should not get so drunk, especially with strangers. He reminds
you of the old Japanese saying:

> 'First a man takes a drink.
> Then the drink takes a drink.
> Then the drink takes the man.'

He says you must always carry your gun with you. You must be
much more careful.''

"Tell him I don't have a gun with me in Japan, but thank him
for his concern. And ask him for the name of the killer, if he
knows it. Or even better, ask him, if the Inagawa isn't behind all
this, who is?''

"He says you are a police investigator, and he is not. So it is
your job to find out. Maybe you were heading in a good direction
when you thought that Shannon had something going on in Atami
besides teaching. It wasn't at the Club Rendezvous, but maybe it
was somewhere else. Many famous and important people pass
through Atami and stop to . . . play.''

"No one at the high school knows anything about such a side
interest,'' Jack said. ''They say she was just a good teacher. And
they should know, because she was watched all the time.''

The bull-shouldered kingpin raised his right shirt cuff and
glanced at his Rolex. He seemed to be considering whether to
break off the interview or to stay just a bit longer. For a moment
his eyes met Jack's, and on a gut level Jack felt that the man knew
something and really did want to help him, but for some reason,
could not do so directly. Finally he spoke.

"He asks if you know the two Japanese words *tatemae* and
honne.''

"No.''

The translator floundered for a second, apparently on his own to
come up with a definition. ''It is difficult to explain, but those two

words are very important in Japanese life. *Tatemae* is the way things are supposed to be. The way people will say they are if you ask them. *Honne* is the way they really are. For example, the *tatemae* is that the police and the Yakuza are on opposite sides. The *honne* is that we often work together to serve the public.''

"So *tatemae* is pretense. And *honne* is reality?"

When the big man heard Jack use the two words, he seemed to assume that Jack understood, and launched into a speech during which Jack heard Shannon's name several times. "He says most Americans live only in *honne*. On the surface. They are direct and strong and are not afraid to say and do what they think, like Brando in *The Godfather*. He says many Japanese live on more than one level. Shannon was very Japanese.''

"So the people in the school are lying?"

"He knows nothing definite. Only rumors of rumors."

"If he wants to help me, why is he being so damned oblique? I need more. I don't know where to look next. He says important people come through Atami—ask him who. Why do they come? What kind of rumors has he heard?"

"He says Atami has everything—the sun, the moon, and the stars. That is why people come to play here during the day and during the night. You must keep doing what you were doing. You were making great progress. That is why they tried to scare you away.''

"They didn't try to scare me. They tried to kill me."

The translator didn't even need to refer to the big man to answer this. "Believe me, if the man who attacked you wanted to kill you, you'd be dead now," he assured Jack. "He only wanted to scare you.''

"Yeah? Well, you say you guys are my friends and you want to help me. So why did that joker in the suit have to kick me in the balls?"

When he heard the translation of Jack's question, the kingpin asked something in Japanese to the tall leader of the four men who had kidnapped Jack. A quick conversation went back and forth in Japanese as the tall man answered his boss.

"My friend says he had to kick you in the balls," the translator finally explained. "We are public servants of the Japanese. We do not want foreigners interfering with Japanese women. He kicked you out of patriotism.''

The bull-shouldered kingpin reached into a desk drawer and produced a small revolver. He stood, handed it to Jack along with a business card, and gave a brief final speech in fast, succinct bursts of Japanese. When he was finished, the translator rendered the speech into English in the same sort of choppy, quick sentences. "He says he is sorry you were kicked in the balls. To make up for it, and since you don't have a gun, he will give you one of his. Be careful. It's loaded. You must not give up—you, like he, are a public servant. There is a phone number on the back of the card. If you get into serious trouble, call that number for help. It is our Tokyo office. Someone there will speak English."

"Thanks. Anything else?"

"Yes. He finds your taste in movies very strange. He says the *Godfather* movies are much better than *Casablanca*. At the end of *Casablanca*, Bogart should have kept the girl. There was no reason for Bogart to send her away with her husband to America. It was weakness and sentiment."

The kingpin nodded to his men, who bowed deeply back. He reached out a hand, and Jack hesitated and then shook—the kingpin had strong, knotty hands with fingers that had obviously been broken several times and knuckles that had disappeared into scar tissue. It was like shaking hands with an old baseball catcher. Then the bull-shouldered man walked to the door and left the room.

"Come," the man with the scar said to Jack, "we'll take you back to your hotel. We gotta put the blindfold back on."

Jack raised the loaded revolver and pointed it for a second at the tall man who had kicked him. No one spoke. The tall man's face remained completely impassive as the barrel slowly lifted from his groin to his stomach and came to a stop pointing at his heart. Jack slipped the safety catch and cocked the hammer, and his finger tightened on the trigger. The tall man watched Jack's trigger finger, and the skin around the right corner of his mouth began to twitch involuntarily. When Jack saw him twitch, he smiled, lowered the gun, and allowed himself to be blindfolded and led away.

16

A spring snowstorm had rolled northward from the Thuner See, sifting inch after inch of snow like powdered sugar on the narrow streets and gingerbread-colored buildings of Creusot. Several miles outside of town, the students of the Creusot school woke to find their castle courtyard and the surrounding grounds powdered and glazed by a deep layer of snow and a crackling crust of ice.

They greeted the storm with mixed emotions. There would be snowball fights and sleigh rides, and perhaps even a ski trip. But the long winter had seemed almost over—patches of brown grass had knitted together as the snow receded, and the first brave crocuses and harebells had splashed bright colors across nearby meadows. It was a shock to look down the Alpine valley that a day ago had been almost clear of snow and ice, and see the same white blanket that had covered the landscape for eight long months.

Conversations about the storm soon gave way to gossip about a much more singular event. Lattimore and Simpson-Smith got the story from Schilling, a Latin tutor, who had a thing going with the nurse's assistant. In the middle of the night the school nurse had been called to the north wing of the castle to see about the old bodyguard of the Mystery Boy. Apparently The Limper, as the boys called the white-haired old Japanese man, had complained of dizziness and shortness of breath.

"His ticker's gone screwy," Lattimore whispered, displaying the vagueness of anatomical terminology that had consistently earned him among the lowest biology grades in the history of the Creusot School. "Tocking when it should be ticking. Problem with the pumps. Cork may pop at any minute."

"Cardiac arrest was their first thought," Simpson-Smith added, raising his eyebrows to show just how serious an emergency it had been. "At his age, at this altitude, they can't take chances with an

191

unstable heartbeat. Soon as the snow lifts, they'll get him to a hospital.''

Simpson-Smith's father was a famous surgeon, but the boy had a reputation among his peers as a notorious liar, and his prognosis was dismissed by most of the students as most probably a gross exaggeration. When the snow began to let up at around noon, however, nearly all the students in the school watched from windows as the old Japanese man limped to one of the school's helicopters and was helped on board. The whirlybird rose straight up through the lightly falling snow and then veered away and soon disappeared between two peaks at the head of the Alpine valley.

"They're taking him to Geneva," Simpson-Smith stated authoritatively to anyone who would listen. "The doctors will never let him back at his age. The altitude and the thin air would be asking for trouble.''

That night at dinner, when the rest of the boys were seated and halfway through their soup course, a whisper suddenly snaked through the room, twisting from long table to table. Soupspoons clattered to the tabletops and necks turned one and all as the Mystery Boy was led in and seated at Headmaster Siegner's own table. It was the closest look they had ever gotten of him, even though seated as he was at the end of the gloomy dining hall, it was difficult to see too much.

He was short and thin as a rail, with black hair cut much longer than the school's regulation length. He sat slumped in his chair with his shoulders hunched and his head faced down toward his plate. He barely seemed to touch his food. Perhaps after long isolation, he was frightened at being in the presence of so many other boys; perhaps he was so haughty, he didn't deign to look at them. As soon as dinner was over, he was led away out a side door, once again refusing to look around at the other boys but instead keeping his eyes on the floor till the heavy wooden door closed behind him.

Speculation on where the Mystery Boy's change of routine would lead ran rampant. "They'll put him in with the rest of us," Lattimore asserted. "We'll take him down a few pegs. I'll teach him to look me in the eye.''

"He'll leave the school," Ali Hassan speculated. "You'll see. He'll be off on the next helicopter.''

"You're both wrong," Simpson-Smith stated flatly. "Someone

new will come to look after him. Someone younger than The Limper, but cut from the same cloth. Wait and see.''

Two days later, The Limper proved them all wrong by returning to Creusot on the same helicopter that had whisked him away. The boys were in lessons, but they heard the copter coming in, and several of them invented pretexts to go to the window and watch. The gleaming metal craft descended onto its pad, and as its rotors slowed, The Limper slowly climbed down from the passenger side and walked across the snow toward the north tower.

His young charge took no more meals in the dining hall, where the other boys could see him.

Jack started with the tall, elegant hotels near the waterfront since they were close together and looked to be the most expensive in town. Whatever the Yakuza kingpin had been trying to tell him in his oblique fashion, it seemed to revolve around the fact that many famous people passed through Atami and stayed in the hotels, and that somehow Shannon might have gotten involved with one of them. Jack began all the way on one end of the shoreline at the Izakaya Hotel and worked his way around the bay.

He began at each hotel by asking if there was anyone there who spoke English. Usually there was, and that person, whether an old bell captain or a nervous maid fresh out of high school, was summoned to translate. Jack next identified himself vaguely as an American police officer, flashed his Bureau identification very quickly, and then produced the picture of twenty-two-year-old Shannon.

The higher staff was summarily assembled and her picture passed from hand to hand, each uniformed employee studying it intently before shaking his or her head and passing it down the line. Throughout the long morning, no one even paused to take a second look. The photograph was always handed back to Jack with sincere apologies and offers of complimentary cups of tea or coffee.

That morning Jack inquired at the Izakaya Hotel, The Tekkyu, the New Togiya, the Atami Grand, the Kikuya, the Izu Dai-Ichi, the Sun Rise, the Takanawa, and the Toryu. He saw a lot of splendid lobbies, exchanged many polite handshakes and bows with managers and bell captains, and came up with absolutely nothing. Everyone was perfectly cooperative, and no one remembered seeing Shannon.

Jack had lunch in a hotel restaurant facing the promenade, and as he ate a small cheeseburger and finished off a dozen or so french fries, he watched the hotels' clientele walk past. It was a sunny Sunday and the jet-set crowd had come down from Tokyo in full force to enjoy the sea air and the lovely bay. This stretch of posh hotels on the Atami waterfront was very reminiscent of Nice and Cannes, and the people who walked by on their way to the beach or back to their hotels were every bit as beautiful and fashionable as the guests at a Riviera resort.

On the sand, young beauties in bright bikinis disported in gleeful twosomes and threesomes, their chatter and laughter borne in like music on the sea breeze. Two sumo wrestlers, bulky and slow as tugboats, cruised majestically by, decked out in bright kimonos and traditional hair knots. Stern-looking dowagers walked poodles on black leather leashes that matched their purses. A young woman whom Jack took to be a teen idol strolled by while three bodyguards tried to keep away a horde of young fans clamoring for an autograph.

Jack sat outside watching the throng for nearly an hour, and didn't see a single other foreigner; for all its glamour, Atami definitely catered to an all-Japanese crowd. He tried to imagine how an American English teacher in this otherwise very Japanese resort might meet and become involved with an important visitor. "Atami has everything—the sun, the moon, and the stars," the Yakuza kingpin had explained. "That is why people come to play here during the day and during the night."

Shannon had had an interest in Japanese art, and Mrs. Taniguchi said she spent a lot of time at an art museum in town; perhaps she had met an artist or made a friend there. She had also apparently been something of a fanatic about learning Japanese, and had used her time in Atami to perfect her command of the language. He wondered if she had taken lessons or found a second job that gave her a chance to practice speaking and writing with native speakers.

The Yakuza chief had denied that Shannon had ever returned to the Club Rendezvous, but he had also said that Jack was on the right track. And Jack had seen for himself how foreigners were prized as exotic attractions. If Barbara Gordon brought in patrons, young Shannon would have been a bonanza. Had Shannon wandered into another nightclub besides the Club Rendezvous? From everything he knew of her and of her job at the school, that didn't seem very likely.

In the back of his mind Jack felt that he was missing a crucial connection—a solution that would grow logically out of what he knew about Shannon and her interests and abilities. But the more he thought about it, the more teasingly it eluded him, and he always found himself returning to practical decisions like which hotels to try after lunch, and whether to poke around the art museum before beginning a systematic investigation of the dozens of nightclubs by the waterfront.

Just as Jack was preparing to leave the restaurant, he spotted Eric Gleason walking along the promenade. He waved, and the young American's acne-pocked face turned in his direction. Gleason hurried over, his owlish features twisting into an angry scowl as he reached Jack's table. "Hi," Jack said.

A long, cold silence. "You got nerve, waving me over."

"What do you mean?"

"You think I can't guess who was behind it?"

"Behind what?"

"Oh, come off it. I cooperated with you, didn't I? Answered all your questions. So I don't see why you had to have them search my apartment when I was out. Fucking cops."

"I didn't—"

"You think I couldn't tell someone had gone through my stuff?" The young American teacher was so furious, it took him several seconds to get his voice back under control. "Whoever you used was just a little clumsy about putting my things back in the right places. The neighbors wouldn't talk, but some of their little kids saw it happen. 'A bunch of men in a van'—sounds a lot like cops, doesn't it? Thanks for setting me up."

"I really didn't—"

"Sure you didn't. You cops are all the same." He turned and stalked off, hurrying away in fast, indignant steps.

Jack paid an exorbitant amount for the modest cheeseburger, his mind turning over the new information. So someone—presumably the Japanese police—had followed up on his lead. When he had talked to Eric Gleason at Atami High School, only three other people—Misako, Principal Kobayashi, and Mr. Endo—had been in the room. One of them had reported back to the Atami police. Had it been Misako? Had she been assigned to him to spy on him? He remembered her visiting him in his hospital room, remembered the honesty in her eyes and the genuine concern she had seemed to have for him. No, he believed her. But the whole thing was suspicious. Feeling uneasy and wondering whether the Japanese police had found anything belonging to Shannon in their search of Eric's apartment, Jack set off for another round of hotel interviews.

He started at the New Fujiya with its mirrored lobby, progressed to the Kanto, which featured pictures in the lobby of its famous gold-plated hot baths, then in rapid succession went to the Ishkawa Gardens, the Riyo, the Mikawa, the Moon Shadow, the Higashi, the Queen Pearl, the Palace, and finished up in the late afternoon at the Marusei with its marble pilasters and rooftop bar. No one recognized Shannon's picture, and Jack didn't get even the faintest hint that anyone was lying or hiding information.

He went back to his own hotel feeling tired and frustrated, had dinner and several bottles of beer brought to his room, watched some Japanese baseball and an absurd TV game show, and finally went to bed early feeling angry and frustrated. His sore ribs ached from a day of continuous walking, and he felt he had exhausted his best shot without turning up even the faintest glimmer of a lead.

Jack lay on his back, his head resting on the hard pillow while he stared up into pitch darkness, and tried to figure his next move. He felt that he had made no real progress in the case since coming to Atami, yet, as the Yakuza kingpin had pointed out, someone had resorted to violence to try to scare him off. So he must be close to something. Using that same strange yardstick to measure progress in an investigation, Walter must have been even closer, since he wasn't scared or warned but summarily killed.

Jack tried to replay in his mind his last few conversations with Walter, when the old detective had told him about the progress he had made so far in the Miles case. It was no use. At that time, Jack's concentration had been focused on the question of why his father had asked him to come to Los Angeles. Thinking back, Jack couldn't recall anything that seemed valuable. They had talked during lunch; they had talked on their way to play catch. Then they had fought in the bar and driven home in silence, and Jack had held back an apology and watched the old man walk away from him, his shoulders moving back and forth, in and out of shadow. And then, the next morning, the knock at his hotel room's door and the news about his father.

Koshijutsu, the Yakuza boss had called it—a lost *ninja* art of attacking by paralyzing nerve centers. It seemed utterly fantastic, yet Jack had felt the steely fingers dig into his own flesh, had felt his own strong body grow instantly rigid.

Jack lay in the darkness feeling Walter's presence suddenly very close all around him. Walter would have known what to do next—he had relied on instincts and followed hunches and had a natural nose for the chase. Closing his eyes, Jack could almost smell the smoke from Walter's Marlboros in the dark room and hear the hacking cough that had shaken Walter's body on the last day of his life. Jack appealed to his father's specter for inspiration, but the ghostly presence furnished no answers.

Jack slept fitfully, waking several times to find himself all twisted up in the futon bedding. He dreamed of his mother as he remembered her from his earliest childhood—a beautiful young woman with the lissome body of a dancer and a sad and gentle voice that coaxed him to sleep every night with half-whispered Irish lullabies. Around four o'clock Jack found himself wide-awake, and after trying every possible sleeping position with no success, he got up and began to dress.

It was pitch-dark out when he left the hotel. The streets of Atami were chill, quiet, and completely empty. Streetlights threw cones of light like tiny squid nets down through the night mist. He walked aimlessly, thinking of his parents buried side by side in the family plot in Rose Hills, resting quietly together in death as they never had in life. He remembered his old grandfather all alone in his white house by the Chickahominy, and recalled his request for great-grandchildren and his admonition that men weren't supposed to go through their thirties on their own.

By the time his grandfather had turned thirty-three, he had already won a Purple Heart, been married for more than a decade, and fathered four children. By the time Walter had turned thirty-three, he had been married for six years, fought in Korea, lost a decision for the California middleweight championship, and fathered Jack. Walter had died one day short of sixty years; Jack was now thirty-three, and if more than half of his own years on earth had already been spent, he wondered just what he had really accomplished.

He had worked hard at the Bureau, but few if any of the cases had meant anything to him personally. He had shared good times with many women, but never found one whom he could truly say he loved, and had never made one love him back with that depth of force and certainty he had occasionally witnessed in the courtships and eventual marriages of some of his Dartmouth friends. He had helped bring no bright-faced children into the world.

Rather, his contributions, such as they were, seemed to all be negative. Again and again angry and disappointed girlfriends had accused him of having wasted their time, and told him he was incapable of giving and receiving love. With excruciating clarity Jack remembered Kate as she had looked that last night in Georgetown, her long auburn hair in disarray, her green eyes glittering with fury, as she had damned him for making her feel so good and then disappeared out his doorway into the rain and out of his life forever.

He had thrown himself into his career and succeeded beyond others of his age and training, but walking these dark streets alone, he keenly felt how shallow professional achievement was when considered next to a true exchange of love and the slow building and maintaining of a family.

He had lost a father without ever telling him that he loved him. Year after year in Washington, Jack had clung to childhood pain and adolescent grudges, never stopping to think that nearly a decade had passed since his mother's death and that maybe it was time to forgive and forget; maybe it was up to him to find the generosity of spirit to reach out and hug Walter to him, and to thank him for bringing him into the world.

Instead, Walter had been the one to reach out. Alone on the dark street, Jack had some sense of how hard it must have been for Walter to write to him, and then to cut through decades of silence and gruff masculine posturing and try to express his love. He remembered sitting next to Walter in the dimly lit Santa Monica bar, watching the old man almost wince as he forced out the words "I love you." How very desperately Walter must have needed the reassurance that, for all his faults, his only child loved him and wished him well. Instead, Walter had heard a harsh, derisive laugh as a reply. Jack speeded up, and his footsteps rang hollowly off the pavement.

Around Jack the sleeping Japanese city was silent and dreary.

The white buildings on the hunched hills floated in and out of wispy vapor, a shimmering phantasmagoria of a backdrop for his sleepless melancholy. This was an old city in an ancient land—a millennium ago, people had walked above this same bay, grown rice and oranges in the same valleys and flats, and been buried beneath the same rocky earth.

The silence Jack fractured with his quick footsteps seemed as deeply rooted as the cedar trees that dotted the lower slopes, and the old graveyards with their crumbling stones and the temples shrouded in night mist and antiquity gave the sleeping city its own sense of dark mystery, far more layered than any riddle Jack had come to Japan to try to unravel. He drew his jacket tighter around his neck as the mist grew so thick, he felt he must be walking through the center of a cloud. For a few seconds even the streetlights failed to pierce the cold miasma, and Jack stood still, holding his breath and thinking of his father's unshaven, deeply lined face and weary blue eyes. Then Jack began to run blindly, almost madly.

As the sky began to grow lighter, Jack found himself down by the ocean, pounding along the same promenade he had lunched near the previous day. Now it was completely empty and dark except for rainbow patches where colored neon from hotel signs flickered across the stones. He stopped by a steel railing and stood there gasping, as the orange sun slowly poked its head above the hills. A chill shook him from chest to spine, and then he had it.

Sunrise.

"Atami has everything—the sun, the moon, and the stars," the Yakuza boss had said. At the time Jack had dismissed it as meaningless, a throwaway expression in a conversation featuring many colorful and no doubt awkwardly translated figures of speech. Now Jack remembered that among the hotels he had visited the previous day were the Sunrise Hotel and the Moon Shadow. "Atami has everything, the sun, the moon, and the stars." He had already visited the sun and the moon and come away empty-handed. Somewhere, in this city that was beginning to wake up to a new dawn, Jack knew he needed to find a star.

At nine o'clock, when the visitor information office opened up, prompt to the very minute posted outside, Jack was the first through the door. "Ohayo gozaimasu, ohayo gozaimasu," the young women said in chorus, striking the low bows and voicing the high-pitched greetings reserved for the first guest of the day.

"Hi," Jack said to the only young woman who spoke English. "A friend of mine recommended a hotel in Atami. I can't remember the exact name of the place, but I think it was 'Star' or at least had the word 'Star' in it."

"Like movie star?"

"Yes."

She thought for a long moment and then shook her head.

"You're sure?"

"Yes."

"What about a hotel not in Atami but on the outskirts? Or even in a nearby town?"

She shook her head.

"It might not be exactly 'Star.' It might be 'starlight' or 'starburst' or anything having the word 'star' in it."

"Sorry," she said. "There is no such hotel. Can I recommend another one? We have many good hotels."

Jack did his best to hide his disappointment, thanked her, and left the tourist information office. He was half a block away when he heard her calling him and turned to see her hurrying in his direction. "Excuse me," she said, "excuse me. After you left, my office manager asked me what you wanted. So I told him. And he says that there was a famous hotel in Atami called the Star, but the owners changed about seven years ago, and they gave it a new name. Now it is the Okawa. On the south side of the city, near Atami Castle. If you want, we can make a reservation for you."

"Don't bother," Jack told her, doing a much better job of hiding his elation than he had a few minutes before of hiding his disappointment. "If it got a new name seven years ago, it can't be the one my friend stayed at and recommended to me. He must've gotten the name wrong. Anyway, thanks for trying to help me."

She turned back toward the office, and Jack set off southward at a brisk pace, the night's doubts suddenly forgotten, replaced by a growing excitement. It took him twenty minutes to reach the Okawa, a large, elegant-looking hotel surrounded by gardens, and flanked by a small stream that ran down from the nearby hills with enough force to spill near the hotel into a glittering fifteen-foot waterfall.

Jack approached the front door and then stopped and turned into the garden at the last possible minute. He headed for the waterfall, and stood there in thought for a few moments. If the Yakuza kingpin had been giving him a veiled hint by mentioning the sun, moon, and stars, then whatever had happened at the Okawa (formerly Star) Hotel had also happened at the Atami Sunrise Hotel and the Moon Shadow. He had drawn complete blanks at the other two. Perhaps at this last one, he'd better play it differently and call in some expert help.

But could he trust her? Jack recalled his doubts about who had told the Japanese police to search Eric Gleason's apartment. It was a difficult decision, but he needed help and he decided to go with his instincts. He would call Misako, he would work with her, but he would also watch her carefully.

Several hundred yards down the street from the hotel, at the foot of the road branching off to Atami Castle and the museum of cultural pornography, Jack found a public phone. He took the business card Misako had given him from his wallet, and dialed the home number she had written in black pen on the back of the card. She answered on the fifth ring. She sounded glad to hear from him, but when he asked her to come and help him, she refused. "I really can't. Captain Sato was very definite."

Her reluctant refusal made him trust her more. He told her about his abduction by the Yakuza at the Club Rendezvous, about his fruitless inquiries at so many hotels, and how he had ultimately made the connection between the Sun, the Moon, and a hotel that had been called the Star when Shannon had lived in Atami. The news excited her, but she still hedged on coming. He begged and cajoled and flirted for several minutes before she cautiously agreed to help him.

Ten minutes later her red Toyota pulled over to the shoulder of the winding shoreline road, and he climbed in. She was dressed casually, in tight-fitting jeans and a lavender blouse, and her hair was loose. "Hi," she said.

"Thanks for coming."

They exchanged smiles and she swung the car out into the street. "I shouldn't be doing this," she said. "I don't want them to know I'm a police officer." She pulled into the parking lot of the hotel. "I'm just here to translate for you. Okay?"

"Sure," Jack agreed, opening his door and getting out, "whatever you want."

The Okawa was like many of the other grand hotels Jack had

visited in town except that it seemed a bit more traditionally Japanese, and perhaps a bit emptier. The gardens surrounding the hotel were all but deserted, and the vast lobby had the feel of an empty athletic stadium. Doormen and car parkers in dark livery and maids in white skirts and blouses stood for the most part idle. In the right corner of the lobby there was a restaurant area and a gift shop with postcards, while in the left corner a small art gallery and exhibition area looked out over the garden.

The desk attendant in the lobby listened to Misako for ten seconds and then bowed and rang for the manager, who soon hurried up, looking fastidious in a dark suit. The process of introduction, explanation, and finally inquiry that Jack had laboriously stumbled through so many times the day before was repeated once again, this time much more quickly and in Japanese. The manager examined Shannon's picture and shook his head; he called in several higher staff members, who also did not recognize the photograph; finally he brought the photo back to Misako and offered free cups of tea or coffee if they would like.

It was an off hour in the restaurant, after breakfast and not quite lunch, and they had the large dining room to themselves. Jack sat facing Misako, looking out the door of the restaurant across the lobby. "I would go back with you to the other two hotels, but it seems pointless," Misako said. "The same people who talked to you would talk to me. They would say the same things. After so many years, even if Shannon had gone to their hotels, they might not remember her. Perhaps the fact that there was a Star Hotel in Atami was just a coincidence after all."

"Is it a common Japanese expression, to say that a city has the sun, the moon, and the stars?"

"No, not common," she admitted. "But who knows what expressions the Yakuza use? If he wanted to tell you something, why didn't he just tell you?"

Jack didn't have a good answer for that one. He looked down into his teacup, and then glanced through the door, across the lobby, into the small art gallery. An old woman sat at an easel working with great concentration. "Misako," Jack said, and pointed.

She looked, but didn't understand.

"Come." He walked quickly across the lobby, Misako trailing a few steps behind. The old woman glanced up at their approach and smiled. She was at least seventy and very probably over eighty, with thousands of tiny wrinkles widening out over her forehead and cheeks. She looked very frail perched on a thick cushion with a blanket over her legs, but her right hand, which held the paintbrush, was perfectly steady. Before her on the easel was a half-finished landscape similar in style to the dozens of small and large ones that hung on the walls all around her.

For a long minute she smiled up at them, and Jack returned her smile. Then he reached into his pocket and fished out the picture of Shannon. Moving slowly and deliberately, the old woman put down her brush and took the picture from him, holding it in the light to see it better. Then she handed it back to him and said something in Japanese.

Jack looked at Misako, whose face showed surprise.

"She said, it's not a good picture of Shannon," Misako whispered. "She said Shannon looks sad in this picture, but she was almost always happy."

"Tell her who we are and ask her how she knows Shannon."

Misako did so, speaking slowly and politely, and the old woman nodded and spoke back. "She says its dangerous to speak to police sometimes, especially when you don't have a good reason to do so. She says, if you like her work, why don't you buy a painting?"

"Which one?" Jack asked the old woman in English.

She reached out toward a large framed picture of a mountain valley, and Jack took it down off the wall. She named a sum, and Jack counted it out without protest, even though it was several hundred dollars in American money. As the old woman took the money from him, she spoke in a low voice.

"She says, once she has talked to us, we must leave the hotel and never return."

Jack nodded at the old woman, promising her with his eyes.

"She says, Shannon came to this hotel to translate for some big-shot businessmen who were staying here. One of them was a man named Ida, and the other was named Miura. They were friends, and both had business interests in the United States, so they needed Shannon to translate letters and documents into natural English. Many times when Shannon came, she stopped here and asked questions about landscape art. She says Shannon was a very nice girl, and that we have to go now and never come back."

Jack bowed to the old woman. "Tell her I like the painting very much."

Misako did so, and received a reply. "She says, she did it from memory. It is a valley near Shuzenji where she used to play when she was a little girl. She says to you good luck, and please go now."

Jack immediately headed out of the hotel, painting in hand, trying to look as if nothing had happened. It was only outside, a block from the Okawa, that he dared talk to Misako about what they had found out. "It fits. I've been trying for days to figure out how Shannon would have met someone in Atami. She was the only American in the city, and her Japanese was superb. If someone needed something translated into English, she'd have been the best person."

Misako suggested going back to the Sunrise Hotel and the Moon Shadow, and within half an hour they were able to ascertain that a Mr. Ida and a Mr. Miura had been frequent guests of both hotels a decade ago. The hotel managers claimed they didn't know much about the two men beyond remembering their names, and that they came to Atami fairly often, usually together, and were both very rich. Both hotel managers repeated their former claims not to recognize Shannon.

The names Ida and Miura struck a chord with Misako. She was sure she had heard them recently, mentioned together, in a context she couldn't now remember. Oddly enough, for his part, Jack felt the same thing. Finally Misako told him that the only way to clear this up was for her to go to the police station and punch the names into the computer there, and that she would tell Jack the minute she found out anything.

He was too excited to return to his hotel room and just wait for her, so she dropped him off at a pachinko parlor several blocks from the station and promised to come right back as soon as she learned anything.

17

The old artist in the gallery of the Okawa Hotel left the lobby as she did at noon every day to drink her tea and eat her lunch on the terrace. She was sitting above the garden in a secluded corner, nibbling a rice ball, when a blow from behind caught her on the back of the head with enough force to nearly knock her off the terrace.

She regained consciousness in one of the small storage rooms in the subbasement of the hotel. The hotel manager, a man whom she had never seen before clad in a gray suit, and a very tall and magnificently built man dressed completely in black with eyes that seemed empty of any human emotion, looked down on her. She tried to move and realized that she was tied to a chair. A gag hadn't been necessary—the small room had no windows, and the basement walls were so thick, no sound could possibly filter up to the hotel guests.

"What did you tell the American?" the man in the gray suit asked her.

She slowly shook her head. "Nothing. He bought a painting."

He slapped her face so hard, it made her ears ring, and for a second she thought she might blank again. But her vision slowly cleared and she saw him bending down low over her. "He didn't come to the hotel to buy art. What did you tell him?"

"Nothing." She shook her head, her eyes filling with tears from the blow and from fear. "Nothing. Please. I'm an old woman. Please . . ."

The man in the suit nodded to the big man in black, who approached her slowly. He seemed to glide rather than walk—she had never seen anyone move quite that way. His hair was cut short in a military-style haircut, and his build was so perfect, it disguised his height and size a little bit. She hadn't realized just how big he was till he stood next to her, looking down with his cold eyes. He reached down to her right hand, which was tied to the arm of the chair, and coiled his large fist around her pinky. With a slow, steady wrench he bent her finger back toward her knuckle.

It was her right hand—the hand she held the paintbrush with. She screamed, a single vibrating wail of pain and protest that went on for thirty seconds or so till the finger broke and she began sobbing.

The man in black took hold of her second finger.

She looked up at him, pleadingly, and saw nothing to plead with—it was like searching for light in a cave.

"What did you tell them?" the man in the suit demanded.

The pain was such that she could only whimper.

The man in black broke her second finger at the joint, and then her middle finger, which snapped in midbone with a surprising popping sound. Her screams contorted her face so that she seemed to almost rise out of the chair.

The same question came again, softly, almost sweetly through the layers of pain. "What did you tell them?"

"Please, oh God, please, oh God . . ."

Her index finger was bent again. And back. It snapped like a winter twig, and hung at a disjointed angle. Her thumb gave the man in black pause for a second, but he adjusted his grip and pushed till the wide joint—slightly swollen from arthritis—gave way.

Her screams ebbed to loud, pained breaths as her head fell over her chest. The man in the suit took her by her hair and lifted her head up so that she faced him. "Listen, old woman," he said. "This is your last chance. What did you tell them?"

Even through the cloud of pain she understood his words, understood what she was being threatened with. "Nothing," she said, and saw his face harden. "I told them the girl used to translate for Ida and Miura. Years ago. That's all. Please, God . . ."

"Reward her for her cooperation," the man in the suit grunted. The big man in black who had broken her fingers squatted down in front of her and looked into her eyes, and she whispered to him, "I have a son in Niigata your age. Please, God . . ."

Then he stepped around behind her, interlocked his fingers so that his palms formed a firm cup beneath her chin, and began slowly and evenly to twist her head around. The hotel manager turned away and vomited in a corner, but the man in the suit continued to watch, fascinated.

In the lobby of the hotel, maids were already removing the landscapes from the walls. An appointment had been made later in the day for a contractor to come in and see about remodeling the gallery space as a souvenir shop.

One look at Misako's face told Jack that she had struck gold. He got into the car without speaking, and she drove off. He could sense her excitement, and he had to force himself not to press her with questions while she navigated the car quickly onto side streets that led up into the less populated hills. Finally, on a steep, rocky stretch of hillside, she pulled the car onto the shoulder and turned to him. "I found Ida and Miura in our computer records."

"Who are they? Do you know where they are now?"

"Yes," she said. "Together."

"Together where?"

She looked down the long slope at the blue bay where a single sailboat glided like a swan before the noon breeze. "They were both murdered, a week apart. Masao Ida was killed first, in the garden of his villa in Shimoda. Then Kenji Miura was poisoned in his favorite restaurant in Tokyo. In both cases, the killer left marks just like that one." And she pointed to the scar on Jack's cheek.

"And, let me guess, in both cases the National Police took over the investigation?"

"Yes."

"Lieutenant Sasaki?"

She nodded.

"What did Ida and Miura do?"

"Masao Ida was the president of Ida Computer Industries—ICI. It's a well-known company with an excellent reputation. Kenji Miura was the president of Dai-Sei Technologies, a very profitable innovator in computer hardware. Both men had extensive ties to computer companies in the United States."

Jack punched the glove compartment so hard, he almost cracked the door. She looked at him as if he must be mad, but he was smiling broadly at her. "That's it," he said. "I knew I had heard at least Ida's name before, but I couldn't remember where. My father mentioned Ida Computer Industries on the way to a ball field to play catch, on the day he died. Dr. Everett Miles had done consulting work there. I never heard of the other guy, Miura, but I have heard of his company, Dai-Sei Technologies. It was another Japanese computer firm that Dr. Miles had worked for. My father was looking into the connections. . . .''

''And then he was killed,'' Misako said, sounding just a bit frightened for the first time since Jack had known her.

''Yes.''

''What should we do?''

''You don't have to do anything,'' he told her. ''Just go back home and pretend nothing's happened. I'll take things from here. I've got more than I need now.''

''But we haven't solved anything. . . .''

''We don't need to solve it. All we have to do is be able to prove that there's a connection between the deaths, and that there's been a cover-up. If the Japanese don't want to listen, I know people in Washington, D.C., I can turn to. One way or another, I've got enough now to force a real investigation. As for Lieutenant Sasaki and Captain Sato and a guy named Captain Charles in Los Angeles, I'll go right over their heads. . . .''

He stopped talking when he saw the way she was looking at him, and then he smiled, and suddenly they both laughed out loud at the same moment.

''It was a nice speech,'' she said. ''Very impressive. Please finish.''

''C'mere, you,'' he muttered, sliding closer to her. His left hand snaked around her back.

''No,'' she whispered, but she did not pull away. When their faces were less than an inch apart, he felt the puff of her breath warmly on his lips. ''Yes.''

Their lips met, and for a long second she did not respond to the gentle inquiry of his kiss. Then she kissed him back, and the fingers of her right hand came up to caress his cheek. Her breath was warm and her lips were so soft, they seemed to melt into his own. She reached down and pushed a button on the CD player, and some lushly layered classical music began. Jack wasn't sure whether it was Ravel or Debussy, but whoever had composed it, it fit the moment perfectly.

''I'm afraid our professional relationship is over,'' Misako whispered.

"Is that a bad thing?"

"Shameful." She ran her hand slowly through his hair, messing it up. "What do your friends call you?"

"Jack."

"Don't you have a nickname?"

"What's wrong with Jack?"

"Nothing," she said, finding some stubble on the scarred side of his chin, which he hadn't shaved for a while, and rubbing the back of her hand over it. With great gentleness she turned her hand over and used her index finger to trace the outline of his scar. "What did your friends call you in college?"

"Jack."

"In high school?"

He put his lips to her ear and whispered through the soft curtain of hair. "Buster."

"Why?"

"I was fighting Golden Gloves. My nose got broken twice."

She drew back. "Why did you keep fighting?"

"My father made me."

"I'll call you Jack."

"You can call me anything you want," he told her, kissing her lips and her chin, and then moving on down her throat. She tilted back her head and shut her eyes. The music got faster and they began to touch each other, gently. Up till this encounter, he had wondered if perhaps she was a cold woman, or if she just didn't like men. Now he saw that quite the reverse was true.

Her breathing grew louder and louder till Jack thought she might come right there in the front seat just from kissing and petting. Their sense of mutual accomplishment at what they had uncovered and their shared fear and uncertainty over what might lie ahead gave the moment of sudden intimacy electric charges of danger and triumph. Her fingers explored his neck and shoulders. She opened her mouth, and their tongues touched, and touched again, and began a cautious dance.

Suddenly a shiver ran through her body. He pulled back and looked at her. Surprising vulnerability showed clearly for a second in her glittering black eyes. "Hold me tight," she requested in a whisper.

He held her so tightly that his biceps tensed to form a protective cage around her, his lips kissing her soft neck and then climbing to whisper in her right ear, ''Good?''

''Good,'' she whispered back.

Around them the afternoon shadows slowly lengthened as the sun began its slow descent toward the bay that sparkled brightly at the foot of the hunched hills. The single sailboat, now halfway to Hatsushima, tacked about and headed home, its white sails falling slack at the turn and then filling suddenly with a strong shoreward breeze.

18

The assassin let himself into Jack's room and closed and locked the door behind him. He wondered if Jack would bring the woman back with him. If so, it would be all the better; he could get them both at once. If not, he would take care of her later that evening. Then this whole business would finally be over, and he could go on his oft-delayed vacation.

They were paying him a great deal for his services, but even so, he was glad to finish. Lately, things had gotten sloppy and poor judgment had been shown, and he hated poor judgment far worse than inefficiency or even outright weakness. He had been against the attack in the alley all along. It had been stupid and ill conceived—he had felt that no matter what injuries he inflicted, the American wouldn't be scared off, that the beating would almost certainly stiffen his determination to push forward.

Anyhow, now that the American had made the Ida-Miura connection, the decision that should have been made long ago had become unavoidable. They wanted it to look like a Yakuza hit—lots of stab wounds and blood everywhere. In addition to his usual short sword, he had brought along two longer ones so that the stab wounds would not all match—the aesthetics of this bloody assignment were by far its most intriguing feature. He had even briefly toyed with the idea of decapitating the American and taking the head with him—he could dispose of it later at his leisure and have the rare treat of eating the eyes. He had finally decided that taking the head might be going too far; they wanted it to be bloody, but not, perhaps, quite so sensational.

The assassin made a quick but thorough reconnaissance of the hotel room, checking to make sure that there were no hidden weapons. It was good that the American hadn't been able to bring a gun into Japan. Not that a gun would have presented a serious problem, but his not having one made matters that much simpler.

The assassin chose a futon closet as the best place to hide, and took his killing sword out of its sheath so that when the moment came, there would be no delay or sounds of metal rattling on metal. He could take the other swords out after the attack, when the killing was finished and it was time for the art direction.

Jack returned to his room several hours later, whistling the theme song from *Casablanca*, ''As Time Goes By.'' After the attack in the alley, he had adopted a crude safety precaution to see if anyone had entered his room while he was out. Before leaving, he carefully placed five hairs in the tatami floor seams near the door. Now, returning, he stopped whistling just long enough to check the hairs. They were all in place.

He ran the bath and undressed slowly, in the main room, moving his arms in experimental circles to see how much pain and stiffness there was in his ribs. He was much better than the last time he had tried it. He took off his pants and shadowboxed for a few seconds in his briefs, throwing lazy left jabs and straight rights as he moved around on the tatami in his bare feet. His punches still wouldn't hurt a twelve-year-old, but he was getting stronger, there was no doubt about it.

He headed into the bathing alcove and dipped his foot in the bathwater. It was as hot as he could stand it. He climbed into the small Japanese tub, his knees up near his chest, his arms spread out on either side of the back rim.

There were only two questions. One was who to talk to first about the connection between Ida, Miura, the Mileses, and the man who had cut his face in the alley. He was tempted to call MacCormack right away, but perhaps he should wait till tomorrow and report what he had learned to the FBI contact at the American embassy. He played with the idea of also turning what he knew over to a major Japanese newspaper. It would be interesting to see what effect national publicity and big headlines would have on Chief Sato, Lieutenant Sasaki, and whoever was controlling them.

The second question was what to do about Misako. He was keenly aware of how little he really knew about her, and her dreams and goals and plans. He did know that Atami was her home and that she was almost fanatically dedicated to her job, which didn't bode well for any kind of a long-term relationship.

Jack settled back in the tub and forced himself to relax. Right now they were both happy, and that was enough. Probably the best thing to do was just to stop worrying about it for the time being and enjoy a much-needed bit of happiness. He took several deep breaths and closed his eyes.

The assassin was very tempted to make his move when Jack first entered the room. He stood up in the closet, hand on sword hilt, and listened as Jack broke off the refrain from ''As Time Goes By'' to check the hairs on the tatami matting. Standing in the dark, the assassin shook his head slightly at the absurd amateurishness of the safety precaution. Perhaps it had come from a James Bond movie or some cheap paperback detective novel.

Jack ran the bathwater, and the assassin heard him walk back into the outer room. Next he would probably start undressing. Would he come to the closet to hang up his jacket? If so, it would be so very easy to slash his neck as he opened the door, inflicting a mortal wound and at the same time silencing him by severing the trachea. Once the American could no longer scream, the assassin could proceed to the more artistic touches demanded by this particular assignment. To get the desired ''blood on the walls'' effect, it would be most expedient to cut the main arteries in rapid succession.

But Jack did not go to the closet. The assassin heard the rustle of a jacket being hung on the back of a chair, and then a shirt being drawn off and tossed carelessly down on the tatami. Next came the sounds of some sort of physical exercise or calisthenic that went on for a minute or so and then stopped. There were no footsteps during the exercise, so the assassin surmised that it was something having to do with the arms; probably the injured ribs were giving him trouble.

Next, one foot thumped down on the matting and then the other, and a second soft thud sounded as a pair of pants joined the shirt on the floor. From the short, sliding steps back and forth across the tatami, and the paced breathing and the snapping of the arms, the assassin knew the American had begun shadowboxing. In its own way, it was rather amusing. When the sliding footsteps were very close to the closet, the assassin was tempted to burst out with a yell and deliver a death blow. Yet still he kept himself back, waiting.

The sliding footsteps stopped as the American walked back toward the bathing alcove. The assassin heard the splash of body entering bathwater and frowned with distaste. In many ways, foreigners really were barbarians. Imagine not taking the time to rinse off, but getting into perfectly clean bathwater still covered with dirt and sweat! Then the American began to sing.

At first the assassin couldn't make out the words. Something about a river. An old man river. Finally he caught the word "Mississippi" and began to understand a bit of the refrain. Timing his movements to coincide with the loudest words in the refrain, the assassin pushed open the closet door and stepped out into the empty bedroom. The plain hilt of his short sword rested easily in his right palm. Old Man River might indeed keep rolling along, but this American, with his deep voice and disgusting bathing habits, would not be sweating and straining much longer.

During his reconnaissance of the hotel suite, the assassin had noted that the mirror in the bathroom was angled in such a way that it provided a reflected view of the short hallway from the bedroom to the bathing alcove. That was unfortunate, but certainly not a serious problem. By keeping low and moving fast, he believed he could remain almost completely out of the angle of view. If the American happened to be looking up, all he would see would be a quick flash at the very bottom of the mirror. And by then it would be far too late.

At the very worst, the American might manage a frightened scream. Since the hotel owner had cooperated by vacating all the surrounding suites, screams shouldn't be a problem. Still, the assassin wanted this job to be quick and quiet. He stood just outside the short hallway to the bathing alcove, listening to the American sing and preparing himself for the kill. When Jack began a new verse—something about getting tired and sick of trying—the assassin took a final breath and flashed forward into the hallway, his body bent over double and less than two feet off the floor, his sword out ahead of him.

As he sped down the hall, the assassin registered that Jack had suddenly stopped singing. His mind functioned with such complete clarity during an attack that even as he moved toward the bathing alcove with tremendous speed, he could see and think about what was taking place around him as if it were happening in slow motion. He heard the American moving inside the tub, splashing, perhaps trying to stand up. The assassin reached the doorway to the bathing alcove and darted through, his fingers tightening on the sword hilt.

The American was standing naked in the tub, a small black gun in his hands. Even as he dodged sideways with tremendous speed, the assassin's mind was trying to figure out how Jack had gotten a gun in Japan without any informants knowing about it, and why he had bothered to bring it with him while taking a bath. When he was six feet away, he lunged forward with the sword, in a dodging, twisting flash. In the half world of slow motion time, he saw the American's trigger finger tighten. . . .

Ever since Walter had pulled a gun on him in the shower and then told him the story about his friend in the narcotics division who had gotten wasted on the can, Jack had never felt completely safe in a bath. In this hotel suite in Japan, Jack had gotten into the habit of throwing occasional glances at the bottom part of the mirror that reflected a view of the hallway. When he caught the flash of movement in the brass strip at the very bottom, he was surprised to find himself already moving as if by instinct, standing and at the same time reaching for the pistol the Yakuza kingpin had given him.

He flicked off the safety catch and began to raise the barrel just as a man dressed completely in black flew through the doorway toward him at incredible speed. Walter's specter had not directly helped Jack before, but as he moved the gun toward the twisting target, an unearthly calmness took hold of him so that he seemed to be aiming and shooting at the same time, guided by instincts that needed no conscious thoughts to direct them.

The first shot went directly through the center of the man in black's forehead, yet the attacker did not stop or even drop his sword. Jack fired again, and saw an eye explode into red pulp as a bullet tore apart the right side of his attacker's face, yet still he came on. Jack pressed himself against the back wall of the bath and fired again, shooting for the heart and seeing the body in black jerk to one side as the bullet tore into his chest. Still the man in black came on, much more slowly, his sword raised slightly to strike downward.

Jack realized that he was not up against a human, because when you shoot a human through the forehead, he keels over, but bullets had no effect on this thing that still came toward him. He fired one final time as the sword came down, hitting the man in black in the neck, and then the sword cut Jack's shoulder, a deep flesh wound but not more than that, as the man in black pitched forward and toppled over, his head striking the side of the tub and then thumping down on the stone floor. The curious-looking short sword splashed into Jack's bath, and sank beneath the water that was already starting to turn bloodred.

The man in black lay still on the floor for a long second. Suddenly he rose up almost to his knees, his magnificently muscled arms and shoulders jerked once, spasmodically, and his right fist punched a large hole in the bathroom's tile wall while his left hand tore a chunk out of the bathtub. He fell back to the floor and lay unmoving, the remaining part of his face fixed in a final grimace of pure, savage fury.

19

The trip itself was fraught with danger—they were having a hard enough time keeping her alive on Shikoku. For weeks she had been living under the shadow of death, moving constantly from town to town and house to house, never sleeping for more than a night or two in the same place. That she had endured this and managed to sustain the struggle and even strengthen the resistance was acknowledged by both friends and foes as a remarkable accomplishment. Her closest advisers told her that setting foot on Honshu was almost tantamount to suicide, but she stared back at them with such quiet determination in her eyes that they set about planning the least dangerous route.

A convoy of jeeps took her over back roads and rough terrain to Naruto, where a speedboat waited. The boat made the crossing in darkness, hugging the west shore of Awaji Island and setting her down with several bodyguards outside of Akashi just before sunrise. Limousines were waiting at the appointed spot. At the sight of the cars, her advisers made one last desperate argument for turning back. Once she got in the cars, they told her, she would be beyond the reach of those who had worked for her husband and who now loved and followed her. Etsuko heard out their arguments, and then, without speaking, walked to the nearest limousine and climbed inside.

Since she had spent weeks leading the underground existence of a fugitive, it was perhaps fitting that the meeting took place in a converted bomb shelter on the outskirts of Kobe. This location was not selected for security reasons—Kobe was a Yakuza stronghold, and the Inagawa had nothing to fear from anyone within the city limits. They were, however, just as anxious that her trip to Honshu remain a secret as she was, so the meeting was held thirty meters beneath the ground in a small, comfortable room.

According to prearranged agreements, she could bring two armed bodyguards with her, but at the last second she decided that such a precaution would serve no practical purpose—if they meant her ill, two bodyguards would not save her; all they would signify was fear and therefore weakness. So she left her bodyguards in the limousines and walked on alone, a single woman descending a steep and narrow stairway in the company of men she did not know or particularly trust.

She wore dark clothes and, for symbolic reasons, a traditional *haramaki*—a length of cotton cloth wound around and around the stomach in samurai times to deflect the thrust of an assassin's blade when entering an enemy camp. The two men who escorted her down the flight of steps stopped at a steel door. One of them held the door open for her—then they took up positions outside the door as she walked through a short hall and through a second door into the meeting room.

The subterranean meeting room had an aristocratic plushness, almost like the smoking room of a British private club. The heavy armchairs were upholstered with dark leather—burgundy and ox-blood—that matched the rosewood paneling. The two men in the room rose out of their chairs at her entrance. Bows were exchanged. They all sat down and there was a long, respectful silence.

One of the men was over ninety and kept silent throughout the meeting. Occasionally he opened his mouth as if to speak, but only licked his dry old lips with the tip of his tongue and went back to listening.

The crime czar himself was sixtyish and silver-haired, and impeccably attired in a dark European business suit. A single thin scar ran down the right side of his face almost to his chin and gave his debonair handsomeness a slightly dark and mysterious dash. He broke the silence first. "I am glad that you had a safe journey."

"Your escort from Akashi was most welcome." They used extremely polite and formal Japanese.

"It was the least I could do. I knew your husband slightly. He was a fine man. And, of course, your great uncle and I had a long acquaintance. My good friend and adviser—" and he nodded toward the silent old man "served with Seiji Muramoto during the war."

"Yes," she said. "I appreciate the long connection."

"If you understand the nature of the connection, then you must also understand our position in the current situation. We of course have our preferences, but we will not take sides. We cannot and will not help you. In fact, it is our belief that the struggle for succession is already over, and that you must acknowledge that unfortunate reality."

She said nothing.

"You were not expecting us to help you?"

"Of course not."

"We are aware that there have been several attempts on your life."

"Your sources of information are very impressive."

"If I may say so, you have acquitted yourself most admirably. There is a time for admitting that future resistance is pointless. If you have reached that moment and would like a third party to arrange a parley, we would willingly serve as intermediaries."

"I haven't come for that either."

He studied her. "Please explain."

"You have a strong presence in Atami."

"This is true."

"And in Los Angeles."

"America is the land of opportunity."

"And, as I said, your sources of information are remarkable."

"Information is the most valuable of commodities."

"You have no doubt heard the rumors?"

For the first time the silver-haired crime czar glanced at his old adviser. They did not need to speak to communicate. "We have no information in this area that you do not have."

"I thought perhaps you might. You seemed to have a . . . tangential involvement."

The Yakuza chief smiled slightly at the delicacy of her expression. "Since, as I said, I am somewhat sympathetic, you will permit me to respond bluntly. If you are referring to the deaths of Ida and Miura—the scars, the mysterious rental cars and passports, et cetera—you are mistaken. And if you are referring to the silly business of the American in Atami, we have no interest in his crazy investigation or the trouble it has stirred up."

"Not to contradict you," she said, "but I had heard there was some contact."

He chuckled. "Your own sources of information are also quite commendable. This American stumbled into our hands. We merely set him back on the street. Throughout this entire affair we wish to remain on the sidelines."

"What about the two attempts on his life? Someone must have helped him?"

"There was only one attempt on his life. The first time they tried to scare him off. Then they tried to kill him. He survived on his own."

"That is . . . rather incredible."

"Yes. But true."

"I had thought that perhaps someone was keeping him alive to use him."

"Go on."

"There were papers missing from Shannon's house in Los Angeles. Presumably they were taken by the police detective, Walter Graham, yet they were not found among his possessions either."

"I have heard this rumor."

"If there really were such papers, the son may have taken them from his father's apartment when he decided to take up this case. Yet he did not bring them with him to Japan, and they are not in his apartment in Georgetown."

"So you think someone may be helping the American stay alive till those papers are located or till the information contained in them leaks out?"

"It seems to be the only explanation for his survival in Atami. I had thought your organization might be tangentially involved."

"We are not. Your theory is an interesting one. But if it's true, how do you explain the latest attempt on the American's life? We have no doubt that they were trying to kill him."

"I can't explain it. Perhaps in his bumbling investigation, he turned up something that threatens them."

"Or perhaps they decided he does not have the papers after all." He looked directly into her eyes. "You know, Matsuda-*san*, it is also very possible that there are no papers and that the rumors are false."

"Yes," she admitted, returning his steady gaze. "That is possible. If you knew anything about the rumors, would you tell me?"

"I do not know anything. If I did, I would not tell you. We do not wish to get involved. This conversation, for example, never took place.''

"Of course not. But thank you all the same for talking with me.''

"You're welcome. I fear we will not have the pleasure of seeing each other again. Please allow me to express my profound admiration. My good friend also respects the courage and judgment you have shown.''

She bowed to both of them. The old man slowly climbed out of his chair to bow back. She looked into his ninety-year-old eyes for a second, glanced back at the silver-haired man who stood urbanely in his dark suit with his heels together and his hands at his sides. Then she turned and walked quickly to the door and exited without looking back.

The doctor worked in silence. Jack asked him a few questions and then gave up and stood quietly, waiting for him to finish. He was almost done when two policemen in riot gear entered the hospital room, rifles in hand, and took up positions by the door. Lieutenant Sasaki, looking dapper as ever, walked in after them and immediately barked out a question in fast Japanese.

The doctor looked up from his work to nod and answer affirmatively. Jack watched the exchange, noting again how the handsome young National Police lieutenant had the ability to walk into a room and immediately command full attention. Perhaps it was his thousand-dollar suits, perhaps an understated, very Japanese type of charisma.

Sasaki glanced at Jack. The lieutenant's quick black eyes showed neither sympathy for Jack's wound nor curiosity about what had happened. Jack returned the cold look and asked him: ''What are you here for?'' Sasaki kept silent. ''Are you here to find out what happened in my hotel room? I already gave my statement to Captain Sato. I'm not talking anymore till I get to see someone from the embassy.''

Sasaki walked closer, took a quick look at Jack's shoulder, and asked another curt question in Japanese of the doctor, who nodded.

''What are you asking?'' Jack demanded, a bit more loudly. Ever since the nightmare attack in the hotel room, he had been asking to talk to an embassy official. Instead, he had been kept alone and in silence except for a brief meeting with the local police. Now he could feel his temper rise close to the breaking point. "Why can't you find me a doctor who speaks English? Who are these two goons you brought, and why do they look like they're ready to fight World War Three?"

Sasaki slowly turned his handsome face toward Jack and said, "These two National Police agents are here to protect your life."

"They're a little late," Jack grunted as the doctor finished bandaging his shoulder and applied the final strips of tape. "What were you asking the doctor?"

Sasaki replied matter-of-factly, as if it should be obvious. "I asked him whether you are well enough to travel. He said you are. That is very lucky, because it saves a lot of time. I must ask you now to please put your shirt on."

"Why? Where are we going?"

"To Narita Airport. And then you are going home."

"The fuck I am. I want to talk to someone from the embassy."

Sasaki smiled. The English words rolled off his lips easily and with nearly perfect pronunciation. "There is no need. Your visa has been revoked. You acquired and used an illegal firearm. You have been associating with Yakuza. The Japanese government no longer feels it can or should protect you, and that if you stay in Japan, you will continue to cause . . . violence. Officials at the American embassy have been fully informed, and have agreed. A protest has been filed with your State Department concerning a violation of the Neutrality Act. I have been given the job—"

Jack cut him off. "I used the gun to defend myself against a professional killer. Or do you think the *ninja* attack in my hotel room might have just been another random robbery attempt?" The sarcasm blew by Sasaki like a light breeze, ruffling only his polite smile. "As for associating with Yakuza," Jack continued, his voice rising, "first of all, they didn't give me much choice, and second, I bet you're on the Christmas list of half the Yakuza in Tokyo."

Sasaki waited for Jack to finish, and then proceeded, completely at ease. "It is not my job to consider your visa problems. The decision to send you home has already been made at a very high level. I have been given the duty of bringing you to Narita and putting you on the next flight to America. Now, please put on your shirt and come with us. Or I can ask one of my men to assist you.''

The veiled threat was made very softly, but Sasaki's meaning was quite clear. Jack glanced at the two policemen by the door and then nodded and finished dressing in silence. It took them a while to walk down to the street, because the two policemen in riot gear insisted on going ahead and fully checking out hallways and elevators before Jack and Sasaki were allowed to follow. The handsome young lieutenant took a revolver out of a hip holster and held it ready all during their descent to the street. Jack had grown up around men who knew guns, and one look at the easy way Sasaki held the police revolver told Jack that while the National Police lieutenant might look like a dandy, he had a long familiarity with guns.

When they reached the street, a dark police sedan was waiting at the curb, its motor idling. Two Atami policemen stood on either side of the car, keeping back a small crowd of curious townspeople and several reporters. The reporters shouted out questions in Japanese, and flashguns popped, as Jack and Lieutenant Sasaki got into the backseat. A police driver, his white-gloved hands already on the steering wheel, pulled the sedan away from the curb. The car had traveled less than a few hundred yards when Jack heard sirens and looked back toward the hospital. The two policemen in riot gear had climbed onto large motorcycles and were now gaining on them, sirens blaring. They pulled even and then moved out to escort positions a hundred yards or so ahead. Cars pulled over to the right and left to let them pass, and they were soon out of Atami, speeding along a major highway. Sasaki took out a package of mints and offered one to Jack.

''No, thanks. But tell me about the show.''

''What show?''

Jack pointed at the driver, and then ahead at the motorcycle escort.

''We just want to make sure that you get home safely,'' Sasaki told him.

''Who do you think wants to hurt me?''

''I would guess a great variety of people,'' Lieutenant Sasaki answered, apparently in good spirits. ''You do not seem to have made many friends in Japan, Mr. Graham. It's a shame. Atami is such a hospitable city.''

"Dr. Miles didn't make many friends here either," Jack observed. "Do you think maybe the same people who threw him off the cliff hired the *ninja* who tried to kill me?"

Lieutenant Sasaki gave a little laugh. "You will be glad to know that I have thoroughly reinvestigated the case of Dr. Miles. The original police finding was quite correct. He was upset over the death of his wife and committed suicide. Truly, it was a tragedy. Scientists are usually not so romantic."

"Well, I'm glad you thoroughly reinvestigated it," Jack told him. "Do you know why?"

Sasaki shook his head and swallowed his mint.

"Because," Jack said, "as soon as my plane lands in Washington, I'm going to go see some friends. Friends who have friends."

"It is good to know such people," Sasaki said. "Please give them my regards."

"I will," Jack promised. "Just between the two of us, I think that with a little help from people I know, this whole stinking thing is gonna blow sky-high. Nobody likes to be on the wrong side of a cover-up, so once the momentum starts, all the right people will do the right things and there won't be any stopping till we find out exactly what's going on and who's behind it. A couple of police careers are going to come to quick, disgraceful ends on both sides of the Pacific. So I'm glad that you personally reinvestigated the case of Dr. Miles and concluded that it was just a suicide. Do you follow me?"

"Of course," Sasaki said, his bright smile still in place. For a moment he was silent, looking through the front window toward the two motorcycle policemen, who seemed to keep exactly the same distance ahead of the sedan. "You know, Mr. Graham, once the world was much simpler. My father was a *chuzaisan* in Tohoku."

"What's a *chuzaisan*?"

"You would say a rural policeman. We lived in a *chuzaisho*—a simple old house with a police office in front and two tiny bedrooms in back. Even for rural Tohoku, it was a very humble house. When it rained, water came in. When it snowed, we had ice in the bedrooms. Most of my father's police work was done through trading gossip with store owners and village leaders and old women. Sometimes I would go with him on his rounds. He rode an old motorcycle that broke down very often. And he would stop to help the farmers, digging ditches or taking in a crop or even spreading manure.''

Sasaki broke off to smooth down his perfectly coiffed hair. ''Now,'' he said, ''things are no longer so simple. East and West are so closely connected that we can fly across the ocean in a day, or pick up a phone and call New York. Or Paris.'' His tone became just a bit more grave. ''Or Washington, D.C. Sometimes it's hard to know what is right or wrong anymore, or when friends of friends will help or when they will not. Sometimes when people are angry enough at you to try to kill you, the Pacific Ocean suddenly becomes a little lake that angry men can leap across. If I were you, I would be most careful. It is a confusing world. I'm afraid that my father would not have understood it. He was a good man, but simple.''

''Well, we have something in common, anyway,'' Jack told him, looking him right in the eye. ''My father was also a cop, and also a very simple man. The one thing he hated was a cop on the take. He used to say they were lower than dogs. He had many faults, but he had a sense of honor.''

The good humor drained from Sasaki's face, and when he spoke, his voice was no longer conversational, but rather, his tone was as cold and hard as flint. ''Honor is a strong word—please do not use it carelessly. As for your father, I believe he had an unpleasant death. A suicide. They say suicide runs in families.''

''Suicide and honor, both are supposed to run in families,'' Jack told him. ''But perhaps not.''

In a flash, the barrel of Sasaki's revolver was a half inch from Jack's forehead. ''There is no need for more conversation,'' he hissed. ''When we reach the airport, we want to make the least possible disturbance. I will personally take you to the gate and put you on your plane. If you create any trouble at all, it will be a most serious matter. And if you should try to escape, it will be my unfortunate duty to stop you.'' The smooth barrel of the gun touched the skin of Jack's temple.

When they reached the airport, the two policemen in riot gear accompanied them as far as the terminal building. Sasaki led Jack into the building and up a series of escalators and hallways till they reached the metal detector. After glancing at Sasaki's ID the security supervisor immediately bowed and waved them through, and they were soon at the Japan Air Lines gate.

The flight was due to begin boarding in less than half an hour. Sasaki gestured for Jack to sit, and sat down next to him. One by one the minutes ticked off and the seating area filled up. It was a mixed crowd: businessmen in suits carrying valises and lap-top computers, groups of college-age Japanese tourists ready to use the inflated yen to see the sights and shop the shops from Fifth Avenue to Rodeo Drive, and Japanese and American parents trying to keep watch on young children who raced about, excited at the impending adventure of the flight.

A serious-looking Occidental man in his forties sat down across from Jack and Lieutenant Sasaki and opened a *New York Times*. He skimmed a few pages, and then switched to a *Wall Street Journal*, his leg shaking nervously. He was wearing a business suit, and to Jack he had the slightly nervous, slightly hungry look of a corporate lawyer or an investment banker traveling first class on business. "I'm just gonna borrow a paper," Jack told Sasaki.

The lieutenant nodded.

Jack stood and walked over to the man with the *Wall Street Journal*. "I saw you finish with the *New York Times*. Can I see it for a sec?"

The man lowered his *Wall Street Journal* and looked at him. "They sell them right around the corner."

"Please. I just need to check one thing."

The man exhaled unhappily, as if to let Jack know he should be able to afford his own paper, and handed him the *Times*.

Jack sat back down next to Sasaki and grinned at him. "Figured I'd better check the weather in Washington. Hope it's not too humid."

Sasaki made no reply—he hadn't spoken since the confrontation in the police car. Jack pretended to glance at two articles, and then took out a ballpoint and began the crossword. Sasaki checked to see what he was doing. "Know a four-letter word for incendiary device?" Jack asked him.

Sasaki didn't bother to answer. He glanced at his watch—there were fifteen minutes till boarding time. He sat back in his seat and watched a pretty blond teenage girl several rows down who was sitting in such a way that her long bare legs were visible under her short skirt halfway up the thigh.

Pausing occasionally as if to think, Jack quickly inked in a number of boxes in the crossword to spell out the message:

Need help. Not a joke. Japanese man sitting next to me is carrying a gun. Trying to plant a bomb on our flight. Act like nothing is wrong, and go get airport security.

Jack got up and walked across to hand the paper back, tapping his thumb with a small movement to call the man's attention to the message in the crossword. "Thanks," Jack said. " 'Preciate it."

Jack sat back down next to Lieutenant Sasaki and watched as the man in the suit read the message several times and then raised his eyes to study Jack. Jack looked back at him, and nodded very slightly. Then, conscious that the man was still watching him, Jack turned to Lieutenant Sasaki and asked him in a loud voice, and with a friendly smile, "So, think we'll have a nice flight?" Sasaki shot him an icy look.

The man in the suit stood up and walked quickly away down the corridor.

Jack yawned, as if bored, and watched Sasaki watch the teenager. She was holding a *Rolling Stone*, flipping through the pages without reading them, and as they watched, she uncrossed her long legs. For a second both men could see right up her skirt to a triangle of white panty. "American girls are pretty damn shameless," Jack muttered to Sasaki. And then, more conspiratorially, "Nice legs, though, huh?"

Sasaki didn't reply, but for a second his attention seemed focused on the shapely bare legs.

"You should see the girls in Los Angeles," Jack told him, checking behind them in one quick glance. There was no sign of the man in the business suit or of airport security. "They hang out outside the high schools smoking cigarettes, looking a lot sexier than that one. And on the beaches around Malibu you see fifty- and even sixty-year-old sugar daddies with teenage girls in microbikinis. It's shameless—a real meat market. A quick line and a fast car will get you anything. You know, you should check it out. A guy with your looks and your morals would do real well. Ever had an American girl?"

Sasaki exhaled slowly, and Jack caught a faint smell of mint on the lieutenant's breath. Once again Jack dared a look behind them, toward the corridor. He spotted the man in the business suit, forty yards away and closing fast, with a group of five burly young airport security men in tow. Jack was glad to see that the security officer who had examined Sasaki's ID at the metal detector wasn't in the group.

"The amazing thing is that she probably knows we're looking at her," Jack whispered to Sasaki as the blond girl slid a bit lower in her seat. She sat for a moment with her legs together, and then her knees slid apart so that the view up her skirt was absolutely unobstructed. "How about that?" Jack whispered, noting the glint that had come into Sasaki's bright eyes. "She's putting on a show for you. . . ."

Jack glanced back. The security men had left the American behind and were now twenty feet from Jack and Sasaki. They had guns and clubs out. Jack stood suddenly, and shouted at the top of his lungs, *"Look out, he's got a gun!"* An American mother sitting across from him screamed and snatched up her three-year-old.

Sasaki half rose out of his chair, and Jack hit him with a very respectable straight right to the point of the chin that lifted the police lieutenant off his feet and dumped him back into his chair. Then Jack began to sprint away. When he heard Sasaki shout, "Stop," he glanced back and saw the little man drawing his gun from his shoulder holster and beginning to take aim. As the gun barrel leveled to point at Jack, the five security men tackled Sasaki from behind. One grabbed his gun hand, and a single shot ricocheted off the stone floor and splintered a large window. Then Lieutenant Sasaki disappeared for a moment in a flailing mass of arms and legs.

Jack knew he didn't have much time. Sasaki would show them his ID and seize control of the situation in seconds, and then word would go out via walkie-talkie and police radio to every security man at Narita. The flesh wound in his shoulder didn't affect his running, but his ribs were still very sore and he had to keep his right hand pressed to his body as he sprinted along. He forced his way up a crowded escalator and then bolted down a very long automated walkway, leaping occasional pieces of luggage like hurdles. Suddenly, several hundred yards down at the end of the long corridor, the two policemen in riot gear turned the corner and headed toward him.

Jack turned to run back the way he had come, but Lieutenant Sasaki and a contingent of security police suddenly appeared at the mouth of the long corridor, a half mile or so away. One of them spotted him and pointed. Jack looked around, forcing his mind to work calmly. There were no turnoffs or emergency exits. There was no chance of slipping by either group of men. Glancing up, he saw that there were a few open windows at wide intervals on the sides of the corridor, all of them more than ten feet off the floor. The nearest window was fifteen feet from him.

Jack climbed on the moving banister and timed his jump—he knew he would only get one chance. He stretched out full length in the air, and his fingers found handholds on the window ledge. For a second he dangled down, watched by hundreds of passengers moving in both directions on the automated walkways beneath. Then a shot rang out, and plaster chipped off the wall six inches from his head. There were screams beneath him. Jack pulled himself up toward the narrow aperture, desperation momentarily dousing the pain in his wounded shoulder. Glancing far down the corridor, he saw Sasaki raise a pistol to take aim. With a final effort, Jack pulled his upper body through the window and looked down at a twenty-foot drop to a gravel road. As he hesitated, his body half out the window, a second shot rang out and Jack felt a burning pain in his right calf.

He jumped and tried to roll when he hit the road, but even so, the impact nearly knocked him senseless. Slowly he got back up to his feet and looked around. He was between two huge terminal buildings, on a ramp leading down to an underground parking lot. He began half running and half limping up the ramp, heavily favoring his left leg. His right calf throbbed, and several times when he put too much weight on it, it almost gave way. And then, like an unasked-for answer to unsaid prayers, a small white Tokyo taxicab emerged from the parking lot and started up the ramp.

Jack jumped out directly in front of the cab and held up his palm to stop it. The car slowed and finally braked to a stop right in front of him. The driver was old and bald and apparently confused by this *gaijin* apparition.

Trying not to limp or let his desperation show, Jack walked over to the side of the cab and opened the back door. He got in and gave the driver a big smile. "Hi," he said. "Take me to Tokyo. Let's go."

The driver continued to gape at him without moving. In the distance, Jack heard the wail of police sirens.

"Do you speak any English?" Jack asked. "Tokyo. Please . . ."

The driver slowly shook his head.

Jack fought through his memory for any Japanese words he could remember. He spat them out almost randomly, the police siren swelling closer. *"Tokyo, kudasai. Onegai shimasu. Tokyo. Domo arigato."*

"Tokyo?" the old man asked.

"Hai." Jack nodded. *"Hai, Tokyo. Onegai shimasu."* His voice had a scared, high pitch and he felt his hands shaking.

The taxi began to move forward up the ramp. "Tokyo," the driver repeated. When they reached the front of the terminal building, Jack ducked down a bit. Three police cars roared past them with sirens blaring and screeched to a stop in front of the terminal building. A half dozen policemen seemed to emerge from the cars at the same second and sprinted toward the terminal entrance, guns in hand. Jack sat back up as they pulled onto an access road and headed for the highway.

"America?" the old driver asked.

"No," Jack said. "Not America. Canada."

The old driver looked baffled.

"Canada," Jack repeated slowly. "You know, Quebec, Montreal, Toronto . . ."

"Ah, Canada-*jin*?" The old driver nodded. *"Naruhodo, naruhodo."* They drove for a long time in silence. Jack rolled up his pants and took a quick look at his right leg. It had only been a glancing blow. Blood had soaked through the fabric of his pants, but the bullet hadn't lodged in the leg, and it didn't look like any serious damage had been done.

"Doko desu ka?" the driver asked as they reached the outskirts of the city.

Jack thought for a second. "Tokyo Station," he said. He thought he remembered once having heard that Tokyo Station was the busiest subway station in the world. If so, all the better. As a wanted foreigner in this fiendishly well-organized country, his only hope for the moment seemed to be to lose himself in the biggest crowds he could find.

SECTION FOUR

Misako

20

The Fleurs de Rong brothel was located just outside of Chiang Mai, and catered almost exclusively to the native Thai population. There were two dozen girls ranging in age from fifteen to twenty-seven, almost all of them from hill tribes like the Shan, the Karen, and the Lao, who had been sold into sexual slavery by families on the wrong side of the starvation line.

Ping, the chubby, middle-aged Chinese proprietress of the brothel, made sure her girls got enough to eat to keep some meat on their bones. Sexual diseases were treated during bimonthly visits by a young doctor from town, who was occasionally paid for his services in hard currency, but far more often in soft flesh.

The Fleurs de Rong was located in an old stone farmhouse that had fallen into disrepair and been rebuilt several times. In its present incarnation, the front of the farmhouse had been fitted with a huge sliding steel door purchased from a machine shop that had gone out of business in Lamphun. Armed bandits from the hills and rowdy drunkards traveling through the countryside had been known to terrorize rural bordellos, and the imposing steel door could be locked from the inside, rendering the stone building virtually impregnable.

Customers' cars would park on the dirt flat in front of the farmhouse at all hours of the day and night. A young guard carrying a shoulder rifle would greet guests, check to make sure they were unarmed, and then signal for the steel door to be opened.

The main room of the brothel was enlivened with several bright carpets and some rickety wooden armchairs arranged around two fire pits that had been dug into the floor. The chairs were almost always occupied by men in their fifties and sixties who drifted in and out of opium stupors, occasionally grunting to the nearest girls to pick up fresh pipes for them from the fires.

The girls did most of the cooking and cleaning in the brothel, and spent a lot of time waiting and gossiping. The private rooms were in the back of the farmhouse, and since most of the girls had regular customers, there was rarely a need for them all to assemble in the main room and show a new guest all the different choices open to him.

On one rainy Tuesday, the sight of a car coming down the dusty driveway occasioned great excitement at the Fleurs de Rong. It was a foreign car—a black Mercedes Benz—looking sleek and luxurious with its coat of shiny black paint and its windshield wipers flicking the drizzle off to either side.

"It's a government official," one girl suggested.

"The police, coming to shut us down."

"Or to get free favors."

"See the license plate? It was rented in Bangkok. Ask Mama Ping if we should run out back and hide in the fields. . . ."

But Mama Ping had taken her old Luger from its hiding place beneath the bar and had slipped outside to stand with the young guard.

The Mercedes pulled to a stop and two men got out. Mama Ping and the guard recognized the driver at once as Mae Hong, a notoriously crooked minor government official in Chiang Mai and a frequent customer at the Fleurs de Rong. A very thin and dignified-looking Thai man in a blue silk suit got out of the passenger side of the front seat and examined the old farmhouse with obvious distaste. He opened a black umbrella and held it above his head while the breeze blew through his white hair. Mama Ping, who had a prodigious memory for faces, returned his stare and decided that she had never seen him before, and that he had the look of a city slicker.

Then Mae Hong opened the car's back door, and a Japanese man stepped out. The girls, peeking out through a small window and several cracks in the wall, exchanged excited whispers at the man's appearance. He was past middle age, but his shaved head and robust physique gave him an ageless quality—he could have been sixty or eighty. He was dressed in elegant black robes, and used a walking stick to partially offset a serious limp. He took a few steps forward and spoke in Japanese to the man in the blue silk suit, who tried his best to shelter them both under the small umbrella as he translated the Japanese man's instructions into Thai for Mae Hong.

"This is an old friend of mine," Mae Hong announced to Mama Ping, indicating the man in the blue silk suit. "A very old friend and a very important man, from Bangkok."

"His name?"

"I have forgotten it," Mae Hong told her with a quick smile. "He is here to arrange a transaction for this other gentleman, who is from Japan."

"What kind of a transaction?" Mama Ping asked suspiciously. The cold drizzle ran down her low forehead to her fat cheeks. She held the gun out of sight beneath her jacket, but her finger never left the trigger. She had been in this business for a long time, and she distrusted situations that were in any way out of the ordinary.

"A very profitable transaction for you," Mae Hong replied. "Now will you let us inside?"

Mama Ping thought for a few seconds. "Anything you can get here, you can also get in the places in town," she finally muttered. "And we both know rich Japanese like this gentleman prefer to take their pleasure in fancy places in Bangkok. Now, tell me the real reason you're here."

Mae Hong glanced at the man in the blue silk suit, as if for permission, and then licked his lips nervously. "You're wrong," he told Mama Ping. "There are things that can be bought here that can't be bought in Chiang Mai, or even Bangkok. . . ."

"Silence," the man in the blue silk suit said, and Mae Hong immediately shut up. "Madam," the city slicker said with dignity, "this is not the place for such a conversation. Let us talk inside."

Mama Ping took the revolver out and held it loosely in her right hand so that it was clearly visible. "Are you with the government? The police?"

"I'm a businessman."

She studied his face and believed him. "Are you armed?"

He took a pistol out of a hip holster and handed it to the guard. "If you try to steal it," he told the guard in a soft whisper, "I will have you hunted down and castrated." He turned back to Mama Ping. "Now, please, let us go in and talk."

She studied his face for a second more, and then nodded and gave the order for the steel door to be opened.

When the three men were inside the main room, Mama Ping, who took a certain amount of pride in her establishment, insisted on showing off her girls. "Please tell him that they are all under thirty, and many under twenty," she told the Thai man in the blue silk suit. "I have them checked for diseases regularly. They're all healthy and happy here, and very skilled at lovemaking. And if it's opium your friend wants, we have a pipe waiting for him."

The man in the blue silk suit duly translated Mama Ping's various claims and offers into Japanese. The old Japanese gentleman listened politely and then responded with a short sentence. "He wants to speak to you in private," the city slicker told Mama Ping. "Do you have an office?"

There was no office, so they went to the largest of the private rooms. The two prettiest girls brought in Thai whiskey, smiling and wiggling for the two rich-looking guests, and then withdrew. Mama Ping shut the door and locked it. She poured whiskey for Mae Hong and the city slicker, but the Japanese gentleman shook his head and held his palm over the top of his glass. Studying him more carefully now that they were at close quarters, she saw the strength of the broad shoulders and massive arms beneath the flowing black robes, and that he wore a very distinctive brooch at the neck of his black robes. On the face of the brooch, a crane stood facing a dragon.

"We're alone now," Mama Ping said. "No one can see. No one can hear. Please tell the gentleman from Japan that he should speak frankly about what he wants. If the girls he saw didn't please him, I can have others brought in. And as for opium—"

"He is not interested in opium," Mae Hong told her. "And he is not interested in girls. But what he wants, he is willing to pay for, and you should remember that it was Mae Hong who brought him here to you. . . ."

This time the man in the blue silk suit silenced Mae Hong with a sweeping gesture of his right hand. For a moment they sat in silence, sipping Thai whiskey and listening to the drizzle on the tin roof. "Madam," the city slicker finally said, "let me come right to the point. This man—" and he indicated Mae Hong "—said that you have a young boy here. Is this true?"

Mama Ping at first shook her head, confused. "Oh," she finally said, "you mean our towel boy? I didn't think of him—he brings clean towels to the rooms." Her face hardened slightly, around the eyes. "But he can't be why you've come here." She frowned, looked across at Mae Hong, and then glanced at the Japanese man. "He's only nine," she said.

"We know," the city slicker said. "My Japanese friend desires to see him. Please bring him here."

Mama Ping considered it for a second. The money would be very good. Then she shook her head. "Tell the gentleman there are places in town Mae Hong can show him. And of course, in Bangkok. And many on Phuket. Not here. I don't run that kind of place. The boy you mention is a great favorite of the girls. I won't do it. No."

The man in the blue silk suit translated her refusal into Japanese for the gentleman in black. He replied immediately.

"He says you misunderstand him," the city slicker explained. "He does not want the boy for any perversion. In fact, the opposite. He may be able to do the boy a great deal of good. But first he must see him. So please bring him here immediately."

The Japanese man saw her hesitate, and reassured her with a frank look. He had a strong, honest face, and his robes lent him a priestlike quality. He took a wallet out and counted out a pile of Thai bank notes, which he handed to her. In bad but understandable Thai he said, "I won't hurt him. I want to help him." She pocketed the money, opened the door, and sent for the boy.

The towel boy arrived in less than a minute, looking very confused. He was a shy, slightly dim-witted child, liked by the girls for his good nature. He wore faded gray shorts and a white cotton undershirt, and it was obvious from his face and coloring that he was of mixed Occidental and Asian parentage. "Don't be afraid," Mama Ping told him, placing a comforting hand on his shoulder. "These men won't harm you."

The Japanese gentleman studied the boy intently in the dim light of the room. He paid particular attention to the boy's face, and to the color of his skin and hair. The skin was a very light tan, between olive and amber, and the boy's wide oval eyes and fair hair gave him a distinctly Amerasian look. He was small for his age, and very thin, and he stood very still with his hands at his sides and his knees pressed together.

"That's the one," the Japanese gentleman said to the man in the blue silk suit. Mama Ping knew no Japanese, but she saw that they had seen what they needed to see, and sent the boy away. She poured refills of Thai whiskey, and as the Japanese man spoke at length in fast Japanese, she waited to see what would come next in this strange encounter.

"Madam," the city slicker began, "the Japanese gentleman would like to know how you came by such a boy."

For a moment she felt very nervous again. "Perfectly legally," she said. "It was charity. I saved his life. He had no place else to go. . . ."

"You misunderstand me. No one is accusing you of anything. Please, just tell the truth. Who was his mother?"

"One of the girls," Mama Ping said. "She was Shan—I bought her myself. She worked here for three years before she became pregnant and ran away."

"Why did she run?"

"She was afraid I would make her get an abortion."

"Would you have?"

Mama Ping kept silent. Above them, the drizzle quickened into a rain that pounded on the tin. The man in the blue silk suit raised his voice to make his next question understood. "Where did she run to?"

"She had family in the mountains near Muang Fang."

"And after she had the boy, she came back?"

Mama Ping nodded.

"Why?"

"Where else could she go? Her family couldn't feed two extra mouths."

"And what became of her?"

"She died of tuberculosis four years ago. A sudden attack."

The city slicker in blue silk paused to sip some Thai whiskey and asked, with apparent disinterest, "And the boy's father?"

"American," Mama Ping said. "From California. Fought in Vietnam and never went home. A little crazy in the head."

"How did he find this place?"

Mama Ping shrugged. "He came for the opium. Friends from town brought him. His Thai was perfect. For about a month he was a regular customer here—he only saw that one Shan girl. He would smoke and smoke, and he drank whiskey like it was water. And then one day he left and he never came back."

"He left before the girl ran away?"

"Long before."

"Do you think they were still in touch when she ran away?"

Mama Ping didn't bother to answer such an idiotic question.

"Where do you think he went after he left?"

"Bangkok," Mama Ping said. "Or Vientiane. Or Tokyo. Or back to California."

"Why do you say Tokyo?"

"I meant that he could have gone anywhere. Who knows where such men end up? He had already been everywhere and done everything."

"But you have no reason to think he would have gone to Japan?"

"No more than anywhere else."

"And you think he had no interest in the boy?"

"None. I don't think he even knew she was pregnant," Mama Ping said. "Most of the time he was smoking opium."

"And when he left, he didn't leave her anything?"

"Nothing."

"So when the mother died, with the father gone, you took the boy?"

"Yes. The mother was popular with the other girls, and they all loved to play with the boy. So I took him and fed him."

The man in the blue silk suit translated all that he had found out to the Japanese gentleman, who listened with his head cocked slightly to one side. At the end he nodded, and made a fairly long speech, looking at Mama Ping as he spoke.

"My Japanese friend says that he would like to make you an offer. Many years ago at a difficult time in his life, he received a favor from an American that changed his life. Before he could repay the favor, the American died. He has never forgotten the favor and he has always felt a debt of obligation. He has come to the conclusion that the best way to repay the debt is to find a poor American child and give him a better life. Sadly, there are legal reasons why he cannot adopt an American child from America. But here in this establishment he has found the son of an American who is not tangled up in silly laws and who could use a benefactor. Of course, you would be well paid for the care you have already shown the boy, and for keeping quiet about this transaction. . . ."

There was more—the city slicker's fancy speech went on and on—but Mama Ping's eyes were suddenly riveted on the pile of money that the Japanese man now produced from under his robe. It was a small fortune.

Half an hour later, three men left the Fleurs de Rong and got into the Mercedes. A few minutes later, Mama Ping led the boy out. He was dressed in black pants and a clean new white shirt, and he walked mechanically to the car. At the door of the car, the boy suddenly panicked and tried to run, but Mama Ping and the guard seized him, and the old Japanese gentleman reached out from inside the car and pulled him inside. The guard shut the car door, and the black Mercedes took off down the muddy road.

That very evening, sedated with a general anaesthetic, the boy underwent a small operation in a private Bangkok clinic. The following morning the Japanese gentleman and the young boy left Bangkok by Air India jet for Delhi. The boy had been washed and his hair had been cut short, and he wore a brand-new suit and fancy shoes that made his feet hurt. The passport he was traveling under had been fabricated rather quickly, but no one questioned it.

From Delhi they flew to Karachi, and then on to Athens, and finally to Bern, where they immediately set out on a hair-raising four-hour drive through the Alps to the tiny town of Creusot.

Of course, it would have been much easier to fly east, but the old Japanese man in the black robes did not want to fly anywhere near Japan. He did not even want to fly over it. He knew he was being unnecessarily cautious, but he believed that men who are entrusted with great responsibilities must take extraordinary precautions.

21

Misako missed the first meeting time and was ten minutes late for the second one. Just as Jack was getting ready to give up, he saw her hurrying through the crowded station toward the little coffee shop he had chosen. He ducked back behind a shelf of books and peered out carefully, watching as she entered the coffee shop and the door closed behind her. His vantage point at the front of the bookstore gave him a wide view of the cavernous north terminal, and he scanned the crowd carefully. Misako waited half an hour for him. When she reemerged and walked away, Jack was pretty sure she had come alone, and that no one was following her.

He left the bookstore and trailed her at a distance of several hundred feet. She headed for the *Shinkansen* ticket counter, perhaps to find out when the next bullet train departed for Atami. Jack sped up and caught her hand when she was forty feet from the ticket counter. At his touch, she whirled around and they looked at each other.

Her eyes were red as if she had been crying. He tried to take her hand, but she pulled away.

"Thanks so much for coming," he began. "I didn't know if you'd even get my message—I couldn't tell if it was your machine. It sounded like your voice, but when you can't understand the words, you can't really tell—"

"Jack," she whispered. Just his name. He shut up and looked at her. Around them, commuters sped by in all directions. "You said you wanted to talk. We should go somewhere quiet."

"I don't think it's safe for me to travel."

She nodded. "You're on every news program. I'm surprised you haven't been picked up yet. Put this on." She handed him a large square cotton mouth mask with elastic straps that fit around the back of his head. He had seen many people in Japan wearing

241

such masks and had wondered whether they were supposed to
filter out pollution or prevent colds from being spread. While it
was ostensibly a mouth mask, when Jack put it on, it covered most
of the bottom of his face. "And this," she said, handing him a
beret. It was too small for him, but he slid it down low over his
forehead so that it almost covered his eyes. "Okay," she said.
"Now, don't talk in the cab. In Tokyo, even the drivers who say
they can't speak English usually can. Don't say a word."

They caught a cab outside Tokyo Station and rode in complete
silence through the city. The cab finally pulled over near the
entrance to a large park, and Misako paid the driver. "Where are
we?" Jack asked her as the cabbie drove off.

"Ueno," she said. "There are many foreigners and tourists
here. No one will notice you."

"Why are there so many tourists?"

"The zoo," she said. "Come."

He followed her through the park, and soon they were walking
through a lovely little zoo, full of Japanese families and groups of
foreign tourists, all looking at the animals so that no one really
studied passersby. They descended a long flight of steps and
strolled past a man-made pond where exotic marsh birds swished
through shallows on sticklike legs. In the center of the park, they
came to a large lake that reminded Jack of the boat pond in Central
Park in New York. They entered the boathouse, and Jack stood by
himself on the dock while Misako rented them a rowboat.

Soon they were out near the middle of the lake, separated from
other boats by a tangle of reeds and a long patch of lily pads.
Around them, on all sides, the skyscrapers of Tokyo soared high
in the afternoon light. Jack shipped the oars. "Well," he said, "I
guess we're alone."

"In Tokyo it's not easy to find a safe place to talk." Misako
studied him carefully. "The news report I heard said that you had
been shot."

"Just a flesh wound in the leg. There's an international phar-
macy in Tokyo Station. I bought some soap and bandages there,
and washed it off in a men's room. I don't think it's anything to
worry about. I've been getting chopped up a lot lately, but I
actually feel pretty good."

"I'm glad," Misako said. "Why weren't you at the coffee
shop?"

Jack hesitated. "The police are looking for me."

"So?"

"I . . . didn't know whether you'd come alone."

"You didn't trust me?"

"If I didn't trust you, I wouldn't have called. But I just had to make sure."

"Which means that you really don't trust me," she said. For a few moments they sat in silence. "Please tell me what you're thinking."

Jack looked into her eyes. Better to get it all out in the open. "You were at Atami High School with me when I found out that Eric Gleason lived in the same apartment that Shannon Miles used to live in. A little while later Eric's apartment was searched by Japanese police. Somebody reported back to them. I'm not saying you did, but somebody did."

She sat very still, watching him with a strange impassivity that seemed to turn her soft features to marble. Sensing that she wasn't about to admit or deny anything, Jack pressed on. "The first time I was attacked, in the alley, I had the distinct feeling the Atami police set me up for it. They took me out, got me drunk, and steered me down the road where the killer was waiting. It wasn't you, but it *was* the people you work for. And finally, when we found out about Ida and Miura, you went off to check their names at the police station. A few hours later, a professional killer tried to murder me in my hotel room. I'm not saying you told, but somebody found out pretty quickly that we had made a breakthrough. So . . . I felt like I needed to be careful."

Misako thought about what he had said, nodded slightly, and then began to cry. She didn't pull out a tissue or turn away, but rather she sat there, not moving a muscle, as one after another, tears squeezed out of the corners of her eyes and ran down her cheeks.

Jack stood up in the boat, walked over to her seat, and sat down next to her. He tried to put his arm around her, but she shrugged him off, and he was surprised to see anger almost passing to rage in her face. "What is it?"

It took her a long time to speak. "Why did you call me if you don't trust me?"

"You're the only person in Japan I did trust enough to call."

"Then take my advice. Go back to America."

"I can't, now."

"You said that once we made the connection between Ida and Miura and Shannon Miles, you had all you needed to force an investigation. Why don't you go home, talk to your people, and do that?"

"Because things have changed. I don't know where I stand back home," he admitted. He told her what Sasaki had told him about how charges had been filed concerning the Neutrality Act. "So when I got to Tokyo Station I called my boss. A man named MacCormack, whom I trust. He wasn't there—they said he was away on an assignment. Instead I got some guy from the Inspector's Division who practically ordered me to get on the first plane home. And he wanted to know where I was calling from in Japan. . . ." Jack broke off and swallowed.

"What's the Inspector's Division?"

"Sort of an internal security bureau within the FBI. They police the police, so to speak."

Misako watched him carefully. The breeze picked up a few strands of her long hair, danced with them for a moment, and then let them fall so that they trailed down the side of her face. She brushed them back with her right hand and waited for him to continue.

"I also called a friend of mine from work—a guy named Monroe. Before I left America, I gave Monroe some things to check out on the Miles case, and I wanted to see if he was making any progress. And I thought maybe he could fill me in on the Bureau scuttlebutt." Even though they were alone in the middle of a lake, Jack found himself lowering his voice. "He told me that lots of funky things are going on all of a sudden. Twice in the last week, men from security have come to talk to him. They know we were friends and they keep asking if I gave him anything or talked to him before I left for Japan. He told them I just came to talk to him about missing some softball games, but the whole thing's made him nervous. And if they're checking with Monroe, then they're checking with everyone."

"What makes you think you can trust this Monroe?"

"I kinda saved his daughter's life," Jack said. "And there are certain people you just know you can trust. MacCormack's like that, too, except that according to Monroe, Old Mac's been out of the office a lot lately. Like maybe they're transferring him or shuffling him around in some way."

"So that he can't protect you?"

"Maybe. Anyway, I don't want to risk going home quite yet. I've got to find out more. And there's no way I can do it without help."

"I understand," Misako said. "I'm sorry your job is in trouble."

"I don't give a damn about the job," Jack told her. "I just want to be free to solve this thing."

"If you solve it, you may even go home a hero. Yes?" She gave him a terrible, sad smile and her voice became so brittle, it sounded as if it might break with every word. "For me, there is no longer any chance of . . . how do you say it? . . . redemption."

"What do you mean?"

"It doesn't matter now."

"Please tell me."

She hesitated a long, long time. When she finally spoke, her voice was a whisper. "Some of what you said was true. I was originally assigned to translate for you so that I could keep an eye on you. It was part of my police job."

"Captain Sato told you to do it?"

"At first. Then I reported directly to the Japanese National Police."

"Lieutenant Sasaki?"

She nodded. "He wanted to know where you went and if you came up with anything interesting on Shannon or Dr. Miles. And he was also interested in anything you might say about your father. . . ." She broke off, looking guilty and greatly distressed.

"Did you tell him anything?"

She nodded miserably.

"What?"

"I told them about Eric Gleason and they searched his apartment."

"Did they find anything?"

"I don't think so."

Jack paused a minute to take it in. "Why did they tell you to stop helping me after the first attack?"

"They didn't. I saw that you were here for an honorable purpose and I felt that spying on you was dishonest. Disgusting. I hated the position they had put me in. So I told them I couldn't do it anymore. I told them you suspected me, and that I couldn't get them any more information.''

"And they let you off the hook?"

"Yes. I went back to my normal police work. I never wanted to do such a . . . dishonorable thing in the first place.''

"I believe you," Jack told her. "What happened next?"

"You called and asked me to come with you to Okawa Hotel. To help you ask questions." She seemed angry at herself at the memory. "I came, very much against my better judgment. I was curious.''

"And they found out?"

"Yes. And they also found out that I used the police computer to check the names Ida and Miura. I didn't tell them, but they found out." She looked down into the water where a lily pad rode a tiny wave. "So I disobeyed my superiors.''

"I know what they tried to do to me—they tried to kill me. What did they do to you?"

"Nothing so . . . dramatic," she said, reaching down with a finger as if to touch the lily pad but pausing in midair so that her finger hung suspended. "They just fired me. But in Japan when you are fired from a job, a part of your life comes to an end.''

"First they told you to pretend to help me, and then they fired you for really doing it? That's ridiculous.''

"I was working with you behind their backs, as you say in English." She raised her eyes from the surface of the water to his face, and he saw her lips tremble slightly with anger. "So forgive me if I am not sympathetic enough about your job difficulties and your request for help. And if you don't trust me, what can I say? I tried to help you. It cost me my career.''

"Can't you do something to fight it? Some kind of appeal process. Strike back at Sasaki and Sato. Show that they're corrupt, and that the investigation into the death of Dr. Miles was a sham. I mean, we're on the right side of this. . . . You were put in an impossible position and you did what you thought you had to. . . .''

Her voice became low and cold. "Now, I'm afraid, you are either speaking from ignorance or trying to make a joke out of the most important thing in my life. This is Japan, in case you didn't notice," she told him, pointing around at the skyline. "Maybe you've read some articles about *Takako Doi* and you think that things have changed here, and that Japan is like America now for working women. Well, it's not. Maybe you think I have some power. I don't. I'm a woman. I disobeyed a clear order from my chief. That's all there is to say. So . . . I'm going home to Hamamatsu."

"Where?"

"It's at the other end of Shizuoka Prefecture."

"What are you going to do there?"

She shrugged. "My father is dead. My mother lives all alone. She's getting old. I will take care of her."

"Misako . . ."

"And I'll think what to do next. Really, a woman in Japan who loses her job should probably find a husband. My mother has several men in mind. I don't know." Her brittle voice finally shattered into lots of tiny pieces. "I . . . don't . . . know."

He put his arm around her loosely, and she let it stay. "Listen," he said. "Will you help me? I'll be a sitting duck in Japan by myself." He gave her his most winning smile. "It'll beat going back to Hamamatsu."

Finally she let the rage out. "So you want my help again? Just like when you begged me to come with you to the Hotel Okawa? Do you have any idea what helping you has cost me?" She shrugged off his arm and looked at him till he shook his head.

"I went to Kyoto University—the second-best college in Japan. After graduation I surprised all my classmates by going back to school—police school. I was the first woman police officer in Atami, but I started out like everyone else, handing out traffic safety information and even cleaning the floor of the station. . . ." The memory made her shake her head from side to side in anger. "You don't know what it's like working in a *kooban*—a police box—on the night shift, having everyone look at you, your fellow policemen leer at you, and then having to make tea for them; you don't know. . . ."

"You're right," Jack told her softly. "I don't know. But I didn't do this to you. Sato and Sasaki did."

"What does it matter?" she asked. "Already my career is gone. What do you want now? Do you want to get me arrested? Or killed? Isn't that the next step?"

Jack had no answer.

"And the only reason you can give me is to smile and say that helping you will be better than going back to Hamamatsu?"

"No," Jack said. "I can give you a better reason than that. You saw the picture of Shannon—she was a nice human being, and somebody brutally killed her. And somebody pushed her crippled husband off a cliff. And that person, whoever he is, will go free if you don't help."

"I never knew Shannon Miles," she replied. "Or her husband. I didn't know Ida or Miura. How do I even know you're right about them? Suppose you're totally wrong? You don't care about your job; you'll just get another one. In America you can do that." She was on the verge of becoming hysterical. "This is a game to you. You haven't given up anything. . . ."

"They fucking killed my father," Jack said in such a loud voice that a couple in a rowboat a hundred yards or so away glanced over. He felt himself trembling, and they both took some small breaths. "They killed my father," he repeated in a whisper.

She waited till she had control over her voice. "I'm sorry about your father. That gives you a good reason. But not me."

"There's only one other reason I can give you. And if it's not enough, you should go back to Hamamatsu."

"What?"

He took her hand and they sat in silence for a while, watching a small goldfish rise up through the murk of the pond to suck down some air. For a second its lips broke the surface and made a tiny O shape. Then it sank back down again.

"What?" Misako asked. "Tell me."

He looked directly into her bright black eyes. A tiny breeze stirred her hair, and he smoothed it down, first with his fingertips and then gently with his palm. She shivered but didn't pull away. Once again, as on the hillside in Atami, Jack glimpsed her hidden vulnerability. Whatever she had suffered, whatever wound she was trying so hard to hide from the world, she bore it nobly, and he empathized with her loneliness. Tenderly cradling her head in his palm and still looking into her eyes, he pressed his lips to hers. She kissed him back.

When they finally separated to breathe, she whispered, "Jack, go home to America. Please."

"I'm gonna see this through, whatever happens. But you don't have to help me. Maybe it would be better if you didn't.'' She reached for him and they embraced, and the small boat rocked back and forth. One of the oars slipped into the water and began to float away, but neither of them noticed.

Later, after they had returned the boat, they sat on a bench by the artificial pond and watched the marsh birds. ''So what do you think we should do next?'' she asked him.

''Even with your help, the police will catch me very quickly. There seems to be only one place to turn.'' He held her hand as a stork walked by, scanning the pond water for an early dinner. ''The only group that's really helped me since I got here was the Yakuza. They got framed, and they really want me to succeed or at least to keep on the trail. So I think I need to go back to them.''

''You can't trust them,'' she said with conviction. ''You don't even understand what they want out of this. Last time they helped you. This time they might kill you.''

''What choice do I have?''

She tried to think of an answer, but couldn't. ''What did your friend Monroe find out from the papers you gave him?''

''A lot of questions, but no answers yet.''

''What questions?''

''He asked me if I knew about Shannon and her husband's interest in skiing. He says it looks like they took a lot of ski trips together.''

''But Dr. Miles was crippled. . . .''

Jack nodded. ''Maybe he sat in the lodge. Or maybe he had some way of skiing with his disability. I know it sounds strange, but a lot of things have been sounding strange lately. I even told Monroe to check up and make absolutely sure that Dr. Miles really was crippled. Just because he spent his life in a wheelchair doesn't mean anything for certain.''

''What else did your friend Monroe tell you about their ski trips?''

''He's checking. Said he'd have more soon. He has to work covertly, so it's taking extra time. Also, he ran a couple of Japanese names by me. Asked me if I'd heard of them.''

''What names?''

''A man named Hara. Apparently Dr. Miles also did a little business with Hara. I forget the first name. Heard of him?''

Misako shook her head. ''Who else?''

"Seiji Muramoto," Jack told her, and she almost fell off the bench with surprise.

"Who is he?"

"He was one of the richest men in Japan. He died recently, in a mysterious plane crash. What did he tell you about Seiji Muramoto?"

"Nothing. Just asked me if I'd heard of him. I said no. He asked me if I knew what a *Zaibatsu* is. I said no. And that was it."

Misako sat very straight on the bench, the alarm showing clearly in the sudden tightness of her face. Her hands slid down between the boards of the bench and found handholds on the undersides of the planks, as if for extra support.

Jack watched her for a few seconds, and then smiled and said, "Fill me in. Who was Muramoto? And what the hell's a *Zaibatsu*? Sounds like a noodle dish."

"I think, in America, you have a saying about seeing the tip of the iceberg," she replied, glancing around, her nervousness increasing by the second. "You see the tip and you think it looks small, but in reality most of the iceberg is hidden under the water. And it is gigantic enough to sink your ocean liner."

"We're heading for an iceberg?"

"I don't know that much about Seiji Muramoto or what happened to him. I know something about the *Zaibatsu*, and I'll tell you what I know later on. Right now we've got to get out of here."

"Why? Where can we go?"

She was silent.

Jack took out the phone number that the Atami crime kingpin had written down of the Yakuza's Tokyo office. He handed it to her, and she studied it with evident fear. "It sounds like we need big protection," he told her. "Will you make the call, or should I?"

"It's too dangerous. We can't trust the Yakuza."

"No choice. It would be easier if you called them, at least to tell them where we are."

She hesitated for a long second, and then saw that he had made his mind up, and nodded. "Okay," she whispered. "Let's find a phone."

He held her hand as they walked among the animal cages. "You seem a little nervous all of a sudden," he said.

Her grip tightened. "I'm not nervous," she said. "I'm scared to death."

22

An innocuous-looking four-door Toyota cruised to a stop in front of the south entrance to Ueno Park, and the young driver and an older-looking Japanese man in the front seat waved to Jack and Misako to get in. Jack opened the back door, but Misako hesitated, suddenly afraid. In the distance, police sirens began to shrill. She glanced at Jack and then got into the backseat, and he followed her quickly into the car. The young driver sped away into the heavy traffic.

The drone of police sirens grew louder. Misako's whole body tensed, as if her worst nightmare were suddenly coming true. The older man in the front seat took out a pistol and turned half around so that he could see out the back window. His movements were precise and unforced, as if he had done this dozens of times before. The young driver guided them skillfully through the crowded streets at high speeds, and then turned off into a narrow alley between tall buildings.

The alley led to even narrower alleys, so that it didn't seem as if the Toyota would be able to squeeze through, but it always just managed. The young driver checked his rearview mirror every few seconds to make sure they weren't being followed through the alleys. Soon the older man put away his pistol, apparently confident that they were free and clear. Neither of the men said anything to Jack or Misako.

The Toyota sped down one last alley, and emerged onto a dingy side street. There was a roaring above them as a train thundered across elevated tracks. Two blocks down, a dog tried to tip over a garbage can. They stopped beneath the elevated tracks and waited at the curb, motor idling. Soon a Lincoln Continental cruised up the block and parked just behind them.

The older Japanese man in the front seat motioned for Jack and

Misako to follow him. He led them over to the Continental and opened the back door for them. Then he got into the passenger side of the front seat while a new young driver sped them on their way without a word.

They changed cars four times in several hours of driving around Tokyo before the older Japanese man, who had remained with them the entire time, produced blindfolds. He spoke a few curt Japanese sentences to Misako, who told Jack, "He says we have to put these on now. They're taking us somewhere."

When they were both blindfolded, the car roared forward onto a highway and then stayed at high speed for perhaps three or four hours, never changing lanes. When Jack was beginning to lose all patience, he felt the car slide over to the right and slow, and then turn off onto an exit ramp. For twenty minutes they navigated local roads, the last few of which were so bumpy, Jack wondered if they were paved. Finally the car jerked to a stop and Jack heard the older man's gruff Japanese once again. "We can take off the blindfolds," Misako announced.

They were on a high bluff, looking down at the ocean waves that broke in on teethlike rocks several hundred yards beneath. Near them, perched on the edge of the bluff so that it commanded a sweeping view of the ocean, was a small, one-story, traditional-looking Japanese house. Beyond it, half-hidden by a grove of cedar trees, was a Western-style compound building. A twelve-foot-high brick wall with spikes at the top ran inland from the very edge of the precipice to a steel gate with a sentry post. From the other side of the gate the wall started again and looped around the far side of the house and the compound building all the way to the cliffs, so that the four- or five-acre property was completely sealed off from the outside world.

The car that had brought them took off back down the drive-way, paused while the gate was opened, and then disappeared from view. The older Japanese man who had accompanied them on their entire journey spoke to Misako and pointed toward the house. "He says this will be our home for a little while," Misako told Jack. "We will find food and everything we need there. He suggests that we make ourselves comfortable."

"Then let's see what's in the fridge," Jack told her. "I'm hungry as hell." Taking her hand, he started up the slope.

The entire little house was a work of art. It was built on a long north-south axis so to the east all three main rooms faced out on a breathtaking view of the ocean while to the west the same rooms offered views of a gravel and cactus garden. At the edges of the garden, scrub pines that had been bent and twisted by the wind cast arabesque shadows on the patterned sand and rocks.

The inside of the house was a study in simplicity. The floors were all inlaid with squares of fresh tatami matting which gave off a slightly sweet, reedlike smell. The frame of the house consisted of black and white wooden beams, interspersed to create pleasing and understated geometric patterns. Sliding shoji screens served as outside walls. They were made of translucent rice paper so that even when all of them were shut, the rooms were suffused with a gentle glow from the outside sunlight. The three main rooms were separated by sliding screen doors, each of which had been hand-painted with seasonal landscapes or seascapes.

Jack had never seen anything like it, and he walked from room to room like a child in his first cathedral. Misako, not quite as awestruck but equally enchanted, walked beside him. They were both particularly captivated by the verandas—the one facing the ocean was of redwood boards polished to such a sheen that they almost looked lacquered, while the ones facing the garden were of split bamboo. On the veranda facing the ocean he put his arm around her. "Not such a bad place, huh?"

"It's nice," she admitted, "but whose is it?"

"Ours for a while. Do you think there's a kitchen?"

The kitchen and bathroom were both Western style, with tiled floors and modern conveniences. A white-haired woman in a kimono was busy in the kitchen, putting the finishing touches on a plate of finger sandwiches. She bowed and spoke in Japanese. "She apologizes for not being ready yet with lunch," Misako told Jack. "She says she'll bring it to us in a minute."

"Tell her we're starving to death and we're furious at her for being late."

"I don't think I'd better," Misako replied, leading him back toward the main room. "She'd probably believe me. This is an old-style Japanese house with old-style servants."

"Any idea where this particular old-style Japanese house is?"

"None. We could be halfway to Osaka or we could be up near Sendai. I can't tell."

"*Dozo, omatase itasimashita,*" the old woman said, hurrying in from the kitchen with a large platter of sandwiches. Misako suggested that they eat facing the ocean, and soon the old woman had them all set up on the veranda, with plates and little bowls of green salad and hot tea. Jack tried a sandwich—they were superb. He grinned at Misako.

"Good?" she asked.

"Maybe we should just stay here and suffer through captivity for a while."

"I don't think we have much choice. Those guards and the fence are to keep people out. But they will also keep us in."

"Whoever brought us here did it for a purpose," Jack responded, "and I'm sure he'll drop in to say hello pretty soon. In the meantime—" he reached for another ham and cheese sandwich "—would you mind telling me who Muramoto is, and whether a *Zaibatsu* is animal, vegetable, or mineral?"

Misako nodded. "At Kyoto University my major subject was modern Japanese history, so I know a little bit more about the *Zaibatsu* than most Japanese." She paused for a sip of tea. "But almost every adult in Japan has heard a lot about them. You have, too, except you don't recognize the word. But you recognize names like Mitsui, Mitsubishi, and Sumitomo?"

"Companies?"

"Now," she said. "But originally, families. In America you had Rockefeller, Carnegie, and the man with the railroads. . . ."

"J. P. Morgan."

"Yes. Fantastically rich families who were major—" she searched for the word "—shareholders in enormous companies that they controlled."

"We called them the robber barons."

"And in Japan, we called ours the *Zaibatsu*. At the beginning of the Meiji period, starting in 1868, powerful samurai families used government contacts to win concessions in one industry or another. Hachiroemon Mitsui began his *Zaibatsu* with silk mills. Yataro Iwasaki started the Mitsubishi empire with a steamship line and a Nagasaki shipyard. The Sumitomo family began with copper mines near Kyoto."

"Were they as rich as the Rockefellers and the Carnegies?"

"Richer," she told him. "You can't even imagine. Between World War One and World War Two, a handful of *Zaibatsu* completely dominated every area of Japan's economy. Mitsui was the biggest of them all—the biggest company in the whole world. It guaranteed more than three million workers lifetime employment.''

They sat there, side by side, legs dangling off the veranda, eating finger sandwiches and contemplating a company that could employ three million people. "So," Jack finally asked, "what happened to the *Zaibatsu*? Did the Japanese government try to break them up the way the American government tried to use antitrust legislation to fight the huge monopolies?"

"You ask a very difficult question," Misako told him. "From what I know of what happened in America, the Rockefellers and the Carnegies controlled their empires by owning a majority of shares in each company. This made them easy targets when the government decided to break their power. In Japan the *Zaibatsu* families didn't control their empires by direct ownership. So it was much more difficult to figure out the extent of their power."

"If they weren't the major shareholders, how did the *Zaibatsu* families maintain control?"

"Loyalty."

"I don't get it."

"Each of the *Zaibatsu* empires was like a little country; they had mines for raw materials, shipping companies for transportation, manufacturing plants, stores to sell products in, and even their own banks. I don't know what you call that. . . ."

"Horizontal conglomerates," he told her. "Spread wide."

"Very wide," she agreed. "But the *Zaibatsu* families didn't need to be major shareholders in each of the companies in their empires. Instead, they relied on very strong bonds of loyalty to the group of companies and, through that group, to the founding family. Some of these family bonds were formed all the way back in the Tokugawa period. They were secret and sacred in an old-fashioned Japanese way." She shrugged her shoulders. "Even modern Japanese people can't always understand such things."

"So what happened to the *Zaibatsu*?"

"After World War Two, during the American occupation, Mac-Arthur and his experts blamed the *Zaibatsu* for being one of the major causes of Japan's military expansionism. They broke up the *Zaibatsu*. And they tried to take all of the power and influence away from the original families."

"Did they succeed?"

"In some cases, yes," she said. "In other cases it was less clear. Many officers in the American occupation were too afraid of the Japanese left to completely destroy the Japanese right. The Yakuza and the *Zaibatsu* both were . . . purged, but not destroyed. Now it's been forty years since the occupation ended. Many of the old *Zaibatsu* companies have slowly regained power." She looked at Jack. "They've even bought up land and office buildings and film companies in America. Their old traditions continue . . . things like exclusive social clubs for executives, and company songs and flags, and lifetime employment."

"And the families themselves?"

"Who knows?" she said. "There are screens behind screens. Certainly many of the *Zaibatsu* corporations today seem to be independent of the original founding families." She paused. "But the old bonds of loyalty were very deep, and many things that were changed by the Americans during the occupation have been slowly shifting back. The best example is the divinity of the imperial family, but there are many others. In the last ten years there has been evidence that some of the original founding *Zaibatsu* families are still tremendously powerful."

"And the Muramoto were a *Zaibatsu*?"

"Not one of the oldest or one of the biggest, but an important one," she said. "The Muramoto were one of a group of latecomers we call the 'New *Zaibatsu*.' Between the wars, the New *Zaibatsu* grew rapidly by exploiting Manchuria and supplying the Japanese military machine. I don't know much about what happened to the Muramoto after the war, except that the son of the founder lived to a very old age and was supposed to be one of the richest men in Japan."

"And he died recently? In a plane crash?"

"Died or was killed," Misako said, taking a small sip of tea. "I know professors in Kyoto who could tell you much more, but that's about the best I can do."

The old woman came and took away the remains of the lunch. Jack waited until she was gone. "So the reason why you got so scared in the park is because we may have somehow gotten mixed up with some heavy hitters?"

"If it is the Muramoto, then I'm sure whatever is going on, there are billions and billions of dollars at stake," she told him. "And the connections of the *Zaibatsu* families to the Japanese government, the police force, the military, and even the royal family itself were . . . incredible.''

"And perhaps still are?"

"Almost definitely still are."

"That might explain how strings are being pulled all over the place."

"Yes," she said, looking out over the expanse of ocean. "Yes, it might. In the National Police force, and in the little city of Atami, also . . .'' She was quiet for a time, perhaps thinking of her lost job. "I think I see a path down the cliffs to the ocean," she finally said. "I'm sure the old woman could find us swimming suits."

"The way she takes care of us," Jack said, "she could probably outfit us with scuba gear. Sure. Let's go."

They swam until the sun started to go down, and then showered in the Western-style bathroom and sat down to a dinner of seafood and vegetable tempura. The batter coating the prawns, eggplant, sweet potato, string beans, and asparagus was so celestially light that it seemed to melt away almost instantly in the mouth. It had gotten chilly, so they ate inside, on a low table with a heater underneath. The old woman brought them pitchers of hot sake that warmed Jack's insides and gave Misako's cheeks a crimson glow. As the old woman cleared away the meal, Misako asked her when they might expect to hear from the owner of the house.

The old woman shook her head. She was just a servant, she explained. Her duties were to cook and clean, and beyond that, she knew absolutely nothing. She in turn asked whether Jack and Misako would prefer to bathe together or separately. Misako translated the old woman's question for Jack, and then asked him, "Is it okay with you if I bathe first?"

He looked at her, conscious of the choice she was really making. She lowered her eyes modestly. "If you prefer to bathe first, I'll wait," she said.

"No, go ahead if you want to. Whatever you want."

While Misako bathed, Jack watched the old woman bustling about the room, laying out two futons side by side. He found himself throwing continual glances at the two mattresses pushed together, and an inner tension made him pace through the little house from room to room. The old woman worked with a slight smile on her face, and Jack wondered if she sensed his nervousness and guessed the reasons for it.

Misako came back from her bath wearing a heavy robe. "It's your turn," she said. "It's a wonderful bath. There's a towel and a robe laid out for you."

The bath was off in its own little room, facing the ocean. The windows of the room had been opened so that the cold night breeze from outside blew off the steam that curled up from the bathwater. The tub was ten feet around and made of redwood, and the water inside it was hotter than any Jack had yet tried. The first time his wounded shoulder and leg touched the water, they stung, and it took him nearly five minutes to immerse himself. When he was finally in the bath, he lay unmoving for a long time, listening to the distant splashing of the waves far below.

After a long, peaceful interlude of what seemed almost like sensory deprivation, he emerged from the bath and toweled himself off. Wearing just the heavy woolen robe that had been laid out for him, he walked back through the house to the bedroom. Misako had pulled the futons apart and was already under the covers of one of them. She turned her head and watched him enter.

"Hi."

"Did you enjoy the bath?" she asked.

"Very much. Where's our old aunt?"

"She's gone to bed in the other house. She wished you good night."

"Oh." They looked at each other in the dim illumination of a single ceiling light, masked by a white paper lantern. He felt himself stiffening under the robe, and wondered if she could see it. "I don't feel tired yet," he said, his voice suddenly husky. "Do you?"

"Yes."

"Misako . . ."

"We should sleep. Will you turn off the light?"

He stepped over to her futon, knelt next to her, and gently stroked her hair.

"I think tomorrow will be a very difficult day," she whispered. "Good night."

He took a deep breath and let it out slowly. "Good night, Misako. Sleep well."

"You, too."

He turned off the light, took off his robe, and got under the thick coverlet. For a long time he lay awake, conscious of how near she was to him. Around the little house, the wind increased till it rattled the shoji screens. Thousands of noises from the outside night blended together into a strange concert of rising and falling sounds, sometimes soft and melodic as a lullaby and then swelling suddenly to a discordant cacophony. Waves split on sharp rocks, and choirs of crickets chirped night masses, and somewhere far in the distance an owl stitched its hunting call into the fabric of black.

Jack tried to separate the different sounds, and to distract himself with thoughts about the case and about what surprises the next day might hold, but he could not drown out the soft, regular breaths sounding a few feet from him. Finally Misako's breathing became shallower and more regular, and he slept himself.

He woke to the crash of thunder and the pounding of heavy rain on the rooftop. A night storm had sailed in off the Pacific, and the little house on the edge of the bluff was directly in its path. Flashes of lightning animated the landscapes on the sliding screen partitions, and rolling bursts of thunder exploded directly overhead.

"Jack?"

White lightning strobed her face, and he saw that her eyes were wide open and that she was looking at him.

"Quite a storm. Like it?"

"No."

"What's the matter?"

"Nothing . . ."

"What, Misako?"

"It sounds silly."

"Tell me?"

"I'm afraid of thunder."

Another burst shook the room, and Misako ducked her head beneath the coverlet. She remained underneath, hidden from view.

Mouthing a silent prayer that the thunder would keep getting louder, Jack lifted his blankets, rolled across fifteen inches of cold tatami matting, and slid beneath the covers of her futon. Lightning flashed and she looked into his face and drew away. For a moment they were on opposite sides of her futon, watching each other in awkward silence, and he wondered if he had made a mistake and should apologize and go back to his bed. Then a tremendous thunderclap shook the little house, and suddenly she pressed her body tightly up against his and turned her face into his shoulder.

The warmth of her naked body flooded over him all at once. Her soft breasts flattened against his chest so that he could feel each of her terrified breaths, her stomach clamped tight to his own, her pelvis unashamedly pressed itself against his groin, and their legs intertwined. He circled her with his arms, tightening his biceps and locking her to him. For a long time he just held her close, feeling her heart beat against his own.

When the rolls of thunder became less frequent, her terror slowly subsided, and she kissed him high on the cheek to thank him. He relaxed his grip and slid his palms slowly over her shoulder blades, down the small of her back, all the way to the curl of her buttocks.

She turned her face to his, and he kissed her very gently on the lips. Even as she returned his kiss, she trembled and pulled her lower body a little bit away from his. "What is it?" he whispered.

"Nothing. I . . . can't explain." Another tiny shiver. She rolled over so that she ended up behind her, with his chest tight to her back.

"Misako?"

They lay inches apart and listened to the rain on the roof. It was raining in bursts—sudden downpours giving way to intervals of weak drizzle. "Hold me," she whispered.

His tongue tasted the smooth skin and tiny hairs on the back of her neck. She made a purring sound. He slid his hands to her sides and up under her arms till he was embracing her from behind, his hands cupping her breasts. She gasped and covered his hands with her own, but she did not try to remove them. Her breasts were full and firm, and he could feel her heart thumping with both of his palms.

She spoke in stutter steps, her mind moving in awkward leaps as her body began to take over. "Please . . . don't do that. . . . It feels so good. . . . Please . . ."

"Why are you so scared?"

"Please . . . you musn't do that."

"Do you really want me to stop?"

"No. Yes. No."

His hands pulled her knees apart, and he bit down gently on the nape of her neck. His right index finger traced up from her knee to squeeze between her thighs, and Misako moaned. She locked her legs around his wrist as his finger slipped deeper. She said something in Japanese that he couldn't understand, but it didn't sound like a command to stop.

Suddenly she rolled over onto her back, her eyes closed, her thighs falling apart. He moved his body between her legs, careful to keep his weight off her, and kissed her gently on the cheek, neck, and lips. She opened her mouth to him, and their tongues sparked. He used his fingers to guide himself gently into her while she lay with her eyes closed and her stomach heaving. He stopped when he was just barely inside of her. Her hands fluttered lightly over his neck.

"Open your eyes," he whispered.

She replied with a moan.

"Look at me."

"No."

"I want to see you feel me inside you."

She half opened her eyes. Still he held back, supporting himself with his arms in a push-up position. He kissed her very gently on the lips. Lightning flashed and she opened her eyes all the way and looked right up at him. Her pupils glowed. She mouthed his name.

"Misako?" he whispered back, thrusting in a tiny bit deeper. She was warm and taut, and every movement further inside was exquisitely tantalizing. "Misako?"

"No. Yes. Please, now. Jack? Jack!"

Her bright pupils seemed to dilate as he drove himself all the way into her in one smooth, strong thrust, and she made a sound in the back of her throat halfway between a whimper and a growl. For a second they were frozen in the wonderful shock of that first deep entry. Then her legs opened a bit more, and they began to make love tenderly.

For a long, sweet interval they moved together with a gentle rhythm, completely lost in their own closeness. The futon was firm beneath her, and her body was soft beneath him, and there was an honesty and a tenderness to their caresses that was in its own way as pleasurable as the electric thrill of their bodies clinging and uncoupling.

After a time her breathing got faster and steadily louder and their rhythm quickened. Gasps turned to moans, and soon he found himself jackhammering her wildly bucking hips. She shouted something that got lost in a clap of thunder, and wrapped her legs around him. Dimly, in a corner of his mind, he felt the pain from his injured leg, ribs, and shoulder, but his body had taken control and would not be slowed or reasoned with.

He looped his arms beneath her knees and spread her out, lifting her slightly and bending her backward so that her legs were doubled back almost onto her shoulders. Her breathing became frenzied as the new position allowed him to slide in and out in long, powerful downward strokes. He felt himself about to come and slowed his thrusts for just a moment. Sliding his hands up her ankles to her heels, he held her by the soles of her feet and drew his arms far apart, spread-eagling her wide.

Her hip movements became spasmodic as he stroked faster and faster. A series of low moans ripped from her throat. The low sounds merged and built to a single urgent vibrating ululation. He came, exploding inside her again and again, continuing to thrust until the very end when he buried himself to the hilt and let the final contractions take place in utter stillness.

For a long time they lay gasping, his arms loosely around her back while his face was buried between her breasts. Finally their gasps leveled off into deep breaths, and he rolled to the side to take his weight off her. Rain drummed on the roof.

He ran his hand through her long black hair, and down the side of her face to her lips. She took two of his fingers in her mouth and bit down gently. "I hope we have some time together," he whispered.

"Don't talk about that now."

"Why not?"

His question hung in the cool, damp air that seemed to be charged with electricity from the lightning. "You don't know what the Yakuza are like. We could both be killed tomorrow."

"At least I'll die happy."

She touched his cheek. "You're such a boy."

"Listen . . . I know you're frightened . . . and worried about your career. . . . But it will work out some way. . . ."

"Shhh." She kissed him on the lips to silence him. The storm slacked off and the pounding rain became a drizzle that whispered intermittently on the wooden roof that covered the little Japanese house at the edge of the cliffs.

23

It was a gathering of the clan. The gangsters began arriving just before noon, their black sedans coming one after another so that the front sentry never seemed to have time to completely shut the iron gate. These first arrivals were all of a kind, fiftyish and tough-looking, with closely cropped hair and dark suits. Many of them were missing the top joints of their little fingers, and all seemed to chain-smoke American cigarettes.

When several of the Yakuza took off their jackets to help move tables into the little house, Jack saw intricate tattoos on their arms. "Are the tattoos a kind of gang symbol?" he asked Misako.

"They were originally used to show . . . fortitude," she told him.

"Sometimes your vocabulary is scary. In what way did the tattoos show fortitude?"

"In old Japan, it was very painful to get a tattoo. The artist used a little tool of bone or wood, with many tiny needles. A gambler or a gangster who wanted a full-body tattoo had to endure weeks of terrible pain, so in a way, getting a tattoo showed that a man had strength and courage."

"And now?"

"There are painless methods. But some of the gangsters still insist on getting them the old-fashioned way."

After fifteen or so middle-aged Yakuza lieutenants had come, the more senior chiefs started to arrive. They came in chauffeured Cadillacs and Lincoln Continentals, and one who looked to be well into his nineties arrived in a long limousine with tinted windows. Among the senior chiefs, Jack recognized the bull-shouldered kingpin he had met in Atami, and waved to him. The kingpin walked over and shook Jack's hand with a powerful grip.

Just then, there was a noticeable stiffening among the assembled gangsters as a Rolls-Royce Silver Cloud pulled in through the gate and rolled to a stop in front of the little house. The gangsters, old and young, all stood at attention as a handsome, silver-haired man in an immaculate business suit got out. He could have passed as the president of a bank if there hadn't been a long, thin scar on one side of his face. Jack had only seen such a wound once before in his life, in photographs in a Heidelberg museum. He recognized it as a dueling scar from live swordplay.

At the sight of the silver-haired man, Misako gasped.

"What is it?" Jack whispered to her. "Know him?"

She nodded. "He is one of the most powerful men in Japan. And one of the most . . . notorious."

"A Japanese Godfather?"

"Be very careful," she whispered. "You have no idea who you are dealing with." The silver-haired crime czar walked toward them, and Jack was surprised when Misako joined the surrounding Yakuza gangsters in bowing nearly to the ground. For a long second Jack was left standing alone, facing the silver-haired man one on one. The crime czar had brilliant, probing black eyes that gave him an almost palpable presence of power and explosive energy kept under firm restraint. As they studied each other, Jack was surprised to find himself slowly backing away. Then two gangsters on either side of him grabbed him and forced him down into a bow, nearly throwing him to the ground.

Low *kotatsu* tables were set up in the three rooms of the little house, and a magnificent banquet lunch was served. Jack and Misako were seated in the room with the crime czar himself and his most senior chieftains. Misako was the only female guest, and she seemed to Jack to be unaccountably nervous; her hands shook during the meal, she knocked over a cup of tea, and she responded to his questions and attempts at conversation with curt, whispered answers. He wondered if the policewoman in her was alarmed at being surrounded by so many gangsters, or if, as a Japanese woman, she felt like an interloper in this otherwise very male assembly.

The food was marvelous. Enormous wooden platters of carefully arranged seafood were placed in the center of each table. Concentric rings of large, sweet shrimps and succulent scallops gave way to prawns and abalone and the biggest crab legs that Jack had ever seen. The centerpiece of each seafood platter was an entire sea bream, its body cut up into dozens of sashimi slices that had been artfully resculpted into the fish's original shape. Several old women hurried back and forth between the tables with tall bottles of beer and pitchers of hot sake, filling any glass or cup that looked even half-empty.

The silver-haired crime czar spoke to Jack only once during the meal. At a certain point he asked Misako for the details of what had happened when the assassin had attacked Jack in his hotel room. Jack told him the story simply and accurately, stopping after every few sentences to allow Misako to translate. When Jack gave a physical description of the assassin, it caused a certain amount of consternation in the room, and when he finished, the Yakuza chief nodded and studied him fixedly for several seconds, as if searching for something and not completely finding it.

When the meal was over, the sliding doors to the other two rooms were drawn open and there was a series of enthusiastic toasts. Finally the stern-faced crime czar told Misako and Jack to come forward, and beckoned his lieutenants to gather more closely around. Chairs were brought for the most important Yakuza leaders and for Jack and Misako, while the other gangsters stood arrayed by seniority, watching and waiting to hear the words of their leader.

The Yakuza chief spoke to Misako, his eyes on Jack. "He asks if you were comfortable here last night," Misako translated. "He hopes the rain didn't give you a cold."

"Tell him I was very comfortable, and thank him for his kind hospitality."

"He says we were very lucky in Ueno. The police came just a few seconds after his car picked us up. They searched the zoo and the whole park area for hours."

"Tell him it wasn't luck. We got away because of his superb planning, and the expert skills of his men."

The silver-haired chief acknowledged Jack's compliment with a little smile, and then spoke at length in fast, confident Japanese. "He says he has taken an interest in your case for three reasons," Misako explained. "First, because you have come so far and braved such dangers to avenge your father's death. That is something he admires greatly. The Yakuza have a relationship between senior officers and junior members that is like the relationship between father and son. It is called *oyabun-kobun*. He says that he considers many of the men in this room to be his sons, and he hopes that they will profit from your excellent example of loyalty.''

Around the room, gangsters were standing stiffly, paying full attention to their leader's every word. Jack wondered how many of them understood English, and could follow Misako's translations of the crime czar's quick, short Japanese sentences.

"The second reason he has taken an interest in you is that you survived an attack—'' she searched for a phrase—''from a master killer. He says that such a thing is very rare and deserves respect.''

"Tell him I just got lucky,'' Jack said. "The next master killer will probably get me.''

Misako translated, and the Yakuza chief grinned, as if to show that he liked a man who could joke about his own death. Then he spoke again in fast Japanese. "He says the last reason why he is interested in your case has nothing to do with you at all. It has to do with a most unfortunate disagreement between two large organizations, and you just happen to be a convenient way for him to further his cause. So in a way, he is using you. He tells you this out of respect for your loyalty to your father.''

"Tell him that, in a way, I'm using him, too. But I do appreciate his honesty.''

The silver-haired leader nodded, stood up, and began to pace, his brilliant eyes flashing from his lieutenants and senior advisers back to Jack, and occasionally swinging to Misako. He spoke passionately, almost theatrically, like a Shakespearian actor delivering a soliloquy. Occasionally he waved his arms for emphasis, and twice he banged his fist down on one of the low tables with enough force to make the teacups rattle.

"He would like you to know that he is very concerned about our younger generation,'' Misako told Jack. "He says young Japanese today lack respect and a sense of tradition. Children are discourteous to their parents, and students speak rudely to their teachers. There were even violent attempts to disrupt the new emperor's coronation. This distresses him greatly. The young Japanese of today have everything handed to them, so they lack character. When he was young, his first job in the Yakuza was sweeping out the headquarters of his gang. For three years he swept twice a day. Many young people today don't have the patience to sweep. He says the violence between gangs that you may have heard about, and the negative images of Yakuza all over the world, are products of this lack of discipline. True Yakuza are humble and honorable, and they have an important role to play in today's Japan.''

The silver-haired chief fell silent, watching Jack. All eyes suddenly turned to him, as if the assembled Yakuza expected him to make an answering speech about America. Instead, Jack said, ''Tell him that that was all very interesting, and ask him what he knows about the Muramoto *Zaibatsu*.''

Jack's two Japanese words produced a sensation in the room. Startled whispers flew between middle-aged lieutenants, and the silver-haired leader glanced significantly at his nonagenarian adviser. Then the Yakuza chief asked Misako exactly what she and Jack had learned about the Muramoto.

She summarized what they knew, and explained that they had no idea how to proceed further or how Jack could evade arrest if he stayed in Japan.

The crime czar aimed a series of quick questions at Jack. ''You understand what a *Zaibatsu* is?''

''Yes.''

''And the history behind them?''

''A little bit.''

''Then you comprehend the power that you are up against?''

''I know they've got billions of dollars.''

''Money is merely one manifestation of power. In Japan we say stature is far more important than wealth. Do you understand?''

''They're all connected?''

''All through the government. And particularly in the police force and the military. The Muramoto originally gained power by supplying the army, so the ties there are very old. You cannot trust anyone.''

''Fair enough,'' Jack said, looking around at the several dozen men assembled in the little house. ''Is it wise to continue this conversation with such a large audience?''

Misako, who had been translating almost simultaneously, hesitated and whispered, ''You must be careful not to insult anyone—'' but the crime czar cut her off, demanding a translation of Jack's remark.

When he heard what Jack had said, the silver-haired leader laughed. ''So you warn me to be careful, too? It is always good advice, *nee*?'' He glanced around the room, his probing eyes moving purposefully from face to face, pausing here and there to meet a pair of eyes or study a facial expression. "The men in this room have all sworn oaths of loyalty to me," he said in a low voice. It was less a boast than a statement of fact. The room had gone still and completely silent, save for the crime czar's near whisper and Misako's equally soft translation. "They have all served well, and they would sooner die than betray me. They are my family and I trust them. I will tell you a great truth, Mr. Jack Graham from America: No matter how rich a man is, if he cannot trust his own family, then he really has nothing.''

"Then again," Jack said, meeting the flashing black eyes head-on, "it sounds like maybe that old Muramoto leader who went down on the airplane trusted his own people a bit too much and also ended up with nothing.''

The silver-haired chief became animated. "Seiji Muramoto was a personal acquaintance of mine, and a true Japanese patriot. The *kuromaku* Yoshio Kodama introduced us at a banquet many years ago, and we drank sake together.'' His voice rose as he spoke with passion. "I can tell you Seiji Muramoto was a man of purest honor, from a distinguished family. He spent two years in Sugamo with the great Ryoichi Sasakawa, and with Nobusuke Kishi, who later became prime minister. And he was a very close friend of Prime Minister Kakuei Tanaka. His father married a woman from the nobility, and his great-uncle was an adviser to the Emperor Meiji! What happened to him was . . . disgraceful.''

"Exactly what did happen to him?" Jack asked.

The crime czar's face darkened in anger, but he chose not to answer the question. "Let me tell you what I will do for the two of you," he said. "We will give you a car, and some cash. We will put you on a road outside of the Kanto region, where the police search is less intense. And we will give you some help in keeping away from the police.''

"That's not enough," Jack said. He sensed that Misako softened his objection in her translation, but even so, he could see the Yakuza chief bristle. Apparently he was not used to being contradicted in front of his men.

"What do you mean?"

"We're stymied now. All the names we have to go on are names of dead people: Muramoto, Miura, Ida. The only name we have of a person who might be alive, Hara, neither of us recognizes or knows how to track down. We need more than just a car and cash. We need to know where to go from here.''

The crime czar walked over to the old man in his nineties, bent down, and had a brief whispered conversation with him. They seemed to come to some sort of agreement, and the Yakuza leader stood back up to face Jack and Misako. ''You mention Hara. His full name is Kitaro Hara, and he is very senior in the Muramoto organization. You will find him on Hokkaido, where he is well-knowh for his wealth and his political activities. He owns several companies north of Asahikawa, and he runs an academy for . . . rightists and radical students.'' He stepped forward, closer to Jack, so that once more they faced each other. ''That is all. It has been most interesting meeting you.''

''The feeling's mutual. And thanks for the hospitality. If you're ever in Maryland, I know a couple of crab houses I'd like to take you to.''

The silver-haired little man in the immaculate suit held out his hand and they shook. ''I'm afraid I will not be traveling overseas in the near future. But thank you for your offer.'' He paused. ''Given the dangers of your situation, I think it would be a bit disingenuous of me to wish you a safe and pleasant journey,'' he finally said. ''So please allow me to give you some good advice instead. If you decide to go after Kitaro Hara, be most careful.'' He spoke the name with barely disguised loathing. ''All snakes bite, but some snakes have more venom than others.''

Jack and Misako were given a leather satchel containing five thousand dollars' worth of Japanese money, most of it in five-thousand- and ten-thousand-yen bills. A young female hair and makeup artist fitted Jack with a blond wig, and with a fake beard and mustache that covered most of his face. Then Jack and Misako were blindfolded and driven to the outskirts of the city of Ishinomaki, where a car with a new paint job was waiting for them, keys in the ignition.

Misako guessed that the car had been stolen and the plates and ID numbers changed so that it was now untraceable. The Yakuza lieutenant who had driven them to the car waved them away onto the open road, and soon they were cruising through a little suburb, completely on their own.

"Well," Jack said, "curiouser and curiouser. What do you think?"

As if in answer, she pulled off the two-lane highway they had been following onto a side road that ran between gleaming squares of silver and brown rice field.

"Why are we stopping?"

"Because I don't know where we're going." In the far corner of the rice field, two women in high boots worked side by side, bent over nearly in half.

"Hara's on Hokkaido, so we want to head north." He saw a look of doubt in her eyes. "I know our friend the Yakuza chief didn't make Hara sound too nice, but what else can we do?"

"I've heard the name Kitaro Hara before—I can't remember where. Before we go all the way to Hokkaido after such a man, we should find out more about him."

"How can we do that?"

"In Kyoto I studied with a professor who's an expert on modern Japanese economic and military history. I'm sure he can tell us all about the Muramoto *Zaibatsu*, and about Kitaro Hara, too."

"The longer we travel around, the more chance we have of getting picked up by the police," Jack pointed out. They sat in the silent car for a while, watching the two old women plant rice. "Then again, I guess it's kind of crazy to just go blundering around Hokkaido asking for Hara's address without knowing anything about him except that a Yakuza chief says he's the worst kind of viper. You think your professor will be able to shed some light on what's going on?"

"I'm sure he will. At least we'll find out what we're up against."

"Okay," Jack agreed. "Let's detour for a quick education."

They planned out a route together, skirting all the major cities, crossing to the Japan Sea south of Murakami and then following the coast so as to stay as far away from Tokyo and the Kanto region as possible. It was early afternoon when they started out, the little car kicking up dust as it negotiated a long, straight two-lane road bordered by concrete drainage ditches on either side. They passed through a monotonous sprawl of large industrial towns, the drab landscapes dominated by nearly identical five- and six-story ferroconcrete buildings with laundry hanging out to dry from narrow balconies.

As they drove, they talked about the Yakuza chief and the admiration he had expressed for Jack's sense of filial duty. Misako asked a few questions about Jack's father, and he soon found himself talking about his relationship with Walter, and describing the old police detective's last days. He explained how his initial reaction to his father's apparent suicide had been guilt, and how over time that guilt had been replaced by suspicion and a desire to find out the truth and get revenge. Now, perhaps, they were finally on a trail that would lead him to his goal.

Jack's description of his father struck a chord in Misako, and soon she had taken over the conversation and was painting a picture of her own father and her childhood in Hamamatsu. She had been born into a happy and prosperous home, the only child of an upper-middle-class couple. After serving in the army, her father had entered the police force and risen quickly to a position of some importance at the central prefectural office in Shizuoka. He had been hardworking and ambitious, and not having any sons, had pushed her to excel more than most Japanese fathers would push their daughters. When she spoke about his death, in his early fifties from a sudden heart attack, Jack could see that she had not yet fully recovered from the blow.

Though Misako opened up to him in talking about her family, and though they constantly engaged in good-natured banter, as the afternoon wore on, Jack became more and more conscious that some sort of awkward barrier had arisen between them. They had made love the previous night, but Misako acted as if it had never happened, and that they were still just good friends.

He didn't know much about the sexual mores of the Japanese, but from the way she was behaving, he couldn't help wondering if she felt somehow guilty about their having slept together. He was tempted to ask her exactly what was wrong, but he decided just to be patient. Perhaps she needed time to work out the intricacies of their daytime working relationship now that it had a romantic dimension.

As they crossed the central spine of Honshu, the terrain grew hilly, and the small, drab towns were soon separated by patches of dense forest. They reached Bandhai-Asahi National Park in the early evening, and followed the shore of Lake Inawashiro. Two thousand meters above them, Mount Bandai soared from the large lake toward the layered clouds that were awash in a high tide of violet sunset.

Last twilight found them on narrow roads, twisting through thick forests and suddenly emerging onto the streets of rustic villages. Some of these villages had thatched huts and unpaved main streets. "We must really be in the boondocks," Jack told her, his voice shaking as the car rattled down a rocky back road. "I haven't seen a streetlight in half an hour, and this road feels like it was built by hand in the Mejii era."

"This is what the Tohoku region is famous for," Misako told him, straining to stay on the winding road. "The Japanese city people call this area *furusato* or 'the old home country.' When businessmen in Tokyo get drunk, they like to sing songs about the simple life of Tohoku."

"But they don't move back here?"

"No. The kind of old-style Japanese life that they like to sing about, and that you can still see here in places, is just a romantic memory for them."

They reached the Japan Sea between Murakami and Niigata, and followed the coastal highway through the darkness. Jack offered to drive, but Misako pointed out that he couldn't read any of the signs, so if he drove, there would be a much greater danger that they would be stopped by police. She began to tire about fifty miles south of Niigata, and turned off the highway onto a two-lane main road. Soon she pulled into the driveway of one of a series of tacky-looking hotels that stood shoulder to shoulder.

The hotels were intentionally gaudy with huge signs and excessive flashing neon, and almost all of them had been built in odd architectural shapes like sailing ships or castles. "Looks like Las Vegas," Jack muttered as Misako steered the car to a private parking space beneath the pink stucco Magic Kingdom Motel.

"It's a love hotel."

"What's that?"

"Japan is a very hard place to find privacy. Walls and floors are thin, and everyone looks into everyone else's business. So young couples, and husbands and wives who can't get passionate at home, and people having affairs, come to love hotels."

"What makes them so private?"

"You get a parking space beneath your room. You don't sign in or check out, so no one sees you enter or leave, and there's no record that you ever came or went. You rent the rooms by the hour. It's perfect for couples who need privacy.''

He followed her up a private stairway. "If the people who run the hotel don't know who's in the rooms, how can they stop guests from stealing the furniture?"

"This is Japan," Misako said, opening the door at the top of the stairs. "No one steals."

It was by far the tackiest and most ornate hotel room Jack had ever seen. The round bed was on a slightly raised daislike platform, carefully positioned beneath tilted ceiling mirrors. Flaring around the edges of the pink coverlet were flaming red satin sheets and pillow covers. The walls were black and shiny, and the floor was covered with a beige carpet so plush that with each step, Jack's feet sank in half an inch.

Misako shut the door behind them and turned on the light. Almost immediately the phone on the bedside table rang. She picked up the receiver and listened, leaning away from him across the bed. "It's the front desk," she explained, holding her hand over the mouthpiece. "They want to know how long we're staying and if we want anything special to eat or drink."

"Get a bottle of their best champagne, and tell them to leave us alone."

"Would a ham sandwich do?"

"That would be fine."

She spoke a few sentences in Japanese into the receiver, and hung up. "I'm going to take a shower," she announced in a businesslike tone.

He waited, and finally she looked at him. "Is it my fault?" he asked.

"What do you mean?"

"Do you feel bad about what happened last night?"

She blushed slightly and shook her head.

"We didn't use any birth control. Is that what's bothering you?"

"I think it will be okay."

"I know there's a lot of stuff on TV here about not sleeping with Americans because they might have AIDS. I was tested back in America. My former girlfriend and I went together. We were both negative. In case you were worrying."

"No. Please . . . you didn't do anything wrong."

They sat side by side on the edge of the large bed. Music played faintly from a ceiling speaker. He put his right arm loosely around her back, and she leaned her head against his shoulder.

"It's just that . . . I don't want to make any promises that I can't keep," she whispered.

He dropped his arm from her shoulder. "Okay."

She kissed him on the ear, stood up, and walked off toward the bathing room. Jack lay back on the bed, tired and confused. In the next room he could hear Misako's shower cascading merrily down on the tile floor, and even the hum of the air conditioner sounded lulling and oddly melodic. Jack closed his eyes and forced himself to relax.

After a few minutes of drifting, he got to his feet and began to explore. A vending machine by the door offered such treats as dried squid and octopus, while a smaller one next to the bed dispensed condoms and various sexual aids. A bedside control panel featured half a dozen switches. Jack tried a few, and the enormous bed tilted and rocked and vibrated.

Misako came out of the bathroom wearing a pink robe tied with a white sash. Her hair was wrapped in a towel, and she smiled at him. "It's a wonderful shower. You can make it so hard, it's almost a massage."

"I'm on my way."

"I'll take the room for six hours. If we leave early, we can be in Kyoto by tomorrow afternoon."

"How do you pay if you never see any of the hotel staff?"

"They put the bill in here, from the outside," she said, pulling out a two-way drawer built into the wall near the door. "And we pay them back the same way, from in here."

The shower was indeed miraculous. Thousands of tiny needles were launched against his face and shoulders in a never-diminishing fusillade that soon had him wide-awake again. By the time he walked out, his skin glowed and tingled. He put on a blue robe and walked out into the room. The bedside lamp was dimmed low, and Misako lay in bed, apparently asleep.

She stirred slightly as he got into bed next to her, but she didn't open her eyes. "Are you awake?" he whispered.

"No. I'm asleep."

He touched her damp hair. "You've been thinking about something all day. Will you tell me what you've been worrying about?"

"You'll be angry."

"Better angry than crazy."

"I like you crazy."

"Please tell me."

She rolled over toward him. "Everything seems to be something it's not. Who's on our side? Who's against us? You said you didn't even know if Dr. Miles was really crippled. If we can't be sure of something as basic as that . . ." She didn't need to finish the sentence. Her eyes in the semidarkness were mistrustful. "A month ago I had a job and a place in a community. I threw it all away to be with a man who says we're doing the right thing. . . . I just don't know what to believe. Who to trust. It's too much. It's too fast. We must both be insane."

He kissed her on the center of her forehead. "I thought it was something serious."

"It is."

"You can trust me. I'm who I say I am—all the good things and all the bad things."

"That's reassuring," she said, "because we seem to be getting into the habit of sleeping together. Good night, Jack. Turn off the lamp." She put her head on his chest and was soon fast asleep.

24

They reached the outskirts of Kyoto just before noon, and detoured around the city proper to Arashiyama on the outskirts of the western precinct. Misako guided the car skillfully along a winding road that followed the curves of a lovely wide river spanned occasionally by picturesque old bridges. "I know a hotel here," she said. "It's far from the city and police patrols. You'll be safe there while I go find Professor Yoshimori."

"Why don't you just call him?"

She pulled off the road onto a gravel driveway that led to a graceful one-story inn. "He lives nearby. I can go see him and be back in less than an hour. Please, let me handle this my way."

Misako left just after one o'clock, instructing Jack not to leave the room or answer the door till she returned. He obeyed for half an hour, and then wrote a note explaining that he had gone for a walk, and headed out through the completely deserted lobby and down the gravel path to the street.

Along the banks of the Hozu River, tiny shops sold snacks, craftwork, and tea. He passed a lovely old wooden bridge that had been reinforced with concrete but retained much of its original charm. An old man in a straw hat with a wide brim leaned against the rail, using a long pole to slowly raise and lower a line into the swirling river. Beyond the bridge the Hozu widened a bit, and three sailboats meandered lazily back and forth, borne along by occasional puffs from the light summer breeze.

The Keifuku-Arashiyama Station was bustling with Japanese families on vacation, local workers on their lunch hours, and an occasional out-of-place-looking foreigner, all hurrying to and fro in the bright sunshine. Jack kept to the side of the station, away from the ticket booths and souvenir stalls, and no one gave him a second look as he reached a phone box and leaned all the way in to hide his face.

Marsha answered groggily on the fifth ring. The long-distance operator had to repeat Jack's name three times before she accepted the call.

"Hi, Marsha."

"Do you know what time it is?" She managed to sound both sleepy and angry.

"Yes. Sorry."

"Hold on," she grumbled. "I'll get him for you. It's like trying to wake a corpse." There was a long pause during which Jack heard Marsha's voice admonishing her husband in colorful language to open his eyes.

Finally Monroe's soporific mumble sounded across the Pacific. "Who? Jack? Hold on for a sec." There was a pause as Monroe walked into another room and picked up the extension. "Hello, Jack?" He sounded much more awake. "What the hell are you doing over there?"

"Standing in a rural train station trying to keep my face hidden."

"I mean what the hell trouble are you causing in Japan?"

"None. I'm just lying low. Why?"

"From the way people around here are acting, I thought maybe you were trying to sandbag the emperor."

"They're still checking up on me?"

"They've sealed off your office. Taken all your papers and books. God knows what they're looking for."

"Who are they?"

"Inspector's Division mostly. The rumor is that a few of them are CIA, and there are a couple of Japanese agents involved, too."

"Have you heard anything about a Lieutenant Sasaki? Lots of star quality and dresses for success."

"Haven't heard of him, but I'm keeping my distance as much as I can. There are a lot of them asking questions and poking around."

"Any idea what they're looking for?"

"You." The one-word answer jolted Jack. He glanced nervously around the station. No one was paying him any attention at all. Thirty feet away, an old woman selected a gift package of assorted crackers and wafers from a stall.

"Is this line safe?"

"I wouldn't be talking to you if I didn't think so. They haven't made the connection between us. I guess you didn't tell anyone you were bringing me those papers."

"No one. Not even MacCormack."

"They've been grilling the hell out of a lot of your old buddies, but they haven't bothered me again. So I think we're safe having this conversation. Which doesn't mean I like it."

"How's MacCormack?"

"Out of the office. Indefinitely. On special assignment, or at least that's the official dope."

"Unofficially?"

"No gossip, no rumors, *nada*. Or as he himself would say, *gornisht mit gornisht.*"

"What have you got for me?"

"Not a lot. Shannon and her hubby traveled almost everywhere from Borneo to Newfoundland. Never went back to the same place twice. Except Switzerland. Every winter for a week or two, regular as clockwork, they headed for the Alps."

"Same place?"

"They flew New York to Geneva, and then headed for Interlaken. From there, it's anyone's guess."

"Skiing?"

"Ostensibly. At least for Shannon. I did some checking on your theory that maybe Dr. Miles didn't really need the wheelchair, and you can forget that idea. He'd been crippled since early childhood."

"What else have you got?"

"Up until two years ago, she traveled with him to Japan. Suddenly she stopped going and let him take his business trips alone. He seems to have been working primarily for a man named Ida. Absolute cutting-edge stuff. Consulted for a guy named Miura, too, but stopped about two years ago."

"The same time Shannon stopped flying with him to Japan. Connection?"

"Maybe. Maybe she just lost her taste for sushi."

"What about Kitaro Hara?"

"Peripheral figure," Monroe said. "Dr. Miles had almost no contact with him for the last five years. But they definitely knew each other."

"And Seiji Muramoto?"

"Our file on him dates back to before the Second World War. He was a personal adviser to Tojo on Manchuria. Fought in several of the big naval battles of the war. Insisted on flying combat missions. Wounded at Leyte Gulf. During the occupation he was in Sugamo Prison as a war criminal. They were gonna hang him, but for some reason they changed their minds. Less than a year later he was free and clear, wheeling and dealing again. After that he kept away from munitions. Gravitated toward high-tech industries. He caught the first wave of the computer boom and rode it. I guess you know about the plane crash?"

"Yes. Anything else?"

"Nothing concrete, but between the two of us, I'd bet dollars to doughnuts the Mileses knew something bad was on its way. They changed their locks and priced a security system, and they were looking to buy a Doberman. In Los Angeles that's all pretty normal behavior, but it seems suspiciously prescient given what happened. And that's it, my friend."

"That's all?"

"Sorry."

"Apologize to Marsha for me. I won't call again."

"You can if you need to."

"I know, but I won't. Listen, all the papers I gave you—burn them."

"I already did. Doesn't look like you'll be coming back to work here very soon. Good-bye, Jack. Take care."

"Thanks," Jack told him. He headed straight back to the hotel, and arrived barely ten minutes before Misako.

"We should go right away," she announced.

"Where?"

"The Tenryuji garden. Professor Yoshimori is there waiting for us."

During the short drive, Jack told her about his phone conversation with Monroe. At first she was upset that he had left the hotel, but when he reassured her that no one had taken much interest in him, she quickly focused on what Monroe had told him. Her tone surprised Jack—she sounded critical and almost angry, as if she believed the papers Walter had taken from the Mileses' house had been largely responsible for getting Jack, and later her also, into this mess, and she was bitterly disappointed they hadn't done more to clear things up. "The Mileses traveled a lot. Dr. Miles worked in Japan for several different companies. Seiji Muramoto had a long and complicated career. It's all things we already knew."

"You can't blame Monroe. He didn't write the stuff, he just checked it out for me."

"Did he ask you where you were calling from?"

"No. Why?"

"Are you sure you can trust him? I don't see why he had to burn all the papers."

"Because he's a careful man," Jack told her. "There was nothing more he could get from them. And yes, I'm one hundred percent sure I can trust him. What about this professor of yours?"

"He has great intellect and no politics." She pulled into the temple parking lot and stopped so abruptly that they were both jerked forward in their seats. "Sorry."

He put his hand on her arm and they looked at each other.

"Government agents are searching your office," she said, her voice a bit shrill. "Your boss has disappeared. They're questioning your friends. And here in Japan, people are trying to kill you. And we don't even know why."

"I don't like it either," he admitted. "But there's not much we can do about it. So let's see what we can learn from your professor."

Jack had never been on the grounds of a Japanese temple before, and he would have taken the risk of walking through the building itself if Misako hadn't counseled against it. "There will be guards and maybe even police. Anyway, the building is just a modern copy."

"What happened to the original?"

"Lost in a fire," she said. "But the garden is genuine, from the fourteenth century. It's one of my favorites in Kyoto."

Jack was grappling with the idea of a six-hundred-year-old garden when Misako waved her arm and a gnomelike figure farther down the path waved back. They caught up to him, and Jack was soon having his hand pumped by an energetic little man who kept repeating, "It's a pleasure, a real pleasure." Yoshimori was under five feet tall, and unlike many older Japanese Jack had seen who managed to look remarkably youthful into their sixties and seventies, the professor's face was wrinkled and sun-splotched, and his hair had thinned to a few wispy white strands.

They sat near the pond, looking out over the placid water that the afternoon sun had turned a coppery green. Seven large vertical stones stood at the back of the pond, endowing the scenery with something of the weird flavor of a floating Stonehenge. "It was modeled after Chinese landscape paintings," Yoshimori explained. "Sung Dynasty. But you're not interested in gardens. Misako says you want to know about the Muramoto."

"Anything you can tell us," Jack agreed. "Especially what's been happening to them lately."

Two dragonflies glided by, dipped down for a second to trace twin streaks on the glasslike surface of the pond, and then lifted off and circled away. Yoshimori made a strange grating sound deep in his throat, and it took Jack a few seconds to recognize it as a chuckle. "The police, of course, insist on calling the death of Seiji Muramoto an accident," he observed sarcastically.

"Why 'of course'?"

Yoshimori looked at him as if he was naive. "Does a snake chase its own tail?"

"I don't quite follow you. The police and the Muramoto *Zaibatsu* may have close ties, but they're separate organizations, aren't they?"

"I'm afraid you will have to abandon Western notions of autonomy if you want to comprehend something so intrinsically Japanese," Yoshimori told him, reeling off the difficult English words with little apparent effort. "The separation you are used to in America between private and public, between parent company and subsidiary, high government official and business leader and gangster chief—put all of that aside for a moment."

"What do I replace it with?"

"A very old and very functional system of ties and obligations, debts of honor and hidden vendettas, that exists, unspoken but very real, in the minds of some of the richest and most powerful men in Japan."

"It's hard to believe that it's still like that. . . ."

"To say that it is as all-encompassing as it was fifty years ago would be a mistake; to say that it completely disappeared as Japan has seemingly been transformed into a modern, Western-style democracy would be a mistake."

"So what did happen to Seiji? His own guys got him?"

"Seiji Muramoto was old. He had no direct heir. He had had two sons, but both had died years before."

"How did they die?"

"The first apparently accidentally, in a car accident. The second perhaps a little less accidentally, on a mountain-climbing trip that ended in the deaths of the entire climbing party. Seiji Muramoto got older and his grasp on the corporate empire got weaker. Some felt he should give up his power, but he refused. We are talking here about billions of dollars, and about power so vast, it is perhaps difficult for people like us to conceive of."

"They got tired of waiting and took him down? They had already killed one or both of his sons, and finally they went after the old man himself?"

Professor Yoshimori looked across the pond at the seven huge stones angled to mimic the shape of the surrounding hills. He didn't need to answer.

"Who did it?"

"Impossible to say."

"Who took over the *Zaibatsu*?"

"Aaah," Yoshimori murmured with more respect. "You ask the crucial question. Unfortunately I have no clear answer. A power struggle broke out. As I mentioned, there was no direct heir. Several of the more important chiefs have been killed . . . men like Masao Ida and Kenji Miura. The Yakuza were implicated in the deaths, but I personally don't think they were really involved."

"Why would someone set them up?"

"Several years ago some Yakuza *sokaiya*—professional stock meeting disrupters—clashed with Muramoto security men. Shots were fired, and two men were killed. There has been animosity ever since. It was handy to try to pin the deaths on them."

"So if it wasn't the Yakuza, then it was somebody from the inside. Ida got rubbed out. Miura, too. Who does that leave?"

"Kitaro Hara," Professor Yoshimori said. "Also a faction based on Shikoku, led by a woman named Etsuko Matsuda."

"A woman?"

"She has blood links to the Muramoto family and she was married to an important young regional chief who died with Muramoto in the plane crash. Since then she seems to have acquired substantial regional power. I heard a strong rumor that she had been killed, but she seems to have surfaced again, and to be continuing the struggle. There are several other regional pockets of resistance to Hara, but one by one he is overcoming them.''

''*Sensei*, what can you tell us about Hara?'' Misako asked in a deferential tone.

''Let us take a walk,'' Professor Yoshimori suggested. They were soon following a narrow path through the lovely garden whose design had been set down in the days of Dante and Chaucer. ''Kitaro Hara is an important man, not just for business reasons but also politically.'' Yoshimori brought his hands together, interlinking his fingers at obtuse angles as if that were how he plugged into his own vast memory. ''Born in Mombetsu, northern Hokkaido, between the wars. Grew up in a poor fishing family. Drafted into the army and sent to Manchuria.''

''Is that where he met Seiji Muramoto?'' Jack asked. ''I know he was an adviser there.''

''It's possible,'' the professor conceded, ''although they would have had nothing in common. Muramoto was an aristocrat's aristocrat. Hara was the other way.''

''Rose up through the ranks?''

''He won many medals for bravery. From what I've heard, he was very bright but completely self-educated. Fanatically loyal to his superiors and the emperor. When the war ended, Hara returned to Hokkaido. He taught *Iaido*—traditional sword-fighting—for a while. And then he suddenly went into business.''

''Maybe with financial backing from Seiji Muramoto? If they had met in Manchuria?''

''It's possible. In any case, within a decade, Hara was one of the richest men on Hokkaido. He had interests in a number of different industries. Lumber mills. Fisheries. Mining companies.''

''Computers?'' Jack asked.

''A very little bit, perhaps. But not like Ida and Miura. Anyway, his financial success allowed him to begin . . . how do you say it? . . . dabbling in politics.''

''He ran for office?''

Yoshimori looked at Jack as if he were naive. ''The politicians in Japan have very little political power. Hara had no interest in campaigning or serving. He founded a political party called the *Katana no Kai*. It was influenced by the political writings of

Mishima Yukio and modeled after the 'Shield Society' that Mishima founded and funded.''

Misako grasped. "I didn't know Hara was behind the *Katana no Kai*."

Jack looked at her.

"There are many such small, very right-wing parties in Japan," she told him. "Among them, *Katana no Kai* is notorious for its use of violence and intimidation. It probably has ten or fifteen thousand members. . . .''

"Closer to thirty," Yoshimori corrected her. "And it's growing. Its philosophy of the innate superiority of Japanese has a lot of appeal in these days when—you'll forgive me, Mr. Graham— Japan has the strongest economy in the world. You see," Yoshimori said, polishing his glasses on his shirt, "the death of Hirohito and the coronation of Akihito ushered in a new era in the national psychology of Japan. Especially for the young on the far right. The generations that lost the war and humbly rebuilt in the shadow of the United States are giving way. Now there are calls for the emperor to formally reassert his divinity, and for Japan to openly take the place to which its financial power entitles it."

"So a group like Hara's, with his organizing skills behind it, could go far?"

"It's not just his organizing skills. He invests his money in his political party."

"And if he becomes head of a *Zaibatsu*, he'll be able to invest far more?"

"Incalculably more," Yoshimori agreed.

"Where is he?"

"On Hokkaido. In a rural area between the coastal cities of Kushiro and Abashiri. I know someone who's been there. He says it's like a fortress."

"Have you ever heard of Dr. Walter Miles or his wife, Shannon Miles, from America?"

"I read about the suicide of Dr. Miles," Yoshimori said. "I know nothing about his wife."

"I think they were both killed by people in the Muramoto organization. Can you think of any reason two Americans might have been involved in this mess?"

"As I remember from the articles I read, Dr. Miles was a famous computer expert. Many of the Muramoto *Zaibatsu*'s companies are in the forefront of Japan's computer innovations. Perhaps there's a connection." They neared the gate, and Yoshimori glanced at his watch. "I should be getting back home."

"Thank you for your time and help," Jack said.

"Thank you, *sensei*," Misako chimed in with a little bow.

Yoshimori looked from one to the other, and a smile brought hundreds of tiny wrinkles to the leathery surface of his face. "You don't have to thank me. But can I give you some advice?"

This time Jack bowed along with Misako.

"Misako has told me only a very little bit about why you are here and what you are trying to do. That is your own business. But I like you, Mr. Graham; and you—" his eyes met Misako's "—are very obstinate, but you were one of my best and favorite students. Please." His voice sank. "Abandon your quest now. The man you are going after has vast resources and a reputation for violence almost unmatched in Japan today." Yoshimori's eyes caught Jack's and held them. "From what I know of him, he guards his privacy like a tiger. And you will understand I am making a great understatement when I say he doesn't like Americans."

The breeze blew through Jack's fake blond hair, and lifted his beard off his chin for a second before slapping it back down. Listening to the professor's warning, he felt for a split second the sheer absurdity of what he had set out to do, when considering the forces ranged against him. Then he thought of his father. And, for some reason, of the assassin who had tried to kill him in the bath in Atami, and who had kept coming on even as Jack blasted away at him. He didn't know what Misako was thinking next to him, but whatever it was, the professor studied them for a time and nodded sadly.

"I see you are determined," he said. "I know a man who operates a fishing trawler. At this time of year, it goes out regularly around Hokkaido and past the Shiretoko Peninsula. He has seen Hara's compound from the ship, and I know he could drop you close by."

"Can we trust him?"

"Absolutely. He owes me a favor. I will talk to him. Call me tomorrow. In the meantime, think about what I said about going back to America." He hesitated, and Jack saw fondness for Misako and what looked like modesty in the old face. "You two look very nice together. You have everything to live for."

*   *   *

Torches fastened to the prows of wooden skiffs spread rippling light like liquid fire on the river beneath Togetsukyo Bridge. Tiny fish rose up from the depths toward the circles of radiance, only to be scooped up in the bills of cormorants held on long leashes by fishermen standing in the boats. Small rings around the necks of the birds prevented them from completely swallowing their catches, and every so often the fishermen pulled them in on their leashes and forced them to regurgitate the little fish onto the decks of the skiffs.

Crowds of Japanese, many in festive kimonos, strolled back and forth along the banks and across the bridge, watching the fishermen and the play of light on the dark river. Jack and Misako walked arm in arm, silently picking their way between clusters of friends, drinking buddies hurrying to or staggering home from bars, and extended families chatting amiably together along the path beside the bank.

Misako was in a very strange mood—Jack couldn't tell whether she was fearful or sad or contemplative, but she didn't feel like talking and he wasn't going to push her. They passed the bridge, and left the crowds and the brightly lit restaurants and gift shops behind. A few other couples were spaced out along the dark path, some walking side by side and some standing motionless as if frozen by the cold moonlight. The moon was full and pale in the sky, its canyons and craters easily visible to the naked eye. The only sounds were the gentle lap, lap of the river against its muddy banks, the rising and falling hum of night insects, and, occasionally, a child's laugh leaping joyfully across the water from a distance.

Now and again a couple discreetly slipped off the path to kiss in the shadows. Misako's arm was looped inside Jack's, and twice her fingers tightened around his wrist as she almost lost her footing on the dark pathway.

They stopped a mile from the bridge, and stepped off the path to the very edge of the river. Jack looked up at the bright moon through a filter of clouds; Misako's eyes were angled downward at the dark ribbon of current. "Buddha said that you can't step into the same river twice," she whispered.

"I thought it was Heraclitus who said that. Anyway, I don't even want to step into it once," Jack told her.

She let his wisecrack hang in the air, unanswered, as if waiting for the night breeze to disperse it. He felt her shiver. "I meant," she finally said, "that it is foolish to try to hold on to too much. When my father was in the hospital, when he was dying, he told me that time flies like an arrow. Fast and always forward. He told me to remember that, and I have."

"My father didn't have any deathbed advice for me," Jack responded. "One evening we were arguing in a bar. The next morning he had a hole in his cranium. But I guess there's a lesson in that, too." They stood together, smelling the mud of the riverbank and the wetness of the water as it flowed past. "Whatever you want, Misako," he finally said in a low voice. "Now or after."

"Now?"

"If you're scared. If you don't want to go to Hokkaido. I completely understand. You've helped me so much. . . . I can manage alone from here."

"And after?"

"After we finish this thing, if we ever do, I'd like to get to know you better, but if it's wrong for you, then it's wrong." She moved her hand to his neck, touched him with two fingers, and raised his collar against the breeze. "I just think maybe you should listen to what your old professor said. We make a good couple."

"He also told us not to go after Kitaro Hara," she reminded him.

"So he's right half the time." They bent their heads at the same moment, and stood for a time shoulder to shoulder and cheek to cheek. "That temple garden today was nice," Jack whispered. "But to me there's something fake about a garden that's so carefully designed and sculpted and . . . manicured. I prefer places like where we are right now. Blown and twisted to whatever way they end up."

"That doesn't surprise me," she whispered back. "I like discipline, but I like wild things, too." She kissed him on the side of his neck and then slid her hand down to his arm. "It's getting cold. We should go back."

The fishermen had given up for the night, and the river was empty of boats and leashed birds. Sounds of revelry still filtered out of a few late night bars, but for the most part, the throngs had retired to their *ryokans* and *minshukus* for the night. Jack and

Misako walked back silently, arm in arm, just the way they had come, till they reached their one-story wooden inn.

Misako got into bed completely naked, kissed Jack lightly on the lips, laid her head on his chest, and was soon fast asleep. He lay awake for several hours, listening to her breathe and thinking about Hokkaido and about a foot soldier who became an industrialist and ultimately turned into a political organizer, and whom everyone seemed to regard as a lethal son of a bitch. Misako shifted in her sleep, and her warm breath fell tantalizingly over his chest and stomach. He stroked her hair, thinking of the cormorants who could catch fish and taste them but were never allowed to swallow. He dropped off to sleep feeling that he was just starting to understand Japan, and to know it as a country of obvious delights and well-disguised but quite formidable torments.

25

Professor Yoshimori called early the next morning, waking them up with good news. "His friend will be happy to meet with us, and maybe even to take us to Hokkaido soon," Misako told Jack as she hung up the phone. "We're supposed to meet them in half an hour in the city."

They drove into Kyoto proper just as the sun rose above the temple roofs. Jack looked eagerly out the window, catching his first glimpse of the famous city as Misako sped them from one major thoroughfare to another. He saw enough to be confused by the contrasts of a metropolis with one foot in the eighth century and the other one stepping toward the twenty-first. Concrete office buildings stood near wooden temples, asphalt roadways led past tranquil gardens, and graceful old-style shops and restaurants stood side by side with McDonald's and Kentucky Fried Chicken franchises.

In the central business district, Misako turned off onto a narrower street that soon led to a series of industrial-looking buildings and warehouses. "Are you sure this is right?" Jack asked her. "Doesn't look like much of a neighborhood."

"This is the address my professor gave me," she said, pulling into the parking lot of a small fish warehouse. "His friend with the boat owns this place."

Yoshimori came hurrying out of the warehouse, waving toward them and bobbing enthusiastically as he walked. A tall Japanese man in a black leather jacket followed him out the door and stood on the steps. "Sorry to get you up this early," Yoshimori said, "but my friend leaves town very soon and I thought you would want to talk to him right away." He led them toward the warehouse. "Come in, come in. This is Yuji Takada. Misako Watanabe and Mr. Jack Graham from America."

Yuji smiled. His face was deeply tanned, his hair longish and unkempt so that even on this completely calm day, it looked windblown. "Sorry. No English," he mumbled.

"My friend may not speak English, but he has the freshest fish in Kyoto," Professor Yoshimori said. "We've known each other for years. You can trust him completely. I will translate for you. Come."

Jack and Misako followed the two men into the warehouse. Wooden tables covered with scales and fish remains stood on the far side of the large room. Three or four muscular young men in jeans and T-shirts were cleaning up the work space, hosing down the tables and loading bones and fish entrails into plastic bags. The young men gave Jack a quick look as he walked in. Misako drew several longer stares, and then the young men went back to their cleaning.

Yuji led the way into a small office just off the main room. Old leather account ledgers overflowed their bookshelves and were piled up in stacks on the floor. He pointed to chairs for Jack and Misako, and then spoke in Japanese to Professor Yoshimori. "My friend apologizes for not being able to offer you anything to eat. He asks if you would like tea or coffee?"

Jack and Misako both refused, and Jack said, "Please ask your friend if he's going near Kitaro Hara's compound on Hokkaido."

When he heard the translation of Jack's question, Yuji did his best to discourage Jack and Misako. He spoke quickly, almost vehemently, so that the professor had to hurry to keep up. "He says the answer to the question is yes, he will be sailing up the northwest coast of Hokkaido. But he warns you that you will both be committing suicide if you try to enter Hara's place. It would be like trying to get into an army base. He respectfully suggests that you go back to America." Yoshimori stopped translating and nodded to Jack. "You will remember, Mr. Graham, that was also my advice."

"Thanks, but we're going," Jack said. "Ask him if he'll take us with him. We're willing to pay, and we won't be any trouble."

"Since you insist, my friend will be very happy to bring you to Hokkaido," Professor Yoshimori told them. He reached into the inside pocket of his suit jacket and pulled out a small pistol. "Please raise your hands above your heads."

Jack glanced sideways at Yuji, who had taken a shotgun from

beneath his desk and was pointing it at them with a very practiced cool. He spoke in hard monosyllables which Professor Yoshimori, ever obliging, translated: "My friend says put your hands up, Mr. Graham, or he will kill you right where you sit."

Jack slowly raised his hands above his head. Beside him, Misako's hands were already in the air. "I'm sorry," she whispered to Jack. And then she said something in Japanese to Professor Yoshimori that made the old man raise his eyebrows and pucker his cheeks in distaste.

"Do you dare to take such a tone with me?" he said back to her in English. "You came to me for information, and I gave you very good advice as well. If you had listened to your old teacher like a student should, my advice would have saved both your lives. You chose not to listen. Now I must say good-bye." Two young men from the outer room entered the office, and Professor Yoshimori put his pistol back into the pocket of his jacket and withdrew a yellow silk handkerchief. He wiped some flakes of dandruff off his spectacles with it, and dabbed at his forehead. "Yes," he said, "it is truly a terrible waste. Good-bye, Mr. Graham. Misako—*sayonara*."

Jack half rose out of his chair to throw a punch at the professor, but before he gained his feet, one of the stocky young men standing behind him pushed him back down. He tried to roll sideways, but at the same moment he heard Misako scream and glimpsed the other young man swinging the butt of a gun down at his head. A shock wave twisted around and around her high-pitched scream, and then he sank into blackness.

For a long while Jack floated back and forth between complete darkness and a very strange realm of sound and light and dimly perceived movement. His arms were tied securely behind his back, and his legs were bound tightly at the ankles. Several times he almost managed to shake himself out of the hazy oblivion, and once he actually opened his eyes and understood that he was in the bed of a large truck traveling quickly down a smooth superhighway. A needle was jabbed in his shoulder, and he floated back into darkness.

When he revived again, the first thing he was conscious of was a cold wind slapping his face. Then the smell of salt came to him, and the roll of high seas, and he heard an engine grinding away somewhere beneath him. Slowly, out of the tangle of sensory images, he remembered what had happened and opened his eyes.

Misako sat next to him, propped up against a steel bulkhead. She saw the movement of his eyes fluttering open and turned to look at him. Her face was badly bruised, and there was a bloodstain on her blouse. Around them was the blue sweep of wide-open ocean; twelve- and fifteen-foot waves tossed into whitecaps and then subsided into gullies.

"Jack?" Misako whispered. "I was worried. . . ."

"How long was I out for?"

She shook her head. "When I woke up, we were on this ship."

"Did they hurt you?"

"I got a very clean kick at the man who knocked you unconscious," she said, with some pride. "I think, perhaps, I shattered his testicles. Then his friend took a very clean punch at me. The next thing I remember, we were on this boat."

Jack looked around the deck of the ship. It was a large trawler, cutting through the high seas at fifteen or twenty knots. The fact that he and Misako had been left up on the deck, in plain sight of the crew, could only mean that all the men on board owed allegiance to Hara. In the distance, beyond miles of tossing waves, the hazy outlines of a land mass were faintly visible. "Hokkaido?" Jack asked her.

She nodded miserably. "Not that it helps, but I'm sorry. About trusting Professor Yoshimori."

"He had me fooled, too."

"But I was the one who suggested we go to him. Probably I killed us both with that suggestion."

Jack was silent for a time. "If Hara wanted to kill us, they would have already dropped us off the deck. So he must want to talk to us about something."

After several hours, a crew member brought Jack and Misako some water in a plastic container. He squirted it into their mouths for them, but refused to talk to them in either English or Japanese, and went away without responding to Misako's entreaties for food. Painful hours rolled by with no further visits by their captors. By the time the sky began to darken, Jack and Misako were in bad shape. The skin of their wrists and ankles had been rubbed raw by the ropes, and their joints ached from being in the exact same position hour after hour. They were both tired and hungry, and as darkness fell and the wind picked up, it grew very cold on the unsheltered deck.

The same guard who had brought them water returned and draped a flannel blanket over them. It helped a bit, but all night long Jack could hear Misako's teeth chattering and feel the blanket moving as she shook with cold. In darkness the trawler plowed steadily northward, the grind of its engine and the slapping of heavy seas against its bow the only sounds. As the night wore on, Jack's wrists went completely numb, and twice his legs cramped so that he had to stretch his legs out as far as possible and beat his heels against the iron deck. His calf, where he had been shot at Narita Airport, throbbed painfully.

He would have liked to talk to Misako, but the shared suspicion that they would be killed the following day made attempts at conversation fizzle miserably. So they shared the flannel blanket and caught occasional fitful stretches of sleep, and waited for dawn.

Soon after the sun came up, the trawler turned toward land. Rocky mountains emerged from the haze, and Jack could make out the bays and points of a rugged and uninhabited coastline. The trawler headed for a bay that was larger than the others, and the waves leveled off as they left the open sea behind.

In the most sheltered part of the bay, a long wooden dock jutted out from towering evergreen trees on the bank into the icy water. Several different large and small boats, including what looked like a large pleasure yacht, were moored to the dock. As the trawler pulled in, a dozen or so gun-toting guards in green khaki uniforms walked out onto the dock to meet it. There was a brief exchange between Yuji Takada and a muscular man who seemed to be the head guard. Then Jack and Misako were unceremoniously half dragged and half carried off the trawler onto the dock.

The guards loaded Jack into one jeep and Misako into another. The jeeps followed a steeply rising road up to a guardhouse that commanded a sweeping view of the bay. Looking back down the hill, Jack saw that the trawler that had brought them was already out of the bay, cleaving a path through the ocean waves toward the northern fishing grounds.

The two sentries in the guardhouse inspected the jeeps carefully before waving them through. Both sentries held Uzis, and Jack was struck by their quiet professionalism. He and Misako must have been a strange catch to take off a fishing trawler, but none of Hara's men displayed the slightest curiosity or desire to talk to them.

The path continued upward to a fifteen-foot-high fence topped with barbed wire. At the only visible gate, sentries with submachine guns tested the ropes that bound Jack and Misako to make sure they were still secure. Finally the jeeps rolled into the compound itself.

Jack had expected a military-style base designed to be functional, and he was completely thrown by the care that had obviously been taken to preserve the natural beauty of the mountainside. It could have been a health farm for yuppies in the Napa Valley, replete with gardens, swimming pools, towering cedars, and even a grove of sequoias. The barracks were graceful one-story wooden structures, built low so as not to break the tree line.

They passed a dozen young men, all dressed in the same standard-issue khaki green uniforms, working hard to repair a stone wall. Beyond the work crew, scattered among logs and boulders, men sat alone reading or meditating. In a flat clearing covered with golden pine needles, twenty men in white cotton uniforms marched up and back, drilling in a martial art. *"Ichi, ni, san, shi, go,"* they shouted, and stepped and kicked in unison.

The two jeeps came to a fork in the path and slowed. Jack's jeep turned right and Misako's headed left. He pivoted in his seat and got a quick look at her. She was facing him, so alarmed that for the first time since he had known her, her vulnerability showed clearly in her face as outright fear. Her long black hair flew behind her bruised face as her jeep took her uphill, into the wind. Then one of the guards in Jack's jeep grabbed him and spun him back around, and dug a rifle butt into his ribs. Jack doubled over, the new pain searing into the old wound, and by the time he had recovered enough to look up, Misako's jeep was out of sight.

The building they took him to was little more than a shed. Two guards carried him inside and threw him roughly to the stone floor. "Will you just untie me and give me some water?" he asked. Without any sign that they had either heard or understood, they left him on the floor and closed and bolted the door, so that he lay in darkness.

*   *   *

Jack had no idea how long he lay on the floor of the shed in pitch darkness. For a while he worked on his ropes, trying to fray them against the stone wall behind him or pry them looser by twisting and contorting his arms and legs, but all he succeeded in doing was rubbing more skin from his already raw wrists and ankles.

Misako was constantly on his mind—he hoped that they were treating her better than they were treating him. The thought of her at the mercy of this all-male private army made him strain again at his ropes in helpless rage. Not knowing whether it was day or night, he finally slept and woke to find both his legs cramped in agonizing knots. He screamed for what seemed like an eternity before two guards entered, carried him out of the shed still screaming, and loaded him into the back of a miniature pickup truck.

It was early morning. The movement of the truck gradually unknotted the cramps in his legs. A thick ocean mist hung over the tops of the cedars, so that their massive trunks tapered into cloud. As they drove higher up the mountainside, the mist grew thicker and lower till it obscured trees and bushes a few feet ahead. It was like driving through a nightmare—Jack's whole body ached and he had no idea where he was being taken, and boulders and rows of shrubs and tree trunks of fantastic girth burst suddenly out of the mist and just as suddenly disappeared.

The jeep finally pulled up near the edge of a bamboo grove. Two guards lifted Jack out of the backseat and carried him through the grove along a narrow path, occasionally brushing green stalks that seemed to part magically before them. The air was thick with the fresh green scent of the bamboo and the heavier, reddish-tinged aroma from the cedar forest beneath.

In the middle of the grove was a clearing, and in the center of the clearing stood a simple wooden teahouse. Jack's guards hauled him up the steps of the teahouse and across polished floorboards. On the front veranda, facing down across the bamboo grove at the fog-wreathed mountainside, a little man knelt, unmoving. He was deep within himself, his head bowed and his hands pressed palmate to his knees, and he didn't look over or give any sign at all of taking notice as Jack was dragged in. The little man was dressed in the same simple khakis that everyone else in the compound wore, and his reverent pose and bald pate gave him the ascetic look of a Buddhist priest.

A tall Japanese man with wire-rimmed glasses and the serious face of a high-level accountant stepped from a corner of the teahouse and spoke to Jack's guards. They bowed and began cutting the ropes that bound his arms and legs. Jack rubbed his wrists together to restore the circulation, and as soon as his legs were freed, he tried to stand. His legs had been immobile for so long that they were unsteady; he toppled forward and lay for a second on the wooden floor. The tall assistant looked down at him with a face completely devoid of sympathy, but the bald man continued facing out toward the bamboo grove, apparently oblivious.

And then suddenly he turned. His face was small and wrinkled like a prune, the skin cracked with age and sun, but the eyes inside their deep sockets lambent with a youthful glow and energy. Jack got to his knees under the scrutiny of those intense eyes and returned the old man's gaze, studying a face that had perhaps originally belonged to an uneducated foot soldier but now bore deep lineaments of wisdom and experience.

After five long minutes, Jack found the silence unbearable. "What have you done with Misako?" he demanded. "She has no idea what this is all about. If you hurt her, you have innocent blood on your hands." Still, only silence. He heard his own voice go up. "Or don't you care about that kind of thing, you sons of bitches . . . ?"

The tall man with the accountant's face spoke in Japanese, presumably translating Jack's remarks. There was no response at all from the little man, who continued to examine Jack from his kneeling pose. A puff of breeze tossed through the bamboo, making the fronds sway in slow motion. Finally the little man spoke. His voice was high-pitched and slightly musical, and even though he spoke in Japanese for his tall assistant to translate, his eyes never left Jack's face.

The tall assistant translated in dry, colloquial American English with a faint Texas twang. "Our chairman, Kitaro Hara, says that you must be very careful what you say and how you act in the next few minutes. Your life depends not only on the words you choose but also on your tone, and how you conduct yourself. Chairman Hara is older than you are, and he deserves respect."

"Tell him I don't owe any respect to the man who killed my father. There are people in America who know I'm here and will come looking for me if they don't hear from me soon."

The little man took his time replying. He seemed to find spoken conversation an unpleasant necessity, and to resort to it only as a last resort after long silences. Finally he spoke, and his somber-faced assistant translated almost simultaneously. "You are mistaken. Your father was killed by a man named Miyazaki, a notorious assassin, on the order of the computer industrialist Masao Ida."

"Why? Why kill Shannon Miles in the first place? Why push her husband off a cliff?"

This time, when he chose to answer, Hara spoke in quick sentences, one after the other so that it almost seemed as if he were chanting. He paused at intervals to allow his translator time to catch up. "After the death of Seiji Muramoto, a struggle for power broke out between three men. Dr. Miles had worked for two of them, Masao Ida and Kenji Miura. He had initially been introduced to them by his wife, who had met them during her teaching days in Atami."

"She met them at the Okawa Hotel," Jack said, nodding. "In those days it was called the Star. She was called in as a translator and met both men."

"Yes, you know a great deal. After she got married in America, she introduced her husband to them. Dr. Miles's most important and most recent consultations had been with Masao Ida. When the power struggle broke out, Dr. Miles attempted to take advantage of the new situation by selling invaluable industrial secrets to Miura. This was a significant betrayal, at a crucial time in the power struggle."

"And Ida found out?"

"Yes. He sent Miyazaki to America, posing as a Japanese businessman, with a second cover as an employee of the Inagawa Yakuza. Ida had hated the Inagawa for several years, since they had interfered with his company."

"Yakuza *sokaiya* broke up some of his stock meetings," Jack offered, remembering what Professor Yoshimori had told him. "So Ida set them up?"

"Exactly. He saw this as a perfect opportunity to take his revenge on Dr. Miles and perhaps make trouble for the Inagawa at the same time. Miyazaki broke into Dr. Miles's home at a time when the professor was away. He found Dr. Miles's wife, Shannon, there, killed her, and made the death look like a suicide."

"And that's when my father got involved?"

"Ida did not want to have your father killed. There was no reason to complicate things further. Pressure was applied on him from his associates to accept Shannon's death as the suicide which it appeared to be. But your father was a stubborn man and he would not let the case go."

"I know. I talked to him about it."

"His inquiries with different Japanese police and consular agencies showed that he was making remarkable progress. So Miyazaki returned to America. He used an ancient *ninja* technique called *koshijutsu*—the paralysis of nerve centers—to overpower your father and then shot him with his own gun and made it look like a suicide. For this work Ida paid Miyazaki twenty thousand dollars, directly into his Swiss bank account. I could give you the account numbers, but it would serve no purpose now."

Jack swallowed at the price tag that had been put on his father's life. "And Dr. Miles?"

"The death of his wife convinced him that Ida's men would soon catch up with him. Deciding that it was pointless to run, especially in his physical condition, and sensing that going to the American police with his story might not protect him, he chose to come to Japan and try to bargain his way out. Ida suggested a meeting in Atami, and Dr. Miles was foolish enough to accept. You know what happened on the cliffs."

Jack nodded. "That explains why Dr. Miles came to Atami willingly, and also why he fought for his life on the edge of the cliff." He kept silent for a time, thinking about everything that Hara had said. "I can't believe this was all about industrial secrets," he finally said. "No matter what Dr. Miles sold to Miura, it couldn't have been worth Ida's having him killed and then going through so much to cover it up."

"You have no idea what Dr. Miles knew and what he sold, and you also don't understand what it means in Japanese terms to betray on that level at such a crucial moment. There was an entire business empire to be won or lost."

"So who killed Miura and Ida?" Jack asked. "And who blasted Seiji Muramoto's plane out of the sky and started this whole thing? Did you?"

The tall assistant looked uncomfortable translating Jack's question. Hara's answer was immediate, and as final as the slamming of a door. "I have answered all of your questions that deserve to be answered. What goes on here in Japan, between members of an organization you know something about but will never be able to comprehend, is of no further concern to you. There remains only the question of what to do with you, and there are only two possible answers."

A middle-aged woman in a snow white kimono bowed her way into the room and carefully handed Hara a cup of hot tea. She immediately withdrew. Hara sipped the tea slowly, inhaling its bitter fragrance as he studied Jack's face a final time. "I have no great fondness for America or Americans," he said through his translator. "Your language disturbs my ears; your smell offends my senses. You should learn to bathe more and talk less."

He lowered the teacup for a moment and looked out across the bamboo fronds that floated above the mist. "Do you like to read history?"

Jack didn't answer.

"I have little formal education," Hara admitted through the interpreter, "but I like to read history very much. Have you noticed how countries are like people?"

"I don't know what you're talking about."

"They have their childhoods, their days of glory, and then they grow weak and die and disappear." The little man suddenly began a speech, which his assistant translated in his flat, twangy, remarkably colloquial English.

"Rome is now only a tourist trap," Hara began. "I have walked down the Via Della Corso and watched the young people of my country shop for handbags and silk ties. The descendants of Genghis Khan and his hordes scratch out a pitiful existence amid the rubble piles of Asia. As for England, not only will she never again rule the waves, but I doubt very much she will even be able to keep up a semblance of leadership in Europe. That mantle has passed to Germany, and if I know the Germans, they will not let it drop a second time."

Jack kept silent, watching the lively black eyes in the shriveled old face.

"Your country has had its three or four decades in the sun, which is perhaps more than it deserves, given its combination of naïveté and oafishness. Now it is our turn. The indignities of defeat and occupation are well on their way to being reversed. We Japanese have a destiny, Mr. Graham. We will seize it and hold it. I believe I will live to see that happen.''

He stopped his speechifying as abruptly as he had started it and focused again on Jack. ''But the question we need to decide now is whether you will live to see the sun set this evening on the mountainside behind us. Despite everything I said about Americans, I believe you are an honorable man. You have come far to avenge your father, and as I explained to you, you have already accomplished that obligation fully and admirably. Unfortunately, after avenging your father's death, you have persisted in investigating matters that really do not concern you, and you have caused me a certain amount of trouble. Now you are in my power. No one knows you are here, and I could have you and your woman friend killed, and simply deny everything. Believe me, I could do this very easily, and I would not feel guilt.''

''I believe that,'' Jack told him, looking him in the eye.

''On the other hand, I'm aware that you are a federal agent, and that you have some loyal friends back in Washington who have some knowledge of your intentions here. If you disappeared, they might become a nuisance to me. I have no desire to expend further time, energy, and money on this trivial matter. That suggests the need for a second possible way of dealing with you.''

Jack waited.

''Suppose I release you. Send you back to America. Give you your meaningless life back. I think I can even guarantee that certain charges relating to violations of the Neutrality Act will be dropped. And in return you give me your word not to pursue this further. You are a young man with many years ahead of you. I will be rid of you and your troublesome friends. Perhaps we will both come out ahead.''

''And Misako?''

''If you wish to die, she will die right here with you. If you choose to go back to your former life, she will go back to her former life also. I have certain connections with the Japanese police that will allow her to resume her job in Atami. The choice is yours, Mr. Graham.''

''I need to talk to her.''

''The decision is yours. You have ten seconds.'' The little man stood and walked to the edge of the porch. The tall assistant shouted a single guttural syllable. Two guards who must have been waiting just outside for the duration of Jack's conversation with Hara hurried into the room. They both held submachine guns, and one look at their faces told Jack they would use them on him without compunction.

Ten seconds. Bits and pieces of what Hara had just told him flashed through Jack's mind as his heart began to race and blood pounded against his eardrums. What was to be gained by dying? Apparently he had already succeeded in killing his father's murderer. Everybody said so, even the Yakuza chieftain. Most of Hara's explanation seemed to make sense. This whole Muramoto *Zaibatsu* thing really was none of his concern. And Misako's life was linked to his own. . . .

"Ten seconds are up. What have you decided?"

"I will go back to America."

The little man nodded. "We will make the arrangements for you. You will be back in your own country in less than two days." He paused, and a serious glint tossed about in the whirling black depths of his eyes. "If you ever give me trouble again, you will be instantly and painfully eliminated. That's all."

Hara turned to face the serene view of trees and sky as the two guards grabbed Jack by either arm and hustled him quickly away.

Jack refused to let Misako come to Narita with him. He hated airport farewells, and he preferred to carry away from Japan a last memory of her in her police uniform walking by the sea, while behind them the old spa city of Atami spread out over the hunched hills.

Matching her step for step, her small palm warm in his own, Jack listened to the wash of the nearby surf and kept his jaws locked together. He wanted to argue with her, to find a way to spend more time with her, but she had made her decision, and he was determined to find the courage to accept it. She had followed him far and risked her life for him, and he owed her the most graceful parting possible.

"Will you fly back to Washington?" she asked him after they had walked nearly half a mile.

"Sure. Plane stops in New York for an hour and then on to D.C."

"Is it nice in the summer?"

"It's okay." He made a tremendous effort to sound conversational and light. "Tell you the truth, it gets pretty hot and humid, but the Bureau's air-conditioned and so's my apartment, and on weekends I sometimes get away to the Chesapeake or I head into Virginia. I've got a grandfather who owns a house on the Chickahominy. . . ." His words caught in his throat, and he let go of her hand. Her fingers trailed down his to his wrist, and dropped off into space.

"Jack," she whispered. "This is hard for me, too. But it'll be better in the long run."

"Let's not talk about it."

A sea gull circled overhead like a small vulture, its hungry cries rising over the rush of the surf. "Okay," she said, with a little smile. "They won't give you trouble back in America?"

"No. I don't know what strings Hara's pulled, but everything seems to be forgiven and forgotten."

"It's strange," she agreed. "I have my old job back, and nobody asks me any questions. Even my next-door neighbors don't ask me where I went."

Jack nodded. "The Atami police gave me back all my possessions from my hotel room. Even the painting from the Okawa Hotel. And Chief Sato came to say good-bye. He wanted to talk about baseball. Like this whole thing never happened."

The gull stopped circling and flew off out over the water. Misako watched the bird glide above the surf. "I'd like you to know that I'm going to miss you."

"My train leaves soon."

She caught his arm. "Jack . . ."

"I should head up to the station."

"I'll walk you up."

"I'd rather say good-bye right here." He raised his hands to her face, his knuckles grazing her lips, his palms flattening out on the warm sides of her cheeks. Slowly he drew her forward and kissed her. "Your father was right," he whispered. "Time flies like an arrow. What a terrible thing to be true." Then he let her go.

"Will you write to me sometime?"

"Sure." He glanced at his watch. If he didn't make the break now, he'd miss his train and they'd end up saying good-bye for another torturous hour. " 'Bye, bright eyes. Catch a lot of Yakuza."

"Good-bye, Jack. Good luck."

He took one last look at her standing in her crisp blue uniform, her black hair stirring in the wind while her eyes glittered with unshed tears. And then he turned and walked quickly away, back up the slope toward the Atami train station.

A pained numbness at having said good-bye to her took hold on the *Shinkansen* ride to Tokyo, so that Jack barely noticed the hour-long trip. He thought back to Hara and the deal the two of them had cut, and tried for the hundredth time to convince himself that he hadn't sold out, but rather that he had completed everything he had come to Japan to accomplish. Soon he was on a Japan Air Lines jet winging his way across the Pacific. He closed his eyes as mingled feelings of success at having avenged his father's murder, and regret for what he was leaving behind in Atami, made him sit back in his seat and clench his fingers around the armrests.

SECTION FIVE

The Stargazer

26

Ten of them crouched motionless in the darkness. It seemed an unnecessarily large number given the element of surprise and the fact that they knew exactly where the boy slept.

They had never all worked together before and they probably never would again, so there was a certain amount of anticipation and curiosity, even among such hardened professionals, as their leader gave the signal to begin. Ten dark shapes crept down like wolves from the high Alpine mountainside toward the Creusot School.

They knew about the guardhouse, the modern weaponry there, and the training the guards had received. The weaponry wouldn't bother them unless they were detected in time for it to be brought to bear, which seemed more than unlikely. As for the guards' training, no matter how thorough it had been, it could scarcely compare to their own. They were from diverse backgrounds and represented many different schools and styles, but they had all spent long decades mastering their disciplines.

They descended through a pass between two jagged crags, and caught their first glimpse of the valley beneath. Tiny waves stirred across the dark lake, gilded with flecks of golden moonlight. The small town of Creusot was silent and still, the windows of the buildings dark.

The sixteenth-century castle that housed the school was a pale silver silhouette against the night sky. Gradually the descent became less steep, until soon they were hurrying across flat, rocky terrain. Skirting the castle's perimeter, they crept close to the north tower.

A half dozen grappling hooks were tossed up and took hold in a bank of narrow windows. Ten dark shadows scaled the rampart. At the top, two men hung back to safeguard their retreat, while eight figures, dressed in black, hurried toward the suite of rooms where they knew the boy was fast asleep. All of them carried guns, and several of them carried swords.

A guard was supposed to be watching the outer door of the suite of rooms, but he had fallen asleep and sat with his back against the flagstone wall, his head drooping all the way over to his right shoulder. He opened his eyes just as the first of them reached him, and blinked at the eight dark shapes. He tried to raise his gun, but before he could get it up more than an inch, a blow from the heel of a hand to his throat snapped his head back into the rock wall. He spilled forward out of the chair, and lay on the cold floor.

The lock on the front door delayed them less than a minute. They fanned out inside the suite of rooms according to the prearranged plan. Two of them searched the living room and guest bedrooms. Three of them, weapons in hand, headed for the bodyguard's room. The other three soundlessly made straight for the boy himself.

The bodyguard woke instantly at the sound of his room's door swinging open, and he moved like lightning. Grabbing his gun, he dove out of bed to the side of the room away from the door, and managed to squeeze off two shots. A hail of answering bullets, fired through silencers, lifted him backward in a bizarre dance of death, his limbs flailing as repeated shots ripped through his chest and turned his face into bloody pulp.

The boy's room was the last on the hallway. The door was open a crack, and the three killers slipped inside. A pink seashell nightlight glowed in a corner. On the other side of the room, behind the bed, a tiny, crescent-shaped window, locked and barred, let in the spectral radiance of the moon and stars. A telescope stood on its tripod, angled up toward Orion. The ghostly light spilled over the partially drawn curtains of a massive four-poster bed. In the gap between the curtains, the outlines of a young, sleeping face could be seen atop a stack of pillows.

The three killers approached, and drew the curtains apart. Still the boy slept, his gentle snores rising slightly at the ends as if he were dreaming in many little questions. He stirred beneath the covers, and as the leader unsheathed his sword, the boy suddenly rolled onto his back and opened his eyes.

For a moment he stared up at the three men without any reaction, his thin features frozen in a mask of complete disbelief and confusion. And then his face pulled taut to his cheekbones, his eyes widened with terror, and he let out a child's scream, as sharp and finely edged as the sword that was slowly raised before his eyes.

A black-cloaked figure bent to the bed, ripped the covers away, and in one motion tore the boy's pajamas off. The man holding the sword waited as the third killer took two quick Polaroid photographs of the boy sitting up in bed, naked, screaming now at full volume. A distinctive birthmark was clearly visible on the boy's left shoulder. The photographs would leave no doubt that their cruel mission had been fulfilled.

As soon as the second picture had been snapped, the man holding the sword effortlessly brought his leg up and sideways so that he almost seemed to be kicking the boy in the throat in slow motion. The high-pitched scream wavered and then broke as the boy was forced backward till he lay flat on his back. Pinned to the bed and silenced, he could only watch in helpless terror as the point of the sword hovered for a second above his rib cage and then flashed downward.

There was a ripping sound as the blade sank in six inches. The child on the bed convulsed. The sword was withdrawn, and almost instantly the cutting edge of the blade swung down in an arc toward the exposed jugular, severing the head from the body with a single quick stroke. Blood fauceted over the four-poster bed. They placed the decapitated head next to the still-twitching body and snapped two more pictures. And then, as quickly as they had come, they turned and hurried away.

The bodyguard's shots or the child's screams had been heard, and a siren began to wail as the killers sped back down the corridor to their waiting fellows. In less than twenty seconds they were all down the ropes, and as searchlights began to sweep the side of the castle and a helicopter took off from near the guardhouse, the ten hired killers split into three groups and began their escape through the darkness.

Two groups got away cleanly. The third was spotted by the helicopter's searchlight, and in the ensuing firefight two of the school's guards were killed and the helicopter forced to crash-land on a glacier. The next morning, there was no trace of the attackers except for their grim handiwork in the north tower. Doctors gave way to dour-faced policemen who laboriously interviewed students and staff about what they had seen or heard. Remarkably few hard details surfaced about the midnight attack. Reporters from Geneva and Lausanne flew to the scene but were not allowed up from the town to the school and had to content themselves with police briefings.

The directors of the Creusot School desperately wanted to avoid further traumatizing their students or attracting more unwanted publicity. With the help of the laconic Swiss police and the relative inaccessibility of the school itself, a pall of silence quickly descended over the entire gruesome episode. Inquiries by worried parents were met with assurances of redoubled security. A brief story made one of the international wire services, but in the hurly-burly of world events, the unexplained murder of an unnamed student was little noticed and quickly forgotten.

Soon the whole story of the mysterious child who had lived up in the north tower and scanned the constellations through his telescope began to seem more like a dream than a real memory. None of the students at the school had known him, no one missed him, and even in the school chapel, no prayers were said for his soul.

MacCormack had grown noticeably older and softer since Jack had last seen him. His jowls rippled as he moved his head, and his ruddy cheeks were fleshy to the point of almost looking puffy. His black eyes were still bright and quick, but at times they jumped far back into their deep-set sockets, like wary foxes never straying too far from their lair.

He had also grown noticeably taciturn, at least when it came to Jack. Gone was the banter, the Yiddish phrases mixed incongruously with the playful brogue. He did not want to know about Jack's adventures in Japan, nor was he forthcoming about his own tribulations in Washington. Instead, all of his energies seemed to be directed toward helping Jack put his days in Japan behind him and getting back to Bureau business.

Arrangements had been made for Jack to visit a surgeon in Baltimore with experience in removing facial scars. After that, staff doctors would examine his lungs, ribs, and leg to make sure that everything was healing properly. "Once you're patched up, take two weeks or so off to recover," MacCormack offered, shifting his weight on his chair. "Then I think I've got an interesting case for you."

"Not that I'm ungrateful for being taken back into the fold," Jack told him, "but aren't you even curious about what happened over there?"

For a second, MacCormack's eyes retreated warily and he tugged at his double chin with his thumb and index finger. "I'm on your side. Don't make this hard. If I were you, I wouldn't discuss it with anyone."

"Why shouldn't I talk about what happened?"

"*Because it's over*. Finished. So let it rest in peace. The important thing now is to get you back in the saddle, working for us again." The big man stood, and extended a meaty hand for a shake. "Welcome home."

Jack took the hand in his own, and looked back into MacCormack's tired face. "What did they ask you?" he whispered. "Who asked? I won't talk to anyone and I'm going to put this behind me and come back to work at the Bureau, but just between the two of us . . ."

MacCormack shook his head very slightly from side to side.

Jack pressed on. "I know you protected me, and did what you could to help me. I'm grateful. Can't we even talk about it?"

And in his own low whisper, as he guided Jack to the door, MacCormack said, "Jesus, lad. You're one of the very lucky ones. Your neck was in the noose. And they're letting you just walk away. So walk, and don't look back."

"I'd just like to know who—"

"You ask too much," MacCormack said firmly, his hand on his doorknob. "And not just from me. Your friends here still have their careers. Don't talk to them. If they've helped you, show your gratitude by never talking about it with them again." He opened the door and propelled Jack outward with a little shove. "Good luck with the surgery. I'll see you in a couple of weeks."

The Baltimore plastic surgeon was skillful and circumspect. He performed the cosmetic surgery without ever asking Jack how he had come to get such an unusual scar in the first place. Later, back in Washington, D.C., doctors examined Jack's bruised ribs, tested his lung, and checked the bullet wound in his leg. They declared that his various injuries were all healing well, and that in time he could expect a complete recovery.

He spent a lonely few days in his Georgetown apartment, watching television and occasionally fingering the playing-card-sized bandage on his right cheek. He was tempted to call Monroe to thank him for all his help and tell him Hara's explanation of the chain of events. After some thought Jack decided to take Mac-Cormack's advice and not to endanger his friend's career any further. So Jack sat alone or went out for long, solitary jogs, trying his best not to think about Misako and Hara and all that had happened in Japan, and in fact thinking about little else.

He missed Misako with an intensity that surprised him. Whether he lay in bed or lifted weights or went for long walks by himself, memories of their afternoon on the lake in Ueno Park and their stormy night in the villa by the sea recurred to him with startling, painful clarity. It was crazy; he reminded himself over and over that they had barely gotten to know each other, yet he couldn't shake the feelings of loss.

In particular he remembered the way she had looked back at him as Hara's men had driven her away in the jeep in Hara's stronghold on Hokkaido. Her hair had flown backward into the wind, and fear, vulnerability, and perhaps even a trace of love had flashed clearly in her bright black eyes. It had been a moment of great danger and therefore great truth—both of them had thought they might die on the isolated mountainside. No one, man or woman, had ever put his or her life on the line for Jack before, and the memory stayed with him.

It got so bad that he was tempted to call her, but he beat down the impulse. He reminded himself of the women who had continued to call and write him for months after he had broken with them. Even as he had politely turned down their veiled attempts at reconciliation, he had marveled at—and in some strange way envied—their ability to forge such strong and passionate bonds. He had even secretly wished that he had the capacity to feel the joys of bonding and the pain of separation the way they were feeling them, instead of remaining detached and coolly rational.

Now he had gotten his wish, and even though the pain and sense of loss kept him awake at night and sent him on long walks along the canal or up to the National Cathedral, he had the strength of will—or perhaps it was really merely foolish pride—not to make the call across the Pacific but rather to bear the loneliness in silence.

To try to put the whole experience behind him, he began discarding all the souvenirs he had accumulated in Japan. He threw out brochures from the many hotels he had investigated in Atami. He donated the painting of the mountain valley of Shuzenji that he had purchased from the old woman artist in the Okawa Hotel to a fund-raising auction for a downtown shelter. Late one sleepless night, he came upon the photographs of Shannon Miles during her teaching days at Atami High School that her friend Mrs. Taniguchi, the office lady, had saved for more than a decade before entrusting them to Jack's care.

He was at the point of throwing out the photographs when he remembered that Shannon's parents had once lived near Boston, and that Mrs. Taniguchi had given him the pictures to send on to them if he could find their current address. A call to Massachusetts phone information revealed that Mrs. Cleary still lived at the address in Weymouth that Mrs. Taniguchi had written down, but that she had an unlisted phone number. Jack decided to mail the pictures in the morning, and be done with the whole mess.

Jack put the pictures aside and tried to get some sleep. It was futile—his mind turned over the same facts and faces and doubts again and again. He wondered why Misako had become his lover and then pulled back so quickly. Hara's explanation of Walter's murder had seemed to tie together a lot of loose ends, yet the more Jack thought about it, the more unsatisfied he felt. MacCormack's uncharacteristic reticence and his warnings not to talk about what had happened in Japan were puzzling and disturbing.

After several hours of tossing and turning, Jack switched on a light and flipped through the photographs of Shannon during her teaching days. Finally he threw on some clothes, took the photographs, and for reasons he himself didn't fully understand, climbed into his blue Mustang and set off northward. It felt good to be getting away from his apartment and out of Washington. Jack pressed down on the accelerator, and the car shot forward.

When he had given Hara his word that he would drop the investigation, Jack's promise had been extracted almost literally at the point of a sword. In no sense did he feel it to be binding. He turned onto the interstate and sped through the darkness toward Baltimore. He wanted to have a look at Shannon's mother and hear about her daughter from her own lips before giving up the investigation once and for all and going back to his job and his life in Washington.

*   *   *

The tree-lined streets of Weymouth seemed prototypically small-town New England—very far removed from Atami, Japan, and the three concrete high school buildings on the hilltop above Izu Taga Bay. As Jack navigated the narrow streets after a long night of driving, he glanced down at the photographs on the front seat next to him. Shannon, red hair flying, spiked a volleyball on the Atami teachers' team. Dressed in shorts and a T-shirt, she competed in the school track-and-field-day races. In the farewell photograph, she stood teary-eyed next to six of her girl students. Jack wondered whether Shannon's parents would really want these mementos, or if, by showing up with them, he was putting to rest his own painful memories of Japan while raking up someone else's deep sorrow.

It was a four-story redbrick building with the name "Admiralty Apartments" painted on the front facade, above a large ship's anchor. In the street outside the building, four teenage boys played an early game of touch football while two girls sat on a car hood watching them and swinging their legs. A postman walked beneath low-hanging maple and elm branches, nodding to almost every passerby, his half-empty sack bouncing around his waist. Norman Rockwell could have painted the scene. Jack was very conscious of intruding on this quiet street; carrying the photographs of Shannon, he felt like an uninvited emissary from a very distant time and place.

Jack entered the lobby of the brick building and ran his finger down the row of names by the front-door intercom. He found Cleary, buzzed, and waited. Seconds passed, and he grew more and more uncomfortable. He even contemplated leaving the photos by the mailbox with an explanatory note. Then a surprisingly husky female voice said, "Hello? Are you here from Delson's about the rugs?"

"Mrs. Cleary," Jack said. "My name is Jack Graham. I'd like to talk to you."

"About what?"

"I have some photographs of your daughter, Shannon, from when she taught in Japan. I visited the school, and a friend of hers there thought you might like them."

"Why didn't you call first?" the voice asked suspiciously.

"I wanted to, but your number's unlisted. So I took the chance and drove out. Will you buzz me in?"

There was a moment of silence while she made up her mind. "I'm on the fourth floor, to the right." The buzzer sounded and he pushed his way in and began climbing. The old building was neatly kept up—the narrow stairs had been freshly swept, and a sign on the third-floor landing warned of wet paint. When he reached the fourth floor and turned to the right, a door ten feet down the corridor popped open as if by magic.

Mrs. Cleary stepped out to look him over. She was nearly six feet tall and slightly stoop-shouldered; a no-nonsense, stern-faced Irish matriarch, still doughty and robust in her midsixties. Her long white hair was covered by a flowery pink kerchief, and she wore a blue cotton apron over her yellow housedress. She stood for a few seconds with her hands on her hips, taking in his unshaven face and rumpled jacket with an appraising look, and then glanced down at the manila envelope under his arm.

He handed the envelope to her, and she flipped quickly through the photographs. A tremor ran across her face, softening the hard lines; she closed her eyes and clutched the envelope to her stomach. She recovered quickly, and looked back at Jack. "Thank you for bringing these to me. Can I get you a cup of tea?"

"It it's no trouble . . ."

"It's the least I can do," she said, holding the door open for him. "Please."

The apartment was in disarray. Furniture had been moved out of some rooms into other ones, and chairs were stacked one on top of the other in the hallway. She guided Jack into the living room, and gestured him toward a faded sofa near a bank of windows that overlooked the street. "Forgive the clutter," she said. "I'm having the rugs done—if those boys from Delson's ever show up. I don't know how they can stay in business. What do you take in your tea?"

"A little milk, if you have it."

"I think I can manage that," she said. "Excuse me. I won't be long." She left the room, and he heard her filling a kettle in the kitchen. Glancing out the window, he saw one of the neighborhood boys run a long square out and make a catch on his fingertips, sidestepping along the edge of the curb to stay inbounds.

The sunlight, streaming through the window, enlivened what would otherwise have been a rather depressing living room. The wallpaper was golden, fading to light yellow in patches. Wedding china was displayed in a mahogany chest that was placed in the center of the far wall to catch the best light. An end table beside the sofa held a collection of snow globes from famous and lesser-known American landmarks: Niagara Falls, Cooperstown, Monticello, and Fort Ticonderoga. On the mantel above the fireplace, a dozen or so photographs framed in silver and gold stood side by side.

Jack walked over and ran his eyes down the row of frozen images. The oldest was a wedding picture, yellowing a bit around the edges, taken outdoors in what looked like a rose garden. Mrs. Cleary was radiant as a young bride, her face turned sideways to stare adoringly at a slightly older groom with an impressive mustache who stood with his arm around her thin waist. Next came baby pictures of Shannon and two little boys, and shots of the happy family of five at a picnic and vacationing on Martha's Vineyard. There were three college graduation photos—one for each of the siblings. Studying Shannon's picture, Jack recognized Yale's Old Campus in the background.

The last photo on the mantel was Shannon's wedding picture. Jack took it down and tilted it with his hands, studying it in the light. It took Jack a minute to realize that Shannon was wearing the same wedding dress her mother had on in the yellowing wedding picture at the far end of the mantel. Dr. Everett Miles sat up proudly in his wheelchair, a rose in his lapel, holding Shannon's hand as if he never intended to let it go. "She never should have married him," Mrs. Cleary commented, balancing teacups and saucers on a tray as she entered the room and crossed to the coffee table.

Jack quickly returned the photograph to the mantel. "Why do you say that?"

"Did you know my daughter?"

"No."

"But you know what happened to her?"

He nodded. She gestured for him to sit on the couch and handed him his teacup on a saucer with two butter biscuits.

"Los Angeles is a dreadful city," she said. "I visited Shannon there several times. Once I was mugged in the airport, with people walking by not fifteen feet away. No one stopped. No one cared. And they call it the City of Angels." Color rose to the old woman's cheeks. "Poor girl, she should never have married the man.

I suppose I shouldn't say it, but I will: She could have done much better. Always had terrible taste in men. Not that the professor wasn't nice enough—I shan't speak ill of the dead. But she was young and so full of life. . . . What kind of a husband could he be to her, I wonder?''

"If she loved him—" Jack began.

"I've no doubt of that," Mrs. Cleary cut him off. "And he treated her well enough. Had a good heart, the professor did. But I never liked the match. Always felt nothing good would come of it. And such a future she could have had . . . dear Shannon. God gave her so many gifts, and then took them away so quickly.''

Jack kept quiet and sampled his tea.

She took a minute to collect herself. "Who did you say gave you the pictures?" she finally asked.

"A woman at the school where Shannon used to teach. They remember her fondly there. She asked me to bring them to you. She said she was a good friend of Shannon's.''

"It was thoughtful of her. And of you. Most thoughtful." She put down her teacup. "Forgive me for saying so, but you have a lonely face for such a handsome young man, Mr. Graham. Are you married?''

Jack shook his head.

"It might make you look happier.''

"There was someone. It's over.''

"I'm sorry," Mrs. Cleary said. "None of my business. Anyway, you're a fine-looking fellow. They'll be lining up. I hope you don't mind my saying so, but you remind me a bit of my George, God keep him. Did you see his picture up there?''

"The wedding picture? He was very handsome.''

"Tobacco was his only vice, and it did him in. Died of a cancer, two years this June." Her voice dropped to a whisper. "A very gentle man. A kind man. How much he suffered.''

"I'm sorry," Jack told her, regretting that he had come. He finished his tea in a gulp. "I really should be going now.''

"Sure, I don't blame you for wanting to rush out. Just a tiring old woman prattling on about her dead and buried.''

"It's just that I have a long drive ahead of me," he told her, putting the saucer down on the table and standing.

"Of course," she said. "So nice of you to bring the pictures for me. Didn't mean to parade my troubles in front of you. It's a problem with spending so much time alone. We give in to bitterness instead of counting our blessings. We should count our blessings every day of our life.''

She walked toward the door, enumerating a new blessing with every step. "My husband was as fine a man as ever I met. We had a long and happy time together. Brought a lovely daughter and two fine sons into this world. We were never rich but never poor. Always food on the table. And always healthy.'' She stopped for a second, lost in her own thoughts. "I guess that's why George's illness was so hard. Neither of us was ever sick a day in our life. We had nothing to prepare us. I'm afraid I didn't make a very patient nurse. . . .'' She opened the door and held it for him. "I hope you get back to Boston in time for your flight.''

And it was only then, hurrying out into the freshly swept fourth-floor corridor and fleeing toward the stairs, that Jack caught the discrepancy. He turned. "Mrs. Cleary?'' But she had already closed the door. He knocked and waited, wondering why he still cared enough to do this.

He heard her footsteps plodding back down the hallway, and finally she opened the door. "Did you forget something, Mr. Graham?''

"No. But I was wondering if I could have a few more minutes of your time.''

She peered out curiously. "My time is far less valuable than yours. Come in again, if you like.''

He followed her back down the hallway, and soon they were seated in the living room once again, watching the sunlight stream through the window at the cabinet with its display of china. "What is it that brought you back?'' she asked.

"I'm afraid I wasn't entirely honest with you before,'' Jack told her. "I wasn't just visiting in Japan.''

"What were you doing there then?''

"I was looking into a series of murders. Including Shannon's. And her husband's.''

She digested his words slowly, pursing her lips and drawing back the pink kerchief so that it covered several stray strands of white hair. "Who do you work for?'' she finally asked. "The police?''

He took out his wallet and gave her his Bureau ID. She studied it and handed it back. "Why didn't you tell me in the first place?"

"I didn't see any reason to. The investigation's over. I just came to drop off those photographs."

She waited, her manner no longer quite so friendly. "So?"

"So when we were walking out, you said you've never been sick a day in your life. But I was under the impression that Shannon left her teaching job at Atami High School six months early to come back to America to take care of you."

Her surprise showed clearly in her face. "And why would I need taking care of?"

"Because you were very sick, according to the teachers at Atami High School."

"Sheer rubbish."

"You weren't seriously ill?"

She shook her head.

"But Shannon did leave her job in Atami six months early?"

She would not deny it, but she didn't seem inclined to help him either. She picked up a doily and ran it through her fingers.

"So if she didn't come back to take care of you, then she left her job in Atami to do something else. And that stuff about you being sick was just an excuse. A good one—even the most serious teachers at a Japanese high school wouldn't blame a twenty-three-year-old American girl for wanting to go home and be with her ailing mother."

Once again Jack paused to give her a chance to fill in the blank. She put the doily down and shrugged. "It was so many years ago. Why even bother to talk about it?"

"Where did she go?" Jack asked softly. "Did she come back to America? Back here to Boston?"

During the deep silence of her refusal to answer, he could hear a clock ticking faintly from a back room. He looked right into her large, watery hazel eyes. Finally she shook her head very slightly from side to side.

"So she stayed? She was perfecting her command of the language. Her friends who I talked to in Atami said she loved Japan. Did she go somewhere to study?"

Once again, after hesitating, Mrs. Cleary shook her head.

"She had a second job?" Jack pressed. "Something exotic? It paid better than just being a teacher at the high school . . . ?"

"The teaching job paid her more than enough," Mrs. Cleary

replied. "I thought you had a long drive ahead of you and were anxious to get going."

Jack shrugged and glanced out the window. The football game had ended. All the players had disappeared except for one teenage boy who sat on the hood of an old black Plymouth Fury, making time with a girl who stood in front of him, smoking a cigarette. Mrs. Cleary's eyes were also drawn to the young couple. Jack looked at her, and as soon as she felt his gaze, she pulled her eyes away a little too quickly.

"You said Shannon had bad taste in men?" Jack whispered.

Her hands were pressed together in her lap, thumb on thumb. She didn't even blink.

"I can see that you don't like to talk about it. I'm sorry to bring it up. But please tell me about him."

"What's the use? Shannon's gone. Nothing can bring her back."

"Just help me a little bit and I'll leave you in peace. Shannon met a man while she was teaching at Atami High School. A Japanese man."

Pain showed clearly in the old woman's eyes.

"She became involved with him," Jack continued. "Somehow she kept it a secret from everyone at the school. Eventually she left Atami with him. She told the other teachers that she was coming home to take care of you, but she really was leaving to be with him."

Mrs. Cleary took a tissue from a pocket of her apron and dabbed her eyes with it.

"Where did they go? Did they stay in Japan?" He bent close to her, reading the lines in her expressive face. "So where was it if it wasn't Japan? There's more than half a year of her life unaccounted for. Did they stay in Asia? Travel? Please tell me."

The old woman's lips slowly came apart, and he intuitively guessed what she would say a split second before she whispered: "Switzerland. Please go now. I beg you."

"Just one more question and then I promise I'll never disturb you again. The name of the man she was with. It was Masao Ida?"

He read her denial in her eyes.

"Miura? Kenji Miura? A wealthy industrialist . . ."

She was staring straight back at him, her hazel eyes brimming with tears.

"It wasn't Miura?" For a moment he was perplexed. Then it came to him. "Hara. Kitaro Hara. I've met him. She was better off rid of him. But I don't understand—"

"No, no, *no*!" she exploded unexpectedly. "Not Hara. It was a long name; I can't pronounce it. He was so wrong for her, so much older, but she was crazy in love with him." Mrs. Cleary's voice was shrill and jumped wildly, with near hysterical fluctuations. "I told her it would never last. But she was deaf to any advice. A man as old as her own father, taking advantage of a young girl like that. She never recovered from it, after he left her. Practically abandoned her. That professor was the first nice one to come along, and she ran to him and hung on for dear life, so shattered she was. Terrible. The whole thing. Terrible."

As his world rocked and then slowly righted itself, Jack managed to whisper, "Muramoto? Seiji Muramoto?"

But Mrs. Cleary had run out of answers and sat on the old sofa with her arms wrapped around her body, sobbing silently into a wadded Kleenex.

27

They met just after midnight in an all-night doughnut shop in Crystal City that was run by a Vietnamese family of seven. The oldest daughter, her high school biology textbook visible on the far end of the counter, got them coffee and glazed doughnuts and went back to her studies. Once in a while one of her parents peeked out from the back room to make sure everything was okay. Jack and Monroe sat facing the street, alone in a world of sugar, dough, glass, and Formica.

"I know you were protecting me, but I'm glad you finally decided to tell me what happened," Monroe said when Jack had finished. "I'd been wondering." He sipped his coffee and smiled. "Quite an adventure you had with this exotic woman companion. Some of us don't lead such exciting lives." He took off his glasses and polished them on the inside of his shirt. "I have to admit I don't see why you were so shaken by what this woman in Massachusetts told you."

Jack fought to keep his voice down. "Because it means that what Hara told me was bunk. Pure *post facto* invention. He was covering up."

"Covering up what? It seems to me that what Hara told you could still be true." Monroe returned his glasses to his nose and looked steadily at Jack.

"Hara knew exactly how far Misako and I had gotten. He made up a story that fit the facts I knew. It was all garbage."

"For example?"

"Masao Ida didn't order Shannon's death, or my father's death for that matter. He couldn't have."

"Why not?"

"Because he was murdered before either of them. I went back and checked his obituary."

322

"That's pretty convincing," Monroe admitted. "But what I don't understand is why you're still digging into this. You've done your bit—more than anyone could have asked. Now you're back home. You're safe. You're healthy. You're about to jump back into a promising career. What the hell, Jack? Even if something in Japan's a little off kilter, you don't have any stake in this anymore."

Jack lowered his coffee cup to the table and slid his thumbnail along the Formica. "They tried everything they could think of to get my father off the case before they finally killed him. He wouldn't let it go."

"It was his job," Monroe pointed out gently.

"Innocent blood had been shed. He was the only one looking into it, and he was damn well going to follow the trail to the end."

Monroe nodded slightly to show that he understood. "What trail are you looking down?" he asked softly.

"Everything Hara told me in that bogus story was designed to make me focus on Dr. Miles and industrial computer secrets. He was steering me away from Shannon."

"What about her?"

"Why do you think she left Japan with Muramoto?"

"Change of scenery. They wanted an adventure. I don't know."

"Why didn't her mother want to talk about it so many years later?"

"She was grief-stricken. Do you know the answers to these questions or are you just fishing?"

"Why do you think Shannon kept going back to Switzerland with her husband?"

Monroe shrugged. "How should I know why she kept going back? Lots of people do. She liked to ski. . . ."

"She had a better reason."

Monroe shrugged. "You want me to try? She was still seeing Muramoto. They were meeting in their old love nest. The marriage to Dr. Miles was just a cover. Unfortunately for Shannon, once Muramoto died, her connection with Dr. Miles got her caught in the cross fire between Ida and Miura. Dr. Miles sold secrets, and she died, even though she was completely innocent of this whole computer secrets thing."

Jack shook his head. "Shannon wasn't killed for her husband's indiscretions. As a matter of fact, it was exactly the other way around.'' Monroe looked totally confused. The Vietnamese girl at the counter closed her biology book and disappeared into the back room so that they were left entirely alone. The doughnut shop was silent except for the hum of the fluorescent lights and the occasional drone of a car passing by in the street. Jack's voice sank down to a whisper. ''Shannon had a secret. I think she killed herself to avoid being forced to reveal it.''

''What secret?''

''What secret would a young woman be willing to die for?''

Monroe watched him, his thin shoulders hunched. He shook his head from side to side.

''They had a baby together,'' Jack told him slowly and clearly. ''Shannon and Muramoto. A direct heir to the Muramoto *Zaibatsu*, whatever exactly that means.''

Monroe leaned forward, his hands suddenly tense on the table, his voice a quick gasp. ''He must've been in his late sixties. She was in her early twenties. I guess it's possible, but. . . .''

''It's the only thing that makes sense. They met in Atami when Shannon was called in as a translator. She and Muramoto had a secret affair. They hid it from his business cohorts and her teaching colleagues. When Shannon became pregnant, they left to have the kid in Switzerland.''

''To avoid scandal?''

''People as powerful as Muramoto don't worry about scandal,'' Jack told him. ''He had more serious things to worry about. He was worth billions. His two sons had both died under mysterious circumstances. He was going to have to turn the whole far-flung empire over to collateral heirs. I met one of those heirs, and I've heard about some of the others. They were sharks. Worse. And the one I met hated Americans.''

Monroe nodded. ''So you're saying that Muramoto was worried what those Japanese heirs would do if they found out that all of a sudden there was a half-American direct heir in their way?''

''From everything I found out in Japan, it seems that the *Zaibatsu*s were really sort of the ultimate family businesses. If the old man had a child, even a bastard child, that kid would have had a strong and direct claim to the whole shebang. Old Muramoto made the decision that no one was going to know about, or be able to get near, his son. So he spirited Shannon off to Switzerland,

and the secret held. Oh, I'm sure there were rumors among the highest circle of the *Zaibatsu*, but no one knew if there really was a kid, or where he was hidden away. Maybe in a moment of weakness Shannon broke down and told her mother, but the old woman kept her mouth shut. When I visited her, I had to practically pry details about Shannon and Muramoto out of her. She never even hinted about a kid."

"How did Dr. Miles fit in?"

"Maybe Dr. Miles was just what he seemed to be, a brilliant scientist who fell in love with a woman with a secret and stayed loyal to her to the end."

"Till they pushed him off a cliff?"

"He fought right to the very brink. I've been there and seen the cliff. They wanted to know where the kid was, and he wouldn't tell them. Just the way Shannon wouldn't tell them. He loved her, so he stayed loyal to her, even though it was somebody else's kid. Kind of noble, in a way."

Monroe tore pieces from his white Styrofoam cup, his eyes alive as he considered the possibilities. "Walk me through this," he said, "and let's see if I understand. Muramoto's own people sabotage his Lear jet. It doesn't really matter who does it."

Jack nodded. "The thing is, they got him."

"Infighting breaks out over the succession, and a lot of top honchos knock each other off. When the dust clears, Hara is the last one standing. Suddenly it's his *Zaibatsu*, which means he's worth billions. Except that maybe a little bit of resistance continues, and there are rumors about a direct heir. Hara sends somebody to find Shannon, but before they can force her to tell where the kid is, she kills herself. Her husband doesn't talk either, so he ends up going off a cliff. Your father looks into both deaths till they decide they better take care of him, too. That about it?"

"More or less," Jack agreed. "The only thing I don't understand is why they didn't kill me as soon as I got to Japan. Maybe it was because I'm an FBI agent and they were afraid that even with their contacts, they wouldn't be able to cover it up. Or maybe they had some other reason. Anyway, eventually they did try."

Monroe squinted in the harsh glare of the fluorescent lights. "Seems to me there's one more question. What's happened to the kid?"

"With any luck, he's still in Switzerland," Jack said. "Hidden away wherever old Muramoto thought he was safest . . ."

Monroe stood up suddenly, knocking into the table so that it quivered on its steel support. "Dear God," he said.

Jack watched him.

"There was something in the paper a week or two ago. You know I read all the unusual little stories. A mysterious attack took place at an exclusive Swiss boarding school, right in the area where Shannon and her husband used to go."

"What kind of an attack?"

"The article didn't go into details. But I remember reading that a ten-year-old boy was murdered." The two men were silent for a long time, looking at each other across the Formica table of the empty doughnut shop. "Listen, Jack," Monroe finally said. "Maybe I'm out of line saying this, but you've done enough—far more than even your father would ever have asked. Whatever problems there were between the two of you, you've atoned for your side of it. Now, let it go. You don't want to keep poking and prying into this. They'll kill you."

"How do I know they won't anyway?" Jack stood up to face him. "I can't count on MacCormack anymore. Will you help me?"

"What are you going to do?"

"I don't know," Jack admitted.

28

Jack's first sight of the Alps from the window of the Swissair jet made him catch his breath. He knew that Hannibal and Napoleon had crossed these mountains with armies, but from this aerial vantage point, the seemingly endless snowcapped Alpine ranges looked to be a totally inaccessible world of unclimbable peaks poking through clouds and mist. He wondered what sorts of fears would drive a man to send his only son to be raised among these mountains, and how that son would be molded and misshaped by the isolation.

Announcements came over the intercom in English, French, and German that the plane would soon be landing in Geneva. Jack brought his seat upright, tilted his head back, and closed his eyes. Serious doubts about what he was doing making such a spur-of-the-moment journey had bothered him all across the Atlantic, and as the plane began its descent, they recurred with even greater force. He still had a week before MacCormack expected him to go back to work at the Bureau. But if MacCormack found out about this trip, in violation of his firm injunction not to talk about or pursue the Japanese case any further, Jack knew he would be fired. Also, by continuing to talk to Monroe, he was putting his friend's career at risk.

Monroe had asked a very good question in the doughnut shop in Crystal City: What was Jack's stake in this? Why continue to push forward? Now, nearing his destination and still very unsure of his own motives, Jack tried to reassure himself that he had not given in to blind obsession. He had invested so much and come so far that he simply had to look into the death of the child. But if all that was waiting for him at the end of the trail was a cold little corpse and no further leads, he promised himself that he would call an end to this long odyssey and begin a new and hopefully happier life far from *Zaibatsu*s and Yakuza and international intrigues.

The jet touched down in Geneva at ten in the morning, and he had five hours to walk around and see the sights before his train left for Bern. He checked his bags and took a taxi to the shores of Lake Geneva. A towering fountain of water, the Jet d'Eau, rose from a jetty far out in the lake. The morning was pristine, the mountain air invigorating, and across the lake in the far distance, Mont Blanc scraped the sky.

He turned right where the Rhône leaves the lake and followed the quai des Bergues along the river. A young couple, honeymooners from the look of them, sat on a bench facing the lovely river. It was easy in such a tranquil spot to become meditative, and as he crossed a bridge over the Rhône, Jack sank for a few minutes into a pleasant reverie. He remembered the morning that he and Misako had walked out to the Atami cliffs, along a pathway that skirted the shore. Her long black hair had tossed about in the strong wind, and as they made the walk around the point, her graceful strides and perfect posture had kept him stealing sideways glances at her. The memory kindled a much stronger tactile memory of how she had felt in his arms in the little house on the edge of the cliff, their naked bodies pressed together while a thunderstorm crashed above them and pounding rain provided a pulse beat for their lovemaking.

A car horn honked him out of his daydream, and he found himself already across the Rhône and advancing through the Place Bel-Air, the center of the banking district. Well-dressed men and women passed by in small groups, discussing money in a dozen different languages. More Middle Eastern oil money was here than everywhere else in the world combined, and as Jack eavesdropped on different conversations, at times managing to identify a language but more often completely at a loss, he got some sense of this strange banking city that was the headquarters for every international organization from the United Nations to the Red Cross to the Boy Scouts.

For the first time, Jack understood that Muramoto and the other parents at the Creusot School had merely done with their children what investors the world over did to protect their financial assets. As he walked down these clean streets, with seemingly impenetrable Alpine ranges rising as barriers, crime and terrorism and all the worries and dangers of the rest of the world seemed a very distant threat indeed.

Jack saw as much of this sober city of Zwingli and Calvin as his time permitted, and just made it back in time to catch a train that ran along the lake to Lausanne and then through the Jura to Bern. In Bern he transferred to a smaller train that stopped for half an hour at Thun and then followed the southern shore of the Thuner See past Spiez, Leissigen, and Darligen to Interlaken.

Exhausted, Jack decided to stay the night in Interlaken. He ate in a small restaurant overlooking the River Aare. A horse-drawn carriage took him back to the Hotel Metropole, where he collapsed onto a comfortable bed and was soon snoring beneath a thick quilt.

The next morning, after a quick *café complet* breakfast, Jack set out for Creusot. From Interlaken a rack-and-pinion railway wound up and down steep slopes till it deposited him in a small mountain town where he boarded a yellow Swiss post bus for the final trip to Creusot.

The three-hour bus ride was both magnificent and terrifying. They stopped again and again in remote hamlets to deliver mail, and by the time Jack finally stepped off the bus in the picturesque little mountain village on the shores of the small, mirror-smooth Lake Creusot, he had to draw his coat together across his throat. A numbing Alpine chill had already crept into the afternoon air.

In a distant valley between rocky crags, the dusk was beginning to collect around the walls and turrets of the sixteenth-century castle that housed the Creusot School. The narrow mountain valley was the very essence of peacefulness and isolation, and he found it difficult to believe that an armed attack had been mounted near such a sleepy town and against such antique ramparts.

Jack found a room in an old chalet whose wide eaves were buttressed by stout half-timbers designed to support tons of snow and ice during the long winter. German was the preferred language, but the old couple who ran the chalet spoke broken English, and with patience they were able to converse. He explained that he was an American policeman, and that he was interested in the attack on the school several weeks before because it might shed some light on a case he was working on. They were able to tell him only the bare details of the incident: The attack had taken place at night, a young student at the school and an older man who was supposed to be his bodyguard had been murdered, and the Swiss police were still looking into the whole affair.

Jack spent that afternoon and evening poking around Creusot, talking to shopkeepers on the short main street as he inspected their wares of woodcarving, torchon lace, and handcrafted leather. He was able to find out little else about the midnight attack, although he did get a better idea of the nature of the school itself. A talkative old woman shopkeeper from whom he purchased a belt chattered on about how the students at the school were drawn from powerful families the world over, and how security at the castle was always tight and had been redoubled after the attack.

Jack dined on a wonderful dish of thinly sliced veal in cream sauce, listening to the tinkling of cowbells as the herdsmen led their flocks down from mountain pastures. He washed the meat down with a delicious bottle of Clevner Stadtberger, and, perhaps because of the altitude, felt noticeably drunk. Returning to his chalet, he glanced up at the clear night sky and marveled at the myriad brilliant stars.

The next morning, washed, shaved, and dressed in his most conservative dark suit, he set off for the Creusot School. He could have taken a taxi from town, but it was only a five-mile hike, and he covered the distance quickly with his long, athletic strides. As he neared the structure, he was intercepted by a guard in uniform, a pistol strapped to his belt. The guard escorted him to the guard-house, where he was kept waiting for fifteen minutes while a flurry of phone calls passed back and forth with the main building. Finally two guards escorted him across an open yard, past a dozen or so glum-looking boys who stopped playing soccer to watch him walk by, to the stately old castle.

Jack was ushered into a large office on the first floor. A double bank of windows offered marvelous downhill views of the town and lake, framed by the peaks that rose up on all sides. The heavy wooden desk, bookcases, and standing clock looked as if they had sat unmoved for centuries. A short, stocky, middle-aged man in a conservative gray suit hurried through a side door and shook Jack's hand firmly and precisely. "I am Peter Siegner, headmaster at Creusot. You are whom, please?"

"Jack Graham."

"You are in law enforcement?" Jack nodded. "You have iden-tification, please?"

Jack handed over his Bureau ID, and the stocky administrator studied it very carefully. Jack took the opportunity to steal another look at the sweeping view of lake and mountains. "Best office view I've ever seen."

Siegner handed back the ID with a slight frown. "Yes," he said. "Over there you can just make out the Jungfraujoch. One day in three it is visible. From the other side of the school it is sometimes possible to see the Schilthorn. May I ask what you are doing here, Mr. Graham?"

Jack hated to claim that he was in Switzerland in an official investigative capacity, but he saw that there was no other way. He had come so far and taken so many risks already; there was nothing to do but take the plunge and hope word never got back to MacCormack. "I'm working on a string of homicides in America. We think the attack on this school may be linked. We'd appreciate your cooperation."

"And you came all this way without calling first or telegraphing or in any way formally requesting our assistance or letting us know that you were coming?"

"We tend to forget the formalities when murder is involved," Jack told him, putting a little bite in his voice.

"Well, I'm afraid you've come a long way for nothing," Peter Siegner responded. "The unfortunate incident at this school is still under investigation by the Swiss police. I will be pleased to give you the name of a police inspector in Bern who has jurisdiction. We have been instructed not to talk about what happened here, and since we value privacy very highly, we will follow that advice rather carefully."

"I'm not after anything that will do any damage to this school, and I certainly don't want publicity on this case any more than you do," Jack told him. "I just need to know who was paying for the boy's stay here, who the man was who was killed with him, and exactly how the attack occurred."

Peter Siegner smiled slightly and shook his head. "I see that, like most Americans, you are used to getting your way. When I say I won't discuss this incident, you should take me at my word. Now, I have some scholastic duties to attend to, Mr. Graham. You will forgive me for being abrupt. I will have someone show you out."

"So where did you send the boy's corpse for burial?" Jack asked the stocky little man as he stepped toward the door. "America? Japan?"

"You may ask whatever you want to Inspector Lehman of the Bern Federal Police. Unfortunately, I think you will find the inspector even less inclined to talk about this case than I am. But I wish you good luck all the same. Now I have business. Please excuse me." Siegner left, and the same two guards who had escorted Jack into the castle led him out. He tried to strike up a conversation with them, and was met with stony silence.

The soccer game in the yard had ended. A half dozen boys were busy taking down the nets, their faces still flushed from running about in the morning air. They stared at Jack as he walked by, closely flanked by the two guards. Jack veered off suddenly toward the near goal, breaking away from his escort so that for a moment he came face-to-face with three of the boys. "Morning," he said. "I'm Jack Graham. A policeman, from America. What can you tell me about the boy who was killed here two weeks ago?"

The boys looked back at Jack, apparently surprised at having been spoken to by a stranger. Jack sensed that they had been conditioned by school policy and long habit not to interact with outsiders. The two guards hurried over and stood on either side of Jack, trying to lead him away. They seemed unsure how to handle the situation. Jack was taller than both of them, and they seemed hesitant to depart from mere escort duty and attempt a show of force. "Please," one of them said in German-accented English, "we will go now."

The shortest of the three boys had a thin, pinched face and sad but very alert-looking hazel eyes. His blond hair had been cropped close to his scalp, and he returned Jack's gaze with curiosity and no visible uneasiness at the presence of the guards. "Did you know the boy?" Jack asked him, bending over slightly to look him full in the face. "Was he your friend?"

A breeze riffled the short blond hair. The boy shook his head.

"What about the bodyguard? Was he Swiss? American? Japanese?"

A slight affirmative inclination of the head.

"Japanese? Did anyone at the school know them? Anyone in the town?"

The guards were slowly stepping up their level of force. They half tugged and half pushed Jack a few feet away. He lowered his shoulder and was able to bull his way back. "Tell me," he asked. "Please."

"He would go into town." The boy's voice was high-pitched almost to the point of sounding girlish. His accent was decidedly upper-class British, his inflection sincere yet oddly listless. "Once a week or so. That's all I know."

"The boy would go?" A slight shake of the head. "The bodyguard would go? What would he go for?"

But before the boy could answer, the guards made their decision. They twisted Jack's arms painfully behind his back and marched him quickly across the yard and out to the road. Jack was tempted to struggle, but the sight of two more guards on their way to help out discouraged him. Soon he was on the road back to Creusot, rubbing his arms to restore circulation while he wondered what to do next.

The bus heading back toward Interlaken left in three hours. Jack walked aimlessly through the small farming town, which looked much brighter and more cheerful in the morning light than it had when he had arrived the previous dusk. He asked himself what a Japanese bodyguard would have come to town once a week for, and came up with dozens of possible answers. Perhaps he had had a fraülein tucked away in the rustic little hamlet, or perhaps he was required to regularly phone or post letters regarding the condition of his young charge.

The owners of the two hotels in town with public phones and postboxes denied remembering a regular Japanese patron. Jack returned to the leather store where he had bought his belt, but the old woman chatterbox was no help at all. Yes, there had been a white-haired Japanese gentleman who occasionally came down from the school into the town, but he had never stopped in her store. At Jack's suggestion that perhaps he might have been visiting a female friend in town, the old woman screwed up her eyebrows disapprovingly and left him at the counter.

Thinking about the dead boy and wondering what had been done with the child's corpse, Jack continued on through the town to the old church that stood on a hillock on the west shore of the lake, its door open and its pews silent and empty. Traversing the nave, he slipped outside through a small door behind the altar, and found himself in the town's old cemetery. Small headstones, many of them knocked aslant by storms of winters long past, ran in jagged rows along the hillside above the placid lake. Jack walked among the stones, examining their inscriptions.

After half an hour of walking, at the very end of one of the rows, he came upon a small headstone that looked as if it had been set up fairly recently. No name or birth or death dates had been chiseled into the white marble; rather, the marker bore only a small representation of a dove in flight. The outlines where patches of sod had been laid over the rocky earth were still clearly visible.

Jack glanced at his watch. The bus would pass through on its way toward Interlaken in less than an hour. He stood motionless next to the grave, facing down the gentle hill so that his eye was occasionally caught by the looking glass of lake that reflected the towering mountains.

Perhaps the last direct heir to the Muramoto *Zaibatsu* was buried in this tranquil spot; perhaps it was a farmer's child from the village. Jack wondered what point there was in trying to inquire further. No doubt the church authorities would be as unwilling to provide information to him as everyone else associated with this case had been.

Even if he could somehow establish the identity of the corpse as Shannon's son, he wondered what good that would do. Headmaster Seigner was no doubt right that the Bern police would not be very cooperative. Jack had no evidence to link the attack on the boarding school to Hara. And even if all his theories about an heir to Muramoto were correct, the only person who could have gained from them was probably buried six feet beneath this humble marker. Jack looked down at the cold and silent lake for a few seconds more, shrugged his shoulders tiredly, and headed back into town.

He settled his tab at the chalet and carried his one suitcase to the bus stop. No one else was waiting yet. Immediately across from the bus stop was a small wine shop that doubled as a tobacconist's. It was at the very center of the little village—near all of the main crossings and the only bus stop. Jack had spent enough time in small towns to recognize this as the place where news from the outside world would be received first and talked about, and gossip from the village passed on. On impulse, Jack crossed to the little shop. A white-haired man with a goatee and a magnificently twirled mustache watched him enter. "Do you speak English?" Jack asked him.

The man nodded.

"Will the bus be on time today?"

Another slight nod. The mustache barely quivered.

Jack ran his eyes over the cigarettes and cigars from all over Europe.

"Are you looking for anything in particular?" The man's English was superb, his German accent barely noticeable.

"A boy," Jack mused, half to himself.

"I beg your pardon?"

"The boy who was killed up at the school." The old man's polite gaze slowly took on a keen shrewdness. "Do you know if he was buried down by the church?" Jack asked.

"Best not to talk of such things. Have you tried these?" The old man pointed to some Davidoffs in a small humidor. "Dominican Republic seed. Very fine cigars."

Jack had Swiss francs to use up, so he selected a half dozen of the cigars. As the old man put them in a bag for him, Jack said, "I've been to the grave. By the lake. Not even a name on the stone." He waited. The old man said nothing. "It's a sad thing when a child dies," Jack tried again.

"Yes, sad," the old man intoned.

"Sadder still when there are no parents there to mourn him," Jack tried to lead him.

"You'd best be getting on. The bus will be coming soon."

Jack ran his eyes along the rows of wine bottles. He picked out an expensive bottle of Heida, and as he handed it to the old man, he was amazed to spot two bottles of sake half-hidden at the end of a shelf.

"Excellent choice." The old man nodded. "From the highest vineyard in Europe. Let me get a bag for you."

Jack gestured toward the sake. "Wouldn't think you'd have too much call for sake here."

"We don't."

"But you keep a few bottles?"

"Sometimes in the summer we get Japanese tourists."

"I understand that the boy who was killed had a Japanese bodyguard," Jack said. "A boy at the school told me the bodyguard used to come into town every so often." He waited, and once again he got no help. "I suppose he needed a drink now and then, and he probably missed his homeland."

"It would be natural," the old shopkeeper replied. He handed Jack the bag containing the Heida. "I hope you have a safe trip back."

"Are there any other Swiss wines you'd suggest I try?" Jack asked him, leaving his wallet, fat with hundred- and five-hundred-franc notes, on the counter.

The store owner met his glance and twirled his mustache thoughtfully. "You might try this Fendant. It's a bit expensive. . . ."

"I'll try it. Make that two bottles. I'm afraid the bus will be coming any minute, so we'd better finish our business quickly."

The old shopkeeper nodded. "I'll pack them in a box for you. They'll be easier to carry." As he worked, he glanced around his shop to make sure it was empty. "He was a fine man," he whispered in a low voice. "A gentleman."

"The bodyguard? You ordered sake for him regularly?"

"A distributor I know in Geneva supplies the Japanese diplomatic community there. Fascinating city, Geneva."

"Fascinating," Jack agreed.

"I lived there for a long time. Had a shop. I prefer it here."

Jack paid for the wine and took the box. "Listen," he said in a half whisper, "tell me about this bodyguard. In a minute I'll get on the bus and you'll never see me again. Was he at the school long?"

"For years."

"What languages did he speak?"

"We spoke English."

"If the boy was buried down at the church, what about the bodyguard? Is he down there, too?"

"I really can't help you about that."

"Why not?"

"Because," the old shopkeeper said, looking distinctly uncomfortable, "I didn't know the bodyguard who was killed. He never came in this shop."

Jack squeezed the package a bit more tightly in his arms as he fought to keep his voice steady. He sensed that if he seemed at all excited, he would scare the old man off. "I don't understand. What happened to the bodyguard you knew? The one you say was a gentleman."

"He was replaced by a younger man a short while before the attack. He left this town, I assume to return to Japan. I was sorry when he came in here to settle his account, but when I heard what had happened at the school, I was glad for him. He was lucky to leave when he did.'

"Very lucky." They exchanged glances. "Did you know his name?"

The old man shook his head. "That's your bus pulling in. Please be good enough to remember what you said about not coming back."

Jack implored the man with his eyes. "I need a name."

"The next bus isn't till tomorrow."

"Please," Jack said. "We can trust each other. You don't know how far I've come for this. Please."

"Takeuchi," the old shopkeeper whispered. "First name, Masanori. That was what he used on his account. Now go and don't come back here." The old man turned and disappeared into the back of his shop. Jack hoisted his suitcase, gathered up his purchases, and just managed to catch the bus, which departed punctually to the minute.

Jack called Monroe from Interlaken, catching his friend just as he was about to set out for work. "It seems like all I do is field phone calls from you from exotic places," Monroe grumbled. "First the Orient, now the Alps. Makes me feel like a damn stick-in-the-mud. What happened at the school?"

Jack told him what he had found out in Creusot, speaking softly and quickly into the bus depot telephone. Thirty feet away, near a row of lockers, a fierce-looking old Swiss woman swept a waiting area that already looked perfectly clean.

Monroe was silent for a time, pondering the information. "So let me guess," he finally said. "You don't think the first bodyguard was just lucky to leave when he did?"

"He was at the school for years. He left town a few weeks before the attack."

"Somebody tipped him off?"

"On one level that makes a lot more sense," Jack agreed. "But then again, if he knew an attack was coming, why didn't he just alert the school? The security force there looks pretty formidable. If they suspected an attack was coming, I think they could have made the place virtually impregnable."

"Maybe he didn't trust them."

"The people at the school?"

"That would explain why he didn't stay. He thought they might set him up." Monroe was silent for a second. "Unless, of course, it was the other way around."

"I don't follow."

"He set them up," Monroe suggested. "He wanted the attack to happen."

"To satisfy whoever was after him? To make them think the attack had taken place and had been successful?" Jack tried to follow the line of thought. "That would explain why he bothered to find a replacement as a bodyguard to take the fall. But it doesn't explain why he didn't try to save the kid."

"Maybe he couldn't. Maybe all he could do was save his own skin."

"Can you run a name through the airline flight manifests for me? Takeuchi. First name Masanori. He probably left Switzerland from Bern or Zurich. If you don't get anything, try Basel and Geneva." Jack gave him the approximate date when the body-guard had left Creusot, and suggested running the name for a few days before and after, just to be sure.

"I'll run it through first thing, and I'll be coming back home early today," Monroe told him. "If you touch down somewhere en route to D.C., call me back and I'll let you know what I've found. I have to tell you, though, from experience, it's a real long shot."

"Understood. Listen, tell me honestly, do you think it'll be safe for you to check this for me?"

"Do you know how many flight records my section runs through in a week? We can't even keep our own records straight, so I can't imagine how anyone could be keeping tabs on us. Now, if it was Japan, after all that went on, I'd be a little more careful. But no one'll even give Switzerland a second look."

Jack made the lovely trip back to Bern without incident, and caught a flight from there to Paris. Despite Monroe's assurances, he worried all the way about having endangered his friend's career. At Charles de Gaulle Airport, where he had a three-hour stopover, he called Monroe. "Did you have any trouble running it through?" he asked worriedly. "Anybody seem suspicious?"

"No problem at all. I put Takeuchi in with two made-up names, and buried the whole request in a monster case that ten of us have been working on for a month. Thanks for worrying, but you really don't need to.''

''What did you get back?''

''I checked Masanori Takeuchi from Basel, Bern, Geneva, and Zurich for a week on either side of the date you gave me. All the major airlines.''

''And?''

''I drew a complete blank. Then I checked as many of the other major airports on the Continent as I could. *Nada.*''

Jack shrugged with disappointment. ''As you said, it was a long shot. Listen, I'll be coming back to work at the Bureau next week. When you get some free time, maybe we can grab a beer. . . .''

''I don't think you'll be coming back here quite as soon as you think,'' Monroe told him.

''Why not?''

''After I ran all those things I told you about through, just for the hell of it I ran Takeuchi through Bern, Basel, Zurich, and Geneva for two months before the date you gave me. A couple of weeks before you think he left town for the final time, he took a big trip. Flew out of Bern.''

''Where did he go?''

''Athens. Then on to Karachi, Delhi, and finally Bangkok. He stayed in Thailand for one week and then came back via the same route. Now, get this. When he came back, he purchased two first-class tickets. The other one was for a Kazuo Ukai. According to passport information, a minor.''

''A child?''

''Yes. I thought about it for a while, and then just for the hell of it, I ran Ukai through for the four airports and dates you originally suggested for Takeuchi. Right when the bodyguard was supposed to be leaving Creusot to avoid the attack. Guess what?''

''The kid left?''

''On the evening you predicted, Kazuo Ukai flew from Bern to London. Along with his father, Konezumi Ukai.''

''His father?''

''The two Ukais flew from London to Toronto. I checked and checked, but they never flew out of Toronto.''

''So they stayed there?'' Jack said. ''In Canada? The body-guard and the child posing as father and son?''

Monroe sounded almost gleeful. "Guess who flew out of Toronto two days after the Ukais arrived?"

"I can't."

"Try."

"Masanori Takeuchi?"

Monroe sounded positively gleeful. "And his son, Morishige Takeuchi."

"So the Ukais flew in and the Takeuchis flew out?"

"Two sets of travel documents," Monroe told him. "Passports, visas, the works. Maybe more than two. Someone was planning this for a long time. From Toronto they headed to New York. Didn't like it there at all, I guess—they left almost immediately for the West Coast. San Diego. Then Mexico City. They hopscotched around Central America a little bit, and then headed back to the States. A week ago they were in Anchorage. Then Seattle, Phoenix, and three days ago the Ukai father and son flew Northwest Air to Portland. That's where I lose them."

Jack tried to drink it all in. "Portland?"

"Yeah. Of course, they're probably not still there. They could have rented a car or taken a bus to just about anywhere, or they might have even had a third set of travel documents."

"Then why didn't they use them before? They always flew as either the Ukais or Takeuchis. And they never rented a car or took a bus before. Why start in Portland?"

Monroe had no answer.

"I'm gonna go see," Jack told him.

"I knew you would. I don't think there's much chance that you'll find anything, but good luck all the same."

Jack hung up and stood still in the busy airport for a time, wondering how many more cold trails he would have to walk down.

Marsha woke suddenly from a light sleep and lay still in bed, listening in the darkness as her husband snored beside her. Gradually she relaxed. It had only been the screen door blowing in the wind. She closed her eyes to try to go back to sleep. The sound of someone stepping on one of the squeaky floorboards downstairs made her body go rigid.

She shook her husband, keeping her palm over his mouth to

shush him. After a few hard shakes, Monroe blinked awake and she removed her hand.

"What's the idea . . . ?" he began.

"There's someone downstairs," she whispered, cutting him off.

"Marsha, for Christ's sake . . ."

"I heard him."

"How many times do we have to go through this?"

"I swear he's down there. I'm scared. What are we going to do?"

Monroe switched on his bedside lamp and stood. "I'll tell you what we're going to do." He threw on a terry cloth bathrobe. "I'm going to take my licensed handgun and go downstairs, and if I find a burglar, I'm going to shoot his brains out. But we both know I'm not going to find anyone because there's nobody here but us chickens. So after I don't find anyone, I'm gonna come back upstairs, get back into bed, and try to get the rest of a good night's sleep."

He took the pistol out of a bottom drawer of his night table, made sure the gun was loaded, and started for the door. "Be careful," she whispered breathlessly.

He threw a disdainful look and walked out into the dark hall. The large house was silent. He switched on the hall light and started down the carpeted steps, peering into the gloom. Nothing seemed amiss. She had done this half a dozen times before, and each time there had been no one downstairs. He had installed a state-of-the-art security system and purchased a Rottweiler, but she had an allergic reaction to the dog, and the security system didn't seem to stop her from waking up petrified several times a year.

He reached the bottom of the stairs and flicked on the light. The entry hall, living room, and dining room were all empty. He peered into the kitchen, decided not to bother with the downstairs bathroom, and headed back for the stairs and his warm bed.

Monroe switched off the first-floor lights, and when he turned toward the stairs, four men were waiting there. Three of the men looked to be Americans. They were large and held guns, two pointed at his head, one at his heart. The fourth man was Japanese and held no gun. He had movie-star good looks and he flashed

Monroe a quick smile before commanding, in fluent English,
"Please lower your gun."

Monroe hesitated.

"Drop it."

Monroe dropped it, and the pistol clunked against the carpeted
floor.

"Is everything okay?" Marsha called from upstairs.

"This doesn't concern her," Monroe whispered to the four
men. "Let's go outside."

At a nod from their Japanese leader, two of the big men ran up
the stairs and confronted Monroe's wife. She opened her mouth to
scream, managed only a series of choking sounds, and finally
produced a high-pitched wail that quivered and immediately
broke. Monroe was dragged up the stairs and allowed to stand next
to Marsha. She buried her face in his chest, and he threw a
protective arm around her shoulders.

"What do you want?" he asked the Japanese man.

"We'll give you anything," Marsha sobbed. "We have money
downstairs. My jewelry box is in the bedroom. Please, we'll give
you what you want."

The Japanese man stepped forward. "I believe you have been
talking with Jack Graham," he said to Monroe. "Where is he?"

"I haven't talked to him since he left for Boston, as God is my
witness," Monroe said.

"Then why your sudden interest in the names Takeuchi and
Ukai?" Monroe's face went ashen. His wife glanced at him and
trembled. "Come," the Japanese man said, "this is not a good
time to play games."

A door opened all the way down the hall, and a fourteen-year-
old girl's voice cried out: "Daddy? Is that you?" No one answered her. "Mom?"

Monroe and the Japanese man's eyes met. "I think you will tell
us what we need to know," he said. "The only question is how
quickly." He nodded to one of his henchmen, who went off down
the hall to get the girl.

29

The head of security in the Portland International Airport was a white-haired woman in her fifties with the face of an angel and the physique of a fire hydrant. She glanced at Jack's Bureau ID and smiled at him with her eyes. "How can I help you, Mr. Graham?"

Jack was feeling remarkably fresh after the long night flight across the Atlantic, and the shorter trip from New York across the continent. He explained that he was looking for a father and son, gave her the date and time, and mentioned the name Ukai.

She nearly jumped out of her chair for joy. "Thank God," she said. "Now, at least, maybe we can clear *that* up."

"Clear what up?"

"A real mess. That's what. Poor Mr. Ukai collapsed just after landing here three days ago. Fell like a log right in the middle of the terminal floor. Double coronary; he never regained consciousness."

"So he's dead?"

She nodded.

"And it was a real heart attack? I mean, there was no sign of foul play?"

She raised her eyebrows a bit. "There was no reason to suspect anything. The doctors seemed convinced."

"And the boy?"

"Well, that's the mess," she said. "We don't really know what to do with him. His passport and visa information don't check out. The Japanese consulate denies any knowledge of a Kazuo Ukai. They're still checking, and we're still checking, but neither of us has much to go on."

"Hasn't the boy explained things?"

"We've tried every language we can think of. He won't say a word. A doctor examined him and said there's nothing wrong with him physically. So it must be psychological. He just stands there quietly, with this look on his face like he's a million miles away.''

"So what did you do with him?"

"Well, we couldn't keep him here," she said. "We sent him over to the police station on Second and Main. They tried with their people, but they didn't get anywhere either. Now I think they're running his name through all kinds of international missing persons banks, and checking with Interpol. I know they were thinking of turning him over to a federal authority if they didn't get any leads in a day or two. It's very sad."

"So the boy's at the police station now?"

She shook her head. "There's a home for juveniles out near Clatskanie."

"Where's that?"

"Two-thirds of the way to Astoria, off U.S. Thirty. It's about a thirty-minute drive along the Columbia River."

"Thanks," Jack said.

She leaned forward, her voice low and compassionate. "He seemed such a strange child. Not frightened so much as . . . sad. Do what you can for him."

"I will," Jack told her. "You can count on that."

He rented a car and was soon on U.S. 30 following the river downstream. He had to fight with himself to stay near the speed limit—several times he caught himself edging up into the eighties. He had so many questions that it was almost better not to think about any of them but just to concentrate on the twisting highway along the pretty river. Soon Jack turned south, away from the river, and following the directions the airport security chief had written for him, he pulled off the road onto a long gravel driveway, past a sign that read: OREGON STATE JUVENILE FACILITY: NO TRESPASSING. ALCOHOL AND DRUG FREE AREA.

He drove through an open wooden gate, and two German shepherds ran to the ends of their chains after him, barking ferociously. The driveway twisted through half a mile of forest and then widened out into a small parking lot. A three-story wooden house, freshly painted a light shade of brown, reared up from the surrounding woods on the far side of the lot. Jack coasted to a stop in the Visitor's Parking space and headed for the wooden building, unsure exactly what he was going to say.

The front door led into a cluttered office. A tall woman in her early thirties was filing manila folders in an old steel cabinet when Jack walked in. She heard the door swing shut, jerked around to see who it was, and then visibly relaxed. "I thought it was one of the boys," she explained. "They're always sneaking in here, even though it's supposed to be off limits." She ran her hand across her forehead in a nervous gesture, catching stray strands of dark hair. "We weren't expecting you for another hour at least. I'll go get Tom or Margaret."

She hurried out before Jack could tell her that she must have him confused with someone else.

He waited a long five minutes, occasionally glancing around at the clutter. Finally three sets of footsteps approached. The tall office worker reappeared, followed immediately by a plump, white-haired woman wearing jeans and a T-shirt with the legend: "Your life is whatever you make it." Trailing her at a distance of three feet was an Amerasian boy of perhaps ten.

The boy dragged his feet across the floor as he walked. His shoulders were as narrow as his hips, and when he swung his arms slightly, the extra movement seemed out of place, as if he was used to keeping still. His face was a perfectly blank mask, from the torpid eyes to the small, flat nose to the expressionless mouth and cheeks that seemed frozen in a half smile of polite disinterest. The dull black eyes emerged from their state of hibernation for a moment to take Jack in from head to foot, and for a split second as their eyes met, Jack felt a certain bond with this lost child. Then the boy's face became a mask once again, and the plump woman bent and began zipping up his little jacket as she spoke to Jack.

"Here he is, all washed and scrubbed and ready for the trip." She struggled with the zipper. "He's a strange one, this one. No trouble, mind you, none at all, but still . . ." She forced the zipper up, actually lifting the boy onto his toes. "I daresay I've seen my share of troubled children, but this one's spooky. Keeps so much to himself. What kind of a child doesn't like to run or play, I ask you?" She tucked his head into a hood, and patted him on the cheek. "Well, maybe he's better at home. So they've found the parents, have they?"

Jack nodded.

"Well, I can't say I think much of them for taking so long to claim him. Still, it's none of my business. The police said to keep him, so I kept him, and now they say to give him to you, so I'll wash my hands of it. My name, by the way, is Margaret Allford. I run this facility with my husband. May I see your identification?"

Jack handed her his ID. She studied it and nodded. "We don't have much contact with federal agencies, so I was a bit surprised when that woman called. I must say, I'm glad she decided not to send that agent from Japan."

"Lieutenant Sasaki?" Jack asked, taking a risk.

She handed him his ID and nodded. "Imagine, she didn't even know if he spoke English. And how were we to communicate, I wonder? By sign language?"

The knowledge that Lieutenant Sasaki, whom Jack had last seen shooting at him in Narita Airport, was on his way to claim this child made up Jack's mind instantly. "Lieutenant Sasaki speaks English quite well," Jack told her, glancing at his watch. "Right now we'd better get going. This little fellow has a plane to catch."

"Well, 'bye, dearie," Margaret said, bending to chuck the boy once more under the chin. "Have a good trip back." The boy regarded her absolutely impassively, appearing to stare right through her to the wallpaper on the opposite side of the room. "Spooky," she said to Jack. "This one's in the Twilight Zone. Good luck with him, Mr. Graham."

The tall office lady held the door for them and smiled shyly at Jack as they went out. The boy got into the front seat without protest, and seeing that the office lady and Margaret were watching them from a front window of the house, Jack wasted a few precious seconds in buckling the boy's seat belt and waving a casual good-bye. Then he started the car, pulled out of the lot, and drove as quickly as he dared down the winding gravel driveway. He had a premonition that they would pass Lieutenant Sasaki on his way in to pick up the boy, and he let out a breath of relief when they reached the main road, turned onto it, and sped away.

They passed suburban homes and two small lakes. The boy sat back in his seat, looking out the window without appearing to notice the green foliage and rolling countryside. Jack smiled wryly. "Well, here we are at last," he muttered out loud. "The two dupes who don't have a clue as to what's going on have finally found each other. Or do you have a clue?"

The boy gave no evidence of listening or understanding.

"Your mom was a nice lady, from everything I've heard," Jack said. "I've seen pictures of her. Very lovely. Shannon Miles. Does that ring a bell? Shannon?"

The child scratched his nose.

"Your father, I didn't know at all," Jack continued. "Seiji Muramoto. Does that name mean anything to you?" It was impossible to tell if the English words were even registering. "Guess he was overprotective, but these father-son relationships can be hell. I had it the other way around, and that wasn't much fun either. Anyway, seems like old Seiji had a lot to protect you from. Are you by any chance familiar with the term *Zaibatsu*?" His scratching completed, the boy lowered his hand to his lap and stared out the window.

Jack shrugged. "Let's start with small things and work our way to the question of what the hell we're going to do." Fishing around in his jacket pocket, he found a pack of spearmint gum. He drew out a stick and offered it to the boy. "Go ahead. Try it." He peeled off the green wrapper, and the boy's eyes took in the foil covering, but he made no move to take it. "Suit yourself," Jack said, stripping off the foil and popping the gum into his mouth. "Do you have a name? I'm Jack Graham."

The boy reached for the pack of gum, which Jack had set down on the front dashboard. He carefully withdrew a stick, peeled off the wrapper and foil, and hesitantly inserted the gum partway into his open mouth. Keeping hold of the end of the stick with his fingers, he brought his tongue up and licked the gum once, tentatively. It was impossible to tell from his expressionless countenance whether he liked it or not, but after a second trial lick, he popped the entire stick into his mouth and began sucking on it.

"No," Jack told him. "Chew it." The boy turned his head slightly to look. "Watch me." He exaggerated chewing, and the boy slowly followed his example. "Great," Jack told him. "Next week I'll teach you how to blow bubbles."

A shot rang out, and Jack's rental car skidded toward the steep shoulder. Jack steered into the skid, fighting to keep the car on the road. Three sedans had closed to less than twenty yards—they were the only cars in sight on a long, straight section of two-lane highway. A second shot took out Jack's other back tire, and the rental car careened across the road, bumped over the lip of shoulder, and rolled down an embankment till it was stopped by two pine trees.

Jack threw himself sideways to cover the boy with his body. The jolting stop as the car hit the tree trunks knocked Jack's head against the front windshield with enough force to stun him momentarily. When he regained his senses, he kicked the passenger door open and half stumbled and half fell out. A dozen or so Japanese men wearing suits and holding pistols stood around the car.

A young Japanese woman dressed in black approached Jack. She was in her early twenties, petite and delicately beautiful except that her face had a long-suffering quality, as if she had withstood tremendous pain. Holding a small pistol steady in her right hand, she examined Jack for a long moment with undisguised curiosity. Then she stepped past him to the passenger door, her pistol raised and its hammer cocked.

"For Christ's sake, leave the poor kid be. . . ." Jack pleaded. She wheeled about to face him. "He doesn't even know who he is. . . ." She pointed her pistol at Jack's heart, and one look at her told him that if he said anything further or moved even an inch, she would shoot him dead on the spot. Around the circle, the men in suits also had their guns trained on him.

Jack stood still and silent, watching helplessly as the woman opened the passenger door, unbuckled the boy, who was still woozy from the crash, and pulled him into the open air. The ring of men holding weapons closed in a step. The boy leaned against the car, blinking his eyes in the bright sunlight. Gradually his gaze became more focused and he seemed to take in the circle of men and to understand his predicament. He glanced up at Jack and then at the woman in black, who still held his arm, examining him intently.

She went down so quickly that at first Jack thought she had fainted. Then he saw that the men standing around in a circle had followed her cue and also doubled in half, and that they were bowing to the boy so deeply that they seemed almost at the point of prostrating themselves. The boy glanced up at Jack. For a moment they were the only two standing upright, both chewing spearmint gum and looking around at the circle of figures bent almost double in reverence. Jack put his arm on the boy's shoulder. "I think you're among friends," he whispered.

*   *   *

Sometimes she went for hours at a time without speaking. She would sit very still, her troubled eyes wandering over her surroundings and always returning to the boy who had become her almost constant companion. She had a habit of folding her fingers into little fists and pulling them inside her sleeves, as if satisfying in a small way a larger wish to withdraw from the outside world. The boy was quite her match when it came to silence and withdrawal from the outer world, and Jack had seen the two of them sit for what seemed like half a day without exchanging a single word.

It was primarily through those long silences that Jack got to know both of them on the roundabout trip back to Japan. She spoke little English, and his Japanese was still limited to a very poor tourist's vocabulary, so they communicated for the most part with glances and occasional bits of sign language, and eventually with half smiles. From the four bodyguards who made the trip back with them, Jack picked up enough snippets of information to put together a reasonably clear picture of who she was and what her stake was in all this.

Her name was Etsuko Matsuda and she was a member of the Muramoto family. Her husband, a rising star in the *Zaibatsu*, had perished along with Seiji Muramoto in the plane wreck. Against all expectation, she had taken over her dead husband's regional organization on Shikoku, consolidated control with an iron hand, and forcefully resisted Hara's succession to the head of the *Zaibatsu*.

Rumors about a direct male heir to Seiji Muramoto, living abroad, had been circulating through the *Zaibatsu* for years. Through a leak in Hara's network, the boy's bodyguard had learned that the child had been traced to Creusot and that an attack was being planned. Not knowing whom to trust, the old bodyguard had set up decoys to take the fall and fled Switzerland with the child. Etsuko's faction, like Hara's, had at first been taken in by the ruse. Both groups had just discovered the whereabouts of the boy and were racing to get him first when Jack had unexpectedly appeared and beaten them to it.

The boy gave few signs of emerging from his near catatonic condition. Now that he had found a partner in silence, his muteness and empty stares no longer seemed quite so unworldly. Sometimes Jack even had the feeling that the woman and child were connecting on a deep, meditative level that he, with his Occidental

tendency toward extroversion, could not fully understand or appreciate.

There was one exception. The boy liked to explore. He seemed
to enjoy gazing up at starry night skies, and to love wide-open
vistas in daylight. During their numerous short and long layovers,
Jack took the boy out for walks, and the child seemed to get a real
thrill out of even a twenty- or thirty-minute hike. His eyes followed every open road and searched out every distant shape on the
horizon, as if he had never dreamed the world was so large. They
stopped for two days in Mexico, and Jack, Etsuko, and the boy
went off for a short hike through the desert. The boy's face lit up
at the sight of such vast empty spaces—it was the happiest and
most animated Jack had ever seen him.

The more time Jack spent with the boy, the more he felt a
responsibility for and even a strange kinship with the child. It
wasn't just that they were both, in their own way, trying to recover
from disastrous childhoods. Jack found something remarkably
touching about a father who had loved his son so much that he had
had to shut him away from everyone and everything. It resonated
with Jack's own mixed memories of Walter, and helped him realize how love and abuse, the best intentions and the worst results,
could sometimes go hand in hand.

From Mexico they flew to Hawaii, the Philippines, and then to
Korea. Jack began to feel more a part of Etsuko Matsuda's silences, and at the same time he had more success in coaxing
responses from her. She was a gracious lady of gentle and faultless
manners, and on layovers between plane flights, the two of them
sipped cups of green tea and sometimes, with the aid of a translator, talked about what to do next. They both shared a common
goal of revenge: she was convinced that Hara was responsible for
the plane crash that had claimed her husband's life, while Jack
was certain that Hara had been behind the deaths of Shannon and
her husband, and therefore had also presumably ordered the murder of Walter Graham.

Jack was impressed by Etsuko's suspicion of everyone and
everything in any way connected to the old Muramoto *Zaibatsu*,
and by the painstaking way she reviewed and rechecked every
aspect of the plans they started to make together. She insisted that
while they made the trip to Japan she would have her people find
out what they could about Monroe, MacCormack, Jack's father,

Misako, and everyone else Jack had trusted or had had extensive contact with during his investigation.

Apart from their hikes together, befriending the boy proved a difficult task. The child seemed to have no sense of playfulness, and almost no desire to interact with anyone in the outside world. Sometimes when Jack clowned in front of him, amusement flickered far back behind the mask of face. Once or twice Jack even thought he saw a faint smile flit across the normally expressionless lips, but for the most part the child looked inward and kept to himself.

They traveled by small planes, evading international flight controls with an ease that surprised Jack. From Luzon they flew to Pusan, and there boarded a small ship that sailed across the Sea of Japan and through the Kammon and Hoyo straits to Uwajima on the island of Shikoku. By the time they set out by car for Kochi, they had worked out a fairly good idea of how to proceed.

30

She came out of the station at half past six, and headed straight for her car. Jack let her get close before stepping out from behind a van and calling, "Misako?" She stared at him for a split second in complete amazement, and then her face lit up with a smile. They embraced right out in the parking lot, and only after thirty seconds or so did she break away to ask: "What are you doing here?"

"Waiting for you."

"I mean in Japan."

"We can get him now," Jack whispered.

"Who?"

"Hara."

She stared at him as if he had gone crazy.

"We need to go someplace where we can talk. I'll explain everything." As they got into her car, he was struck with how his body reacted to her nearness and touch. Just sitting next to her on a car seat made his stomach tighten.

She drove along the coastal road, past the New Akao Hotel and Atami High School, in the direction of Ito. During the ride, Jack told her everything that had happened to him in Boston, Switzerland, and Portland, leaving out only the meeting with Etsuko Matsuda and her men and the fact that they had all traveled back to Japan together.

Misako's face registered great surprise when he told her that Shannon and Seiji Muramoto had had a child together, and that that child still lived. Jack studied her very keenly at that moment, and he felt certain that whatever else was the case her surprise was genuine. Midway between Atami and Ito she turned uphill, along a small road that wound through mekon orange orchards. The small fruit trees were dwarfed by a single line of cherry trees planted at twenty-foot intervals just off the road.

When they were more than half a mile from the highway, Misako pulled over to the side of the road and they got out. She had fallen silent—he knew that she must be thinking furiously. The sugary aroma from the ripening fruit mixed incongruously with the tangy salt smell from the bay a few hundred yards below.

"I was very sorry after we said good-bye," she said as they began to walk alongside a row of trees. "I thought I would never see you again."

"I missed you, too," he told her truthfully. "Kept me awake at night."

"You never wrote."

"I didn't think you wanted me to. God, but you look beautiful." She came to him then and they embraced on the hill between the orange trees.

They resumed walking down the muddy row, holding hands as the afternoon began to darken slowly toward dusk. "So after you found the boy, what happened?" she asked.

"I came back to Japan with him."

"Wasn't that dangerous?"

"Very dangerous. The boy's a walking target here, and I'm not too well liked either."

"Why did you come back?"

"For five million dollars."

She stopped and looked at him.

"Don't you think Hara would pay five million dollars for the boy? I bet he's already spent nearly that much trying to kill him. As long as Seiji Muramoto's child is alive, Hara's usurping the throne. The boy's death would give Hara security and even a kind of legitimacy. He'd pay five million with a smile."

Misako thought about it for only a few seconds and then shook her head. "You don't care about money that way."

"I'm American. Don't you know all Americans want to be millionaires? I wrecked my career over this; I might as well get something out of it. So instead of going back to work at the Bureau, I'll use the five million to buy a villa and some land in Tuscany and spend the rest of my days sampling local Chiantis and eating fresh pasta. What the hell. Why not?"

"I don't believe you," she told him.

"The point is that Hara will believe me."

He saw the confusion on her face.

"It couldn't be simpler. When I talked to Hara on Hokkaido, he was pretty explicit about his loathing for Americans. He thinks we're all clumsy money grubbers without any ideals. So we offer him a deal. He gets what he wants, and I get what he thinks I want. I think he'd believe five million dollars was my motivation. Don't you?''

Misako didn't hazard an answer.

"It's important that you think it'll work, because you're the one person who's gonna have to convince him that I'm for real."

"How can I do that? Jack, I don't want to get involved in this again. The last time I tried to help, it turned into a nightmare."

They were standing at the end of a row, and the gentle light of dusk brought out all the soft beauty of her face. He took her hands, and held them palm up in his own, his fingers crossing her love lines at right angles. "Listen," he said. "It's time to come clean."

"I don't understand that expression."

"It's time for us to be totally honest with each other. Do you remember in Ueno Park when you confessed that you'd been spying on me for the Atami police and Lieutenant Sasaki?" She nodded slowly. "Well, I trusted you after that. But now I know you switched back to Hara. During our trip across Japan you fed him information."

She managed a look of absolute shock. Her eyes widened, the skin tightened over her cheekbones, and her mouth opened slightly in a remarkable imitation of an involuntary gasp.

He held her hands a little tighter. "I didn't suspect a thing till I got back to America. But once I found out about the boy, I was able to work backward."

She stood very still, watching him and occasionally moving her head slightly from side to side in silent denial. He spoke in the emotionless tone that he had perfected in mock courts in law school.

"One of the things that never made sense to me was the way Hara seemed to change his mind about me. He could have had me killed as soon as I arrived in Japan, but he just tried to scare me off. Then he pulled an about-face and tried to have me chopped up in my room, but I got lucky and survived. After that, as you and I traveled across Japan together, Hara apparently decided to keep me alive and on the scent. As if he needed something from me at that point."

"What could he need?"

"He didn't know where the boy was. Gradually he found out that I knew, or at least that I had the means to find out. So he got us back together and let me do his work for him."

She was watching him very carefully, no longer even shaking her head in denial.

"See, I figure it was like this. When I first got to Japan, Hara didn't yet know about Monroe and the papers I had taken from Walter. I was a minor annoyance to him at that point. He could have had me killed just as he had had my father killed, but I guess even Hara doesn't go around killing the federal agents of other countries if there's another way of handling a situation. So he set you up to spy on me, and eventually tried to scare me away by that first attack."

Jack smiled and stroked his right cheek—the plastic surgery had been a success, and all traces of the strangely shaped scar were gone."But I didn't go. In fact, I became something of a pest. And I began to make some of the connections that my father had started to make about Ida and Miura. So Hara changed his mind and decided it would be better to have me killed. He still didn't know where the boy was, and he probably suspected that I might be able to help him find out. But there was a rumor at that time that his only real rival within the Muramoto organization—a woman named Matsuda on Shikoku—had been killed, so I'm not sure Hara even felt the need to find out where the boy was anymore. He had control. End of story.

"Then two things happened. I survived the assassin's attack in Atami. And it turned out that the rumor was false and that this woman on Shikoku was also still very much alive and putting up resistance. So when I escaped at the airport, Hara sent you back into action to spy on me again. Monroe and I were doing their work for them, so they let us continue. When Monroe found out that Shannon made regular trips to Interlaken, and I told you about it in Kyoto on our way to meet Professor Yoshimori, you passed on the information to Hara."

"That's not true. I never—"

"The timing works perfectly. Hara immediately began setting up the attack on the Creusot School. His killers made it to Creusot in less than a week."

"He could have traced the boy a million other ways," she protested.

"After you relayed that info about Switzerland to Hara, he had all he needed from Monroe and me. We'd found the boy's school for him, and now he just needed me out of the picture. So with your help, he staged that kidnapping thing, concocted a story that seemed to make a lot of sense on the surface, and sent you and me home. The kidnapping was kind of clumsy, by the way. Even at the time it seemed to me to be a little bit of a coincidence that your old college professor just happened to be so closely tied to Hara's organization. But you did a good job with the acting, and the bruises on your face were convincing, so I swallowed it. Did you find it harder to lie in a foreign language?"

"Jack," she said. "Don't. Please."

"I would think it would be easier. Speaking a foreign language always involves a certain amount of acting, no matter how fluent you are in it. And if you say the wrong thing or slip out of your role for a second, you can blame it on language interference. And then, of course, you had another advantage. I was really starting to care for you."

Pearl-like tears strung together in the corners of her eyes. "You have no facts. . . ."

"It's crystal-clear in hindsight," he told her. "You told me your father was in the military and then a police officer in Shizuoka. I've seen how the police operate, and where their loyalties lie. It was stupid of me not to put it together at the time. Tell me, was your dad actually in the *Zaibatsu* or was he just a right-winger?"

"My father was conservative and tradition-minded, like all of his colleagues," she said bravely through her tears. "He was never involved with any *Zaibatsu*. And as for me—"

"As for you, I can see why you were so nervous when we were taken to the Yakuza stronghold. That wasn't in the plan, was it? If the Yakuza suspected you were doubling up and really working for Hara, they probably wouldn't have been quite as hospitable as they were. Was that why you slept with me that night? Fear and guilt? Were you trying to throw me and our hosts off the scent by introducing a little romance? I'd prefer to think that my charm and the thunderstorm had something to do with it."

She took a deep breath and turned away from him, to look downhill. The sun was setting, and the choppy waves that crawled across the bay seemed stitches of white froth on an ink-dark fabric. Then she turned back, and exhaled very slowly. "If Hara knew that we had become lovers, he never would have trusted me," she whispered, her wet eyes shining. "That's the way Japanese men think about Japanese women. You're right that I was afraid that night—especially after we made love. I was terrified of what I was starting to feel for you and what would happen to both of us if Hara decided he no longer trusted or needed us."

"He would have killed us?"

"You can't imagine what it was like for me," she hurried on, her tears flowing freely. "When I was fired, I had nothing. All my work, gone. Then they said if I'd cooperate for a day or two, I'd get my job back. And then everything just went out of control . . . including between us . . . and I didn't know what to do. I told you again and again to go back to America."

"I remember you did. I wouldn't go."

She raised her eyes to his, and despite the tears, her gaze was steady. "You were going to continue the case on your own. They would have killed you. Cooperating with them seemed to be the only way for us both to stay alive. To put things back the way they were. I could get my job back. You could go back to America. And I was starting to fall in love with you, and I was afraid for both of us. . . . What else could I do?"

Jack ripped an orange off a tree and threw it the way an outfielder throws a baseball. It sailed out across the orchard before disappearing beneath the tree line far down the slope.

"Tell me what else I could have done," she asked again, her voice rising.

"I guess nothing."

He bent to pick another orange, and she caught his wrist and pulled him upright. Her tear-streaked face was just a few inches from his own. "Yes, I come from an old Japanese family with a conservative police tradition, but I've done so much to move away from that . . . and make myself a modern woman. My mother had an arranged marriage when she was still in high school. I've been to college. To graduate school in America. I've learned your language. Do you think I can fake these tears? That I don't feel love as strongly as you do?" For a moment she couldn't continue. "Do you think I don't care for you? That I didn't, almost from the day we met? That I don't right now?"

He put his arm around her back and drew her even closer,

looking into her glistening eyes as if trying to read the fine print on her innermost soul. She stared back without blinking. She shivered slightly, but did not break the stare. "Yes," he finally whispered. "I believe you."

"I can't tell you what it was like having to lie to you. Having to keep pushing you away. To pretend not to want to make love. Having to say good-bye."

"And for me," he said. "All during our trip across Japan, I couldn't understand why you were pulling away."

"I felt so guilty. How could you ever trust me if I were to tell you the truth?"

"Back in America, when I figured out that you had thrown in with Hara, I felt terribly betrayed."

"But you believe me now?"

He kissed her, his lips salty with her tears.

"What will we do, Jack? They'll kill you. They'll find out you're here, and where the boy is, and they'll kill both of you."

Jack shook his head. "They'll never find the boy."

"Why not?"

"That's my problem," he said. "Now, listen to me for a second. I want Hara. He killed Shannon and her husband and a host of others in cold blood. He ordered my father's death. He turned us against each other."

She watched him, silently, her right hand on his left shoulder, her body so close to his that he could feel her breasts against his chest.

"He doesn't know that I know you were feeding him information. And he certainly doesn't know what we feel for each other, and that you and I are working together now. So he'll trust you. We'll set up an exchange." Jack talked faster, his words running together with excitement. "He brings the money. I bring the kid. He brings one bodyguard on his side. I bring you on mine."

"He won't believe you would agree to such a plan," she told him.

"Of course he won't. So we give him another level. I'm trying to set a trap for him. You pick out a small group of policemen. Say three or four. Not Atami police . . . I wouldn't trust them anymore, and he knows that. But police you've known since the academy. Or even friends of your father whom you've known all your life. What matters is that Hara believes that I still trust you. He knows that I worked with you and traveled with you and trusted you right up to the end, so he would believe that I'd trust you now.''

''That's true, but I still don't understand. What happens to the policemen?''

''We tell them everything. The three or four cops are waiting for us when Hara and I arrive to make the exchange. I expect them to arrest Hara with the blood money as a final piece of evidence. Hara knows you're really on his side and you're bringing people loyal to him. But you really bring honest cops and we nail him. He goes to jail—hopefully for the rest of his lousy life. I can pin at least two murders on him, and maybe as many as five or six. Plus he's gonna show up with five million dollars, which should prove our whole story pretty well. You get a key role in bringing a multiple murderer to justice, which shouldn't exactly hurt your career when the dust clears away. I avenge my father. And maybe the two of us end up together.''

''All of those things would be wonderful,'' Misako told him. ''But such a plan can never work.''

''Why not? You don't think Hara'll go for it?''

She thought about it. ''He might. As you say, the boy represents the only challenge to his power.''

''Well then, what's the problem? You can't find three or four policemen we can trust?''

''I can,'' she admitted. ''Hara has a lot of influence over certain factions, but I know many policemen who are outside of his control. There are mixed feelings among the Japanese police, and in the army, too, about the influence right-wing politicians have. I know several senior police officers who would pretend allegiance to Hara and who we could really trust. They would love to arrest him and strike a blow against the power the extreme right has been exerting.''

''So what's the problem?''

''I'm scared. Hara will suspect something.''

''Sure he will. But he'll go along with it.'' Jack stroked her face. ''His own low opinion of Americans will kick in. Faced with the chance to get the boy, he won't be able to resist. And we'll nail the bastard.'' Jack's fingers slowly slid across her cheeks, still wet with tears, and down her small chin.

She closed her eyes and tilted her head back slightly.

He could feel the blood pounding through her jugular as he pressed his lips to her throat. They were alone among the orange trees, as the evening breeze rustled the leaves and carried to them the faint crashing of the waves from the bay far below.

"I love you," she whispered.

"I love you, too."

"Make love to me, Jack."

"Here?"

"Yes."

"Now?"

"Yes."

He lifted her like a rag doll, and placed her back gently against the trunk of a nearby cherry tree. In seconds his pants were around his ankles while her panties dangled from a nearby low-hanging branch. She wrapped her legs around his hips and locked her lips against his. As their tongues danced and he began to move inside her, he was so lost in the moment, he didn't remember whether he loved her or hated her, trusted her or despised her.

The Ton Katsu restaurant was in Asakusa, between the Hana-yashiki Amusement Park and the Ginza Line subway. Lieutenant Sasaki was waiting for Jack at the best table, by a window with a view of the street. He stood when Jack entered and extended his hand for a shake, smiling his movie-star smile.

Jack glanced down at the proferred hand and said, "You don't like me and I don't like you. Let's keep this on a business level."

"As you like," Sasaki responded, sitting back down. "I ordered for you—I hope you don't mind. Breaded pork cutlets are all they serve here."

"That will be fine," Jack said, sitting opposite him. They had the whole front of the restaurant to themselves. Japanese pop music played softly, further screening their conversation from anyone who might happen to sit nearby. "Do you have an answer?"

"Mr. Hara agrees," Sasaki said. "He is anxious for the exchange to take place at the soonest possible time. This week if possible."

"I don't see why not."

The waitress brought them their breaded pork, with heaps of

shredded cabbage, small mounds of potato salad, hot mustard, and several tomato wedges. Jack sampled a piece—the meat was tender and juicy.

"I must congratulate you on your good fortune," Sasaki said after swallowing and wiping his lips with a napkin. "You are soon to be very rich. Mr. Hara is most anxious that you are pleased with your side of the arrangement. Once this transaction is completed, he of course is interested in what I think you would call in America 'keeping things quiet.' He would like to know your plans."

"Tell him I'm as interested in keeping the whole thing quiet as he is. My plans are to leave Japan immediately. I don't plan to come back. Beyond that, I don't think it's any of Hara's business what I do with his money."

"He is also concerned for the boy's safety till the transaction takes place."

"I wouldn't think the boy's safety would exactly be his biggest worry," Jack observed wryly.

Sasaki grinned. "I think we understand one another. But allow me to explain. You are probably aware that Mr. Hara is not the only one interested in this boy. To be frank, we have reason to believe that at least one other group knows you have him and that you are back in Japan. It would be very unfortunate for both you and Mr. Hara if they were to find the boy before the transaction is completed."

Jack stared back, his face completely blank, but in a corner of his mind he rejoiced that the smoke screen was apparently working. "No one will find the boy before we swap. I know you're looking and you haven't found him. They won't either."

"Mr. Hara suggests that perhaps leaving the boy with a third party would be the safest way."

"It's not open for negotiation," Jack said.

Sasaki ate another small piece of pork. His table manners were fastidious to the point of being almost comical. "Of course, we are assuming that the boy is indeed who you claim he is. I am advised to tell you that there are ways of telling, and that Mr. Hara himself will make the determination. If you are trying to cheat us, things will not go well for you."

"He's real," Jack said. "But if you don't believe me, why don't you just call the whole thing off?" Secretly Jack was very happy that Hara had a few doubts about whether the boy was genuine. Hara had been set up to kill the wrong boy in the Swiss school, and he didn't want to make the same mistake twice. So this time he would come himself to make sure. The fact that Hara needed to personally confirm the child's identity was some insurance against him having them all killed before the exchange could even take place.

"Mr. Hara is concerned by the question of how you and the boy were able to enter Japan without being detected by the normal passport controls. And, of course, since we know where you are but we are unable to determine the whereabouts of the boy, the two circumstances taken together seem to suggest that you have been receiving outside help. This possibility is very worrying for Mr. Hara."

Jack laughed in his face. "I bet it is. It probably also doesn't sit very well with you. All your connections and resources and you couldn't find the boy before I did, and you couldn't tell when or how I came back to Japan. And you can't even find the boy now. I'm surprised Hara still wants to work with you."

Sasaki went on eating, but the pupils of his eyes seemed to shrink and harden a tiny bit, to two black gemstones.

"He gets the boy. I get the money. That's the deal and that's all he needs to know," Jack said. "If he doesn't trust me, let's just call the whole thing off. As you say, there are other parties that I think will do business for the boy."

"That will not be necessary." They finished their pork cutlets, and the waitress took their plates away. "There is one final matter to be discussed," Sasaki said across the empty table. "The place and time where the exchange is to take place are, of course, of great importance. Mr. Hara is willing to let you choose both, as long as you choose a place on Honshu and give him one day's notice."

Jack stood up. "Sorry," he said. "What I told Misako to tell you about that still stands. I'll call three hours beforehand and tell you where to find us."

"For many security reasons, that plan is simply not adequate. You must compromise a little bit."

"I don't have to do anything. If Hara doesn't like it, that's his problem. Good-bye, Lieutenant. As always, it's been a pleasure."

Sasaki stood to face him, his smile flashing, his voice icy. "The pleasure," he said, "has been all mine."

31

Jack took the direct bus from Shinjuku to Kawaguchiko Station in the Fuji Five Lakes Region. The tourist season was coming to an end, and he had the back half of the bus to himself. Jack had a 9-mm revolver, courtesy of Etsuko Matsuda, in a shoulder holster beneath his jacket. If everything went well, he knew he wouldn't have to use it, but whenever he moved, the tug of the metal against his ribs reminded him that his long journey was speedily nearing a conclusion. The Neutrality Act be damned; Jack's heart pounded with excitement as the perfect cone of Mount Fuji floated into view in the far distance.

He arrived at Kawaguchiko Station in the early afternoon, followed the crowd through the main exit, and headed down to the lake. A brisk five-minute walk brought him to the shore of Lake Kawaguchi, where Misako was waiting nervously. She smiled at the sight of him, and then frowned. "Where's the boy?"

"Nearby. We'll get him on the way. I want to keep him out of any harm's way as long as possible. Your friends have gone on ahead of us?"

"They left here an hour ago," she told him. "By now they should have arrived and hidden themselves." She shrugged her shoulders as if slightly amazed. "I thought this was a crazy idea, but it may just work. There was no trouble convincing Hara that the policemen I chose would side with him. As you said, he still trusts me, and he overestimates his influence among the police."

"They'll make the arrest when the time comes?"

"Yes. The unsolved deaths of Miura and Ida have been an embarrassment to the police. As I said, I never thought this could work, but now I'm starting to believe it."

"Then let's call Sasaki from the station and start the ball rolling. It should take Sasaki and Hara less than two hours to make the trip, which doesn't give us much lead time.''

She nodded and they set off. At the station, she called Sasaki while Jack went off to get the boy. As prearranged, the child was sitting quietly on a bench at the station's south exit, watched discreetly by one of Etsuko's bodyguards. The boy was dressed in a gray jacket, and sitting by himself on the long bench, he had never looked smaller or more alone. He smiled very slightly when he saw Jack. Without a word or sign to the tall bodyguard, Jack took the boy by the hand and led him away. "I want you to know I did my best for you," Jack whispered to him as they walked away. "We're both due for a little luck.''

Inside the station, Misako had Sasaki standing by on the line. Jack took the receiver, and she examined the boy while Jack described to Sasaki exactly where the transaction would take place. Sasaki assured him that he and Hara would leave immediately, and that they had the money with them.

"What's the matter with him?" Misako asked Jack after trying to speak to the boy in Japanese and English. "Is he drugged?"

"No, he's just never been much of a conversationalist.''

"What a strange child.''

"You'd be strange, too, if you'd had his childhood. Let's go.''

The bus ride to Lake Shoji, the smallest, most isolated, and prettiest of Fuji's five lakes, was uneventful. At the very back of the bus Jack spotted the tall bodyguard who had been waiting with the boy at the station. When Jack, Misako, and the boy deboarded at Lake Shoji, the tall bodyguard stayed on the bus—he had covered them as long as he could. The three of them started off along the hiking trail that led from the lake toward the distant Mount Fuji. An autumn chill crept into the afternoon air, and the cone of Mount Fuji was occasionally obscured by fogbanks.

They soon reached the outskirts of a forest. The boy balked at the tall trees growing so closely together that in places, their long limbs locked, blotting out the light of the sinking sun. Jack and Misako each took one of his hands and led him on. The narrow trail was empty—it was already off season for climbing Mount Fuji, and far too late in the day for anyone to begin the long trek through the dense forest.

"The Japanese call this forest Aokigahara," Misako said as they walked through low-hanging mist that all but obscured the trail twenty feet in either direction. "It means 'Sea of Trees.' I've never been here before, but it's famous in Japan because compasses don't work here. Underneath the earth a magnetic lava field. Many years ago it was very dangerous, and even today people get lost and never find their way out." For a moment her voice quivered as the fog became a thick shroud twisting around them so that they could barely even see their feet. "Why did you choose such a place?"

"It's isolated, but it's near a major tourist spot, and it's only a few hours from Tokyo. It's exactly what Hara would think I would choose." They reached a bend in the trail where a much narrower side trail cut away into the underbrush. "This is where we turn off. Hold him tight."

For the first hundred yards or so they were able to walk three abreast. Then branches on either side began to brush their faces and they soon ended up single file. Jack led the way; the boy trudged silently in the middle, and Misako brought up the rear. The height and girth of the surrounding old-growth trees were oppressive—insect trills and strange animal calls added to the sense of mystery and danger.

Jack threw occasional quick looks backward, but the trail behind them was completely empty. He felt fairly sure that Hara wouldn't try to snatch the boy along the route, but would wait for what he thought was a perfect setup later on. Since Hara had a trap already set and waiting to be sprung, it didn't make sense that he would try anything now. Even so, each time Jack glanced backward, his fingers touched the stock of his gun.

After half a mile the narrow trail began to widen and soon spilled out into a vast forest clearing. Jack knew the three policemen Misako had chosen were hidden nearby, but looking around, he saw only clumps of tall grass and scrub pines, hemmed in by the dark curve of the tree line on all sides. They walked farther into the clearing. The sun was just above the tree line now, giving the sunset haze a purplish bloom. For a few moments the cloud cover parted and they saw Mount Fuji rising majestically in the distance. Soon it was once again swathed in mist and hidden by cloud.

They waited mostly in silence, occasionally walking about the clearing to keep occupied and stay warm. Misako rubbed her hands together nervously every few minutes, until Jack finally took her hands in his own. He looked into her eyes. "Don't worry so much."

"It's just that I'm cold."

"Is there anything I should know?"

She looked straight back at him, even as her body shivered. "I love you," she whispered. "And from you? Should I know something?"

He shook his head, squeezed her fingers once, lightly, and then released her.

They heard the chop-chop of the rotors long before they saw anything. Jack, Misako, and even the boy glanced upward at the sound that built in volume and seemed to come from a source very near them and low to the forest. Then the landing lights appeared over the tree line, and finally the whirlybird itself hovered into view.

Jack took the boy's hand as the copter began to descend. Both of their grips tightened as the roar grew louder. The boy was plainly frightened by the noise, while Jack had dreaded this moment for weeks. In many ways, this was the biggest gamble of the whole plan. Hara could easily have them all gunned down from the helicopter. But Jack was banking on the fact that the old man would want to see the boy for himself. Sasaki had communicated enough doubts about the exchange and what third parties might somehow be involved for Jack to conclude that Kitaro Hara would at least pretend to keep his side of the exchange.

The rotor wash bowed the scrub pines and flattened the tall meadow grass as the craft inched downward and came to rest in a flat area thirty feet from them.

As the rotor slowed, Lieutenant Sasaki got out of the driver's side of the helicopter and waved to Misako and Jack. He was dressed nattily in a gray tweed sport jacket with pilot's goggles that he had pushed up on his forehead like a ski mask. He crossed the distance between them in quick strides, bowed slightly to Misako and smiled pleasantly to Jack, and then bent for an intense scrutiny of the boy. Finally he nodded, stood back up, and said, "Please wait here."

He crossed back to the helicopter and helped Kitaro Hara down from the passenger side. The old man seemed very out of place getting out of the helicopter; the anachronism was compounded by how perfectly Lieutenant Sasaki was suited to the scene. Hara held a leather suitcase in both hands as he walked slowly across the grass.

The old man stared down at the young boy with the penetrating yet cold-blooded gaze of a scientist about to dissect an important test animal. He bent, unzipped the boy's gray jacket, and roughly pulled the boy's shirt open. A distinctive birthmark was visible on the child's left shoulder. Hara nodded and turned his attention to the boy's features.

At first the boy met the old man's stare, but soon he turned his head away and finally hid his face behind his arm. The old man nodded; it was clear that in the boy's face, Hara had recognized the inherited features of his old *Zaibatsu* boss, Seiji Muramoto.

Hara walked by Misako, barely giving her a glance, to Jack. For the first time since their encounter in the teahouse amid the bamboo forest on Hokkaido, Jack stared into the gleaming black eyes of the man who had ordered his father's death. Hara spoke a few contemptuous words in Japanese and held out the suitcase. "He says he knows that in America you like to count your money in public," Sasaki translated. "Please go ahead."

Jack took the briefcase from him. He opened the clasp and glanced inside at the stacks of hundred-dollar bills tied neatly with colored string. Jack closed the lid. "I don't need to count it," he told Sasaki.

Hara walked over to the boy who shied away from him and tried to hide behind Misako's legs. The old man grabbed the boy's hand, and at that moment shouts broke out from the surrounding meadow and three policemen with guns drawn charged forward. Their heavy-booted footsteps thudded nearer and nearer as they sped across the shadows toward the knot of people and the helicopter.

Lieutenant Sasaki and Kitaro Hara stood frozen in stunned surprise as the three men in dark blue uniforms reached the center of the meadow and pointed guns at them. The policemen were tall, serious-looking men. One of them grunted at Lieutenant Sasaki, who looked as if he wanted to argue, but then slowly raised his hands. A second policeman spoke a sharp command to Hara, who released the boy's hand and answered back in harsh Japanese. The policeman cocked his revolver, and Hara fell silent and raised his hands. The policemen took out handcuffs and approached Hara and Sasaki, guns at the ready.

The third policeman, whose shock of white hair and anvil of a jaw gave him a gruff, straightforward look, spoke to Misako in quick Japanese. "This is Sergeant Morashita," she said. "I have known him for years. He says our surprise has worked, but we must be very careful now. Hara may have men nearby. He needs to know if you really came alone with the boy, or if you brought some protection of your own."

"I came alone," Jack said, feeling very confused.

"He says you must tell him the truth. He feels there were other people involved in choosing this site and keeping the boy hidden. If you have been working with other people, you must tell him quickly. All our lives depend on it."

Sergeant Morashita studied Jack carefully. In the background Jack could see the other two policemen snapping handcuffs on Hara and Sasaki. For a moment Jack hesitated. "The boy and I did this alone," he repeated.

Again Morashita spoke. "He asks if there were any plans involving other people later on," Misako translated, her voice catching some of the sergeant's evident concern. "Are there other people on the outskirts of the forest or back in Tokyo? He thinks someone was following you into this clearing. Is your agency in America involved? You must tell him."

Jack began to deny it and then fell silent, bewildered as to what to say and whom to trust.

Misako saw Jack's hesitation. "I've known Sergeant Morashita since I studied at the police academy," she told Jack. "He's risking his life to help us. They all are. If you know something, you should tell it."

"There's nothing," Jack finally said. "This was the plan, and it worked."

Misako touched his chin lightly with her index finger. "Jack? You're sure?"

"Yes. We should go."

As if on cue, the policemen turned and pointed their guns at Jack and the boy. "Don't move," Sergeant Morashita growled in perfectly fluent English. "Give me that suitcase. Now, put your hands up."

Jack slowly put his hands up and glanced at Misako. She stepped away to help Hara and Lieutenant Sasaki remove their cuffs. When their hands were free, she turned back and met Jack's look. Their eyes locked and he saw that she had never been really his; despite the excitement and drama of the moment, anger welled up in his heart against her and he took a half step toward her. She drew back, and one of the policemen stopped Jack by cocking his pistol.

Hara walked over, retrieved the leather suitcase, and nodded to the policemen. They snapped the cuffs that had been on Hara and Sasaki on Jack and the boy, hands behind their backs. Hara spoke one short sentence in Japanese, which Sasaki gleefully translated. "Mr. Hara asks you to please give his regards to your father. Now, you will please follow these men into the woods. . . ."

Sasaki's sentence was cut off by a burst of sound and light. Searchlights lit up the center of the meadow, and a quick barrage of gunfire downed all three policemen in an instant. One writhed on the ground, moaning. The other two fell and lay silent.

Lieutenant Sasaki moved like lightning. At the first sound of gunfire, he dropped to his knees and scuttled back toward the helicopter, moving bent over but at great speed. A command to halt was barked from nearby. Sasaki slowed and then darted forward again, leaping up and grasping the helicopter's door with his right hand. A single shot caught him in the spine and made him cry out and curl backward. A second shot sounded, and his head jerked forward. He dangled for a second from the door handle by one hand and then fell to the ground and lay still.

Jack stood close to the boy. From around the edges of the clearing, shadowy figures began to emerge. They all wore dark grays that matched the dying light, and their hoods and face masks gave them the aspect of a platoon of submachine-gun-toting phantoms, anonymous yet sanguinary, mute yet menacing.

One of the gray shapes walked forward to face Hara, and threw off its mask and hood. Etsuko Matsuda and Kitaro Hara were almost the same height, and for a long moment they looked into each other's faces without speaking. Watching the confrontation, Jack could not help being impressed by the old man's equanimity. Hara had lost everything in a few short minutes, yet his face remained calm and his expression betrayed no great apprehension.

Etsuko Matsuda spoke to Hara in a low, clear voice, and Jack didn't need to understand her Japanese to know that it was a summons to die. Her lovely face was stern and coldly vengeful—an angel of death without any trace of hesitation or remorse.

Still, the old man looked at her, standing stock still less than a foot from her, his eyes moving over her face as if searching for something far less tangible than mercy.

For a second the quick black eyes in the wrinkled face jumped to the boy, and Jack felt the hatred behind the stare. From the boy, Hara's eyes moved up to Jack's own, and he looked into the features so annealed with pride and pain that they already seemed tempered into an ageless death mask. Then Hara returned his gaze to Etsuko, bowed his head slightly, and walked slowly off out of the center of the meadow. She followed him at a distance of three steps, and the circle of gray-clad phantoms parted slightly to let them out.

Watching Hara's bald pate bob up and down as he shuffled into darkness, Jack felt no exultation at finally attaining revenge, but only relief mingled with pity. On some unexpected empathic level he had understood the loathing that had danced in the old man's eyes when they had been turned on the boy and finally on Jack himself.

A montage of memories momentarily blurred the twilight: rebellious Japanese students riding minibikes on the grounds of Atami High School, Yakuza who patterned themselves after American movie gangsters, drunken Japanese cops who fantasized about Marilyn Monroe–style American blondes as the unattainable epitome of female sexuality, and American fast-food restaurants diluting Kyoto's rustic charm.

Thinking back to the encounter with Hara in the teahouse on the Hokkaido mountainside, Jack remembered that the little man had portrayed Japan and America as locked in a life-and-death struggle. Hara believed with all his heart that it was a struggle that Japan would win, yet Jack had seen enough of modern Japan to understand that even if it became the most powerful nation in the world, the distinctively Japanese qualities that Hara loved and to some extent embodied were the very price of that victory. And with this insight, Jack felt he could understand to some extent the bitter hatred in the old man's eyes as he had looked upon the American who had thwarted him and the half-American child destined to inherit control of the *Zaibatsu* empire that he had so coveted, and that stretched back as a living connection to Japan's noble samurai past.

A single gunshot split the silence. All heads turned toward the spot, but the gathering darkness was impenetrable. Misako was the first to react. She began fumbling to undo Jack's handcuffs, the key shaking in her hand. "I picked men who I thought were loyal," she whispered. "Hara's influence extended much further than I knew. Further than anyone knew. But now he's dead and we can spend the time together that we always wanted."

The cuffs snapped open and Jack slowly raised his wrists and felt the blood flow back in. She pressed herself close to him, searching his eyes with her own. In response to his silence and look, she suddenly reversed tack. "Jack, I was forced," she whispered, glancing around at the circle of shadowy shapes which seemed to be closing in bit by bit as the light died. "I didn't want to help them, but I had no choice. They were going to kill me. You must believe me. You're the only one who can speak up for me now. . . ."

He looked into her entreating eyes, and for a second he almost reached out to her. Then Jack remembered his father's corpse with the whole back of its head blown off, and Monroe and his wife and daughter tortured and murdered in cold blood. He slapped her hard, and she stumbled back several steps and fell in the tall grass.

He walked over, grabbed a wrist, and hoisted her up. The gray shapes had pulled back, and the two of them were alone together at the edge of the clearing. "They won't kill you," he told her. "My friends found out that your father was involved with the *Zaibatsu* years ago in Shizuoka, so we never trusted you to choose honest cops. But I got them to agree to spare your life."

A thin stream of crimson blood trickled out of a corner of her mouth and she wiped it away. "Do you . . . believe . . . that I still love you?" she whispered.

"I feel sorry for you," Jack told her. "I think you're so confused that you don't know who or what you're loyal to. The mouth speaks English. The heart is Japanese. Part independent policewoman, part lackey to a gangster . . . You say you love me, but you were setting me up. . . . How can you stand to live that way? Jesus, it must tear you apart."

The wind blew her black hair across her forehead. She had never looked lovelier.

"Anyway, I saved your life for you. . . . Now, get the hell out of here."

She reached out and very gently touched his cheek where the

scar used to be. Then she turned and walked silently away into the twilight.

Jack stood frozen, watching as the darkness and the tree cover swallowed her up. Finally Etsuko Matsuda, her eyes gleaming with the cold light of revenge, her hair tied behind her in a single long braid, walked up to Jack. "Come," she said softly, and then when he gave no sign of hearing or moving, she repeated it a bit louder. "Come away now."

Postscript

They walked for a mile and a half along the Chickahominy to where a mudbank stroked the current flat so that it ran smooth as glass over a stretch of pebble-encrusted shallows. On the sides of the mudbank, cattails curled in scattered clumps, in places leaning out over the water, and in other places shying back toward dry land.

A few hundred yards from the large white colonial house, the boy stopped to rest. It was getting along toward evening, so Jack left them and went on ahead by himself to see about dinner. His grandfather's house had been newly painted that summer, and it sat on its bend in the Chickahominy neat and pretty as a picture postcard. On the front lawn, a dozen or so neighborhood boys kicked a soccer ball back and forth in a hotly contested free-for-all without rules or teams.

"Tommy's coming by with a couple'a bushels of blue-claws," his grandfather told him. "I've got some sweet corn and potato salad. There's pie for dessert."

"Sorry to put you to such trouble."

"Oh, it's no trouble at all. Actually, I kind of like doing it." The old man almost sounded embarrassed at the admission. "Nice having people around." They stood together in the living room facing out toward the river and watched Etsuko and the boy stroll slowly toward the house, side by side, with the sun sinking behind them. "They're good together," the old man finally grunted.

Watching Etsuko walk toward the house, her long hair loose and trailing behind her in the breeze, reminded Jack painfully of Misako. He still thought of her several times a day: of their time together crossing Japan, of their lovemaking, and of their last walk to the clearing. Jack forced himself to try to respond to his grandfather. "She lost a baby of her own, and he grew up without parents, so . . . ." He couldn't finish.

The old man looked at him carefully. "You okay?"

"Sure."

A long silence and then a whisper: "What the hell happened to you over there?"

"Nothing."

His grandfather nodded, and they watched in silence as Etsuko and the boy clambered up the bank. The woman and child held hands and ended up pulling each other down almost as much as they were able to help each other up.

"She's good with him, but you're even better," the old man said.

"You don't even want to know what we have in common," Jack told him, but he knew the old man was right. Since the nightmare evening in the clearing in Japan, Jack and the boy had forged a strong friendship, built, at least in the beginning, on a mutual recognition of common pain and loneliness. They shared long walks and silences, and both seemed to get something out of the other's brooding presence.

In some ways, it was the deep and effortless father-son bond that Jack had never been able to create with Walter; they never talked and they never fought—the boy simply trusted Jack completely and unquestioningly, the way one trusts a member of one's family. Lately the child had shown some signs of coming out of his shell, and Jack had managed to forget Misako enough to try to encourage these brief flashes of normality from a kid who had never even begun to learn how to have fun.

Etsuko came in and joined them in the living room. The walk and the chill of sundown had given her cheeks a flush of color. "Hungry?" the old man asked her.

"A little bit." Her English, when she used it, was getting much better.

"Boy likes the river, doesn't he?"

"It's a very beautiful place," she said.

"Well, it's really just a glorified shack," Jack's grandfather muttered, but Jack saw that her words made the old man happy. "We're having blue-claws for dinner. Wait till you taste 'em."

For a minute the three of them were quiet together, watching the Chickahominy round the bend and flow off into the sunset. She threw Jack a glance, and he shook his head slightly in response. "I haven't asked him yet. We'll do it now."

"Ask me what?" the old man wanted to know.

"Etsuko has to sort things out for a while," Jack told him. "It's still too dangerous for the boy to return to Japan with her. She's looking for a safe place to leave the boy. Someplace isolated, with people she can trust. She'll provide two full-time bodyguards. I told her I thought the boy could stay here for a while." Jack paused and then added, "I can stay, too—there's sort of a house-cleaning going on in my old section of the Bureau right now, and they won't bring me back till it's over. So a little fishing might be the right thing. If you want us."

"Tell Etsuko the boy is welcome for as long as she wants. We'll take good care of him. But we don't need her bodyguards."

"You don't know what could happen. . . ."

"I've got a gun if it comes to that."

"I've got a gun, too," Jack told him. "Take my word for it, we shouldn't turn down the bodyguards."

The old man examined Jack's face. "Whatever. Tell her he's welcome, and that it'll be my pleasure. Boy's got the temperament to be a good fisherman. With my experience and a little of your luck rubbing off . . ."

Etsuko suddenly glanced around. Jack immediately sensed and understood her alarm. "Where did he go?"

The child had never wandered away before. Always, when brought to a place, he stood silently, gazing off into space with his eyes vacant and disinterested till someone came for him. But now he had disappeared.

Etsuko drew her pistol. They ran through the house, whipping from room to room, and came back empty-handed into the living room. They all had the same thought at the same moment and scanned the river, but there were no signs of life on the bank or out in the gleaming, swirling current. Etsuko's face was drawn tight in controlled panic.

"I'll call the police," the old man said, hurrying toward the phone. "You go out to the river. . . ." Then he stopped short and stared.

Seeing his stare, Jack and Etsuko joined him by the window that faced out toward the front lawn. The boy stood on the edge of the grass, watching the soccer game. The ball rolled close to him, and two of the neighborhood boys gestured for him to kick it to them. He hesitated for several seconds and then stuck out his right foot and tentatively pushed the soccer ball with his toe. It rolled across the grass and the game resumed.

A moment later the heir to the vast Muramoto *Zaibatsu* ventured forward onto the lawn, clearly terrified at what he was doing yet moving ahead, doggedly, step by step. Soon he was swept up in the melee of swirling, shrieking, laughing children, and became part of the game.